# The Travelling Cat Chronicles
## by HIRO ARIKAWA

**Over two million copies sold worldwide. Translated into over thirty languages**

*It's not the journey that counts, but who's at your side.*

Nana is on a road trip, but he is not sure where he is going. All that matters is that he can sit beside his beloved owner Satoru in the front seat of his silver van.

Satoru is keen to visit three old friends from his youth, though Nana doesn't know why and Satoru won't say.

Set against the backdrop of Japan's changing seasons and narrated with a rare gentleness and humour, Nana's story explores the wonder and thrill of life's unexpected detours. It is about the value of friendship and solitude, and knowing when to give and when to take.

**At the heart of this book is a powerful message about the importance of kindness. It shows, above all, how acts of love, both great and small, can transform our lives.**

www.penguin.co.uk

**HIRO ARIKAWA** is the million-copy-bestselling author of *The Travelling Cat Chronicles*. Her brand-new homage to cats, *The Goodbye Cat*, brings together seven cats as they weave their way through their owners' lives. Featuring all the irresistible wit, wisdom and warmth that thousands of readers across the world love so much in her storytelling, *The Goodbye Cat* is published into multiple languages. Arikawa's latest book, translated into English by Allison Markin Powell, is the bestselling, much-loved modern classic, *The Passengers on the Hankyu Line*. She lives in the city of Takarazuka, Japan.


**PHILIP GABRIEL** is a highly experienced translator from Japanese, and best known for his translation work with Haruki Murakami.

# The Travelling Cat Chronicles

# &

# The Goodbye Cat

### Hiro Arikawa

Translated from the Japanese by Philip Gabriel

doubleday

TRANSWORLD PUBLISHERS
UK | USA | Canada | Ireland | Australia
India | New Zealand | South Africa

Transworld is part of the Penguin Random House group of companies whose addresses can be found at global.penguinrandomhouse.com.

Penguin Random House UK, One Embassy Gardens,
8 Viaduct Gardens, London SW11 7BW

penguin.co.uk

First published in Great Britian in 2025 by Doubleday
an imprint of Transworld Publishers
Publication rights for this English edition arranged through Kodansha Ltd, Tokyo

*The Travelling Cat Chronicles* was first published in Great Britain in 2017 by Doubleday
an imprint of Transworld Publishers
*The Goodbye Cat* was first published in Great Britain in 2023 by Doubleday
an imprint of Transworld Publishers

*Tabineko Ripôto* copyright © Hiro Arikawa 2015. All rights reserved.
First published in 2015 in Japan by Kodansha Ltd, Tokyo
English translation copyright © Philip Gabriel 2017
Publication rights for this English edition arranged through Kodansha Ltd, Tokyo
Text illustrations by Yoco Nagamiya

*Mitorineko* copyright © Hiro Arikawa 2021. All rights reserved.
First published in Japan in 2021 by Kodansha Ltd, Tokyo
English translation copyright © Philip Gabriel 2023
Publication rights for this English edition arranged through Kodansha Ltd, Tokyo
Text illustrations by Yukata Murakami

Copyright © Hiro Arikawa 2025

The moral right of the author has been asserted
This book is a work of fiction and, except in the case of historical fact, any resemblance to actual persons, living or dead, is purely coincidental.

Every effort has been made to obtain the necessary permissions with reference to copyright material, both illustrative and quoted. We apologize for any omissions in this respect and will be pleased to make the appropriate acknowledgements in any future edition.

No part of this book may be used or reproduced in any manner for the purpose of training artificial intelligence technologies or systems. In accordance with Article 4(3) of the DSM Directive 2019/790, Penguin Random House expressly reserves this work from the text and data mining exception.

Typeset by Six Red Marbles UK, Thetford, Norfolk
Printed and bound in Great Britain by Clays Ltd, Elcograf S.p.A.

The authorized representative in the EEA is Penguin Random House Ireland,
Morrison Chambers, 32 Nassau Street, Dublin D02 YH68.

A CIP catalogue record for this book is available from the British Library

ISBN: 9781529959871

Penguin Random House is committed to a sustainable future
for our business, our readers and our planet. This book is made
from Forest Stewardship Council® certified paper.

# PAWS FOR THOUGHT

'Anyone who has ever unashamedly loved an animal will read this book with gratitude, for its understanding of an emotion that ennobles us as human beings, whether we value it or not.'
*GUARDIAN*

'Arikawa has a lightness of touch that elevates her story to a tale about loyalty and friendship... while speaking to our basic human need for companionship.'
*JOHN BOYNE*

'Bewitching... as self-possessed and comforting as – well, a cat.'
*SUNDAY TELEGRAPH*

'It has the warmth, painterly touch, and tenderness of a Studio Ghibli film – and it is a delight to read.'
*FINANCIAL TIMES*

'A book about kindness and love, and about how the smallest things can provide happiness.'
*STYLIST*

'Prepare to have your heart strings tugged by this quirky tale... It's a deceptively gentle story that you won't need to be a cat lover to fall for.'
*SUNDAY MIRROR*

'Heart-wrenching but uplifting.'
*RED MAGAZINE*

'This is the book I am giving everyone... the book I am recommending to anyone buying something Japan-related or cat-related, and, quite possibly, the book I am placing in someone's hand when they ask me what my favourite book is. For a bookseller, that is the highest accolade a book can ever receive.'
*A WATERSTONES BOOKSELLER*

# Prologue

# The Cat with No Name

*I* AM A CAT. *As yet, I have no name.* There's a famous cat in our country who once made this very statement.

I have no clue how great that cat was, but at least when it comes to having a name I got there first. Whether I like my name is another matter, since it glaringly doesn't fit my gender, me being male and all. I was given it about five years ago – around the time I came of age.

Back then, I used to sleep on the bonnet of a silver van in the parking lot of an apartment building. Why there? Because no one would ever shoo me away. Human beings are basically huge monkeys that walk upright, but they can be pretty full of themselves. They leave their cars exposed to the elements, but a few paw prints on the paintwork and they go *ballistic*.

At any rate, the bonnet of that silver van was my favourite place to sleep. Even in winter, the sun made it all warm and toasty, the perfect spot for a daytime nap.

I stayed there until spring arrived, which meant I'd survived one whole cycle of seasons. One day, I was lying curled up, having a snooze, when I suddenly sensed a warm, intense gaze upon me. I unglued my eyelids a touch and saw a tall, lanky young man, eyes narrowed, staring down at me as I lay prone.

'Do you always sleep there?' he asked.

I suppose so. Do you have a problem with that?

'You're really cute, do you know that?'

So they tell me.

'Is it okay if I stroke you?'

No, thanks. I batted one front paw at him in what I hoped to be a gently threatening way.

'Aren't you a stingy one,' the man said, pulling a face.

Well, how would *you* like it if you were sleeping and somebody came by and rubbed you all over?

'I guess you want something in exchange for being stroked?'

Quick on the draw, this one. Quite right. Got to get something in return for having my sleep disturbed. I heard a rustling and popped my head up. The man's hand had disappeared into a plastic bag.

'I don't seem to have bought anything cat-suitable.'

No sweat, mate. Feline beggars can't be choosers. That scallop jerky looks tasty.

I sniffed at the package sticking out of the plastic bag and the man, smiling wryly, tapped me on the head with his fingers.

Hey there, let's not jump the gun.

'That's not good for you, cat,' he said. 'Plus it's too spicy.'

Too spicy, says you? Do you think a hungry stray like me gives a rat's about his health? Getting something into my stomach right this minute – that's my top priority.

At last, the man liberated a slice of fried chicken from a sandwich, stripping off the batter, laying the flesh on his palm and holding it out to me.

You want me to eat right out of your hand? You think you'll get all friendly with me by doing that? I'm not that easy. Then again, it's not often I get to indulge in fresh meat – and it looks kind of succulent – so perhaps a little compromise is in order.

As I chomped down on the chicken, I felt a couple of human fingers slide from under my chin to behind my ears. He scratched me softly. I mean, I'll permit a human who feeds me to touch me for a second, but this guy was pretty clever about it. If he were to give me a couple more titbits, scratching under my chin would be up for grabs, too. I rubbed my cheek against his hand.

The man smiled, pulled the meat from the second half of the sandwich, stripped off the batter, and held it out. I wanted to tell him I wouldn't say no to the batter, either. It would fill me up even more.

I let him stroke me properly to repay him for the food, but now it was time to close up shop.

Just as I began to raise a front paw and send him on his way, the man said, 'Okay, see you later.'

He withdrew his hand and walked off, heading up the stairs of the apartment building.

That's how we first met. It wasn't until a little later that he finally gave me my name.

From that moment on, I found crunchy cat food underneath the silver van every night. One human fistful – a full meal for a cat – just behind the rear tyre.

If I was around when the man turned up to leave food, he'd wrest some touch-time from me, but when I wasn't there he'd humbly leave an offering and disappear.

Sometimes, another cat would beat me to it, or the man would be away and I'd wait in vain till morning for my crunchies. But, by and large, I could count on him for one square meal a day. Humans are quite flighty, so I don't rely on them a hundred per cent. A stray cat's skill lies in building up a complex web of connections in order to survive on the streets.

Acquaintances who understood each other, that's what the man and I had become. But when he and I had settled into a comfortable relationship, fate intervened to change everything.

And fate hurt like hell.

I was crossing the road one night when I became suddenly dazzled by a car's headlights. I was about to dart away when a piercing horn sounded. And that's when it all went wrong. Startled, I was a split second late in leaping aside, and *bang!* the car rammed into me and sent me flying.

I wound up in the bushes by the side of the road. The pain that shot through my body was like nothing I'd experienced before. But I was alive.

I cursed as I tried to stand up, and even let out a scream. Oww! *Oww!* My right hind leg hurt like you wouldn't believe.

I sank to the ground and twisted my upper half to lick the wound, only to find – good Lord! A bone was sticking out!

Bite wounds and cuts I can mostly look after with my tongue, but this was beyond me. Through the wrenching pain, this bone protruding from my leg was making its presence known in no uncertain terms.

What should I do? What *could* I do?

Somebody, help me! But that was idiotic. Nobody was going to help a stray.

Then I remembered the man who came every night to leave me crunchies. Maybe he could help.

Why this thought came to me, I don't know – we'd always kept our distance, with occasional stroking time in thanks for his offerings. But it was worth a try.

I set off along the pavement, dragging my right hind leg with the bone jabbing out. Several times my body gave out, as if to say, *I can't take it, it's just too painful. Not one. More. Step.*

By the time I reached the silver van, dawn was breaking.

I really couldn't take another step. This is it, I thought.

I cried out at the top of my lungs.

*Oww . . . owwwww!*

Again and again I screamed, until my voice finally gave out. It killed me even to call out, to be honest with you.

Just then, I heard someone come down the stairs of the apartment building. When I looked up, I saw it was the man.

'I *thought* it was you.'

When he saw me close up, he turned pale.

'What happened? Were you hit by a car?'

Hate to admit it, but I messed up.

'Does it hurt? It looks like it.'

Enough of the irritating questions. Have a little pity for a wounded cat, okay?

'It sounded like you were desperate, the way you were screaming, and it woke me up. You were calling for me, weren't you, cat?'

Yes, yes, I certainly was! But you took your time getting here.

'You thought I might be able to help you, didn't you?'

I guess so, Sherlock. Then the man started sniffing and snuffling. Why was *he* crying?

'I'm proud of you, remembering me like that.'

Cats don't cry like humans do. But – somehow – I sort of understood why he was weeping.

*So you'll do something to help, won't you? I can't stand the pain much longer.*

'There, there. You'll be okay, cat.'

The man laid me gently in a cardboard box lined with a fluffy towel and placed me in the front seat of the silver van.

We headed for the vet's clinic. That's like the worst place ever for me, so I'd rather not talk about it.

I ended up staying with the man until my wounds healed. He lived alone in his apartment and everything was neat and tidy. He set out a litter tray for me in the changing area beside the bath, and bowls of food and water in the kitchen.

Despite appearances, I'm a pretty intelligent, well-mannered cat, and I worked out how to use the toilet right away and never once soiled the floor. Tell me not to sharpen my claws on certain places, and I refrain. The walls and door frames were forbidden so I used the furniture and rug for claw-sharpening. I mean, he never specifically mentioned that the furniture and the rug were off limits. (Admittedly, he did look a little put out at first, but I'm the kind of cat who can pick up on things, sniff out what's absolutely forbidden, and what isn't. The furniture and the rug weren't *absolutely* off limits, is what I'm saying.)

I think it took about two months to get the stitches out and for the bone to heal. During that time, I found out the man's name. Satoru Miyawaki.

Satoru kept calling me things like 'You', or 'Cat' or 'Mr Cat' – whatever he felt like at the time. Which is understandable, since I didn't have a name at this point.

And even if I *had* had a name, Satoru didn't understand my language, so I wouldn't have been able to tell him. It's kind of inconvenient that humans only understand each other. Did you know that animals are much more multilingual?

Whenever I wanted to go outside, Satoru would frown and try to convince me that I shouldn't.

'If you go out, you might never come back. Just be patient, little cat. Wait until you're completely better. You don't want to have stitches in your leg for the rest of your life, do you?'

By this time, I was able to walk a little, though it still hurt, but seeing how put out Satoru looked, I endured house confinement for those two months, and I figured there were benefits. It wouldn't do to be dragging my leg if a rival cat and I got into a scrap.

So I stayed put until my wound was at long last totally healed.

Satoru always used to stop me at the front door with a worried look, but now I stood there, meowing to be let out. Thank you for all you've done. I will be forever grateful. I wish you lifelong happiness, even if you never leave me another titbit beneath that silver van.

Satoru didn't look worried so much as forlorn. The same way he seemed about the furniture and the rug. It's not totally off limits, but still . . . *That* sort of expression.

'Do you still prefer to live outside?'

Hang on now – enough with the teary face. You look like that, you'll start making *me* feel sad that I'm leaving.

And then, out of the blue: 'Listen, Cat, I was wondering if you would become my cat.'

I had never considered this as an option. Being a dyed-in-the-wool stray, the thought of being someone's pet had never crossed my mind.

My idea was to let him look after me until I recovered, but I'd always planned to leave once my wound was healed. Let me rephrase that. I thought I *had* to leave.

As long as I was leaving, it would be a lot more dignified to slip out on my own rather than have someone shoo me away. Cats are proud creatures, after all.

If you wanted me to be your pet cat, then, well, you should have said so earlier.

I slipped out of the door that Satoru had reluctantly opened. Then I turned around and gave him a meow.

Come on.

For a human, Satoru had a good intuitive sense of cat language and seemed to understand what I was saying. He looked puzzled for a moment, then followed me outside.

It was a bright, moonlit night, and the town lay still and quiet.

I leapt on to the bonnet of the silver van, thrilled to have regained the ability to jump, and then back on to the ground, where I rolled and scratched for a bit.

A car drove by and my tail shot up, the fear of being hit again ingrained in me now. Before I knew it, I was hiding behind Satoru's trousered legs, and he was gazing down at me, smiling.

I made one round of the neighbourhood with Satoru before returning to the apartment building. Outside the door of the stairway to the apartment on the second floor, I meowed. Open up.

I looked up at Satoru and saw he was smiling, but again in that tearful way.

'So you *do* want to come back, eh, Mr Cat?'
Right. Yeah. So open up.
'So you'll be my cat?'
Okay. But sometimes let's go out for a walk.
And so I became Satoru's cat.

'When I was a child, I had a cat that looked just like you.'
Satoru brought a photo album out of the cupboard.
'See?'
The album was full of photos of a cat. I know what they call people like this. *Cat fanatics.*
The cat in the photos did indeed resemble me. Both of us had an almost all-white body, the only spots of colour being on our face and tail. Two on our face; our tails black and bent. The only difference was in the angle of our bent tails. The tabby spots on our faces, though, were exactly alike.
'The two spots on its forehead were angled downwards, like the Chinese character *hachi* – eight – so I named him Hachi.'
If that's how he comes up with names, what on earth is he going to choose for me?
After *hachi* comes *kyu* – nine. What if he picked that?
'How about Nana?'
What? He's subtracting? I didn't see that coming.
'It hooks in the opposite direction from Hachi's, and from the top it looks like *nana* – the number seven.'
He seemed to be talking about my tail now.
Now wait just a second. Isn't Nana a girl's name? I'm a fully fledged, hot-blooded male. In what universe does that make sense?
'You're okay with that, aren't you, Nana? It's a lucky name – Lucky Seven and all that.'

I meowed, and Satoru squinted and tickled me under my chin.

'Do you like the name?'

Nope! But, well. Asking that while stroking my chin is playing foul. I purred in spite of myself.

'So you like it. Great.'

I told you already – *I do not*.

In the end, I missed my chance to undo the mistake (I mean, what's a cat going to do? The guy was petting me the whole time), and that's how I ended up being Nana.

'We'll have to move, won't we?'

His landlord didn't allow pets in the apartment, but he'd made an exception for me, just until I got back on my paws.

So Satoru moved with me to a new place in the same town. Going to all that trouble to move just for the sake of one cat – well, maybe I shouldn't say this, being a cat myself, but that was one fired-up cat lover.

And so began our new life together. Satoru was the perfect roommate for a cat, and I was the perfect roommate for a human.

We've got along really well, these past five years.

As a cat, I was now in the prime of life, and as Satoru was a little over thirty, I guess he was, too.

One day, Satoru patted my head apologetically.

'Nana, I'm sorry.'

It's okay, it's okay. No worries.

'I'm really sorry it's come to this.'

No need to explain. I'm quick on the uptake.

'I never intended to let you go.'

Life, be it human or feline, doesn't always work out the way you think it will.

If I had to give up living with Satoru, I'd just go back to the way I was five years ago. Back when the bone was sticking out of my leg. If we'd said goodbye and I'd gone back to life on the streets, it would not have been a big deal. I could go back to being a stray tomorrow, no problem.

I wouldn't have lost anything. Just gained the name Nana, and the five years I'd spent with Satoru.

So don't look so glum, chum.

Cats just quietly take whatever comes their way.

The only exception so far was the night I broke my leg and thought of Satoru.

'Well, shall we go?'

It seemed Satoru wanted me to go with him somewhere. He opened the door of my basket and I got in without making a fuss. For the five years I'd lived with him, I'd always been a sensible cat. For instance, even when he took me to my bête noire, the vet, I didn't make a racket.

Okay then – let's go. As Satoru's roommate, I had been a perfect cat, so I should be the perfect companion on this journey he seemed so intent on making.

My basket in hand, Satoru got into the silver van.

# 1
# The Husband without a Wife

*L*ONG TIME NO SEE.
   So began the email.
   It was from Satoru Miyawaki, a childhood friend of Kosuke's who had moved away when he was in elementary school. He had moved around quite a bit after that, but they never completely lost touch, and even now, when they were both past thirty, they were still friends.
   *Sorry this is out of the blue, but would you be able to take my cat for me?*
   It was his precious cat, which 'unavoidable circumstances' were preventing him from keeping any longer, and he was now looking for someone to take care of it.
   What these unavoidable circumstances were, he didn't say.
   He'd attached two photos. A cat with two spots on his forehead forming the character *hachi* – eight.
   'Whoa!' Kosuke couldn't help saying. 'This cat looks exactly like Hachi.'
   The cat in the photo looked just like the one Satoru and Kosuke had found that day so many years ago.
   Kosuke scrolled to a second photo, a close-up of the cat's tail. A hooked tail like the number seven.
   *Aren't cats with hooked tails supposed to bring good fortune?* thought Kosuke.
   He tried to recall who had told him that. Then he sighed, realizing it had been his wife, who'd gone to live

with her parents for a while. Kosuke had no clue when she'd be back.

He was beginning to get the faint sense that maybe she never would.

The ridiculous thought crossed his mind that perhaps if they'd had a cat like this, things might have been different.

With a cat hanging around the house, a cat with a hooked tail to gather in pieces of happiness, maybe they'd be able to live a simpler, more innocent life. Even without any children.

Might be good to have the cat, he was thinking. The cat in the photo was good-looking, a lot like Hachi, with the hooked tail and everything. And he hadn't seen Satoru for a long time.

*A friend asked me to take his cat for him, so what do you think?* Kosuke emailed his wife, and she answered: *Do whatever you like.* A tad cold, he thought, but since she hadn't replied to a single email since she'd left, it felt good to hear from her, at least.

He began to wonder if his wife, a true cat lover, might actually come home if he took in the cat. Perhaps if he told her he had adopted the animal but didn't know how to look after it and begged her to help, perhaps she would come back solely out of sympathy for the cat.

No. Dad hates cats, so that won't work. He caught his own knee-jerk reaction; he was worrying, as usual, about what his father might think.

This was exactly why his wife had got fed up with him. Kosuke was the one running the business now, and there was no need to worry about how his dad would feel about things. Yet still he did.

So, partly as a reaction against his dad, he threw his name – Kosuke Sawada – into the ring as a candidate willing to take in his childhood friend's cat.

Satoru wasted no time coming over to Kosuke's place, arriving on Kosuke's day off the following week in his silver van, along with his beloved cat.

When he heard a car engine outside his shop, Kosuke wandered out to find Satoru pulling into the shop's parking lot.

'Kosuke! It's been ages!'

Satoru took his hands off the wheel and waved out of the open driver's-side window.

'Just hurry up and park,' Kosuke urged. He was excited to see Satoru. The guy hadn't changed at all since he was a kid.

'You should have parked at the end. It's easier.'

There were three parking spaces for customers right in front of the shop and Satoru had pulled into the spot furthest from the entrance, where a small shed and piles of boxes made it a tight fit.

'Ah, is that right?' Satoru said, scratching his head as he got out of the van. 'I didn't want to take up a space in case a customer needed it. Well, it's done now.' He took the cat basket from the back seat.

'Is that Nana?'

'Yep. I sent you a photo so you could see how his tail is shaped like a seven. Great name, don't you think?'

'I don't know if I'd call it great, exactly . . . You always choose kind of quirky names . . . Like Hachi.'

Kosuke ushered them into his living room and tried to get a good look at Nana's face, but all Nana did was give a moody growl and turn himself around. When Kosuke peered inside the basket, all he could make out was the black hooked tail and white rear end.

'What's the matter, Nana? Nana-chan . . .?'

Satoru tried to coax Nana out, but eventually gave up.

'Sorry about that. He must be nervous about being in a different house. Give it some time and I'm sure he'll settle down . . .'

They left the basket door open and sat on the sofa together to reminisce over old times.

'You're driving, so alcohol's no good. What would you like to drink? Coffee? Tea?'

Kosuke brewed two cups of coffee. Satoru took his carefully and asked, innocently enough, 'Is your wife here today?'

Kosuke had intended to avoid the issue but, after an awkward silence, failed to come up with a plausible excuse.

'She went back to her parents' place.'

'Oh . . .'

Satoru's face was hard to describe. A *sorry I didn't realize that was such a sore point* kind of look.

'Is it okay for you to make a decision about the cat on your own? Won't you two quarrel about it when she comes home?'

'She likes cats. In fact, taking the cat might lure her back.'

'Yeah, but not everybody likes the same type of cat.'

'I forwarded those photos of Nana to her and asked her what she thought, and she said I should do whatever I like.'

'That doesn't sound like she's on board with the idea.'

'It's the only time since she left that she's answered one of my emails.'

*Taking the cat might lure her back* – Kosuke had said it as a joke, but he was actually hoping it might be true.

'She's not the type of woman to chuck out a cat. And if she never comes home, then I'll look after it myself. Either way, I don't see any problem.'

'I see,' Satoru said, backing down. Now it was Kosuke's turn to ask the questions.

'But tell me, why can't you keep the cat any more?'

'Well, it's just that . . .'

Satoru gave a perplexed smile and scratched at the thinning hair on his head.

'Something came up, and we can't live together any more.'

Something clicked. Kosuke had known something was awry when Satoru, who had a nine-to-five job, had offered to work around Kosuke's day off and come over in the middle of the week.

'Have you been laid off?'

'Not exactly, well – in any case, we just can't live together any more.'

Kosuke didn't pursue it, since Satoru seemed reluctant to talk about it.

'Anyhow, I've got to find a home for Nana, and I've asked a couple of friends.'

'I see. That can't be easy.'

It made Kosuke want to take the cat even more. As an act of kindness. And besides, it was for Satoru.

'What about *you*? Are you okay? Your – plans for the future, and everything?'

'Thanks for asking. As long as I can get Nana settled, I'll be fine.'

Kosuke sensed he shouldn't probe any further. Resisted the *if there's anything I can do, let me know* line.

'You know, when I saw the photo, I was amazed. Nana's the spitting image of Hachi.'

'Even more so when you see him in the flesh.'

Satoru glanced back at the basket still sitting on the floor, but it didn't look like Nana was intending to show his face any time soon.

'When I first saw him, I was surprised, too. For a second I thought it *was* Hachi.'

That was impossible, of course, but the memory saddened him, nonetheless. 'What happened to Hachi?' Kosuke asked.

'He died when I was in high school. His new owner got in touch, told me it was a traffic accident.'

Even now, this must have been a painful memory for Satoru.

'It's nice that they let you know, though.'

At least the two of them, who had both loved the cat, could mourn together. Satoru must have cried alone many times since.

'Sorry, I seem to be getting sadder and sadder here,' Satoru said.

'Don't apologize, you idiot.'

Kosuke made as if to lightly punch him and Satoru playfully swayed to avoid it.

'Time goes by before you know it,' Satoru said. 'It seems like yesterday when you and I found Hachi. Do you remember?'

'Remember? How could I forget?' Kosuke smiled, and Satoru gave a little embarrassed *ahem* laugh.

∽

A SHORT WALK FROM THE SAWADA Photo Studio, up a gentle slope, was a housing complex. Twenty-five years ago, this was considered an up-and-coming area, with rows of model showroom-like houses and fashionable condo units.

Satoru's family lived in a cosy condo in the neighbourhood. Satoru and his parents: the three of them.

Satoru and Kosuke had started going to the same swimming club in second grade. Since he was little, Kosuke had struggled with skin allergies, and his mother, convinced that swimming would make his skin tougher, had made him go, but Satoru had a different reason for going. He was such a fast swimmer people said he had webbed hands, and the teachers at his school had recommended he learn to swim properly.

Always a bit of a joker, Satoru, when they had free swimming time, would pretend to be a salamander and crawl along the bottom of the pool, then playfully pop up and pounce on the other pupils. 'What are you, some kind of *kappa*?' the swimming instructor had said, irritated, and the nickname Kappa – a kind of mythical water imp – stuck. Depending on the instructor's mood, he sometimes called him Webfoot, too.

Once lessons began, though, Satoru was in the advanced class for kids who could swim fast, while Kosuke was in the ordinary class that included all the kids like him with allergies.

Despite all the Kappa and Webfoot antics, when

Satoru swam at speed down the lane he looked incredibly cool. Kosuke and Satoru were good friends, but at those times Kosuke found Satoru a little annoying. *If only I could be like him*, he thought enviously.

But one day he saw Satoru clowning around, diving into the water and cracking his forehead on the bottom, and he was no longer so envious.

It was early summer, and they had been going to the swimming club for two years.

They always met up at the bottom of the slope below the housing complex to walk to swimming club together, and on this day Kosuke was the first to arrive. Which is why he was the one to discover the box first.

A cardboard box had been left below the post with the map of the housing complex on it. And the box was meowing. Hesitantly, Kosuke opened the lid and saw two white balls of downy fur. With a sprinkling of tabby patches here and there.

He stared silently at them. Such helpless, soft little things, he thought. They were so tiny he hesitated even to touch them—

'Wow! Cats!'

From above him, Satoru's voice rang out.

'What's up?' he said, crouching down beside Kosuke.

'Somebody just left it here.'

'They're so cute!'

In silence, the two boys timidly stroked the fluffy fur for a few moments, then Satoru spoke.

'Do you want to hold him?'

*You have allergies, so don't ever touch animals* – Kosuke could hear his mother's scolding voice in his head, but he couldn't just stand and watch Satoru give them a stroke. Kosuke had been the one to find them, after all.

He scooped one of them up in his hands and placed it on his palm. It was so light!

He wanted to carry on stroking them, but they were going to be late for swimming. Reluctantly, they peeled the kittens off them and returned them to the box.

They agreed that they would look in on the kittens on the way back, and raced down the road to the swimming club. They were a few minutes late for class and the instructor slapped them both on the head.

After class, they fell over themselves to get back to the bottom of the slope below the housing complex.

The box was still there, under the sign, but to their dismay, now there was only one kitten inside. Someone must have taken the other one.

It seemed to them that the fate of the remaining kitten lay in their hands. A kitten with tabby patches on its forehead in the shape of the character *hachi*. And a black hooked tail.

The two of them sat down on the grass beside the box and gazed at the little kitten curled up in it, sleeping soundly. How could any child not want to take this tiny, soft little creature home?

What would happen if we did take it home? Each boy knew exactly what the other was thinking.

Kosuke knew his mum would be against it because of his allergies, plus his dad wasn't so keen on animals.

In contrast to Kosuke, Satoru was quick to come to a decision.

'I'll ask my mum.'

'That's not fair!'

Kosuke's reaction was fuelled by something that had happened at swimming club a few days before. A girl Kosuke was keen on saw Satoru swimming in the advanced class and murmured, 'He's pretty cool.'

Satoru could swim fast, he didn't have any allergies, and his father and mother were both kind people, so if he took the cat home they were sure to accept it. So not only did the girl Kosuke liked praise Satoru, but now he would get to keep this soft, tiny creature – that just wasn't fair, was it?

When Kosuke told him this, Satoru looked hurt, as if he'd been slapped. Kosuke felt ashamed.

He'd simply been getting something off his chest, that was all.

'I mean, I found him first,' he finally blurted out.

To which Satoru, honest to a fault, said, 'I'm sorry. Yes, you did find him first, Kosuke, so he's your cat.'

Kosuke regretted having snapped at his friend, but all he could manage was a small nod. They parted a little awkwardly, and Kosuke carried the cardboard box with the kitten inside it home.

His mother, surprisingly, wasn't against keeping the kitten.

'Perhaps it's because of the swimming, but you haven't had any allergic reactions lately, so as long as we keep the house really clean, I think it should be okay.'

The main obstacle was his father.

'No way! A *cat*? Are you insane?'

That was his immediate reaction, and he refused to change his mind.

'What if he scratches everything with his claws? Looking after a cat costs money, you know! I'm not running a photo studio to feed some cat!'

Kosuke's mother supported her son, but that seemed to make his father even more resistant to the idea. Before they had dinner, he ordered Kosuke to take the cat back where he'd found it.

So Kosuke, on the verge of tears, trudged back to the slope below the housing complex with the cardboard box held tightly to his chest.

But put the box back under the sign? He couldn't bring himself to do that. And so he found himself heading for his friend's house.

'My dad said I can't keep the cat.' Standing at the door sobbing, Kosuke finally managed to get the words out.

'I get it,' Satoru said, and nodded. 'Leave it to me. I have a great idea!'

Satoru disappeared inside the house. Kosuke waited at the door, guessing that he was going to ask his mother if he could keep the cat, but then Satoru reappeared, with his swimming bag slung across his shoulder.

'Satoru, where are you going with that?' his mother called out from the kitchen. 'We're going to have dinner as soon as your father gets home!'

'You go ahead and eat!' Satoru called out, slipping into his trainers at the entrance. 'Kosuke and I are going to run away from home for a while!'

'What?'

Satoru's mother was always so graceful and gentle. Kosuke had never heard her sound so stern.

She seemed to be in the middle of deep-frying tempura, so although she wasn't happy about it, she couldn't come to the front door. Instead, she just popped her head out from the kitchen.

'Ko-chan, what is he talking about?' she asked.

But Kosuke was equally clueless.

'Come on,' Satoru said. He pulled Kosuke by the hand and they ran out of the house.

'I read this book at school the other day,' Satoru explained. 'A boy found a stray puppy and his father got angry and told him to take it back where he had found it, but he couldn't bring himself to do it so he ran away from home. In the middle of the night, his father came looking for him and, in the end, he said he would let him keep it, as long as he looked after it himself.'

Satoru rattled on excitedly.

'What we're doing is exactly the same, Kosuke, so I'm sure it'll work out! The only difference is it's a stray cat, not a dog. And you have me to help you.'

Apart from it being a kitten, not a puppy, Kosuke had the feeling that his situation was quite different from the one in the book, though he was, admittedly, quite attracted by the idea of his father feeling sad and giving in if he ran away.

He decided to go along with the plan. The first thing they did was go to a small supermarket and buy some cat food. 'We'd like food for a kitten,' they told the man at the cash register, and the man, whose hair was dyed red, said, 'Try this,' and handed them a can of paste-like meat. The man had looked intimidating at first but turned out to be unexpectedly kind.

Then they had dinner in the park of the housing complex. Satoru had grabbed some bread and sweets from his house, and the two of them made do with that. They opened the can of cat food for the kitten.

'So, by "middle of the night", I'm guessing we need to hang out here until about twelve.'

Satoru had prudently packed an alarm clock in his bag.

'But won't my father have a total fit if I stay out that late?'

Kosuke's father seemed friendly enough outside the house, but with his family he was an obstinate man with a short fuse.

'What are you talking about? We're doing it for the cat, aren't we? And besides, he'll forgive you in the end, so it'll all work out.'

In the book, the father had forgiven his son, but caught up in Satoru's blind enthusiasm, Kosuke didn't feel able to say what was on his mind, namely that his father had a very different personality, and he doubted that the plan would succeed.

As they whiled away the time playing with the cat in the park, a few people, out for a stroll, called out to them, among them a woman walking her dogs.

'What are you doing out this late? Your family will be worried,' she said.

They were too well known in the neighbourhood. Kosuke started to wonder if they'd chosen the wrong spot, though Satoru didn't seem at all concerned.

'Don't worry about us,' he told the woman. 'We're running away!'

'Is that so? Well, you'd better go home right now!'

After a fifth woman had come up to them, Kosuke finally raised an objection.

'Satoru, I don't think this is how you run away from home.'

'I know, but in the book the father came looking for them in a park.'

'Yeah, but this doesn't make any sense.'

At that moment, they heard a voice calling through the cool air: 'Satoru!' It was his mother. 'It's late, and enough is enough. Come home now! You've got Kosuke's family worried, too!'

Satoru flinched. 'There's no way they could have found us so quickly!'

'You didn't think they'd find us?'

Had Satoru seriously believed they could hide from their parents when there were all these strangers around who seemed to know them?

'I'm sorry, Mum!' Satoru shouted. 'But we can't be found yet!'

'Come on, Kosuke!' He grabbed the cardboard box and ran with it to the gate leading out of the park. Kosuke could do nothing but follow. It felt like they were straying from the storyline Satoru had described, but there should still be time to put that right. Surely there would be. Well, maybe.

They managed to shake off Satoru's mother and were sprinting down the slope away from the housing complex when all of a sudden there was a roar.

'Come back here!'

The roar came from Kosuke's father. It was probably too late now to put anything right. Maybe we should just apologize, Kosuke was thinking, but Satoru shouted: 'It's the enemy!'

The story had taken a different turn now.

'Run for it!'

By now, they'd completely lost sight of the narrative they were supposed to be sticking to. For the time being, all Kosuke could do was chase after Satoru, who was determined to keep running.

His portly and generally sedentary father couldn't keep up and they lost him after they'd rounded the first corner, but now the street was totally straight. There was nowhere to hide.

'Kosuke, this way!'

Satoru had raced inside the small supermarket where they'd bought the can of cat food. A smattering of customers were flipping through magazines while the red-haired clerk listlessly restocked a shelf.

'You have to hide us! We're being chased!' Satoru shouted. The clerk looked over at them doubtfully.

'If they catch us, they're going to get rid of him!'

Satoru showed the cardboard box to the clerk and a siren-like yowl rang out from it.

The clerk stared at the box for a moment, then headed to the back of the shop, motioning for them to follow. They passed through a door and the clerk pointed to the back exit.

'You're a lifesaver!'

Satoru scampered out, followed by Kosuke.

He turned and gave a small bow of thanks, and the clerk wordlessly waved a hand at them.

From there, they scurried from place to place, but they were only children and there was only so far their legs could carry them.

Finally, they ran to their elementary school. Satoru's odd little plan to run away from home had caused quite a disturbance, so much so that the news had got around the neighbourhood, and as they legged it into the school grounds, all the grown-ups were hot on their heels.

They prised open a window, one that all the pupils knew was out of kilter and didn't lock properly, and slipped into the school building. The adults had no idea how to get in, so they ran around helplessly outside, while the boys made their way up to the top floor.

They spilled out on to the roof and could at last put down the cardboard box with the kitten inside.

'I hope he's okay. He was quite shaken up.'

There was no sound coming from the box so they quickly opened it. The kitten was nestled in a corner. Kosuke hesitantly reached his arm inside to touch it—

*Pyaaa—!*

The kitten started to howl even louder than before.

'Sssshhhh! You'll give us away.'

The two boys tried to calm the kitten, but cats don't often listen. Crouched down and shushing at each other, they could hear voices calling out.

'I hear a cat!'

'It's coming from the roof!'

The grown-ups had started to gather down below.

'Kosuke, enough!'

One angry voice rose up from the crowd, that of Kosuke's father. From his tone, it was easy to guess that his son was in for a beating.

Kosuke, in tears, turned on Satoru.

'It didn't work! You lied, Satoru!'

'It isn't over yet. We can still pull this off!'

Again, a voice called out from below. 'Satoru, come down here right this minute!'

Satoru's father had joined their pursuers.

'We can go up the fire escape,' someone piped up, and it became clear that Kosuke's father, his face burning with rage, was already climbing the stairs.

'It's all over now,' Kosuke mumbled, holding his head

in his hands. Satoru ran over to the railing on the roof. He leaned over it and shouted, 'Stop! If you don't stop, he's going to jump!'

A murmur ran through the crowd below.

'*What?*' Kosuke was horrified. 'What are you doing, Satoru?!'

When he grabbed Satoru's sleeve, Satoru gave him a blazing grin and a thumbs-up. 'A comeback!' he said. It wasn't what Kosuke had been hoping for, but it did seem to be enough to stop Kosuke's father dead in his tracks.

'Satoru, is that true, what you said?' Satoru's mother yelled from below.

'It's true! It's true!' Satoru yelled back. 'He just took off his trainers!'

'Oh my god!' People were screaming from below.

'Kosuke, calm down now, kid!' This from Satoru's father, while Kosuke's father roared, 'Stop buggering about!' Even from up above, it was clear he was furious. 'Stop whining! I'm coming up, and I'll drag you down from there if I have to!'

'Don't do that, Mr Sawada! Kosuke's really going to do it!' Satoru shouted, to stop him. 'If you come up here, he'll jump off, and he'll take the cat with him!'

Satoru turned to Kosuke with a grave expression on his face. 'Kosuke, could you, like, kind of straddle the railing?'

Kosuke replied that no way was he going to risk his life over all this.

'But look, you want to keep the cat, don't you?'

'Sure, but . . .' For the sake of a cat, did you really have to go this far?

For one thing, the story Satoru had read about the boy running away hadn't ended up with him and the puppy jumping to their deaths.

'Listen! Can't we ask first whether it's okay to keep the cat at your house, Satoru?'

'What?' Satoru looked as startled as a pigeon shot with an air rifle. 'You mean, it's okay for *me* to have the cat? Man, if you thought that, you should have said so!'

Beaming, Satoru called out to the crowd down below.

'Dad! Mum! Kosuke says he wants us to have the cat—!'

'Okay, okay. But first talk Kosuke out of jumping!'

A storm of misunderstanding still seemed to be swirling through the crowd of grown-ups, who didn't have a clue what was going on.

~

SATORU, YOU REALLY WEREN'T TOO bright as a child, were you?

I could hear Satoru and Kosuke's conversation from inside my basket. I'd never heard such a mad story in my life.

'It was after we came down from the roof that things got heavy.'

'Your dad thumped us pretty hard, Kosuke. I remember, the next day my head looked like the Great Buddha in Nara.'

The cat that had thrown the whole neighbourhood into such an uproar was my predecessor, that cat Hachi, apparently.

'Speaking of which, Hachi was a male tabby, wasn't he? Aren't male tabbies supposed to be quite rare?' asked Kosuke.

Is that so? Well, since Hachi and I have the same markings, I must be a pretty rare specimen myself.

I had pricked up my ears to listen in, and Satoru said, smiling, 'Well, the thing is . . . I asked a vet about it and he said his markings are too few for him to be classified as a tabby.'

'Really? Other than his forehead and tail, it's true – he was pure white.'

Kosuke paused. 'Man,' he said, raising his arms then crossing them in front of his chest. I could see all this through the gaps in my basket. 'I was thinking that if I had told my father it was a valuable male tabby I might have been able to convince him to keep it.'

Kosuke looked over at the basket. I quickly turned my head away so as not to meet his eye. Too much bother if he tries to get all friendly on me.

'What about Nana? His face looks exactly like Hachi's, but what about his markings?'

'Nana can't be classified as a tabby either. He's just a moggy.'

Well, *excuuuse me*. I glared at the back of Satoru's head, and he went on:

'But, to me, Nana's much more valuable than a male tabby. It's fate, don't you think, that he looks just like the first cat I ever had? When I first laid eyes on him, I knew, someday, he had to be my own precious cat.'

Harrumph. You're just saying that because it sounds good. I know what you're getting at. But still.

Maybe that's why I saw Satoru crying that day. After I was hit by the car and had dragged myself back to his place. He mentioned that Hachi had died in a traffic accident.

Satoru must have thought he was going to lose another precious cat to a car accident.

'That was one good cat, Hachi. So well behaved,' Kosuke said.

To which Satoru replied, with a smile, 'Though he wasn't very athletic.'

According to what I heard, he was the type whose legs went all spongy when someone grabbed the back of his neck. A cat who couldn't catch mice, in other words. Pretty pathetic, if you ask me. A real cat would immediately fold in its legs.

Me? I'm a real cat, naturally. I caught my first sparrow when I was less than six months old. And catching something with wings is a lot trickier than catching any four-legged land creature, believe you me.

'When he was playing with a catnip toy he'd go dizzy, chasing it around.'

''Cause he was usually pretty placid.'

'What about Nana?'

'He loves mouse toys. The kind made out of rabbit fur.'

Hold on a sec. I can't let that pass. Since when did I *love* that awful fake mouse?

It smells like the real thing, so if you throw it near me, of course I'll fight with it, but no matter how much I chomp on it, no tasty juice comes out. So when I finally calm down I'm worn out, and the whole thing's been a total waste of time, d'you understand?

There's that manga on TV sometimes where the samurai cuts down a dingbat and sighs, 'That was a waste of a good sword.' To me, that's kind of how it feels. You've hunted down yet another useless thing. (By the way, Satoru prefers the shows with guns.) The least they could do would be to stuff those toys with white meat. But could I take this complaint to the pet-toymakers? Stop worrying about what the owners think and pay some attention to your *real* clients. Your real clients are folk like *me*.

In any case, after one of those pointless chases, I usually let off steam with a good walk. But Satoru usually tags along, and that makes it hard to do any successful hunting.

What I mean is, the minute I spot some decent game, Satoru interferes. Deliberately makes some careless noise or movement. When I glare at him, he feigns ignorance, but all that racket gives us away, thank you very much.

When I get upset and wave my tail energetically from side to side, he gives me this pathetic look and tries to explain.

'You have lots of crunchies at home to eat, don't you? You don't need to kill anything. Even if you catch something, Nana, you barely eat it.'

You idiot, idiot, idioooootttt! Every living creature on earth is born with an instinct to kill! You can try to dodge it by bringing in vegetarianism, but you just don't hear a plant scream when you kill it! Hunting down what can be hunted is a cat's natural instinct! Sometimes we hunt things but don't eat them, but that's what training is all about.

My god, what spineless creatures they are, those that don't kill the food they eat. Satoru's a human being, of course, so he just doesn't get it.

'Is Nana good at hunting?'

'He's beyond good! He caught a pigeon that landed on our porch.'

Right you are. Those blasted birds get all superior in

human territory. I thought I'd show them what's what. And Satoru, all teary-eyed, always asked, 'Why do you catch them if you're not going to eat them?' If that's the way you think, then don't interfere when I hunt on our walks.

And didn't Satoru complain about pigeon droppings on the laundry he'd hung out to dry? He'd be happy if I chased away the pigeons, and I'd get to hunt. Literally, two birds with one stone, so why the complaints? And by the bye, ever since that incident, the pigeons have never come near our porch again, but have I heard a word of thanks? Still waiting!

'It was a real problem that time,' Satoru said. 'A sparrow or a mouse I could bury in the bushes next to the apartment building, but something the size of a pigeon, that's a different story. I ended up burying it in a park, and the only conclusion anybody who spotted me, a thirty-year-old man burying a pigeon, could come to is that I was a pretty dodgy character.'

'There are more and more weird things happening these days, too.'

'Right. Every time someone passed by, I would say apologetically, "I'm so sorry, but the cat did it," and they'd look at me really oddly. And wouldn't you know it, that was the one occasion Nana wasn't with me.'

Ah, so he had an awkward time, did he? I should have been with him. But Satoru didn't tell me, so it's *his* fault, and I'm not going to apologize.

'Sounds like Nana's wilder than Hachi was.'

'But he's quite gentle sometimes too, like Hachi. When I'm feeling depressed or down, he always snuggles up close . . .'

Not that hearing these words made me happy or anything.

'Sometimes, I get the feeling he can understand what people are saying. He's pretty bright.'

Humans who think we *don't* understand them are the stupid ones.

'Hachi was a very kind cat. Whenever my father had a go at me and I went to your house, Satoru, he'd sit on my lap and refuse to jump off.'

'He understood when people were feeling down. When my parents had an argument, he'd always side with the one who had lost. It made it easy for me as a child to tell who had won and who had lost.'

'I wonder if Nana would do the same, too?'

'I'm sure of it. He's pretty kind.'

Hachi seemed to be a decent sort of cat, but going on and on about *Hachi this* and *Hachi that* made me think, *If a cat that's dead was so good, maybe I should die too, and let them see how they like that.*

'I'm sorry,' Kosuke suddenly murmured. 'I should have taken Hachi from you back then.'

'There was nothing we could do about it.'

Satoru sounded like he didn't hold a grudge. Instead, looking at Kosuke, it seemed to me that he was the one who did.

～

THOUGH SATORU'S FAMILY BROUGHT Hachi up, it was as though Kosuke did the job half the time.

Whenever he went over to Satoru's, he played tirelessly with Hachi, and Satoru sometimes took the cat over to Kosuke's house.

At first, Kosuke's father stubbornly refused to let

Hachi in the house, so they played in the garage, but before long his mother let them bring the cat inside, if not into the studio, and little by little his father got used to it. He warned them not to let Hachi sharpen his claws on the walls or the furniture, but sometimes, when he passed by, Kosuke's father would say a few nice things to Hachi.

Kosuke regretted that he couldn't have Hachi himself, but he was very happy when his father played with him. It felt like his father was meeting him halfway. He even hoped that, if he ever found another stray kitten, this time he would be allowed to keep it for himself.

Because it was a very special thing – to have your own cat in your own home.

Whenever he stayed overnight at Satoru's, sleeping on the futon beside his bed, he'd often be woken in the early hours by four feet clomping over him. Feeling the weight of a cat's paws pressing into your shoulders in the middle of the night – not much beats that.

He would glance over and see Hachi curled up in a ball on top of Satoru's chest. Perhaps finding it too hard to breathe, Satoru, still asleep, would slide the cat beside him. Lucky guy, Kosuke thought. If he were my cat, we could sleep together and I would let him walk all over me.

'My father seems to have taken a liking to Hachi, and I'm thinking, maybe, if we find another stray kitten, he might let me keep it.'

'That'd be great! Then Hachi would have a friend.'

The idea made Satoru happy, and on the way to and from swimming club he'd kept an eye out for another box with a kitten inside it.

But there never was another cardboard box with a kitten inside left under the housing complex sign.

Of course, it was a good thing that no more poor cats were abandoned. Because, even if they had found another cat, Kosuke's father still wouldn't have let him keep it.

Two years had passed since Hachi had gone to live at Satoru's. Kosuke and Satoru were now in the sixth grade of elementary school.

As autumn shed its leaves, their school organized a residential trip. Three days, two nights, in Kyoto. Kosuke could do without the temples – they all looked the same to him – but he was overjoyed to be staying away overnight with his friends, far from home.

And having more spending money than he'd ever imagined to buy souvenirs with was exciting, too. There were plenty of things he wanted to buy for himself, but he also had to remember to buy presents for his family.

One day, when they were in a souvenir shop, Satoru had a worried look on his face. 'What's wrong?' asked Kosuke.

'Um, I'm wondering which one to buy.'

Satoru was looking at various kinds of facial blotting paper on a cosmetics display.

'Mum asked me to buy some blotting paper, but I've forgotten which brand she wanted.'

'Aren't they all the same?'

Satoru didn't seem to know one way or the other, so Kosuke said, 'Why don't you buy her gift another time?'

'Okay, I guess I'll get something for Dad.'

'Yeah, you should. I'll get something for my dad, too.'

They wandered around a few shops, and Kosuke was

the first to decide what to get. A good-luck *maneki-neko* cat keyring, the cat with a banner on its back that read 'Success in Business'. Of course, there was an ulterior motive behind this choice: his father might begin to like cats.

'Oh – that's great!' Satoru's eyes sparkled at the comical expression on the *maneki-neko* cat's face. 'But we don't have a family business, so that slogan wouldn't work.'

'There're lots of others besides "Success in Business".'

Satoru figured that the two slogans on banners that made most sense for his father were 'Health Comes First' and 'Road Safety'. A third read 'Harmony in the Home', but he wasn't exactly sure what that meant.

Satoru ended up picking the keyring with the 'Road Safety' banner, because he thought the *maneki-neko* cat resembled Hachi.

He hadn't bought the blotting paper for his mother, but said he'd look for some the following day.

But after lunch the next day, Satoru was gone. When their class assembled, their teacher explained that 'Miyawaki-kun had to return home before us.'

'Ah – poor Satoru!'

His classmates all murmured to each other how sorry they were. They imagined themselves in Satoru's place, having to go home early.

'Sawada-kun, do you know why?'

Kosuke had heard nothing. Satoru had gone home without saying a thing even to his best friend, so something very serious must have happened.

And Satoru hadn't even bought the blotting paper for his mother. She'll be disappointed, Kosuke thought, when only his father gets a souvenir.

That's it! Kosuke had a sudden flash of inspiration.

I'll buy it for him, that whatchamacallit blotting paper. But how am I going to work out which brand she wants?

As he was puzzling over this, their school group went on a visit to Kinkakuji, the Temple of the Golden Pavilion. This glittery temple was unique, totally different from all the sober-looking ones they'd seen up till then. There were squeals of disbelief among the students when they saw it. 'Man, that's gaudy!' was the consensus. If only Satoru could be here to see it, Kosuke thought, his heart aching.

During their free time, a couple of girls in his class were hanging out in a souvenir shop, and when he spied them, Kosuke was struck by another flash of inspiration.

The girls will know! Blotting paper is something girls use.

'Hey!' Kosuke called over to the girls, who were twittering away to each other like a pair of chirping birds.

'Do you know a brand of blotting paper? It's supposed to be kind of famous?'

They both shot back the same reply.

'You mean Yojiya. Yojiya! They have it in that store over there.'

The girls were about to head over there themselves, so Kosuke went with them.

The cheapest blotting paper was over three hundred yen and, thinking how much spending money he had left, Kosuke hesitated.

But Kosuke felt sorry for Satoru, having to go home in the middle of the school trip. And he was Satoru's best friend.

Satoru probably feels worse about not getting the gift for his mother than having to go home early, he thought. And Kosuke was the only one who understood that.

He had no clue what was so special about this blotting paper, but he went ahead and bought a pack, with its distinctive drawing of a *kokeshi* doll on the wrapping. The package was so thin and flimsy-looking he was doubtful that Satoru's mother would really want it, but that's what Satoru had decided on.

'Sawada-kun, did your mother ask you to buy Yojiya paper?'

'Nope. Satoru's mother asked him, and he was searching for it in all the shops. But he went back without buying any . . .'

'You are such a good guy, Sawada-kun!' the girls gushed. It was not a bad feeling.

'Miyawaki-kun's mum will love it. It's a famous brand.'

Is it really that famous? Kosuke was surprised, and at the same time relieved. He was convinced now that Satoru's mother would appreciate the gift, no matter how flimsy it seemed.

I should have bought the same thing for my mother, he thought, but he'd already bought her a present the day before. Buying two presents for her would push him over budget, and he could picture his father's face. He abandoned the idea.

They arrived home on the evening of the third day.

'I'm back!'

Kosuke held out the presents he'd bought and was about to tell his parents all about the trip when his father poked him.

'Stop messing around!'

But all he was doing was giving them their presents. The thought made him want to cry.

His mother had a serious look in her eyes. 'Change your clothes, we're going over to Satoru's.'

'Satoru had to leave early. Has something happened?'

His mother looked down, searching for how to put it, but his father didn't mince his words.

'Satoru's parents passed away.'

*Passed away.* The words didn't register, and Kosuke stood there blankly.

'They died!' his father grunted.

The moment Kosuke understood, the tears started to flow. It was as if a dam had broken.

'Stop your blubbering,' his father said, poking him again, but the tears wouldn't stop.

Satoru – *Satoru, Satoru . . .* My god . . .

Kosuke had gone over to Satoru's just the day before they had left for their school trip. He had been playing with Hachi and Satoru's mother had said, 'You have to get up early tomorrow for your school trip, so you'd better be getting home soon. You're welcome to play with Hachi any time.' Kosuke suddenly fell silent.

'It was a car accident. They swerved to avoid a bicycle that came out of nowhere . . .'

They missed the bike, but the two of them didn't make it.

'Today's the wake, so we should go.'

Kosuke changed into the clothes his mother had laid out for him and the three of them set off. Just as they reached the bottom of the slope leading to the housing complex, Kosuke realized he'd forgotten something.

'You can get it later!'

He stood up to his father, telling them they could go on ahead, and finally managed to persuade him to give him the house key.

'What an idiot!' he heard his father mutter as he trotted on.

The wake was being held at the local community centre.

A couple of women dressed in black scurried around, and Satoru sat vacantly in front of the two coffins at the altar.

'Satoru!' Kosuke called out.

'Um,' Satoru said, nodding. It was as if his mind was elsewhere. Kosuke had no idea what to say.

'Here you go.'

Kosuke pulled out a thin paper packet from his pocket. The present he'd run back to fetch when his father had called him an idiot.

'The blotting paper your mother wanted. It's Yojiya.'

Satoru burst into tears; he dropped his head while his small body shook with his sobbing. It was only later, when Kosuke had grown up, that he understood the full meaning of the word 'lament'.

A young woman came over quickly and huddled over him. She spoke in Satoru's ear, and from the way she was rubbing his back to comfort him, she seemed to know him well.

'Are you a friend of Satoru's?' she asked.

'Yes, I am,' Kosuke replied, standing up straight.

'Would you take him home so he can have a rest? This is the first time he's cried since he got back.'

Kosuke said he would.

The woman's eyes, puffy from crying herself, broke into a smile.

'Thank you,' she said.

Throughout the funeral, Satoru had sat rigidly next to

the young woman. There were other people there who were apparently relatives, but they didn't seem so close to him.

Satoru's classmates had gone, too, to light incense and pray. All the girls sobbed, but Satoru had greeted them without shedding any tears himself.

Kosuke was impressed by how Satoru had held up. But, at the same time, it felt as if his friend had drifted away somehow and wasn't really there. If Kosuke were in Satoru's place, if his father – the one who had called him an idiot – and his mother had passed away at the same time, he knew he wouldn't be able to hold it together like that.

Kosuke took Satoru by the hand and led him home. On the way, Satoru's words were broken up by tears.

'The good-luck charm for my father came too late. And I didn't get a present for Mum . . . Thank you for buying it . . .'

Only Kosuke could have worked out what he was saying, so incoherent with sobs were his words.

When they got to Satoru's house, Hachi was waiting on that day's newspaper near the front door. He seemed unfazed by Satoru crying like an animal and padded towards the living room as if guiding them. When Satoru collapsed on the sofa, Hachi jumped up on his lap and licked Satoru's hand over and over.

When they'd found Hachi he'd been only a kitten, but now he seemed more grown up than Satoru.

After the funeral, Satoru didn't come back to school. Every day, Kosuke would take homework over to his house, and they would play silently with Hachi for a while, then Kosuke would go home.

The young woman stayed at Satoru's house the entire

time. It turned out she was Satoru's aunt – his mother's younger sister.

Is he going to live with her here? Kosuke wondered; he would drop in on Satoru even on days when there was no homework to deliver. His aunt knew his name, greeting him with a 'Hello, Kosuke,' whenever he came by. But she was quieter than Satoru's gregarious mother and the house now felt strange to him.

'I'm going to move,' Satoru said one day.

The aunt was going to be Satoru's guardian, but she lived a long way away.

Ever since Satoru hadn't come back to school, Kosuke had had an inkling that this might happen, but when it did it felt as if a hole had opened up in his heart.

He knew that whining about it wasn't going to change anything. He stroked Hachi as he lay curled up on Satoru's lap, without saying a word. Today, too, Hachi was gently licking Satoru's hand.

'But Hachi will go with you, won't he?'

That way, Satoru wouldn't be so lonely.

But Satoru shook his head.

'I can't take Hachi with me. My aunt moves around a lot with work.'

And Satoru, too, looked like he knew that whining about it wasn't going to change anything. But that's just too much to bear, Kosuke thought.

'What'll happen to him?'

'Some other relatives say they'll take him.'

'Do you know them well?'

Satoru shook his head. This made Kosuke angry. How could Hachi be taken in by people Satoru didn't even know?

'I'll . . . I'll ask if we can have Hachi at our place!'

Hachi had been looked after by Kosuke half the time anyway. If Kosuke could take care of Hachi, then Satoru could come to his place to see him.

Even his father had shown an interest in Hachi whenever he visited.

But his father's view hadn't changed a bit. 'No way! A cat? Are you kidding?'

'But Satoru's mum and dad are dead! And now, if Hachi has to stay with people he doesn't even know, think how sad he'll feel!'

'He knows them. They're relatives.'

'Satoru said he doesn't know them!'

Distant relatives you hardly ever see are, to a child, like total strangers. Friends are much closer. Why don't adults understand that?

'In any case, it wouldn't work. Cats live ten, twenty years sometimes! Do you want to take responsibility for it your entire life?'

'Yes!'

'That's pretty cheeky for someone who's never earned a penny in his life.'

His mother, perhaps thinking this was getting out of hand, stepped in on Kosuke's side, but his father still wouldn't budge.

'I feel sorry for Satoru,' his father went on, 'but these are two different things. Go and tell him you can't do it!'

There was no way a sixth-grade boy was going to make him change his mind, so Kosuke headed towards Satoru's, crying fat tears all the way. His legs felt like lead as he climbed up the slope from the bottom of the housing complex.

When they had first found Hachi, Satoru had done everything he possibly could to enable Kosuke to have him. His attempts had been misguided, but he had given it his all, done his very best.

And the upshot was that Hachi had gone to live in Satoru's house.

'I'm so sorry,' Kosuke said, still crying, his head on his chest. 'My dad said I can't have him.'

*Damn you, Dad. Don't you see what Satoru means to your son?*

'It's okay,' Satoru said, smiling through his own tears. 'Thank you for asking.'

On the day Satoru moved, Kosuke was there to see him off. Unbelievably, Kosuke's father came with him. 'Of course I'm coming,' his father had said, 'since we know Satoru so well.'

Seeing his best friend off before he moved away, Kosuke had never felt such deep contempt for his father.

At first, the boys exchanged letters and phone calls frequently, but as the days passed, the calls and letters naturally became less regular. One reason for this was Kosuke's shame at having shirked his duty towards his friend by not taking Hachi in.

If they had been able to see each other from time to time, their closeness would have eased his sense of awkwardness, but as they were not able to meet, time only made his feelings of guilt grow.

However, they never stopped sending each other New Year cards.

These always included a brief note saying that they should get together sometime, and they continued through high school and on into college. But the intervening years in which they hadn't seen each other made it all the harder to arrange to meet again.

At the Adult's Day ceremony, all Kosuke's old classmates were reunited to celebrate their turning twenty. Many who now lived outside the prefecture came back especially. But Satoru wasn't among them. Where was he attending his Adult's Day ceremony? Kosuke wondered.

Kosuke and his classmates must have had fun at the ceremony, because afterwards, for a while at least, they continued to get together on various occasions. It was still a bit soon for a high-school reunion, but it was just the right time to wax nostalgic about elementary- and junior-high-school days.

Kosuke, who still lived in the prefecture, was put in charge of organizing the elementary-school reunion. It was decided that all his sixth-grade classmates should be invited.

As he was in charge, he decided to send an invitation to Satoru.

Satoru phoned in reply. His voice had not changed. Though they hadn't talked in years, their conversation was as lively as if no time at all had passed. Satoru rattled on and on, as if making up for all the years of silence.

'It was fun talking to you again. Well, see you!' Satoru said, and hung up. Moments later, he called again. He'd forgotten to mention the class reunion. Of course he would come.

After this, they kept in touch more regularly. Satoru was living in Tokyo, but now that they were adults distance wasn't so much of an obstacle.

Satoru graduated from a college in Tokyo and got a job

in the city. Kosuke graduated from a nearby college and found a job locally.

It was three years ago now that Kosuke had taken over his father's photographic studio.

Even after Kosuke had grown up, he and his father didn't get on, and when his father's health failed he shut up shop and moved to the countryside a short distance away. He was from a family of local landowners, so he had various plots of land in the area.

For a time, his father kept the photo studio closed. But after a while, keeping it at all seemed like too much trouble so he decided to sell it off. He'd often announced his intention to do this, but even so it made Kosuke a bit sad.

He'd been around photos ever since he was a child. His father, hot-tempered and overbearing most of the time, became cheerful and kind when teaching him about photography, and once he'd even given him an old camera. Kosuke had picked up a lot about photography, or at least his father's version of it, and when he was older he had helped out occasionally with photo sessions at the studio.

It was only through photography that he and his father had got along. Which meant that now that their connection with photography had ended, their relationship could only get worse.

And Kosuke couldn't bear that. He talked things over with his wife, and urged on, too, by the fact that his own job wasn't going well, he told his father not to sell off the studio but to let him take it over.

His father was unexpectedly overjoyed, and nearly burst into tears.

Ah, even this late in the game, maybe this would mark a change for the better.

'At least that's what I thought . . .' Kosuke almost spat the words out.

'Did you two have a bad argument or something?' Satoru asked anxiously.

'What with my father being so arrogant and selfish, maybe I shouldn't have tried so hard to be a good son.'

After he had reopened the photo studio, his father still interfered, turning up and meddling.

He'd give his opinions on how to run the place, what direction the business should go in, and generally boss Kosuke around. On top of this, he'd make inappropriate remarks to Kosuke's wife.

'You'd better have a child soon so there'll be someone to take over the studio,' he told her.

Kosuke and his wife were having trouble conceiving, and this was causing them a lot of stress. Kosuke's mother would sometimes warn her husband to watch his tongue, but hearing candid advice from his wife only made him more obstinate, a condition he never seemed to outgrow.

Finally, Kosuke's wife conceived a child. That had been last year. But during the first trimester of the pregnancy, when things were touch and go, she had a miscarriage.

His wife was deeply upset, and she found the words his father spoke in an attempt to comfort her extremely hurtful.

'Well,' he had said, 'at least we know now you can have children.'

Kosuke was incensed. *Why is this man my father? I don't know how many times since I was a child I have felt this way about him. Ever since the day he rejected Hachi.*

'After that, my wife went back to her parents' place. Her

parents, naturally, were furious. Even if I try to apologize, they don't want to listen.'

His father showed no remorse at all. 'Young women these days are so touchy,' was all he could say.

'Sometimes I just wish he'd drop down dead.' Kosuke blurted this out as if to himself, and quickly apologized. 'Sorry about that,' he added. Perhaps he'd inherited this insensitivity from his father. The idea appalled him.

'Don't worry about it,' Satoru said, smiling. 'There are all kinds of parent–child relationships. I never wanted my parents to die. But if I'd had other parents, I don't know how I would have felt. If your father had been my father, Kosuke, I don't know if I would have been able to love him.' He burst out laughing. 'Some people really shouldn't become parents. There's no absolute guarantee when it comes to the love between a parent and their child.'

This was an unexpected view, coming from Satoru.

'I hope your wife will come back soon,' he added.

'I don't know. It's not just her father-in-law she's upset with.'

She must be disgusted with her husband, who had never been able to stand up to his father. Kosuke had a habit of swallowing whatever he wanted to say. Repeated patterns of childhood behaviour have long-term consequences. All Kosuke ever did was mumble ineffectually about the ridiculous things his father said in that high-handed tone of his.

'Does your father still really meddle that much?'

'And we don't have as many customers these days, either.'

People weren't going to photographic studios on special occasions like they used to. It was all part of the changing times, but Kosuke's father blamed it on his son; he thought he was spineless. And he started interfering even more, saying he needed to take charge of the business again. And still, Kosuke could never bring himself to stand up to his father and argue back.

∽

ME, ON THE OTHER HAND, I'm not like that. If things aren't good, I have no problem saying so. Because cats are creatures that can say no.

And the idea of being taken into the home of a man because he hoped that his wife, who likes cats, would be tempted back? I swear, with all the feline dignity I can muster, this gets a definite no from me.

'I wonder if Nana's finally got used to it here.'

Kosuke stood up from the sofa and knelt beside my basket, placing his hand gently on the top.

Just try it – try pulling me out by force from this basket and I swear I'll scratch so many lines on your face you'll be able to play checkers on it for the next three months.

*Chi chi chi* – Kosuke made friendly little sounds and stuck his hand into the basket. I hissed and bared my teeth. Yep, that's off limits. Cross that line and, believe me, you'll live to regret it.

'He still doesn't seem to want to come out.'

Kosuke withdrew his hand.

'Hmm. Doesn't look like it's going to work.'

'You know . . .' Satoru began hesitantly. 'If you're going to get a cat, I think it might be better if you and your wife find a new one together.'

'What do you mean?'

'If you take my cat, it'll be like you're getting back at your father for Hachi.'

'I'm sure he doesn't even remember rejecting Hachi.'

'But you do.'

At this, Kosuke fell silent.

I'm not denying that Kosuke wanted to take me for the sake of their friendship. But I wouldn't let him deny, either, that taking me, with my resemblance to Hachi, would have *something* to do with ghosts of the past.

Neither would I let him maintain that it had nothing to do with his wife having left him because of that difficult father of his.

'I think it would be good if you and your wife got a brand-new cat,' Satoru said. 'One with no strings attached.'

Kosuke pouted like a child. 'I loved Hachi. I really wanted to adopt him back then.'

'They look similar, but Nana is his own cat. He's not Hachi.'

'But you felt it was fate when you met Nana, because he looks like Hachi, didn't you? If you were fated to have Nana, then it should be my fate, too.'

Jeez. *Humans*. Even when they grow up, they just don't get things. Makes me sick.

'My Hachi died. Back when I was in high school. Your Hachi, Kosuke, is still alive.'

That's right. Satoru, in his mind, had already laid Hachi to rest and moved on. So Hachi's place and my place were different.

But that's not true of you, is it, Kosuke? You know in your head that Hachi's dead, but emotionally you can't accept it, right?

If you don't mourn a dead cat properly, you'll never get over it. Even if you feel able to mourn the death of a cat you've heard nothing about for years, it's a little late to feel truly sad about it, isn't it? One other thing:

You want me to replace Hachi, Kosuke. Up until now, Satoru has loved me as Nana, but now you expect me to be Hachi's stand-in? *Not going to happen!*

And even worse is your troublesome father and wounded wife being added to the mix. I am an exceptionally wise cat, but there's no way I'm going to be part of that drama, burdened with all those depressing human relationships as they fondle me. It's more than I want to take on.

'You and your wife should find a new cat and make him your own. Leave your father out of it. He might complain, but just ignore him and get a cat, if that's what you want to do.'

Kosuke didn't reply, but he looked like he finally understood.

So when he stuck his hand inside the basket again I allowed him to stroke me, as a kind of farewell gift.

It's about time you cut the strings and got over your father. Cats, you know, are independent from their parents six months after they're born.

Satoru put me and my basket back into the silver van.

He stood on the pavement, talking with Kosuke. He seemed reluctant to say goodbye.

'Oh, by the way,' Satoru said, slapping his forehead as if remembering something. 'In the city, they have photographic studios that take photos of pets, and they're really popular. There are more people than you'd think who want to have cute photos of their pets.'

Kosuke seemed quite keen on the idea. 'Have you had professional photos taken of Nana?'

Satoru smiled mischievously. 'Not yet. But if the Sawada Studio becomes a pet studio, then maybe I will.'

Kosuke broke into a smile. 'It'd be fun to hurl a new business idea in my father's face, too.'

Satoru was now in the van. He wound down the window. 'One more thing,' he said to Kosuke. 'When I was twenty, you invited me to a class reunion, remember?'

'Oh, that old story.' Kosuke laughed.

'It made me so happy.'

'Why are you bringing that up now?'

''Cause I don't think I ever told you how happy it made me.'

'Oh, *stop*,' Kosuke said, trying to change the subject.

'I won't,' Satoru said jokily. 'Thank you. I never thought I'd get a chance to come back to this town.'

Satoru finally drove off.

'Sorry, Nana,' Satoru said, turning towards me in the back seat. 'I thought it was better for him to get his own cat than to take you. But I'll find someone to have you, someone I can trust completely.'

No worries. I mean, I didn't ask you to do this in the first place.

If you had forced me to stay there, things would have been pretty terrible for you and Kosuke, you know? By that, I mean half a year's worth, perhaps, of chequerboards on your faces.

Satoru glanced at me in the back seat, where I was now sitting in a tidy ball, my tail around my front legs. He let out a yelp.

'Nana! How did you get out?'

Didn't you know? That lock on the basket doesn't work very well, and it's easy-peasy to unlock it from the inside.

'So you can open it? I had no idea. I'll have to buy a new one.'

You find out I can open the basket, and that's all you can say? Even that day when you took me to the one place I never, ever want to go, the vet's, I didn't try to run away.

'On second thoughts, maybe there's no need. Even if you've known how to get out all along, you still listened to me.'

Exactly. Satoru should be thankful I'm such an exceptionally bright cat.

I stretched up, placing my front paws on the passenger window, and enjoyed the passing scenery for a while, then curled up on the seat.

Some kind of rock music was playing on the car radio, and the bass sounds vibrated in my stomach. Not exactly my thing.

Cats have their own preferences when it comes to music. Did you know that?

I pressed my ears down and waved my tail around in an attempt to make my feelings known to Satoru. It didn't take him long to understand.

'Oh, I see, you don't like this. What's on the stereo, I wonder?'

Satoru switched to the car stereo and a light orchestral melody started playing. Okay, this wasn't so bad.

'My mother used to like this. Paul Mauriat.'

Hm, not bad at all. I could picture doves about to fly off, a happy vision from the feline perspective.

'I never knew you liked cars so much, Nana. If I'd

known, I would have taken you to all kinds of places.'

Saying I like cars is a little inaccurate. Aren't you sort of forgetting that a car broke my leg?

I just like this silver van, that's all. 'Cause it was mine even before I met Satoru.

Okay, so whose place are you going to take me to next?

∽

AFTER KOSUKE HAD WAVED OFF Satoru and Nana, he went back inside and found a text on his phone.

It was from his wife.

*Did you take the cat?*

He was about to reply, but decided to call instead.

He had a feeling that this time she might answer.

The phone rang seven times. Nana's lucky seven.

'Hello?' His wife's tone was flat and a little distant.

Now it was up to Kosuke to cheerfully, delicately, soften that hard voice.

'I was thinking,' he said evenly. 'What about if the two of us got our own new cat?'

# 2
# The Unsentimental Farmer

THE DAY WE SET off again, music filled the silver van once more, the kind that sounds like a magician is about to whisk a dove from a hat.

Satoru said the title was 'Necklace of Olive'. How come there was no dove in the title? If it were up to me, I'd put one in. How about calling it 'The Special Relationship Between a Dove and a Silk Hat'?

'It's nice to have good weather again today, isn't it, Nana?'

Satoru was in a great mood. All cats get sleepy when it rains, and I was wondering: does weather affect humans physically, too?

'Going for a drive isn't much fun if it's not sunny.'

Ah, so it was a question of mood. Humans are so easy-going. A cat's behaviour is controlled by real-life factors, and for strays the weather can be a matter of life and death. Our success rate in hunting changes, too.

'We'll take a break at the next service station.'

Unlike when we went to Kosuke's place, the road we were taking on that day had very few places to stop. Satoru said it was called a motorway. Basically the only time the silver van stopped was when Satoru announced that we were heading to a *service station*.

Satoru said this was the road we had to take if we intended to travel far away, and this trip was indeed a long one. It was the previous morning that the silver van had left home. We drove along the highway all day, then stayed overnight at a place where they allow pets.

With it being such a long trip, the space in the van had been compartmentalized. So, if you'll excuse me a second.

As I slipped off the passenger seat towards the back of the van, Satoru asked, 'Something wrong?' and glanced at me.

'Ah, sorry . . .'

Yeah. My toilet was on the floor at the back. A new one Satoru had bought which had a hood so the litter didn't fly all over the place.

This way, Satoru and I could go as far as we wanted in our silver van.

I thought it would be great if we could travel together like this for the rest of our lives.

'Nana, we're just going to pull into a service station—'

Okey-dokey, I answered vaguely, raking up the litter between my legs.

Once Satoru had parked at the service station, he pulled out my food and water bowls from the back. He placed them on the floor of the van side by side, filling one bowl with crunchies and the other with water from a plastic bottle.

'I'm going to go to the toilet, too.'

Satoru hurriedly shut the door and strolled off. He looked like he really had to go, but he was such a good owner he had taken care of my needs first.

I was wetting my whistle with the water when I heard a tapping on the window. Not *again*.

I glanced behind me and then up to see a young couple, faces plastered against the glass, staring in my direction. The pair had goofy smiles.

'A cat!'

You got that right. A cat I am. So? A cat eating his crunchies isn't so rare a sight, is it?

'Oh, look – it's eating. How sweet!'

'So sweet!'

Hey, you idiotic couple. How would you like it if somebody pointed at you while you were eating? And today happens to be a chicken-breast-and-gourmet-seafood blend.

How come cat lovers spot me every time? Whenever we take a break, they swarm around me. Pretty amazing, if you think about it.

If you guys were the ones who fed me, then I'd be as sweet to you as the quality of the food merited, but Satoru's the one who feeds me. So let me focus on my food. Okay?

I decided to ignore them and dived back into my crunchies. With some screeches and giggles, they seemed to give up and wander away.

But only moments later I felt someone's red-hot gaze on me. I looked up despite myself, and this time it was a scary-looking, goblin-like old man's face plastered to the window.

Yikes! I jerked away on reflex, and the old man looked really hurt. Come on – anybody would shudder if they were suddenly confronted by that kind of face while they were having a snack. Not my fault, now, is it?

The old man looked upset but kept his face up against the window, staring at me.

'I'm guessing you like cats?'

This from Satoru, who'd come back. The old man, a bit flustered, replied, 'Sure is a cute little kitty.' *Cute little kitty?*

I looked up and meowed. On the other side of the window, Satoru smiled and nodded.

'Would you like to stroke him?'

'Are you sure?'

The old man started to blush like a girl. Satoru opened the door and I clambered over to the seat. The old man reached out and I let him stroke me. His face began to glow. But just then—

'No way! A cat!'

The shriek came from a clump of *gyaru* – girls with dyed-blonde hair and thick make-up – who were passing by.

'I want to stroke it! Can we touch him after you?'

Get lost! I bared my teeth and made my fur stand on end, and the group of *gyaru* shrieked again: 'Oh my god – he's angry!' and ran off.

'But I wanted to give him a stroke—' the tall one whined.

'It's okay. That kind of cat with those eyebrow markings isn't that cute anyway.'

*Excuse me?!* This insult was so unfounded my face went into a kind of flehmen response. I curled back my upper lip and bared my front teeth like a tiger.

'You *are* cute, Nana! Very cute!' Satoru hurriedly interjected. 'Those girls are a bit loud, and I'm sure their sense of what's beautiful is different from most people's. Let's just let it go.'

'No, he really is a cute cat,' the old man said. 'Nana, you said his name is?'

'Yeah. Because his tail's hooked into the shape of a seven.'

I didn't think we needed to explain the origin of my name to every passing stranger, but Satoru was always so conscientious when it came to things like that.

'Is he maybe the type that doesn't let people touch him much?'

'Yes, he's very choosy about who he allows to touch him when we're out and about.'

'I see,' the old man said, smiling even more broadly. Then he gave me one final lingering pat on the middle of my back and walked off.

'Kind of unusual, isn't it, Nana, for you to let a passer-by stroke you for so long?'

True enough. How should I put it? I was making amends – a sort of atonement. No need to analyse it any further.

The van had been driving along for a while when I next stretched up to look out of the passenger window. The sea!

'I think you'll like the sea, Nana.'

Until then, I'd only seen it on the TV in Satoru's front room, which I used to watch from my blanket in the corner. To see it now for real was going to be amazing.

And it was! The sparkling, deep-green water was completely stunning, but more than that was the idea that underneath that water lurked all the delicacies that made up my gourmet seafood blend. Oops! I had started to drool at the thought of it.

'If, like last time, you end up coming back with me, let's stop by the sea properly.'

What? Stop by the sea? Might I be lucky enough to catch one or two of those delicacies?

The sea was soon out of sight, and I drifted off for a bit. When I lazily opened my eyes again the scenery had become tranquil and countrified. Now we were sliding past green rice paddies and broad fields like a whirligig.

'Oh, you're up? We're almost there.'

Just as Satoru said, the van soon pulled up in the front yard of a farmhouse. It seemed functionally constructed, large and practical. Nearby was an annexe of sorts, and a shed. Beside it was parked a smallish truck.

I took the initiative and leapt on to the back seat, into the opened basket. I've learned that when you go into an unknown house, it's best and safest to be in a place you're used to, one where you can barricade yourself in.

Satoru opened the back door and picked up the basket with me inside.

'Satoru Miyawaki!'

At the sound of a welcoming voice, I peered through the bars and saw a man in work clothes and a straw hat heading towards Satoru, hand held high.

'Yoshimine, how have you been?' Satoru's voice was excited, too. 'You're looking good.'

'I work outdoors all the time, so your body naturally gets strong. Haven't you become a little thinner?'

'Have I? Guess it's the unhealthy city lifestyle.'

The two of them clapped each other on the back and headed towards the main house.

'Did you have any trouble finding my place?'

'No, the sat-nav made it easy.'

'Still, I didn't think you'd come all this way from Tokyo by car. Flying would have been faster, and cheaper. Going by road must have been a bit pricey?'

Absolutely. You have the tolls on the motorway, service stations, the pet-friendly little hotel we stayed in last night. By the time we got here, Satoru had opened his wallet several times.

'But if I had flown, then Nana would have been stored

in the luggage hold, which is dark and noisy. One time, I took another cat on a plane and it was terrified for the entire day after we landed. Cats can't understand why they're in a situation like that, and I'd feel bad if Nana had to go through it.'

Okay, I might be terrified, but I'm a little offended that he'd think that Hachi could make it, but I couldn't. Surely I'm more intrepid than Hachi. After all, until I was an adult, I survived as a stray on the streets.

Instead of worrying about me, you should worry about all the money you've spent on this trip.

Inside the main house, Yoshimine showed us into the living room. Satoru placed my basket in a corner and opened the door.

Yoshimine was crouching in front of my basket.

'Mind if I take a look at Nana?' he said, peering in.

'Sure, but it might take a bit of time for him to feel comfortable enough to come out.'

'No problem.'

What do you mean, *no problem?* I tilted my head in puzzlement and, just at that instant, a thick arm shot into the cage.

Hey, what—?

The fat arm grabbed me by the scruff of the neck and, without so much as a by-your-leave, dragged me out, then dangled me high up in the air.

Wh-wha-what the hell do you think you're doing, you barbarian!

'Good! He's a proper cat.'

What the hell do you mean by *that?*

'Hey!'

Satoru, horrified, gave Yoshimine a healthy shove in the back. 'What do you think you're doing?'

'I just wanted to make sure he's a real cat,' Yoshimine explained, holding me against him with his thick arm. I tried to kick myself free, but that thick arm just took my kicks and didn't budge an inch.

'What do you mean?'

'Look, you hold him like this, see?'

'Don't hold him like that!'

'If his back legs fold up when you do this, it means he's a real cat.'

Let me go! I put my legs together and kicked off against Yoshimine's arm, flopping around like a salmon. Finally, I was able to break free.

I twisted my body around and landed perfectly on my four paws. Keeping my belly low to the ground, I turned to meet Yoshimine's eye, and he said, 'Whoa!' and clapped his hands.

'One fine cat you've got here. Well coordinated, and smart, too. An outstanding cat. I underestimated him.'

'Yeah, I guess so.'

That can't be true. Of course I'm well bred, *but still*. Satoru interrupted, in sync with me: 'But still – that's not the point!' Great minds think alike. 'Why did you grab Nana by the neck like that? It startled him!'

'The reason is, I found a stray recently that isn't a real cat. If Nana turned out to be like that one, there wouldn't be much point, from a farmer's perspective, in having him. So I just wanted to check him out.'

This unpleasant guy came over to try to play with my tail, which I was waving slowly to show my displeasure.

I spun around, only to find an orange tabby male kitten beside me. He'd appeared out of nowhere and was meowing and trying to cling to my hooked tail. What a pain.

Yoshimine grabbed the kitten by the scruff of the neck and picked him up. The kitten's legs drooped down in a line.

'This one isn't a real cat. See?'

True, this kitten didn't seem equipped with the natural abilities of most cats. He was the kind – like Hachi – that would never catch a mouse. Even if he could hone his skills through training, he would never be a true hunter like me.

'He's still just a kitten, you shouldn't treat him so roughly . . .'

Satoru reached his hand out, fluttering it in the air in a *stop that* gesture. Yoshimine thrust the kitten at him.

'Here. Feel free to stroke him, if you like.'

'I'd love to.'

Satoru was a dyed-in-the-wool cat lover, like I said. Go ahead and get all lovey-dovey with that kitten. See if I care.

IT HAD BEEN A LONG TIME since Yoshimine had received an email from his former junior-high classmate Satoru Miyawaki.

He had just been thinking about him when the email arrived.

After a few quick words to bring him up to date, Satoru issued his request.

*I know this is a bit sudden, but could you take my cat for me?*

*He's really precious to me*, he went on, *but unavoidable*

circumstances make it impossible for me to keep him, and I'm looking for someone to adopt him.

There were two things Yoshimine could read in this message.

One was that his cat-devoted friend had once more found a cat he loved, and two, that once again he was having to part ways with it.

When it came to cats, Daigo Yoshimine could take them or leave them. If there was one in the house, he'd notice it and look after it, but he wasn't passionate enough about them to adopt one himself. He felt the same way about dogs and birds.

But having a cat on a farm did have its advantages. On farms, mice inevitably caused damage, and a cat was a pretty good means of control.

He tapped out a reply.

*I don't think I'd look after a cat the way you do – I treat them like cats, not like pets – but if you're okay with that, I'd be happy to take him off your hands. If you can't find anyone else, then let me know. Rest assured, I'll make sure he's looked after.*

Satoru wrote back thanking him. *I've promised to show him to one other person first,* he said, *but if that doesn't work out, I'll be counting on you.*

A month later, Satoru wrote back again, asking if he could bring the cat over for Yoshimine to meet.

And, by coincidence, it was during this time that Yoshimine happened to find the kitten.

'I was driving down the highway in my truck when I saw him lying by the side of the road like a limp dishrag. I wouldn't have been able to forgive myself if I had just left him there.'

'I see . . .'

Satoru seemed to melt with the orange tabby kitten on his lap. Cat lovers have a special place in their hearts for kittens.

'You did a good job bringing up this teeny guy. Was it hard?'

'I needed the vet a few times. But there're other folk in the neighbourhood who have cats, and plenty of people ready to give advice.'

Because it was the countryside, people weren't all that particular about the way they brought cats up.

'It was a lot easier once he started eating cat food.'

Satoru burst out laughing. 'I'm trying to imagine you feeding a kitten milk from a bottle. You're lucky, aren't you,' Satoru said to the kitten, tickling him vigorously under the chin, 'to be taken in by such a kind owner?'

'I'm not that kind. I was hoping he'd catch a mouse or two around the place, but he's not a real cat and I feel a bit let down.'

'So, now that he's recovered, are you going to throw him out of the house?'

Yoshimine looked put out by Satoru's teasing tone.

Satoru stroked the kitten in his lap in contented silence. Then he said, 'I get it now. That's why you were asking whether Nana was a real cat or not.'

'If I bring up two of them and they're both useless, then all that cat food is a total waste.'

'I knew you wouldn't turn Nana down.'

'Well, I can't exactly refuse a guest who's driven all the way here from Tokyo just for a cat.'

'I get it,' Satoru responded, as if he didn't really accept this explanation.

'By the way, what's the kitten's name?'

'Chatran.'

'That's pretty silly.'

'Is it?'

Yoshimine had asked around the neighbours who owned cats, and one person had said, 'An orange tabby? That reminds me of Chatran.' He liked the name and decided to use it.

'Since that movie *The Adventures of Chatran* came out, it's become a bit of a cliché to call an orange tabby Chatran.'

'Hmm. I didn't know that.'

And this Chatran with the silly name recognized a real cat lover and was fully relaxing in Satoru's lap, stretching his paw on to Satoru's cheek.

'This brings back memories. I used to have a cat who did this.'

Satoru never named this cat he used to have to Yoshimine. He felt that if he spoke its name aloud, all the pent-up affection and sadness would break his heart again.

And even someone who knows nothing about the universal benefit of cats could understand that.

Yoshimine had transferred into the junior high school in the spring of his second year.

'This is Daigo Yoshimine, who will be joining us as your new classmate.'

The form teacher was a striking woman who'd won some Miss Something-or-other contest back in college, but Yoshimine had disliked her from the start.

When she explained to the class, in great detail, why

he had moved to their school, she made it sound very close and intimate and oozed sympathy.

He had gritted his teeth and let her words wash over him, but what he couldn't fend off was the timing.

'Yoshimine-kun's parents are busy with their jobs, so he's transferred here and will be staying with his grandmother. We should all admire him, for enduring the loneliness of being away from his parents. I'd like you all to be friends with him.'

He understood then that her overly intimate manner was because she felt sorry for him. And, deep down, that disgusted him.

Even to an immature class of junior-high-school students with little worldly experience, it was crystal clear that this was the worst possible way to introduce a new student to his classmates.

'Yoshimine-kun, why don't you say a few words?'

Yoshimine turned to face the teacher. 'Why did you tell everyone about my family like that without my permission? I never asked you to.'

A murmur rippled through the classroom. The teacher was taken aback, her smile faltering. 'I – I thought it would help you settle in.'

'No, in fact it makes me uncomfortable. I want people to be friends with me without my family being a part of it.'

'I understand, but the thing is . . .' the teacher mumbled. There was no way this was going to turn out well.

Yoshimine turned to face the other students.

'Hi. I'm Daigo Yoshimine. There's nothing special about my family, so I hope we can just get along like anybody else.'

A deathly hush descended on the classroom. Right from the start, he'd put them off.

As for his form teacher, she looked on the verge of tears.

'Where do you want me to sit?'

Just then the bell went, signalling the end of form time, and the teacher left the classroom in a hurry.

'Just sit down on any empty chair.'

It was Satoru who said this, pointing to some seats at the back.

First period was over, and while his other classmates eyed the new boy warily, keeping their distance, Satoru approached him without hesitation.

The next class was science. Yoshimine gathered his textbooks and left the classroom, with Satoru leading the way.

'Listen.' Something was bothering Yoshimine, and he had to ask. 'Are you being nice to me just because of what the teacher said?'

'Not at all,' Satoru replied. 'I thought it was all pretty childish. On both parts.'

'You mean me, too?'

'That teacher likes to be super-kind to kids who have issues going on at home. She doesn't mean any harm by it.'

Something about the way he said this – the desire to be kind and mean no harm – made Yoshimine feel he had something in common with Satoru, a kind of connection.

'Right after I entered this school, in freshman year, she did the same thing to me, so I get where you're coming from. When I was in elementary school, my parents died in a car accident and now I live with my aunt. But that doesn't mean I want to go out of my way to tell everybody in class about it.'

The circumstances Satoru had so casually mentioned were so much more serious than Yoshimine's. So surely the teacher must have put on an even more annoying display of concern.

'But you don't need to complain about every little thing. Just take it as it comes, be grown-up about it.'

A little too philosophical, aren't you, for a second-year junior high schooler? Yoshimine thought, but what Satoru said made sense, so he didn't argue.

'Still,' Satoru said with a grin. 'To tell you the truth, I felt good when you said that. Back when I started school, I wanted to say what you actually did say.'

Yoshimine changed the subject.

'What's your name?'

'Satoru Miyawaki. Nice to meet you.'

He didn't have to say anything like *Let's hang out*, for by this time they were already friends.

From day one, Yoshimine hadn't got on with his classmates or his form teacher, but being friends with Satoru made life at school go more smoothly.

Satoru had also apparently straightened things out with the teacher. Yoshimine had no idea how he had won her over, but one day she stopped him in the corridor and tearfully apologized.

'I'm so sorry, Yoshimine-kun. I didn't understand how badly you were feeling.'

Yoshimine felt as if some huge misunderstanding was about to occur, but it was too much trouble to explain things, so, following the advice to be *grown-up* about it, he ended the encounter with a quick 'It's okay.'

'Don't worry, Yoshimine-kun,' his teacher added. 'I won't mention your family situation again.'

So it seemed there was still some major misunderstanding about his family situation, which only Satoru correctly grasped.

'My parents,' Yoshimine had explained to him, 'both work really hard and love their jobs too much.'

His father was in R&D at a top electronics company, while his mother worked in foreign investment for a multinational trading company. They were hardly ever at home, and Yoshimine often went days without seeing them.

'Since spring, they've both become even busier, and they can't seem to find any time for their family. Including me.'

His parents had tried to offload responsibility for their son on to his older brother, and their preoccupation with work had quickly led to total neglect of the household.

'So they decided to send me to live with my grandmother on my father's side until things settled down.'

But he didn't think it was a big deal, so he found it embarrassing when his teacher went all gushy over how sad he must be. Because there are lots of kids with much tougher backgrounds. Take Satoru, for instance.

'Hey, Yoshimine.' A classmate called out to him from the corridor, putting an end to their conversation. 'You interested in joining the judo club?'

'Nope.'

The classmate's shoulders drooped in disappointment, though he didn't stop trying, dangling the possibility of him being a regular on the team. 'So – what do you say?' he asked.

'I say no thanks,' Yoshimine replied.

With his sturdy build, he was continually being invited to join the school sports teams, but Yoshimine turned them all down.

'Aren't you into school clubs?' Satoru asked.

'I don't like sports much,' he replied. He certainly had an athletic physique, but he disliked games with too many rules.

'What about other kinds of clubs?'

'If there was a gardening club I might join.'

His grandmother's family were farmers and he had always enjoyed digging in the soil. His grandfather had passed away a few years before, and his grandmother had only just been managing to keep the family plots going, so Yoshimine had been pitching in.

'There's a greenhouse in the corner of the school grounds. I wonder if anyone's using it.'

The greenhouse had been on Yoshimine's mind ever since he had transferred to the school.

'I've never even thought about it. You interested?' Satoru asked.

'My grandmother's crops are all outdoors. I've never worked in a greenhouse.'

'You really are into farming, aren't you?'

Yoshimine thought that was the end of the matter, but Satoru brought it up again later.

'I looked into the gardening club thing. They stopped a few years ago, because membership numbers fell. But if you're interested, the science teacher said he'd run it, even if it's just the two of us. And we can use the greenhouse.'

Two things surprised Yoshimine. One, that Satoru had

actually looked into it. And two, that he was planning to take part himself.

'You want to be in the club, too?' Yoshimine asked.

'I'd like to give it a try.'

'But you're not into gardening or anything like that, are you?'

'I wouldn't say I'm not interested. I just haven't had anything to do with it up till now. I've never known any farmers.'

'Really? Nobody? Not even, like, your grandfather or your grandmother?'

A total city boy, Yoshimine thought, but Satoru waved a dismissive hand.

'It's not that,' he said. 'My parents didn't have much to do with their relatives. My grandparents on my mother's side died when she was still young, and my father didn't seem to get on with his parents that well. The first time I met them was at my parents' funeral, and we didn't talk much.'

Yoshimine understood now why Satoru's aunt had taken him in. If your parents died and your grandparents were in good health, it's likely that's where you'd go. Pretty unusual for a single woman to take a young boy in.

'I reckoned this might be my only chance to give it a go,' Satoru said, laughing. 'I've dreamed about living the country life. Like in Miyazaki's film *My Neighbour Totoro*, do you know it?'

And so the two of them revived the gardening club. Yoshimine's grandmother also invited Satoru over to their home to experience life on a working farm.

Satoru was a latchkey kid, since his aunt worked all day, so he began to go over to Yoshimine's home, and sometimes stayed over for the weekend.

'I hope you will be good friends,' Yoshimine's grandmother said to Satoru – what grandmothers typically say when other children come to play. 'I always wonder if Daigo – she called him by his first name – 'is getting on with the other children at school. I hope he isn't being bullied.'

'I wouldn't worry about that. I don't think there's any chance Yoshimine would ever be bullied.'

'What d'ya mean?' Yoshimine said, poking him in the ribs.

'You know exactly what I mean,' Satoru said, poking him back.

His grandmother, who had been worried that Yoshimine might not make any friends in his new school, was overjoyed when he brought Satoru home. Very soon, she started calling him Satoru-chan.

'Shall I buy a video game or something you can play with Satoru-chan?'

She asked this because she was concerned that he might be getting bored, always helping out in the fields.

'I already have some,' Yoshimine replied, 'and so does Satoru.'

Satoru genuinely enjoyed helping out in the fields – it was a kind of pastoral hobby.

'We're doing the gardening club at school together, too, and I think he really likes farm work,' Yoshimine explained to his grandmother.

'Really? Then that's fine,' his grandmother responded. 'At any rate, you've made a good friend here. So I won't worry about you.'

His grandmother didn't just say this once, but at every opportunity. As if reassuring herself.

'I guess Grandma still sees me as a little kid,' Yoshimine said, a trifle embarrassed.

With Satoru being so good-natured, and her grandson's best friend to boot, Yoshimine's grandmother fussed over him, and Satoru grew very attached to her.

'You're lucky,' he told Yoshimine. 'I wish I had a grandmother like yours.'

He'd never been close to his grandparents, and seemed to enjoy having a relationship with an elderly person.

'If you're okay with an old woman like me,' Yoshimine's grandmother told him, 'then consider this like your own grandmother's house.'

Yoshimine never teased his friend about his obvious envy of his grandmother. He knew that Satoru tended to keep his distance from his aunt and had no other relatives he could become close to.

'Come over any time. My grandmother likes you a lot, too.'

One afternoon, during class, Yoshimine was feeling uncomfortably hot. He glanced out of the window and saw heat shimmering up from the ground. It was the time of year when the temperature was often over thirty degrees.

He suddenly pushed his chair back and stood up, causing a stir of excitement in the class.

'Yoshimine! What do you think you're doing?' his teacher scolded.

'Nothing,' Yoshimine said casually, and walked out of the classroom.

'Hey!'

At times like these, it was Satoru's role to step in.

'What do you mean, nothing?' he called.

'I'll be right back.'

It was Satoru, not their teacher, who ran out of the classroom after him.

'What's wrong?' he asked Yoshimine, when he finally caught up with him.

'The greenhouse. I forgot to open the vent this morning. It's so hot now, the plants are going to boil.'

Inside the greenhouse, they were growing tomatoes and other vegetables, as well as tending some orchids, a hobby of the science teacher. Tomatoes don't do well in the rain so the roofed-in environment was perfect for them, but this region generally had a temperate climate and when it got too hot in the summer they suffered.

'Why not wait until break? It's only another thirty minutes.'

'But it's the hottest time of the day. We have to cool it down as soon as we can.'

'You could have pretended you had to go to the bathroom or something! It'll be your fault if they close down our club.'

'Then you go and explain.'

'Jeez,' Satoru muttered, and made his way back to the classroom.

'Yoshimine's been attacked by guerrillas!'

Satoru's report had the classroom in uproar.

Though Yoshimine threw the class into chaos on such occasions, before the summer vacation they got a bumper crop of tomatoes and other vegetables and were able to save their teacher's orchids as well.

When he was sharing out the vegetables with Satoru

and the teacher, Yoshimine ended up taking a portion of tomatoes that was a little larger than the others. Yoshimine's grandmother's outdoor-grown tomato plants had been hit hard by the long rainy season and hadn't yielded quite what she'd hoped.

'Take more. There are just the two of us in our house, so I don't need so many,' Satoru said, and Yoshimine burst out laughing. There were only two in Yoshimine's home, too, and one of them was extremely old. Satoru had a comeback for that: 'But you eat much more than I do.'

In the space of one semester, Satoru had learned a lot about farming, and had picked up on the fact that Yoshimine wanted to grow greenhouse tomatoes as a sort of insurance policy against his grandmother's tomatoes failing. Grateful, Yoshimine went ahead and took three or four extra, dropping them happily into his bucket.

'I'm going back home the first week of the summer holiday,' Yoshimine said.

'I get it,' Satoru answered instantly. 'I'll take care of the greenhouse while you're gone.'

Their first crop was in already, but there were a lot more that would ripen later.

'This is the first time you've been home since you came to this school, isn't it? Hope it goes okay.'

Satoru understood the situation, which is why he didn't just say, *Oh, that's nice*. Yoshimine's parents weren't taking any time off work to see their son; he was just putting in a token appearance. 'If they ripen while you're away, I'll take some tomatoes over to your grandmother's.'

Yoshimine's grandmother gave him a lift to the airport in her little van, and he flew back to Tokyo.

Nobody was there to meet him at Haneda airport.

He boarded the airport shuttle for the ride home, to a condo in a residential suburb. After a whole semester at his grandmother's, the apartment seemed even smaller and more cramped than before.

His parents were as preoccupied as ever.

About three days after Yoshimine had arrived home, both his parents, surprisingly, came home from work early. His mother cooked them dinner, a rare thing, and the three of them sat down together to eat.

After dinner, his mother made them tea. The whole thing had Yoshimine confused.

His father, seated opposite him at the dining table, spoke first, a serious look on his face.

'We have something important to tell you.'

His mother came over and sat down next to his father. This couldn't be good.

'The thing is, Mum and I have decided to get divorced.'

Ah – just as I thought, Yoshimine said to himself.

He had known that someday it would come to this.

'Daigo, do you want to come and live with me, or your mother?'

He looked at his parents' expressions and was forced to confront a reality he couldn't avoid.

His parents waited expectantly, each hoping he would choose the other.

'I'm sorry.' He was finally able to squeeze out the words. 'I can't decide right now. I want to think about it a little more.'

His parents were clearly relieved that they wouldn't have to deal with the problem straight away.

'Can I go back to Grandma's place tomorrow?'

Confronted with the fact that neither parent wanted him, he no longer had any idea how he was supposed to behave.

Naturally, they didn't stop him, and he flew back the following day. The airline took good care of unaccompanied children, and he was actually grateful that his parents weren't there to see him off.

His grandmother came to pick him up at the airport and drove him briskly back home in her small van.

'Mum and Dad said they're getting divorced.'

'Is that right?' his grandmother replied.

'I don't know which one I should live with.'

'Well, it doesn't really matter, because you can live with me.'

Yoshimine felt a huge lump in his throat.

'You have a good friend here, too, Daigo, so it's all okay.'

*You have a good friend here. It's all okay,* his grandmother murmured, over and over, as if reassuring herself.

His grandmother had known what was going to happen from the moment her grandson had first come to live with her.

The lump in Yoshimine's throat grew bigger and by the time they arrived home, it had started to hurt.

'I'm going to run over to school.'

He changed into his uniform. Even in the holidays, they weren't allowed at the school unless they were wearing it.

'Why don't you wait until a bit later? It's the hottest time of day now.'

'I'm worried about the greenhouse.'

Shaking off his grandmother's objections, Yoshimine

rode his bike to the junior high. As he pumped the pedals he felt the lump in his throat sink to the pit of his stomach.

Satoru's bike was parked in the bicycle racks.

Inside the greenhouse, Yoshimine found him happily plucking tomatoes and cucumbers.

'Hey.'

As Yoshimine stood in the doorway to the greenhouse, Satoru let out a funny-sounding 'What the—? Weren't you supposed to come back a little later?'

'Yeah, stuff happened.'

They washed the vegetables in the sink, and in the shade of the school building Yoshimine told Satoru what had happened. Out of the corner of his eye, Yoshimine watched the baseball team doing fielding practice in the shimmering heatwaves radiating from the schoolyard.

'When they left me with Grandma, I didn't think anything major was going on, since my parents had always kind of left me to my own devices. But it's turned out to be a big deal.'

So the form teacher's sympathy was justified, after all.

'They were planning to get divorced all along. And they wanted me to understand that. I'm such an idiot.'

Satoru had been listening in silence, but now he broke in. 'That's not true,' he countered. 'You were just trying not to think about it.'

Yoshimine felt that lump in his throat again. *Get over it*, he urged himself.

*Daigo never gives us any trouble, and that makes things so much easier.*

If I had been a bad kid who *did* give them a hard time, *then* what would have happened?

Ever since he was little, he had known his parents were both overly fond of their jobs and weren't particularly interested in him. Which is why he tried his best to be the kind of child who wouldn't require too much of their time and effort, the kind who wouldn't get under their feet.

Being a kid who never gave his parents any trouble would at least stop them being in a bad mood and keep things settled on the home front. In that way, Yoshimine, who was always the one holding the fort, could breathe easy.

And the few times that the whole family was together, things did go smoothly. But maybe all he'd done was to prioritize what was easy in the short term.

There's a proverb that says a child is the glue that keeps a husband and wife together. A child who was never any trouble might keep things peaceful from day to day, but when push came to shove, that child would finally come unstuck.

Maybe the kind of kid who needed more parental affection and made trouble would have been the glue that would have held their marriage together.

*Enough.*

Yoshimine shook his head hard to put a stop to the thoughts spinning around in it. There's no use thinking about something that can't be undone. It'll just let this lump grow bigger. It's already pretty big.

'Still,' he said aloud. 'Parents get divorced all the time.'

He tried to say it casually, but the tail end of his words wavered.

'You had it a lot harder than me, didn't you, Satoru?'

'But I never once experienced my parents acting like I was a nuisance, because they were gone.'

There was nothing Yoshimine could say to that. The lump in his throat burst at long last.

When his sobbing finally subsided, Satoru asked, 'Want one?' and held out in his soiled fingers a luscious red tomato.

∽

REALLY, NOW, I THOUGHT, looking at Satoru.

I was out of the basket. Not sure why, but Satoru had left the door open, telling me to come out whenever I felt comfortable, but the thought of that tabby kitten with the stupid name, Chatran, invading my space was unbearable, truth be told.

Hey, tabby. You know your owner was abandoned by his parents, too. But the tabby was so engrossed in playing with his toy mouse he didn't hear me. When are you going to realize how pointless it is to play with a fake mouse, eh?

Having a decent conversation with an itty-bitty kitten this young was out of the question. He was of the age when he'd eat, leap around a bit, then suddenly flop down asleep in the middle of whatever he was doing, as if his batteries had run down.

Even when he was in the middle of saying something, if a breeze made the curtain flutter he would drop everything and leap at it. Was I that silly when I was his age? I think I had a bit more sense than that. Well, cats mature emotionally at different rates. I felt sorry for the poor kid, compared to a rare, wise cat such as myself.

Stitching together his fragmented history, I gathered that this orange tabby was the runt of the litter, and when his mother had moved home, he hadn't been able to keep up and got left behind.

A fact of life in the feline world. Kittens that are awkward to bring up, or slow, are easily abandoned. No matter how hard she tries, a mother cat has only so much milk, and she won't waste any on a lethargic kitten.

One of my siblings was like that. Overshadowed by the rest of us, it was the kind of kitten you were never sure was there or not, and one day we suddenly noticed it was gone, as if it had never existed.

This orange tabby was on the small side for his age; to be honest, not the type you'd expect to make it in life. Yoshimine had done a great job bringing him up. And despite him being the ill-mannered kind who'd grab you by the scruff of the neck the first time he met you, Yoshimine hadn't just looked the other way when a troublesome kitten turned up, so it was clear to me he was an individual who had a lot of love to give.

Even people who are big and strong are sometimes thrown in the gutter. If he'd been a cat, Yoshimine would have been the top priority in the litter.

Okay, be that as it may . . .

You probably shouldn't have made it, little kitty, yet you've been given a new lease of life, so shouldn't you show some gratitude to Yoshimine for that? Yes, you. I'm talking to *you*.

The orange tabby looked as though he was listening for a moment, but then, clearly not getting what I was saying, he started to play around with my tail. Hmm. Guess I'll have to simplify this a bit.

Tell me, do you like Yoshimine?

I seemed to have got through. As he chewed on my tail, he nodded. Hey, that hurt. I flipped my tail up.

If you like Yoshimine, don't you want to make him happy?

The orange tabby grabbed my tail again and recommenced chomping with his mini jaws.

I told you, that hurts! I flipped it up again.

You do know Yoshimine wants cats to catch mice for him, don't you? So, if you can become a real cat who can catch mice, I'm sure Yoshimine will be very pleased.

The orange tabby stopped his chomping for a moment. I seemed to have struck a chord.

But the way you're behaving, forget it. You're useless. You couldn't even catch a lizard, let alone a mouse.

Okay, what if I teach you the basics of hunting? And not just hunting, but train you to hold your own in a fight with other cats. Yoshimine will be worried if you lose every scrap.

Putting everything in simple terms like this, I think I got through to the kitten. He sat up straight and asked me to teach him. Good. In the cat world, good manners are a must.

I was about to lead the orange tabby into an Intro to Hunting when Satoru said, 'Oh! Look, Yoshimine. They've started playing together.'

'Aren't they fighting?'

'No, Nana's going easy on him.'

This isn't a game, folks, I'm teaching. Whatever.

'If they carry on together like this, maybe I can convince you to keep Nana for me.'

Well, I'm doing my thing here, so you chaps keep doing whatever you're doing. Don't mind us.

Satoru watched as the orange tabby pounced on the toy mouse the way I taught him to, and his eyes narrowed into a smile.

'He's so excitable, just like the cat I used to have years ago.'

You're right about that. When he's supposed to crouch quietly and blend in, he madly waves his tail around instead. I stretch my tail out smoothly, but this little kitten waves his around like a helicopter. And when he crouches down ready to pounce, he keeps his body way too high off the ground.

'What was Nana like when he was little?'

'I found him when he was a grown cat, so I don't know what sort of kitten he was. I wish I could have known him then. I'm sure he was adorable.'

You're right there. My level of cuteness when I was a kitten was such that passers-by vied for the privilege of leaving me a little something to eat.

'Now that you mention it . . .' Yoshimine said, as if suddenly remembering something, 'did you see that cat you adopted ever again?'

'Unfortunately, no. It died when I was in high school.'

'I see,' Yoshimine said, his voice respectfully mournful.

'I wish you could have seen him. Sorry about that. But I really didn't want the word to get back to my aunt.'

Whoa there, Satoru. What on earth are you hinting at here?

I ordered the orange tabby to run through the exercises I'd taught him on his own, and turned my attention to Satoru and Yoshimine's conversation.

૭

YOSHIMINE'S PARENTS' DIVORCE went through without

a hitch, his father getting custody of their son. This was because Yoshimine wanted to live with his grandmother. It also meant he could avoid the inconvenience of changing his last name.

As if they had been set free, both his parents went off on overseas postings, and appeared to be doing well. And, as ever, Yoshimine found that living with his grandmother suited him down to the ground.

A year passed and, during the first semester of their last year in junior high, the class went on a school trip to Fukuoka.

Yoshimine realized that something was bothering Satoru only after he'd found out what had happened on a previous school trip – that Satoru's parents had died in an accident.

Satoru had looked glum from the moment they departed. On their first day in Fukuoka, when they had some free time, he was uncharacteristically quiet, even though he was with his usual group of friends.

Yoshimine was concerned that the trip had tapped into depressing memories, but with all the other students around it was hard to find an opportunity to talk to him about it.

After dinner, when they were browsing through the souvenir shop in the hotel, he finally found his chance.

'Are you okay?'

Satoru looked worried. He glanced up at Yoshimine and said in a low voice, 'I was wondering if I can get to Kokura.'

From Hakata Station in Fukuoka to Kokura was about twenty minutes by the Shinkansen train. So of course it was possible. But only if they weren't on a school trip. Which they were.

Always alert to the dangers of the students wandering off, the teachers chaperoning the trip had set up a tight surveillance system. The daily activities were scheduled to the minute. After checking into the hotel, it was strictly forbidden for students to go out on their own. A teacher was always stationed at the hotel entrance. If a student were to try to slip out to have fun at night, there was a very real risk that they might be sent home.

So for Satoru to go to Kokura on his own was, in the circumstances, not an option. Yet the obedient, sharp-witted Satoru wouldn't have said such a thing unless he had a very good reason.

'How come?' Yoshimine asked.

So Satoru told him.

It had to do with the cat he'd had back when his parents were still alive. When they died and his aunt took him in, he'd had to give up the cat, and relatives in Kokura had adopted it.

'My aunt's always so busy I can't ask her to take me to Kokura just to see the cat . . . So I was wondering if, when we have a free moment during the day, I could slip away and go there to visit it.'

'Do you really want to see the cat that much?'

'He's family,' Satoru replied.

'I see,' Yoshimine said, folding his arms. He'd never had a pet himself, and had no particular fondness for cats.

But for Satoru, that cat was something he and his parents had all loved, the one remaining family member from that happy time they shared before his parents died. It all made perfect sense.

Okay, then.

So it's just a cat, but it is, after all, a *cat*. For his friend, the one and only cat in the world.

'Let's do it.'

But then Satoru hesitated. 'Yeah, but . . .' He trembled.

'We have three hours till lights-out. You know your relatives' address, don't you?'

It turned out to be in an apartment building not far from Kokura Station.

'If we skip having a bath, we'll have plenty of time. But you won't have a cent left to buy anything afterwards.'

A round trip to Kokura would cost several thousand yen.

'We can't tell anyone in our group. If they knew, then they could get into trouble, too. When it's time to go for a bath, we'll tell them we'll be down in a minute, and then we'll make our getaway.'

'I'll go on my own. I don't want anyone else to get mixed up in this.'

'Come on, mate. I'm your best friend.' And with that, Yoshimine slapped him on the back.

They hadn't been allowed to bring any clothes other than their school uniform and pyjamas, so the choice was between those. They'd both brought jerseys to wear in bed, so they opted for those, since they wouldn't stand out as much as school shirts and blazers.

When it came to their turn to go down to the bath, they pretended to need more time to get ready for it.

They waited three minutes, then left their room. They avoided the main entrance, because of the teacher standing guard, and headed straight to the emergency exit they had scouted out earlier. The doorknob on the fire exit had a plastic safety cover, which made it obvious if anyone used the door. If a teacher found the cover missing, there would be an immediate roll call.

'What should we do?' Satoru asked anxiously. 'The teachers will check this when they make their rounds.'

'We go up,' Yoshimine said, yanking him over to the lifts. 'If we rip that cover off a door on another floor, they won't notice.'

In order to isolate the noisy students from the other guests, all their rooms were adjacent. If they ripped the cover off the knob on a floor where only regular guests were staying, it was possible it would go undetected.

The hotel rooms started on the fifth floor, and they'd heard that students on school trips were always housed on the fifth, sixth and seventh floors. When they got out at the eighth floor the hallway was so quiet they couldn't believe how peaceful the hotel could be.

'Okay, let's go.'

They yanked off the safety cover, pulled open the heavy fire door and hurtled down the stairs. Exiting on the ground floor, they reached a service entrance, through which they headed, trying to look nonchalant. Suddenly, a voice called out from behind them, 'You there!'

Startled, they turned around and saw a hotel employee.

'Aren't you students on a school trip?'

Oh god, Yoshimine thought. The hotel employees must have been warned to keep an eye out for escapees.

'No, actually we're not!' Yoshimine shot back, starting for the door.

'Hold it right there!' the man shouted, heading after him.

'Run for it!'

Yoshimine darted off, Satoru chasing after him.

'Somebody stop those boys!'

The employee's shouts immediately led to more obstacles being put in their way, but, running this way and that, trying to avoid all the people who were joining the pursuit, they finally came to the hotel's main entrance.

Standing guard was the form teacher Yoshimine had met on his first day – the pretty woman who'd been so sympathetic.

'Yoshimine-kun! Satoru-kun! What are you doing?'

Satoru thought Yoshimine might give up at this point, but when Yoshimine shouted, 'Let's go for it. Sod the consequences!' he sped up with his friend. The teacher raised her arms to stop them, but they slipped past her and leapt on to the crowded pavement outside the hotel, laughing all the way.

They might as well have used the main entrance to start with.

They kept on running, to shake off any pursuers, and Satoru shouted breathlessly at his friend, 'Listen! Tell people I went out 'cause I was dying to go out at night and have some fun.'

'Okay.'

As they made their way down unfamiliar streets, they asked for directions, and in about twenty minutes they had arrived at Hakata Station.

They were at the window for train tickets to Kokura when they heard someone calling from behind them.

'Hey! You boys!' It was a PE teacher, one of the chaperones.

They were escorted back to the hotel, called into one of the rooms where the teachers were staying and firmly scolded.

'Where on *earth* did you think you were going?'

They hadn't agreed on a story beforehand and weren't sure how to get through this. They glanced at each other, wondering who should go first.

'Satoru-kun.' This from the kindly teacher. 'Maybe being on a school trip was hard on you?'

Oh, the beautiful teacher, Miss Empathy. Well just stop it, Yoshimine thought. Drop the sympathy. Don't try to protect Satoru by bringing that up.

'No, that's not it,' Satoru replied in an even voice, though his face had turned pale. 'I just wanted to get out and have fun in the town. That's all.'

'Don't lie to me. I know you're not that kind of boy.'

Yoshimine nearly burst out laughing. What do *you* know about Satoru, Teacher?

*Tell people I went out 'cause I was dying to go out at night and have some fun.* Satoru didn't want anyone to know he was trying to get to Kokura to see a cat.

'Satoru, I'm sorry. I've had enough.'

Yoshimine looked as though he was about to give up. The teachers' attention turned to him.

'It's my fault, ma'am. I was dying to eat some Nagahama ramen. And I was asking for directions at the station.

'Thing is,' he went on, 'I had ramen at an outdoor stall once in Tenjin with my parents, back before they got divorced. Since we weren't far from there, I remembered my parents and memories of those good times. Satoru just tagged along with me.'

Their circumstances were different, but both boys were no longer with their parents. That was justification enough – two lonely boys wanting to cheer each other up.

'Yoshimine . . .' Satoru was about to say something, but Yoshimine cut him off. 'It's okay,' he said. He needed his friend to keep quiet if he really didn't want the world to know about his precious cat.

The teachers remained silent and stern, but they were clearly uncertain how to proceed.

'I understand how you feel, but rules are rules. You can't just go off on your own during a school trip,' said the PE teacher sourly.

They should have just bowed their heads and apologized then and there. Both of their guardians were contacted and, as an example to the rest of the students, their punishment was to sit in the hallway, in uncomfortable formal *seiza* style, legs tucked under them, until late in the evening.

As soon as he got home from the trip, Yoshimine asked his grandmother a favour.

'Grandma, *please*, there's something I really, really need to ask of you.'

He wanted his grandmother to call Satoru's aunt to apologize. To apologize for getting Satoru mixed up in all this.

His grandmother knew her grandson had never been to Tenjin with his parents, but she did as requested, no questions asked.

'I'm so sorry that Satoru-chan got yelled at because of what Daigo did.'

Satoru's aunt seemed embarrassed. 'I'm the one who should apologize,' she said. 'Yoshimine-kun wanted to abandon the idea but, apparently, Satoru dragged him along.'

So that was how Satoru had explained things at home.

'I know you two wouldn't break the rules without a very good reason,' Yoshimine's grandmother said later to him.

He felt choked.

This kind and considerate grandmother died some ten years ago, at a ripe old age.

Satoru had moved away when he graduated from junior high, but Yoshimine had continued to write to him, and when he told him of his grandmother's passing Satoru had come a long way to attend the funeral.

When he was thanked for attending, Satoru smiled. 'She was my grandmother, too, wasn't she?' he said. Yoshimine nodded, his eyes filling with tears.

His father, who was in charge of the funeral, had no intention of taking over the farm, and placed the house and its land in the care of nearby relatives, who had already got used to farming the fields and rice paddies when Yoshimine's grandmother was no longer able to.

Yoshimine had proposed that he take over the farm, but was persuaded otherwise. Apparently, the farm wouldn't make him much money and it would cause him a lot of trouble when it came to finding a wife.

'Well, as my relatives predicted, no marriage prospects so far,' Yoshimine told Satoru now.

'Well, if I were a woman, I would definitely be interested,' Satoru said.

'If you know any women who share your values, be sure to introduce me to them.'

Smiling, Yoshimine poured more *shochu* into his glass. Now that they had checked the fields for the evening, it was time for a couple of drinks with dinner.

Satoru had some beer with his, but later drank only barley tea. He had never been much of a drinker, and had recently become even less able to hold his liquor.

'I was hoping that before I leave tomorrow, I might pay a visit to your grandmother's grave,' he said.

The grave was in the hills behind the house. In Yoshimine's small truck, it would take less than five minutes to get there.

To celebrate his friend's visit, Yoshimine had planned to stay up late with him, but with an early-to-bed-early-to-rise habit drilled into him, he didn't even make it to midnight.

∽

SATORU AND YOSHIMINE WENT out first thing in the morning in Yoshimine's truck, talking as they drove about the night before.

Perfect, I thought. I have my own little something to take care of while they're gone.

Hey, orange tabby. Yes. *You.*

You remember what I taught you yesterday, don't you? We're going to go over how to handle yourself in a fight.

I crinkled up my nose and flattened my ears back. Okay, when you see an angry cat like this, what do you do?

The orange tabby followed suit, crinkling up his nose, laying his ears back, arching his back and making the fur on his back and tail stand on end.

Excellent. Well done.

Now, the final test. When I make an angry face, instantly strike a fighting pose. Impress Yoshimine. Listen, we need to have this nailed before I leave. So keep on your toes.

The orange tabby was full of spirit. Just then, Satoru and Yoshimine came back.

Timing it perfectly, so they were just coming into the room, I signalled to the orange tabby to adopt a fighting stance.

The kitten puffed up the fur all over his body like an exploding ball of wool. He was determined to show Yoshimine his best stance.

'*What the*—?!' Satoru sounded totally confused. 'They were getting on so well yesterday. I wonder what's happened all of a sudden.'

Who knows? Kittens are pretty impulsive. Perhaps he changed his mind?

'Maybe he's already forgotten about yesterday.' Yoshimine looked puzzled, too.

'Well, let's see how it goes for a while. He might just be in a bad mood.'

Satoru was planning to leave in the morning, but held off until the afternoon. He tried out a few things, including putting the kitten and me in separate rooms for a while.

Unfortunately the kitten continued performing until we left. Every time I urged him on, he took up his best fighting pose. He was really into it, for a kitten. If he kept this up, he might actually make something of himself.

'Why don't you leave Nana here and see how it goes? Give him a few days and they might get used to each other,' suggested Yoshimine when he got back from his morning farm chores.

'I don't think so,' Satoru said doubtfully. 'Nana got furious and hid in his basket, so it doesn't look promising. It's too bad, but if they don't get on, forcing them to be together is sort of cruel.'

'Really? That's too bad. He's such a good cat.'

*Yoshimine, I don't dislike you, so don't think badly of me, okay?*

*But I'm still not ready to leave that silver van for good.*

Satoru still seemed a bit sad about the whole thing, but with the little orange tabby looking so angry, wearing that ominous look, he finally gave up on the idea. Holding my basket to his chest, he climbed into the silver van.

'It really is a shame.'

'You say that, but you look pretty happy about the whole thing.'

To Yoshimine's teasing, Satoru gave only a 'Hmm' in reply. His remark seemed to have hit the nail on the head. 'Well . . .' he went on, 'it's true I'm going to find it hard to part with Nana.'

'If you like him so much, why do you have to give him away?'

*Oh. You threw that pitch right down the middle, didn't you, Yoshimine? A straight pitch, just like when you stuck your hand inside my basket when we first met.*

Satoru looked perplexed and didn't reply.

'Never mind,' Yoshimine said, not pressing the point. 'If you ever have any trouble, come round, okay? I may not have any marriage prospects or savings, but one thing is certain – farmers never lack for food.'

'But you see how Chatran and Nana are.'

'They're not going to kill each other, and if it comes to that, we can just force them to live together even if they don't want to. They're just animals, you really don't need to worry so much about whether they get on.'

'That's absurd. When animals are under too much stress, their fur can fall out.'

'If it really doesn't work out, then I'll set it up so you can stay in one of the unoccupied houses in the village. People are afraid their houses will deteriorate so they want someone to live in them. The village is doing its best to attract young people to come here from the city, too.'

'Thank you.' Satoru smiled, but his voice was still a bit shaky. 'If I really can't find a solution, then I'll definitely take you up on that.'

'Good. I'll look forward to it.'

Satoru and Yoshimine shook hands firmly.

'Thank you for everything. I'm pleased I was able to pay a visit to your grandmother's grave.'

He got into the van, but just before he started the engine Satoru said, 'Oh, that's right,' and rolled down the window. 'Yoshimine, do you remember the name of that cat I used to have?'

Yoshimine shook his head.

'He was called Hachi. He looked just like Nana, right down to the marks on his face like the Chinese character for eight. And Nana got his name because his tail looks like the character for seven.'

Yoshimine burst out laughing. 'You said Chatran's name was kind of corny, but the names you come up with are cheesy, too.'

'One names them according to the way they look, and the other is into clichés. I'd say it's a tie.'

Satoru beeped his horn lightly and drove off down the lane.

*

'You shouldn't act up like that, Nana, getting all upset over a little kitten.'

Ahem. You said you were going to leave me there, but do you really think that's gonna fly?

'I am a little relieved, though. That we can go home together.'

This I already knew.

'Like I promised, do you want to stop by the sea on the way back?'

Sounds great! I wonder how many of the delicacies in my usual gourmet seafood blend are really in there?

So the silver van headed towards the beach. Too much bother to stay in the basket, so I balanced on Satoru's lap as we bumped down the rough lane towards the sea.

When we got out of the van, Satoru scooped me up and hoofed it down the slope that led to the shore, but me, I clung on for dear life.

'Hey, Nana. What are you doing with your claws? It hurts!'

No way. *No. Way.* What is that *rushing* sound? I've never heard anything like it! What *is* it, that monstrous roar?

And there it was. The sea – spread out before my very eyes. An endless expanse of water rolling relentlessly towards us.

'Look, Nana. The sea. Aren't the waves fabulous?'

Fabulous!? What are you talking about? How optimistic humans can be, to think that this enormous mass of rolling water, this soaring energy – is *fabulous*!? I don't know about humans, but if any cat got caught up in it, that would be the end of it, for sure!

'Let's go down by the water's edge.'

NO. WAY.

'Nana! Ouch! That hurts!'

I slipped out of Satoru's arms, struggled to grasp higher ground, and leapt right up on top of his head, where, I have to admit, there wasn't much hair.

'Your claws! Nana, don't scratch me with your claws!'

This is no good. I need a safer place than Satoru's head! Humph!

I pushed off and landed on all fours on the ground. Then, scuttling as fast as I could, I dashed in the opposite direction from the shoreline.

'Nana!'

I ran straight up on to a nearby bluff and settled down at the base of a pine tree growing at an angle from the bare rock.

'Why do you have to go all the way up there? Come down here!'

Not gonna happen. If I'm not careful, I'll get swept away by a wave and die!

'Come on down from there, Nana. It's too hard for me to climb up!'

In the end, Satoru, with great care and awkwardness, clambered up the bluff to rescue me.

From my first experience of the sea, I learned a valuable lesson.

*The sea is where you go to reminisce when you are far away from home.*

Delicacies of the sea are not something cats should catch by themselves. It's quite acceptable to allow humans to prepare them for us.

'My scalp is full of scratches. It's going to sting when I shampoo, that's for sure.'

Satoru muttered a couple more complaints, but then gave a little chuckle.

'But you know, I never imagined you'd be that afraid of the sea. I've seen a side of you I've never witnessed before, but it's good to know you don't like it.'

I do like it, viewed from a distance. The sea, that is.

The van drove smoothly along the shoreline. I gazed at the glittering dark-blue water, my tail happily raised to the sky.

Until then, my life had been limited to the modest territory of Satoru's apartment and a small area around it. A decent-sized territory for a cat, really, but pretty modest compared to the vastness of this world.

A cat could never see all the sights the world has to offer in one lifetime. There's just so much out there.

Satoru?

Since we had embarked on our journey, I'd seen the town where you spent your childhood. And a farming village. And the sea.

I wondered what new scenes we would see together before this journey was over.

# 3
# Sugi and Chikako's Hotel for Pets

*Relax with your beloved pet while enjoying a breathtaking view of Mount Fuji.*

This was the slogan with which Shusuke Sugi and his wife Chikako launched their bed and breakfast three years ago.

The whole thing came about when the company Sugi worked for started to struggle and began to explore the idea of voluntary redundancy. Around that time, a B&B next to the fruit orchards owned by Chikako's parents came up for sale at a greatly reduced price, and the couple bought it, lock, stock and barrel, and opened it up for business. They considered part of its appeal would be to offer a discount to guests wanting to do pick-your-own in the orchards next door. This worked both ways, for it would benefit the orchard business to have customers referred to them, which was another reason they decided to take the plunge.

In the end, though, the B&B's biggest selling point was that they allowed pets.

It was Chikako who came up with the idea.

Using the first and second floors, plus a small cottage in the grounds, they were able to lodge guests with dogs or cats separately. Dogs and cats each had their own floor and, as long as they got on with their own kind, they could enjoy life off the lead or outside their basket. Issues of compatibility were left to the owners' discretion.

Very few B&Bs in the area allowed both dogs and cats; most places catered just for dogs. Some of the larger inns accepted both, but most of them demanded that pets remain on a lead or in a basket.

Sugi was more of a dog person, so at first he wasn't sure about his wife's idea, but after the B&B had been running for three years he had to admit she'd been very perceptive.

In addition to Chikako's family business, there were plenty of other orchards and wineries nearby, and within their prefecture this area attracted a lot of tourists – but a B&B where cats could stay, stress-free, was almost unheard of. Word of mouth and repeat business led to an increase in cat-owning guests, and these days, guests with cats outnumbered those with dogs.

Chikako loved all cats, and cat-owning guests always received a warm welcome, but she'd never been happier than with the guests who were arriving today.

Chikako had been on the second floor making the bed in the sunniest twin room and now, dirty linen in hand and humming a tune, she made her way downstairs.

'You seem pretty upbeat,' Sugi said. He'd tried to make it sound casual, but it came out sounding oddly churlish. Chikako looked at him, puzzled.

'Aren't you happy? Satoru Miyawaki is bringing his cat for the very first time.'

'Of course I am, but . . .' Sugi said hurriedly, trying to gloss it over. 'I was just wondering if his cat will get on with our pets.'

Their own pets were a dog – a Kai Ken breed – and a brown tabby cat. The Kai Ken was a three-year-old male named Toramaru, while the brown tabby cat was a twelve-year-old female named Momo. Toramaru (*tora* meaning 'tiger') got his name from the distinctive orangey brindle fur that certain Kai Ken dogs have, while Momo, which means 'peach', was named after the main crop of the orchard.

'Don't worry so much. It'll be fine. Our little ones are used to having guests.'

Sugi persisted, despite Chikako's teasing smile. 'Satoru is giving away his cat, you know. I'm sure he can't be too happy about that.'

The man they were expecting was their mutual high-school friend Satoru Miyawaki.

An email had arrived in Sugi's inbox saying that, though Satoru loved his cat very much, there was a compelling reason why he couldn't keep him any longer, and he was looking for someone to take care of him.

No explanation of what this *compelling reason* was, but when Sugi noticed in the newspaper that a large corporation had started to lay off employees, he didn't pursue the matter. Satoru's company, as he recalled, was a subsidiary of that corporation.

If an organization that big is beginning to lay people off, Sugi pondered, then I guess it's only to be expected that my old company would do the same. He was lucky to have left his local firm when he did.

'But if we take on his cat, we can give him back at any time, can't we?' Chikako said, and laughed. 'I'm thinking of it more as a temporary arrangement. I'll take good care of him while we have him, of course. That goes without saying.'

A temporary arrangement. Sugi hadn't considered that. Chikako was always so positive and forward-thinking. Always looking on the bright side. Calling Sugi *prudent* made it sound positive, but the fact was he tended to be far less optimistic, the exact opposite of Chikako.

'There really must be some sound reason for him to give away his cat all of a sudden . . . But one day, I know, Satoru will come back for him.'

Chikako seemed to believe categorically that Satoru's love for his cat would overcome all obstacles. When it came to cat love, the two of them had always been on the same wavelength.

Bed linen in hand, Chikako went into the laundry room. 'Get down, Momo.' Their cat seemed to be asleep on top of the washing machine. 'Satoru says his cat is named Nana. Make sure you get on with him now.' Chikako sounded like she was singing as she said this. 'Oh!' she called loudly. 'Darling, make sure you tell Tora the same thing.'

Both dog and cat were equally important to them, but, in practical terms, there was a clear division of duties. Chikako, the cat person, was in charge of Momo, while Sugi, more on the dog side of the divide, handled all things Toramaru.

*Whenever there's anything major happening in our family we need to inform both our dog and cat* – this proposal by Chikako had become a firm family rule.

Sugi slipped his feet into the sandals he had left at the entrance and went outside. When the weather was fine, during the day they let Toramaru have free run of a special fenced-off space in the front yard. Sugi's father-in-law, who prided himself on his carpentry skills, had built a kennel for Toramaru.

'Tora!'

Hearing his name, Tora wagged his curled tail energetically and leapt up to his owner. He could jump so high it looked like he might one day bound over the high fence, so, to be on the safe side, whenever guests arrived, they put him on a lead tied to his kennel. The expert who had given them the dog told them how the breed divided into two types – the slimmer types who were built for chasing deer, and the thicker-set types who were good at chasing wild boar. Toramaru was a textbook deer type.

For two days, Satoru would be the only guest, so Sugi had let Tora off his lead.

'Satoru is coming this evening. The friend I told you about.'

Sugi had acquired Toramaru three years earlier when they first opened the B&B, but right about that time, Satoru was moved over to a busy section of his company and had little free time to visit him and Chikako. Sugi had been able to see him occasionally when he went into Tokyo to purchase food for the B&B, but it would be the first time in three years that Chikako had seen him, and the very first time for Toramaru.

Satoru had always seemed very busy with work, so Sugi presumed his job must be secure, but with staffing cutbacks there could be many factors at play.

'This is the first time you'll meet Satoru and Nana, Tora, and I hope you'll get on with them.'

Sugi gave Toramaru's head a brisk rub, and the dog gave a throaty growl. Rough stroking like this was one of the real pleasures of having a dog. If he tried the same with Momo, he thought, she'd probably lunge at him, claws bared.

'You be on your best behaviour, okay?'

Toramaru looked searchingly into Sugi's eyes, then gave another husky growl.

THAT DAY, THERE WAS NO doves-about-to-pop-out kind of music playing in the silver van.

Perhaps thinking he'd have a break from the car stereo, Satoru had the radio on instead. A little while ago, a refined-sounding older gentleman had been enthusiastically introducing a book on some programme or other. Apparently, he was an actor.

He talked elegantly, yet occasionally he would use unexpected language: words like 'cool' and 'awesome', and even for a mere cat like myself, hearing this gentleman rattle on and on about how *awesome* a book was really made me smile.

All well and good, but no matter how appealing a book might be, I can't read it. As I explained earlier, most animals are multilingual when it comes to listening, but reading is beyond us. Reading and writing seem to belong to a special linguistic system that only humans possess.

'Hmm, if Mr Kodama, the host of the programme, likes the book so much, maybe I should read it,' Satoru murmured. When he was at home, he spent more time reading books than watching TV; he'd even been known to shed the occasional tear as he turned the pages. If he ever caught me watching him during one of these moments, he would look embarrassed and say, 'Stop staring.'

The book programme came to an end, and after a while a nursery song began to play.

*Put your head above the clouds, look down on all the other mountains around . . .*

Sometimes it's nice to hear this kind of gentle singing. Though the melody was making me sleepy.

*Hear the thunder roll above . . .*
*Mount Fuji is the highest mountain in all of Japan . . .*

Hm? At this last line, I sat up, rested my paws on the passenger-seat window and craned my neck to see out.

For a while now, there had been a huge triangular mountain plonked down in the distance.

'Oh, did you make the connection, Nana?'

Humans always underestimate our language skills. Just 'cause they can read and write, there's no need to act all high and mighty.

'That's right, it's a song about Mount Fuji. Great timing, don't you think?'

When that triangular-shaped mountain, with its base spread so wide, loomed closer, Satoru said, 'That's Mount Fuji.'

On TV and in photos, it looks just like a triangle that has flopped down on to the earth, but when you see it in real life it feels overwhelming, like it's closing in on you.

It's the highest mountain in Japan at 3,776 metres, and there's even a mnemonic device for people to remember the elevation: Let's all be like Fuji-san, *Fuji-san no yo ni mi* [three] *na* [seven] *ni na* [seven] *rou* [six] – there are many higher mountains around the world, but as a free-standing single mountain it's unusually high. Satoru rattled on and on, explaining all kinds of facts in great detail.

I get it, how great it is. You don't need to go on and on. It makes total sense why there is a song dedicated to it. Yada yada.

You really have to see it with your own eyes, though. If you've only seen it on TV or in photos, it'll always remain just a triangular mountain sitting there. Like it was to me until right this moment.

Being big has its advantages. Just as being a big cat makes it easier to get by in life.

Still, this mountain *was* pretty darn amazing.

I wonder how many cats in Japan have seen the actual Mount Fuji. Unless they live around here, there can't be too many.

Our silver van was like a magic carriage. Every time I got into it, it carried me to a place I'd never been before.

At that moment, we were without doubt the greatest travellers in the world. And I was the world's greatest travelling cat.

The van veered off the main road and drove into a thick, lush forest.

The branches of the trees on either side had bunches of white paper bags hanging from them, apparently to protect the peaches growing on them – to keep the insects off and help the fruit ripen.

After zigzagging for quite some time, finally a large white house appeared in front of us.

'We're here, Nana.'

This must be the bed and breakfast Satoru had talked about – the inn, run by some friends, that accepts pets. Today, the place was reserved just for us.

As the van pulled into a parking lot big enough for about ten cars, a man Satoru's age came out to greet us.

'Sugi!'

Satoru gave him a wave and unloaded his bag from the van.

'Is this your only bag? I'll help you.'

'Apart from Nana, I only brought a change of clothes, as it's just the one night.'

Sugi took hold of his friend's bag, and Satoru carried me in my basket, and together they climbed the gentle slope to the B&B entrance.

'What a wonderful place this is. Is that a dog run?'

On the way up the slope was a fairly large fenced-in space with what looked like a kennel near the back.

'I wanted a space where my dog could run free.'

'A Kai Ken, isn't it? I remember you saying you had one.'

From inside the basket, I sniffed at the air. A disgusting smell that belonged to that perennial rival to cats.

I squinted through the bars and watched as a hard-faced brindle dog sprang to his feet and stared challengingly in my direction.

'Yeah, his name is Toramaru.'

'Is he okay living with a cat?'

'Of course. We have Momo, you know. And lots of guests bring their cats.'

'Ah, that's right . . .'

I'd already heard from Satoru that they had a middle-aged female cat named Momo. She was twice my age, he'd said. I was still fairly young, so would we get on?

'Hey there. Hello. Glad to meet you, Toramaru,' called Satoru, holding his hand over the fence.

Hold on a minute! Don't go speaking to that dog! I glowered from inside my basket.

This Kai Ken who went by the name of Toramaru cast

a sharp glance our way and growled and bared his yellow teeth.

'Is he in a bad mood then?'

The instant Satoru inclined his head – *ruff!* – the dog barked at him.

'Whoa!'

As you might expect, Satoru quickly pulled his hand back from the fence.

Hey! Knock it off, hound!

Every single hair on my body was now standing on end.

If you're going to pick a fight with Satoru, then I – a cat with a strong sense of pride – am not going to just sit here and take it! If you don't want that nose of yours cut to shreds, then apologize right this instant, you mangy mutt!

'*Tora!*'

Sugi scolded him, but the mutt didn't stop his miserable yammering.

Satoru tried to soothe me, too.

'It's okay, Nana. Just hang in there.'

He was holding the door of the basket closed from the outside because he knew I was quite willing to have it out with that stupid dog if I had to.

'I'm really sorry,' Sugi said. 'He's not usually like this.'

'No, it's okay . . . I wonder if we did something to upset him.'

'What's going on?' A woman hurried out of the front door. A pretty woman wearing an apron. 'Is Tora angry?'

'It's no big deal. Hi, Chikako. How are you?' This from Satoru, who waved his hand at the woman.

'Satoru! I'm so sorry. Is everything all right?'

'No worries. I'm not used to cats or dogs getting angry with me, and it startled me for a second.'

That's true. From an animal's point of view, Satoru was a pretty stress-free human, the kind that passing dogs and cats found no reason to pick a fight with.

An impudent dog like this leaping out at him was definitely a first.

'I'm so sorry. I really am,' Sugi apologized, making another *knock it off* gesture at the dog. Toramaru let his curled tail droop. Serves you right, you stupid hound.

'It's fine. Really,' Satoru said, trying to smooth things over. 'He seems like a good, dependable dog. Maybe I look a little dodgy to him?'

Satoru tried again, reaching over the fence to scratch the dog's neck. The mutt quietly allowed him to stroke him, but it was obvious to me he was still sulking. Try flashing those gnashers at Satoru again for even a split second, mate, and you'll have *me* to deal with!

Through the bars, the dog and I exchanged some seething, hostile looks, but Satoru was then shown inside the house, so there was an unavoidable pause in the action.

We were shown a lovely sunny room on the second floor.

'After you get settled, come down,' Chikako-san said. She turned and went nimbly down the stairs.

Well, I'll take a look around the room, then. I easily unlatched the door of the basket from the inside and slipped silently out. The neat little room had wooden flooring, and from a feline point of view looked perfectly cosy.

'Oh, hello there, Momo.'

At the sound of Satoru's voice, I spun around to face the doorway. A small, dignified, brown female tabby was sitting quietly in the corner. Double my age, but still quite limber, from the look of things.

Nice to make your acquaintance, Momo greeted me, in a dignified voice quite in keeping with a dignified tabby. I hear you and Toramaru have already squabbled.

I let out a sniff. That dog has no manners. Baring his teeth at humans who try to say hello to him – he couldn't have been well brought up.

I was thoroughly sarcastic in my comments, and Momo smiled wryly.

Please forgive him. Just as your master is precious to you, so Toramaru's master is precious to him.

Your master is precious to you so you bark at your master's *friend*? That doesn't compute. *At all.*

As if sensing my displeasure Momo gave another wry smile.

I'm really sorry. I believe our master is not quite as strong a character as your master.

I still didn't get it. I refrained from objecting, though, because I didn't want to be disrespectful to an older lady.

∽

'HE SEEMS TO BE GETTING ON well with Momo.'

Satoru had come down to the lobby-cum-lounge and, with a smile, he was pointing upstairs.

'They're in the bedroom, getting to know each other better. Now, if only Toramaru could be friendlier. Maybe he's angry that I brought a cat along?'

'He should be used to guests bringing cats by now.' Chikako tilted her head, puzzled, and offered them some herbal tea.

'Darling, you did explain things to Toramaru, didn't you?' Chikako scolded Sugi jokingly.

'Of course I did,' Sugi pouted, his tone a little snappy.

*You be on your best behaviour, okay?* Sugi had said, as Toramaru gazed into his eyes. So why did he then bark at Satoru?

Maybe Toramaru had detected some discomfort in Sugi?

'Wow, this is delicious,' Satoru said as he sipped his tea, and Chikako beamed.

'I'm so happy! Our guests seem to like it, too. The herbs are from our garden.' Chikako looked over at Sugi sternly. 'The first time I made herbal tea for him, he said it was like drinking toothpaste.'

One silly slip of the tongue back when they had first got married, and Chikako still bore a grudge. Thinking about this, Sugi had often wished he could follow Satoru's lead and be shrewder in dealing with things. But, in truth, Sugi found openly praising anyone a bit embarrassing.

'It's slightly sweet. What do you put in it?' Satoru asked.

'Stevia.'

'Ah, that makes sense.'

'This is why I enjoy talking to Satoru, because we can talk about things like this!'

'Your business seems to be doing well,' Satoru said, clearing his throat.

'It is. Targeting guests with cats was a smart move,' Sugi said.

'All *my* idea,' Chikako returned.

'Indeed. Entirely the wife's doing,' Sugi added. 'But

what about you? Are *you* doing okay? Giving away your cat . . . all of sudden?'

Sugi had found it hard to ask this question in an email, so he had planned to do it when they were face to face.

'Yeah, well . . . you know . . .' Satoru gave a troubled smile, and when he did, he suddenly looked very old.

'I heard the business group your company belongs to has started to lay people off.'

'It's not really that . . . There are other things involved.'

Chikako gave Sugi a stealthy wink to signal him to stop. *Okay*, he signalled back.

'I was so relieved when you said you'd take Nana for me. I've asked quite a few people now, and taken Nana to see them, but somehow it just hasn't worked out.'

'There's one thing I'd like to say upfront, Satoru,' Chikako said, sitting up straight. 'We're thinking of it as temporary. We'll take good care of Nana, of course, but if things work out for you so you can take him again, we'll have no problem if you come back for him, any time.'

Satoru looked as though this had really struck a chord, and for a moment he pursed his lips and looked at his feet.

That face – lips pursed, trying his best to keep his feelings in check – was one both Chikako and Sugi had seen before.

Suddenly Satoru looked up and smiled.

'Thank you. I'm sorry to be so selfish, but it really makes me happy to hear that.'

༄

SATORU HAD BECOME A MUTUAL friend, but Sugi had been the first one to form a bond with him.

In the spring of their first year in high school, the three of them were all in the same class.

In their new form room, students from their previous junior high tended to group together, weighing up the situation, wondering who to make friends with. Satoru wasn't hanging out with anyone. There didn't seem to be anyone else from the school he had just come from.

They learned later that he'd arrived from another prefecture during the spring holidays and had taken the transfer exam, which was why he didn't know a soul.

It was during one of the periodic exams that they became friends.

Sugi had crammed all night for the exam, and his head was stuffed with mathematical equations and English vocabulary. He was on his bike, heading to school, pedalling as gently as he could, in case some unexpected jolt or vibration drove all the facts he'd memorized from his brain.

Along the road to school, he spied a face he knew. That looks like Satoru from my class, he thought, as he drew closer. Satoru had got off his bike and was standing beside a wide ditch.

The ditch was the width of a stream, an agricultural irrigation channel lined with concrete on both sides, about as deep as a child was tall. Satoru was staring down at it, a serious look on his face.

Sugi wondered what he was up to, but didn't have much time to spare before school started. Their eyes had met, so he thought he'd just give him a nod and pass on by, but he began to feel that that would make things awkward later, so after he'd gone on a little bit, he stopped.

'What're you doing?' Sugi asked.

Satoru looked over at him, as if surprised. He must have thought Sugi would just cycle by.

'Um, I found something a little troubling, that's all.'

Satoru pointed down at the ditch, where Sugi could now see a small dog shivering. The dog had managed to scramble on top of a tiny sandbar where gravel and dirt had piled up, and his thick white-and-brown fur was soaked and plastered to him.

'It's a Shih Tzu.'

Sugi knew the breed, because Chikako's family had one. They ran a fruit orchard, loved animals, and ever since she was a young child they'd had several dogs and cats, which was something that drew customers in. And Sugi had always envied their attitude to animals.

Sugi's family lived in company housing; his father was a middle-management company employee, and because of his mother's allergies, the only pets she would allow were hairless ones such as goldfish or turtles. His dream had always been to have a dog, but this was never going to happen in his own house, so being with Chikako's family at least came close.

'He must have fallen in.'

'I guess so,' Satoru said, nodding. There were no steps down to the ditch that they could see.

'He's not the type of dog you'd expect to be a stray, so I reckon he must have wandered away from his home and got lost . . .'

At Chikako's, during the day they let their dogs run free in the orchards so the customers who came to pick fruit could enjoy their company, but at night they always made sure they were brought inside the house.

'Go on ahead. You don't need to stick around,' Satoru

urged him, but for Sugi it was a delicate decision. If it emerged later that he'd ignored a poor little dog that had fallen into a ditch, then Chikako would be pretty upset.

'Yeah, but I'm worried about him.'

Glancing at his watch, Sugi got off his bike. He was going to be late for school, but if he got there before first period he'd still be able to take the exam.

'Let's sort this out as quickly as we can.'

Satoru smiled. 'You're a good guy, Sugi.'

All he'd been worried about was Chikako's reaction, and he found this praise from Satoru embarrassing.

'If we go down there, our ankles will get soaked.'

The sandbar where the Shih Tzu was standing was too far away to leap to from either side of the ditch. The water was full of algae and grass so they couldn't see the bottom, and they were reluctant to take their shoes off in case there were any pieces of glass.

Sugi noticed a pile of boards left on the side of the road, the remnants, perhaps, of some scaffolding. He ran over and pulled one out.

'If we angle it down near the dog, he might be able to use it as a bridge and climb along it.'

'Maybe.'

But even with the board right in front of it, the Shih Tzu didn't react.

They tried calling, but the dog just stood there trembling, not taking a single step.

'Maybe it can't see it,' Satoru said, a serious look on his face. 'If you look at him closely from the side, his eyes are a bit cloudy. He might be getting cataracts.'

It was hard to tell the age of the baby-faced dog, but its coat was definitely a bit worn.

'Amazing that the little guy made it this far!'

There was a busy motorway nearby; it was a miracle the dog hadn't been run over. Perhaps it had fallen into the ditch because it couldn't see properly.

'I'm going to go down. If I use this, I won't get wet.' Satoru put a foot on the board they'd stretched out towards the dog.

'Be careful, it's dangerous.'

The board was old and weathered. It might not even hold a dog's weight, let alone that of a high-school boy. Just as these thoughts were going through Sugi's head, the board let out an ominous creak.

'Whoa!'

Satoru swayed on the board, and in an instant, it had split completely in two and collapsed into the ditch. There was a loud splash and a spray of water as Satoru landed on his rear in the ankle-deep stream.

*Woof woof woof.* The Shih Tzu barked, and started to splash his way blindly through the water.

'Wa-wait!'

Satoru scrambled to his feet and tried to follow him. But his splashing only scared the Shih Tzu even more, and he didn't stop. You wouldn't know he was old and half blind, the way the dog tore through the water.

'I'll run ahead and climb down! We'll catch him. Don't let him get away!'

Sugi hared down the road, past the fleeing Shih Tzu, and took a flying leap into the ditch.

There was an explosion of water. The Shih Tzu leapt into the air and screeched to a halt. Then he spun around and started to race back the way he had come.

'He's coming back your way. Grab him!'

Satoru leapt towards the dog like a goalie. The Shih Tzu made a tight turn, trying to slip past, but Satoru managed to snag a hind leg. Panicked, the dog chomped down on his hand.

'Ow!'

'Hang on! Don't let go!'

Sugi whipped off his blazer, threw it over the Shih Tzu and grabbed him. Swaddled, the dog finally gave up his struggle.

'You okay?' Sugi asked.

Satoru smiled wryly. 'This could be pretty serious,' he said, showing his hand. Spots of blood were bubbling up. For such a little creature, the dog certainly knew how to bite.

'You'd better get to the hospital.'

No chance I'll make that exam now, Sugi thought.

They took the dog to a police station beside the motorway, but when they went to the hospital there was a problem. Satoru didn't have an insurance card. Being high-school students, they didn't have enough cash either, so they ended up handing over their school ID cards and promising to come back and pay – and finally Satoru was treated.

By the time they got to school, second period was just finishing.

They went to the faculty office and explained to their form teacher what had happened. The whole thing sounded like a joke, but Satoru's resemblance to a drowned rat, and his bandaged hand, must have convinced her, for the teacher accepted their version of events.

'What happened to you guys?' asked Chikako, playing the concerned older sister as the boys returned to the classroom.

When she heard about the rescued Shih Tzu, she wanted to see him, so they stopped at the police station on their way home from school. Satoru was concerned about the dog, too, so the three of them went together.

The old Shih Tzu with his cloudy eyes was on a lead in the corner of the lobby, bowls of dry dog biscuits and water next to it. No one had reported a missing dog.

'He really is quite old. I don't think he can see well at all.' Chikako knelt down in front of the dog and waved her hand in front of his eyes. The Shih Tzu was slow to react.

'I was wondering if we could ask you to take him,' said a middle-aged police officer. 'Looking after lost dogs isn't really a policeman's job, so we can't keep him here for very long.'

'If you can't keep him here . . . then what will happen to him?' Satoru asked.

The officer tilted his head. 'If the owner doesn't appear in the next few days, he'll go to the pound.'

'How could you!' Chikako snapped. 'You know they'll put him down! If the owner doesn't turn up in time—'

Satoru, pale and silent, nudged Sugi in the ribs. 'How about keeping it at your place?' he suggested. Instead of arguing with the officer, Satoru seemed to be looking for a practical solution.

'No can do. My mum is allergic to any animal with fur. What about yours, Satoru?'

'We're in company housing and they don't allow pets.'

Chikako, who was still carping at the police officer, turned around. 'It's okay,' she said. 'We'll keep him at ours.'

'Are you sure you can make that decision right now? Shouldn't you ask your parents or something?'

Satoru seemed alarmed by her snap decision, but Chikako just glared at him in irritation.

'Well, we can't just leave him here!'

Chikako called home from the payphone in the lobby. Almost an hour later, her father pulled up at the station in his small truck. They loaded her bike on to the truck bed, and Chikako got into the passenger seat and held the Shih Tzu on her lap.

'Okay, see you soon!' she called. 'Satoru, if you're worried about him, you can come and visit him at my place!'

'Ah – thanks.'

Satoru seemed a bit intimidated by Chikako's forceful manner.

Then Chikako was gone, like a storm departing, and the boys burst out laughing.

'That Sakita-san is really something.'

'She sure is. She's always had strong views when it comes to animals, ever since she was little.'

'Have you known her since she was a kid?' Satoru wanted to know.

'We're childhood friends,' Sugi explained.

'I get it,' Satoru said, nodding. 'So that's why Sakita-san calls you Shu-chan?'

'I told her to drop that.'

'What's wrong with it? She's your cute, dependable childhood friend.'

The way he'd casually called her *cute* startled Sugi. Chikako was spirited, kind and, yes, cute. He'd always known that. Still, Sugi had never spoken about these things out loud.

It made him feel like he'd lost out.

'But will her family really be okay about taking in an unknown dog without any warning?' Satoru asked.

'It'll be fine. Her family are mad about animals. They have five or six dogs and cats already.'

'Really? Cats, too?'

'Chikako's more of a cat person.'

'I see,' Satoru said, smiling. 'I love cats, too. I wouldn't mind making sure the Shih Tzu's okay, but it would be nice to see her cats, too.'

Sugi was hit by another wave of anxiety. It was clear Satoru and Chikako were going to get on well.

That evening, Chikako phoned Sugi. The fact that he had missed taking the exam in order to rescue the dog had made an impression on her.

'By the way,' she asked, 'which one of you found it?'

Sugi wished he'd been the one who'd come across the dog – the thought of saying this had crossed his mind. *But if I had, I probably would have just let him be. Perhaps the most I would have done would have been to check on him on the way home.*

'Well, we were both passing at about the same time.'

A little white lie.

'But I think Satoru actually spotted him first,' he added hastily.

'We haven't spoken much up till now, but Satoru's a pretty good guy.'

Chikako seemed to like Satoru a lot. He had known she would.

The three of them often talked together after this. And Satoru and Sugi often went to Chikako's house to see how the Shih Tzu was settling in.

Whenever Sugi went to see Chikako, he'd be put to work helping out in the orchards, as would Satoru. From the way he spoke, Satoru seemed like a real city boy, but he was, surprisingly, used to farm work, and Chikako's family quickly grew fond of him.

The stray Shih Tzu's owner never did materialize, so the Sakita family ended up keeping him permanently. Satoru felt badly about it and said he'd try to find somebody to take the dog, but Chikako waved this away.

The younger Shih Tzu they already had got on with the new one – they were like parent and child – and, typically for Chikako, she referred to the latter as 'the Shih Tzu Miyawaki gave us'.

The cats at the Sakitas' were friendlier to Satoru than to Sugi. They had, from the start, sensed that Sugi was more of a dog person. Things evened out, though, since the dogs were much friendlier to him than to Satoru. 'The Shih Tzu Miyawaki gave us', perhaps remembering how Satoru had been the one to chase him down, was friendlier to Sugi than to Satoru, who had found him.

One day at school, Satoru was leafing through the part-time jobs listings in the newspaper. The end-of-term exams were approaching, and their teachers had joked with them not to pick up any more stray dogs.

'Are you looking for a holiday job?' Sugi asked.

'Yeah . . . I was wondering if there're any with a decent hourly rate.'

'How come? Isn't your allowance enough?'

'No, it's just that I want to take a trip during the summer holiday, and I'd like to go as soon as possible.'

'Where to?'

'Kokura.'

Sugi didn't know the place.

'It's in Fukuoka prefecture. Just before Hakata,' Satoru explained.

Sugi knew exactly where he meant, but couldn't understand why Satoru would want to go there, instead of to Hakata, which was much larger.

'I have some distant relatives there,' Satoru explained. 'They took in our cat when we couldn't have him any more. I haven't been to see him at all since then.'

I see, Sugi thought. It's not Kokura he wants to visit, but a cat.

'Why couldn't you keep it?'

He asked this casually, but Satoru gave a troubled smile. He seemed unsure how to respond, and Sugi was just thinking that maybe he should change the subject when a shadow loomed over them.

'I heard, I heard.' Laughing her usual audacious laugh, it was Chikako.

'Man, you're always sticking your nose into things, aren't you?' Sugi teased her.

'Shut it,' she shot back. 'I know exactly how you feel – wanting to visit your beloved cat. I'll pitch in and help!'

'Do you know where I can get work?' Satoru asked.

'And where you can begin this very weekend!' Chikako answered.

'Really? If there's a job that good, then tell me about it, too.' Sugi had been starting to think about finding a summer job himself.

'Having a part-time job during term time is prohibited, but there is an exception: "This shall not apply to helping out with a family business." And if it's helping with a classmate's family business, if you apply, you can get permission to work just at the weekends. They consider it part of social studies.'

In short, she was telling Satoru he could work in her family's orchard.

'The pay isn't much, but I'll ask them to pay you weekly, so if you start work now, you should be able to go on your trip at the beginning of August.'

Satoru stood up, so excited he nearly kicked over his chair.

The crop was ready to harvest and a lot of customers were coming to pick fruit in their orchard. Sugi joined them to work there on Sundays, except during exam time. The hourly wages were even less than working in a small supermarket, but by the time the school closing ceremony was over, Satoru had been able to put away about 20,000 yen.

'What are you going to use your money for, Shu-chan?' Chikako asked.

'I haven't thought about it.'

Which wasn't exactly true. 'Hey, do you want to go and see a film?' he said, trying to make it sound as if he'd just come up with the idea.

'Your treat?' As he expected, she leapt at the idea.

'Okay. I mean, you did get me the job and all.'

'Great! Maybe I'll sponge a meal off you as well.'

Only just managing not to physically jump for joy, smiling, Sugi said, 'Okay, okay.'

'Great. You weren't joking, were you? Don't you dare change your mind later on!'

Chikako, totally thrilled that Sugi would be footing the bill, certainly wasn't viewing this as a date. But for now that was okay.

There was no need to rush things.

On the first day of the last week of July, Satoru failed to show up for work.

It wasn't like him – he was always so conscientious – and he hadn't even been in touch to explain his absence. Sugi wondered what was up.

Satoru turned up an hour late.

'I'm very sorry I'm late,' he said, his face pale and stiff.

'If you don't feel well, you should take some time off,' Chikako's father said, but Satoru insisted he was fine.

At lunchtime, Chikako's parents told the three of them to come back to the house. Satoru was looking paler than ever.

'What's wrong? Has something happened?' they asked. But again, he obstinately insisted it was nothing, and wouldn't say any more.

Chikako, silently watching, spoke up. 'Has something happened to your old cat?'

Satoru's lips tightened. He dropped his head and screwed up his eyes. Finally he allowed the tears to flow.

'He was hit by a car,' he muttered, his voice broken, and then he couldn't say anything more. It seemed he'd just got the news that morning.

'You were really fond of that cat, weren't you?' Chikako said, putting her arm around his shoulders, to which Satoru murmured back, 'He was family.'

Why had he been forced to give him away? When Sugi had asked him earlier, he hadn't responded. If the cat had been regarded as part of the family, it was even more puzzling.

If he was this grief-stricken at the news, he shouldn't

have given the cat away in the first place, thought Sugi, somewhat uncharitably. Perhaps he was a bit jealous of the other two and their shared love of cats.

'He was the cat we had back when my parents were still alive,' said Satoru, which put Sugi in his place. God was punishing him, he figured, for having entertained a nasty thought about his poor friend.

'. . . And you hoped to be in time to see him.' Chikako's kind words were so full of warmth.

Why am I such a low, mean person, when all I want is to be the kind of man Chikako won't be ashamed of? thought Sugi.

He hadn't realized that Satoru's parents were dead.

But even if I had known, I would never have been as sympathetic as Chikako.

'What are you going to do about the job? Will you carry on?' asked Sugi.

Beside him, Chikako gave him a *Really? Now?* type of look.

'There's no point in going to Kokura now,' Satoru said, and gave a faint smile.

Chikako interrupted him. 'You really should go. Save up your money and go over there to say goodbye.'

Satoru blinked in surprise.

'You have to mourn your cat properly, or you won't get over it. Don't just sit here fretting about being too late. Go there and mourn him. Tell him you're sorry you didn't make it in time, that you wanted to see him.'

Sugi knew very well how deeply these words resonated with Satoru, because even he, who'd thought those mean things, was starting to tear up.

Satoru smiled, and decided to get back to work.

*

Towards the end of the summer holidays, Satoru set off on his trip.

When he came back again, he looked like he'd put the past to rest.

He'd brought back some souvenirs for Sugi and Chikako. For Sugi, some Hakata ramen he'd asked for, and for Chikako, for some reason, he brought back some blotting paper and a hand mirror he'd bought in Kyoto.

'Wow! This paper is Yojiya!'

Apparently, it was some famous cosmetics brand, and Chikako was ecstatic. A friend of hers called her over and she gave a hurried 'Thank you!' and rushed off.

'So you stopped in Kyoto, too?' Sugi asked, and Satoru nodded.

'I was on an elementary-school trip to Kyoto when my parents were killed in a car accident. My mother had asked me to buy Yojiya blotting paper as a present for her. I looked all over but never managed to find it. A friend later managed to find some and bought it for me, but I never bought it myself.'

'What about the hand mirror?'

'I just thought that I'd like to buy that for Chikako.'

It hurt to hear all this.

Chikako should be the one to hear this. But Sugi didn't want her to.

He began to wish it had been somebody else who'd run into Satoru the day they rescued the Shih Tzu.

He didn't tell Chikako what Satoru had told him about Kyoto. He suppressed his guilty conscience by convincing himself that, if Satoru really wanted her to know, he'd tell her himself.

Now, he was constantly worried that he was losing his advantage of being Chikako's childhood friend.

She was always calling Satoru by his last name, Miyawaki, while she always called Sugi 'Shu-chan'.

Some time passed before he saw any significance in this.

If Chikako had known Satoru's feelings, she would, no doubt, have been drawn to him.

Unlike himself, shamefully struggling to be the kind of man Chikako could be proud of, Satoru was already there.

And there was that terrible experience he'd been through as a child.

In spite of losing his parents so young, having his precious cat taken away from him, and now not being in time to see it again, Satoru blamed no one for his troubles, didn't see any of it as unfair.

If it were him, Sugi would give himself over to the tragedy to make it work in his favour. He would make all sorts of lazy excuses, perhaps even exploit it to attract Chikako's affections.

How could Satoru be so relaxed and natural? The more Sugi got to know him, the more he felt driven into a corner. Satoru was a rival he would never be able to beat.

He started to feel the lesser man despite his privileged upbringing, and though he had more to be thankful for than Satoru, he began to feel dissatisfied with life. He started arguing with his parents over nothing, saying malicious things, sometimes reducing his mother to tears.

*I have everything I need in life, so why am I such a mean, small person? Why can't I be kinder than Satoru, who has so much less?*

Chikako, too, had been brought up like Sugi, never

lacking a thing, yet she never felt like this when she was with Satoru. She seemed to naturally enjoy being with him. And this made Sugi feel even more cornered.

If things went on like this, he knew he was going to lose Chikako. And he had loved her for so much longer!

'I wonder if Satoru has a special girl he likes.'

These words spilled out from Chikako one day when Satoru wasn't with them.

It was the final blow. Sugi felt crushed.

Later, Sugi found himself saying, 'I've always loved Chikako. Ever since we were kids.'

This confession was directed not at Chikako but at Satoru.

Sugi had expected that when Satoru heard this, he would put a lid on any feelings he himself might have for Chikako. He had deliberately confessed his feelings to Satoru, while pretending to seek his advice.

Satoru's eyes opened wide in surprise and, after a moment's silence, he smiled. 'I get it.'

You do get it, right? You, of all people, should definitely get it.

Thus Sugi neatly stopped Satoru from declaring his feelings to Chikako, and in the end Satoru stepped aside without ever saying a word about them.

In the spring of their last year in high school, Satoru changed schools. His aunt, who was his guardian, often moved around with work.

Sugi was truly sad that his friend was leaving, but all the same felt a rush of relief. At the time, he felt, *Now things will be okay.*

'How can you be such a good person when you've been so unlucky?'

Sugi was grumbling away before he realized what he was doing. It was the wine they'd opened at dinner. He had thought it was a good opportunity to treat Satoru to some local wine, so he'd bought some Ajiron red. This variety had a sweet fragrance and taste, and if you didn't watch yourself it was easy to overdo it.

Chikako was out of the room having a bath, her absence another reason Sugi had let down his guard.

Satoru smiled wryly. 'I don't know if I'm a good person or not. But either way, I wasn't unlucky.'

'What are you talking about? Are you denying that life's treated you unfairly, and trying to make me feel bad by not admitting it?'

'I don't know what you mean. The wine must have gone to your head. Try sobering up a bit before Chikako finishes her bath.' Satoru pulled the wine bottle out of Sugi's reach.

---

We cats get all limp and squishy when we have catnip; for humans, wine seems to do the trick.

Satoru would occasionally drink alcohol at home. He'd down a few while watching one of those games with balls that humans like – baseball or soccer – and start feeling happy, and soon tumble sideways on to the floor.

If I inadvertently passed near him, he'd grab me and hug me to his face, saying 'Nana-*cha–n*' in a syrupy voice, and I couldn't stand it. So I tried to keep my distance. Plus he stank of alcohol.

There had been times when he drank away from the house and came back smelling of liquor, but he was always in a good mood. So I used to be convinced that when humans drank it always made them cheerful. Like catnip for cats.

I'd never encountered someone like Sugi, who got all gloomy and moody when he drank. When Chikako went to have a bath, he suddenly started pouting at Satoru, almost like he was cowering before him.

If drinking isn't fun, then why do it? I was hanging off the top of the TV in the sitting room, eyeing the two men as they talked, until Satoru finally removed the bottle of wine from the table.

By the way, I became really fond of the TV there. Ours at home was thin and flat like a board, but the one there was more of a box, very enticing for a cat. Plus, it was faintly warm, and made my tummy feel toasty. Fantastic in the winter, I imagined.

It's really old, Momo told me. In the past, all TVs were this shape, apparently. Going from this perfect design to an impractical flat shape is, if you ask me, a step backwards, technology-wise.

Momo told me that you could tell how old a cat was by whether or not they knew about these boxy TVs. In that house, Chikako gave priority to making things comfortable for cats and she dismissed the idea of getting one of the flat TVs. A splendid decision, in my opinion.

Why the glum look? If you're bored of it, then I'll have it back, Momo said to me.

She was stretching out her long limbs on a nearby sofa. She'd allowed me, the guest, to take her special seat on top of the TV.

It's not that I'm bored. It's just . . . I cast a glance at the worn-down Sugi.

I thought they were friends, but it doesn't look as though Sugi likes Satoru very much, Momo suggested.

That can't be true, I said.

Don't think he wants him here. And yet he went out especially yesterday to buy that wine. Said he'd like Satoru to try it.

Why flare up at Satoru like that then? Why say things about Satoru's character, as though he's *upset* that he's such a good person?

He likes him, but he also envies him. My master wants to be like your master.

I don't get it. Satoru is Satoru, and Sugi is Sugi.

Exactly. But the master seems to feel that if he could be like Satoru, then Chikako would love him more.

Dear me, it sounds like it's a pretty big thing for him.

Chikako used to really like your master, is what I gather, Momo clarified.

This was going way back. Way before Momo was born, when these humans were young. She said she heard it from the cat who lived with them previously.

What did Satoru think? Did he like Chikako, too?

*If a woman who held on to an old boxy TV for the sake of a cat was Satoru's wife, now that might be really wonderful,* is what I was thinking.

Well, that's not something we know. It's just that, when it comes to Chikako, the master seems to have a guilty conscience regarding Satoru, said Momo.

Sounds like an awkward business to me. I mean, Chikako ended up choosing Sugi and became his wife, so what's the problem?

Among cats, when a female chooses a mate, it's a very clear-cut thing. Not just among cats, but with all animals, the female's judgement about love is absolute. Of course, I haven't experienced true love myself, having been looked after by Satoru since I was young. I was a little too gentle to have won the heart of a female when I was young. If I'd had a bigger face and a sterner expression, I might have. Like Yoshimine. If he were a cat, he'd definitely be a hit with the ladies.

But it makes sense now.

That mutt of a dog is Sugi's, isn't it?

Dogs the world over just aren't very level-headed about things. Their master says jump and they ask, 'How high?' So perhaps Sugi's dog is trying to take the side of his gloomy master.

With cats, though, the master can throw a tantrum but cats don't necessarily jump. Cats always follow their own path.

Toramaru was still young and lacked subtlety.

In the evening, they let the dog inside the house, but led him immediately to another room. He didn't come at us barking like he did when we first met, but since he had been so terribly rude to Satoru, he and I were on high alert.

'Well, well, you seem to have had a few already.'

Chikako was out of the bath.

'Are you going to bed now?' Chikako asked, as though pacifying a child, to which Sugi replied, 'Nope,' shaking his head like a spoiled brat.

'If you and Satoru are staying up, then I will, too.'

Chikako and Satoru looked at each other with a smile. Their faces were glowing. Is a drunk really that endearing? To me, it just looks embarrassing. Crikey, I really hope I don't look like that when I sniff a bit of catnip.

After a while, Satoru said, 'I'm feeling sleepy now, so I'm off to bed. Come on.'

Satoru helped Sugi to his feet, but perhaps he was heavier than he expected, or his body more limp, because he began to stagger. Chikako got up quickly to help prop Sugi up.

In this way, the two of them got Sugi to bed.

∽

NOT LONG AFTER SATORU moved away with his aunt, Sugi started going out with Chikako.

They were both aiming to get into the same college. They talked it over and decided on a university in Tokyo. Chikako was planning to help out with the orchard business in the future, so if she didn't go to college outside the prefecture, she would end up spending her whole life within the confines of the district she grew up in. It was an entirely natural, innocent desire for a young girl to want to spend some part of her life in the big city.

They both passed the university entrance exams, and Chikako was to live with relatives in Tokyo while Sugi would stay in the dorm. It was a double room, and he was a bit concerned about whether he'd get on with his roommate, but the dorm had two points in its favour – the low rent and the convenient location.

He and his roommate arranged to meet up before the college entrance ceremony, and Sugi set off, map in hand, down the unfamiliar streets to locate his dorm.

The winding backstreets confused him and he wandered round in circles for a while, but he finally arrived, not too much later than the scheduled time.

He was filling out forms at the reception desk when it happened.

'Sugi!'

He didn't know anyone yet and turned around uncertainly. When he saw who it was, he was stunned.

'Satoru!' he said, before his brain froze. It was great to meet an old friend like this in an unfamiliar place, but at the same time the question of why Satoru was here, paired with his still-guilty conscience, began to play on his mind.

'I heard from Chikako that she was applying to this college, and I thought maybe you were, too. I see I was right.'

'You heard from her? You mean, you guys met after you moved away?'

'No, not at all. She wrote to me.'

This was back when high-school students didn't all have mobile phones.

'I gave you guys my new address, remember? And Chikako wrote me a letter. I never got a letter from *you*, though,' Satoru said, teasingly.

'Hey, but I did call you a few times.'

'Well, I guess when friends grow up, they lose touch. It's the same with my pals from junior high, though we talk a lot on the phone. When I got that letter from Chikako, I thought, Wow, girls really are conscientious. We've written to each other a few times since.'

And in one of the letters Satoru had apparently read about which college Chikako was applying to.

'Chikako never told me you were applying here, Satoru.'

'That makes sense, since I never told her. I reckoned, if one of us didn't get in, it would feel kind of awkward.'

Now that he understood, Sugi realized there was nothing to it. But still he had his suspicions – and that was the problem.

'Since we're both here, why don't we ask them if we can share a room?' Satoru asked. 'My roommate hasn't appeared yet, and if we arrange it now it shouldn't be a problem.'

Satoru had been in the dorm for a week already, and his kind nature meant he had already made a network of acquaintances, so they managed to swap roommates.

Chikako was delighted that Satoru was attending the same college, but sulked about not being told. 'Why didn't you let me know?' she asked. She had been just about to write a letter to him to let him know that she and Sugi had both got into the same college.

The first semester flew by, and before they knew it the second semester had started.

'Sugi, I got a gift from one of the second years.' Satoru showed him some cans of beer, an upmarket brand that was seldom discounted.

Twenty was the legal drinking age, but for college students that was just official policy, and in the dorm drinks were circulated even between under-age students. They made sure, though, that things didn't get out of hand, and were careful to avoid the eagle-eyed dorm mother whenever there was alcohol around.

'Oh, then I'll cadge some snacks to go with it.'

Dorms students often got food parcels from home, and if the students shared whatever they received, they could all get some pretty nice things. Sugi had just received some juicy grapes, and, trading up, he managed to talk a student hailing from Hokkaido into letting him have some salmon fillets and sweets that were a speciality of the student's hometown.

Satoru would get merry when he drank, but he wasn't much of a drinker. Two cans of beer were all it took before his eyes grew bloodshot.

For some reason, the talk turned to an in-dorm romance. A freshman, quite a frivolous guy, had made repeated moves on an older girl in the dorm and kept getting shot down. The other guys found it funny, but also tried to cheer him up.

'How many times has he been rejected?'

'Eleven, so far.'

Satoru, the informant, passed this on to Sugi, and chuckled. 'It's so funny – he won't give in. He said that during the second semester he's going to hit the twenty mark.'

'What for? Is he aiming to break some kind of record for being rejected? He's lost sight of the goal!'

'I know, but I kind of envy that sort of recklessness.'

Satoru's red eyes sparkled.

'You know, in high school I sort of had a thing for Chikako.'

The one thing Sugi had hoped never to hear.

'But since you were there, I reckoned it was hopeless. Still, even if I had been rejected, I wish I'd at least told her.'

*I wish I'd at least told her.* If he had, then history would have been different.

Unable to keep it in, his voice cracked. 'Please. Don't ever tell Chikako.'

*I wish I'd at least told her.* History might still be different, even now.

'Please.'

Miserably bowing his head, Sugi thought, how shameful can I get? I know very well how miserable I look, yet I still go ahead and beg him.

Satoru seemed touched by his words, and his eyes widened a little. Just as they had when Sugi had asked for advice and shut him down. 'Don't worry about it.' He smiled. 'You two probably have a stronger relationship than you think you do.'

So Sugi was, in the end, successful in keeping Satoru quiet.

Sugi graduated from college, returned to his hometown and, after a few years, married Chikako. Satoru came to the wedding.

History wasn't going to be rewritten now – they'd come too far for that.

Still, sometimes Sugi would get a bit panicky when he thought of Satoru. Punishment, he thought, for having suppressed his friend's words all those years ago.

If he took in Satoru's cat, it would be a thorn in his side that would torment him for the rest of his life. But still.

Satoru was clearly troubled about what to do with his cat and had come to ask for his help, and since Sugi had won out with Chikako through unfair methods, he felt it was his duty to help.

It might seem weird for such a petty and cowardly guy like me to do this so late in the day, Sugi thought, but I really do like you, Satoru. You've had a much, much harder life than I have, yet you've always remained generous and kind. You blow me away.

I've always wanted to be more like you. If only I could be.

∽

THE NEXT MORNING, ANOTHER meeting between the dog and me was arranged.

After breakfast, Chikako left the dining room to fetch him.

'Be a good boy this time, Tora,' Chikako cautioned him as he stood behind the fence. Sugi, looking worried, was pacing around the dining room. Satoru looked a little worried, too. The only ones who kept their cool were Momo and yours truly.

Breakfast for me was a special tuna blend with a side of chicken breast, so I was feeling pleasantly full. Give it your best shot, you hound.

The door to the room swung open.

The dog had planted himself in the doorway and was staring hard in my direction. He avoided Satoru's eyes.

Too damn right.

Yesterday, on several occasions, Sugi had scolded the dog, reminding him that Satoru was his good friend and that he mustn't bark at him. That being the case, there was only one other he could turn his fire on.

You want it, pal, then I'm more than ready for you.

The dog began to bark at me in such a frenzy he looked on the verge of losing it.

Ignoring the cries of the humans, I arched my back as high as it could go and made my fur stand on end. You don't fool around, do you? Momo murmured. High praise, indeed.

The dog would not stop barking. Satoru rushed over to hold me down so I wouldn't leap out at the stupid dog.

As long as you're here, the master and his wife will be thinking of Satoru! It's painful for my master if his wife remembers him!

I don't need to hear that. If it's a house with a stupid hound like you in it, then I'm calling the whole thing off on my own!

If it came to a fight, I was several leagues above this mutt.

You may talk big, but I bet you've never been in a life-and-death scrape. Bet you've never been in the kind of fight over territory where, if you lose, you'll have nothing to eat for days, have you, you spoiled, high-and-mighty hound?

I gave him an earful of the kind of spiel I'd perfected over the course of numerous scenes of carnage. The kind of rough language to which I can't subject you polite ladies and gentlemen.

Momo, surveying all this with total disinterest from her perch atop the TV, smiled. Pardon me, I told her. My one regret is besmirching the ears of a refined lady like yourself with such language.

Go home, damn you! The hound was close to tears, and still barking his head off.

A piddling three-year-old dog who's always worn a collar thinks he's going to beat me? Not in a hundred years, my friend. Momo's lived twice as long as me, and I've lived twice as long as *you*, pal.

I won't allow someone in this house who reminds the master and his wife of Satoru! Besides—

Shut it! Say any more and I'll make you regret it!

I had to admire the dog, though, since he still wouldn't shut up. He really was wound up.

*Besides, your owner smells like he's not going to make it.*

*I told you to shut it!*

'Nana!' Satoru yelled at me.

I had escaped from his grasp and swiped the dog with my claws.

*Ruff!* The dog's scream rang out. Three neat rows of wounds now ran down his brindled muzzle, and three lines of blood were faintly oozing out.

But still Toramaru didn't put his tail between his legs.

Several times, he looked as though he was about to lower it at least, but then he forced it up again. And growled more deeply.

'*Stop it*, Nana! You'll hurt him!'

The fight was already won, so I meekly let Satoru pick me up. 'I'm so sorry.' Satoru apologized over and over to Toramaru, and to Sugi and Chikako.

'It's okay. I'm just glad Nana didn't get bitten.'

Chikako, turning pale, let out a sigh. Sugi gave Toramaru a good rap on the head with his fist.

'If you had really bitten Nana, he would have died, you know!'

For the first time, Toramaru let his tail sag between his legs. And he glared at me regretfully.

*Okay, I understand. I won't count that among my victories.*

'I'm sorry. I really appreciate you saying you'd look after Nana for me, but I'm going to take him back home.' Satoru sounded quite sad about this. 'It wouldn't be good for Toramaru, either, to have to live with a cat he doesn't get on with.'

Satoru fetched the basket. As I stepped in obediently, I glanced back at Toramaru.

Thank you, Toramaru.

Toramaru looked a little dubious.

I came here on a trip with Satoru. Not to be left behind here in this house. I was trying to come up with a plan so we could go home together, and thanks to you it has all worked out smoothly.

Toramaru lowered his eyes and tilted his head, and Satoru and I headed towards the silver van.

They brought Toramaru out on a lead to see us off. Sugi kept a tight hold of it, wrapping it a few times around his hand.

Momo came out of her own accord to say goodbye. It's been a long time since I've seen a fight as definitive as that, she said, paying me a compliment.

'I'm so sorry it's turned out this way. I'm just glad Nana didn't get hurt.'

'We really did hope to look after him.'

Sugi and Chikako apologized, one after the other, but that only made Satoru uncomfortable. Which was understandable, seeing as how the only one who actually hurt anyone was, in the end, *moi*.

As usual, before Satoru got the van on the move, the old friends seemed to find it painful to say goodbye.

Even after Satoru was behind the wheel, Chikako kept saying she had forgotten to give him this or that, and handed him one present after another: her home-grown herbs, some fruit, and more fruit.

We really had better be going.

'Oh, by the way,' Satoru called out of the open window. 'When I was in high school, I really liked you, Chikako. Did you know that?'

The way he said it was pretty blasé. Sugi's face stiffened. And Chikako said – *'What?'* Then she blinked like a pigeon that had just been shot by a peashooter, and gave a little laugh. 'That was so long ago. Why bring it up now?'

'Yeah, I guess you're right.'

The two of them chuckled. Sugi stood there, astonished, then gave a late-to-the-party laugh.

He might have been laughing, but he looked almost ready to cry.

The van had started moving down the drive when there was a shout.

'Toramaru!'

Toramaru wrenched hard, struggling to break free of the lead.

Hey, cat!

Toramaru was calling me.

You can stay! The master was laughing with the missus and Satoru, so it's all okay now for you to stay!

You idiot. I told you I had no intention of being left behind from the very start.

'Tora, can't you at least behave when we're saying goodbye!' Sugi tugged angrily at the lead.

Don't be cross with him. He was trying to stop me leaving.

But what with Tora barking his head off earlier, Sugi thought he was still angry.

'Is he upset?' asked Satoru. He looked in the rear-view mirror at the receding figures. 'His bark sounds different from before.'

That's why I like you, Satoru. You're perceptive about things like that.

The silver van gave a little beep of its horn before turning a corner, sending dust into the air and leaving the bed and breakfast far behind.

'It would have been perfect if they could have looked after you.'

There you go again, Satoru. That's just sour grapes. Mount Fuji's now well behind us.

If you intend to come and fetch me back one day, then you shouldn't leave me there in the first place.

I was standing on my hind legs and pawing the top of the back seat to see out of the rear window, and Satoru laughed. 'The sea might not have been your cup of tea, but you do seem to have taken a liking to Mount Fuji.'

'Cause Mount Fuji doesn't make that belly-shaking roar, and doesn't have that perpetual motion that'll swallow me up.

'I hope we can see it again together. Yeah, let's do that someday. And let's visit Sugi and Chikako again. We had such a nice view of Mount Fuji from our bedroom, and also – you liked that old picture-tube TV, too, didn't you?'

Yes, that's the ticket! That box-shaped TV was perfect. Just the right size to lie down, all toasty warm. Say, Satoru, what if we were to get a box-shaped TV like that?

'Sorry that ours is the thin type. They don't sell tube TVs any more.'

Ah, such a pity.

But that's okay. I can think of it as a special attraction for when we visit the Sugis next time.

And one other thing: the next time we visit, I bet you Toramaru will wag his tail at us.

∽

IN THE EVENING, A RESERVATION came in at the bed and breakfast for that night.

'Maybe we should keep Toramaru tied up.'

'True, he might still be worked up because of his fight with Nana.'

Sugi took Toramaru outside and chained him to the kennel. Then he turned to Chikako, who had followed him.

'About what Satoru said a little while ago . . .'

'What? Are you bothered by that?' Chikako asked.

Ouch. That hit home. 'No, it's not that,' Sugi stammered. 'I was just wondering how you would have taken it if Satoru had told you he liked you when we were still in high school.'

'Who knows?' Chikako said, shrugging. 'Unless we could go back in time, I don't know how I would have reacted.'

A spot-on answer, to which he had no reply.

'It might have been nice, though, to be a young girl wavering between the affections of two boys.'

'Wavering?'

This took him by surprise and he couldn't help but ask her what she meant.

'Of course I would have wavered.' Chikako laughed. 'If I'd had two boys liking me at the same time, then that would definitely have piqued my interest.'

Sugi felt like weeping, but managed to control himself.

I don't know which of us two she would have chosen, he thought. But at least I was included in the line-up.

And he felt his sense of inferiority and jealousy diminish a little.

The next time I see Satoru, I know I can be a much better friend.

Now that is a happy thought.

# 3½

# Between Friends

A HUGE WHITE SHIP was docked beside the wharf of the harbour.

The mouth at the bow was open wide and Satoru told me that we were going to drive our van right into it. It swallowed up any number of cars into its belly and yet it didn't sink. I must say, humans really do create some amazing things.

I mean, who in the world came up with the idea of floating a huge lump of iron on top of water? Must have had a couple of screws loose, whoever it was. It stands to reason that a heavy object will sink. No other animal in the world would try to defy the laws of nature, but humans are a very peculiar species.

Satoru hurried over to the ferry terminal to buy our ticket, but when he came back his face was all flushed.

'I'm afraid we've got a problem. They won't let you travel as a passenger like me, Nana.'

He explained that he had written my name on the passenger form.

When the official at the reception desk found out that Nana Miyawaki (age six) was a cat, he had a good laugh, apparently. Sometimes Satoru can be spectacularly dense.

'Shall we get on board?'

A string of cars was already lined up and driving into the gaping mouth of the ferry, and I was starting to feel just a little bit anxious.

'Nana, why is your tail all puffed up like that?'

Oh, come on. If, worst-case scenario, the ship does actually sink, we'll be thrown overboard into the sea, won't we? I don't think I can imagine a fate more terrible.

I recalled the sea we'd visited when we were on our way back from Yoshimine the farmer's, and how that vast expanse of water, the weighty crash of the waves, had made me feel. The thought of being flung straight into it made even an intrepid cat like me shiver. Cats are no good at swimming and detest the water (though there are a few exceptions; some cats actually like to have a bath, but these are just instances of spontaneous feline mutation).

Even Satoru would have great trouble swimming to shore with me perched on top of his head clinging on for dear life.

Despite my misgivings, the silver van entered the belly of the beast. Walking with his suitcase in his left hand and my basket in his right seemed to wear Satoru out. Not long ago, he could have carried both easily.

Maybe I should walk on my own?

I scratched at the lock of the basket from the inside, and Satoru told me to stop. He tilted the basket so the door was facing upwards. Whoa, I said, and slipped backwards on to my bottom.

'Animals aren't allowed loose on the ferry, so you'll just have to be patient.'

By animals, this would include dogs, too, I assumed. Fair enough. There are plenty of hotels that allow pets in general but turn away cats. They complain that cats sharpen their claws on the furniture, and so on. But for guests with cats, all they need to do is add an extra fee to cover any repairs, right?

Plus, this *animal smell* that bothers humans is much less strong in cats than it is with dogs, am I right?

Even so, this *dogs okay, cats not okay* attitude is really offensive from a feline perspective. In that sense, it's much easier to accept if neither cat nor dog is allowed. The upshot? I was liking this ferry.

Satoru took me to the pet room in the ship, where all the travelling animals were kept.

It was a spartan, neat room, and several spacious cages were stacked up to the ceiling. Today, there seemed to be a lot of passengers travelling with animals, for almost all ten of the cages were occupied. There was a white chinchilla, but that was the only other cat. The rest were a mix of dogs of varying sizes.

'This is Nana. Please be nice to him until we arrive.'

Satoru went out of his way to greet the passengers already in the pet room, and put me into one of the cages.

'Will you be okay, Nana? You won't be too lonely?'

Lonely, surrounded by all these other dogs and a cat? Hardly! In fact, I'd prefer somewhere more peaceful. The dogs seemed to want to talk, and because there were so many of them, they were all yapping back and forth. And muttering complaints about me, like, *Well, look at this, will you? A mongrel moggy that the human dragged in.* Well, hey, sooorry!

'I really wish we could have gone the whole way in the van. I'm sorry about that,' Satoru said.

Not to worry. It's only for a day, so I can put up with it. Cats might not seem it, but we are nothing if not patient.

On this trip, it seems like we'll still have a long way to

travel even after the ferry has docked. And Satoru gets tired easily these days.

'I'll come as often as I can to check on you, so if you get lonely, just hang in there.'

Any chance you can refrain from the over-protective comments in front of the others? You're embarrassing me.

'Hello there. I hope you two cats will get on.'

Satoru was peering into the cage just below mine, the one with the chinchilla in it. I was in my cage, so I couldn't see, but since the moment we arrived it had been curled up in a corner.

'This one seems lonely, too. Maybe he's feeling afraid, with all the dogs around today.'

No, you guessed wrong. The curled-up chinchilla's tail had been twitching all this time, and it was obvious to me that what he was feeling was annoyance and irritation at the dogs' incessant chatter.

'Okay, I'll see you later, Nana.'

His suitcase in hand, Satoru left, closing the door carefully behind him.

And the dogs immediately tried to make conversation.

*So — tell me — where ya from, and where ya headed? What kind of guy is your master?* In an instant, I understood exactly how the chinchilla felt, curled up there in disgust, and I copied his way of dealing with it.

I was still curled up in the back of my cage, pretending to be asleep, when the door opened wide and in stepped Satoru.

'I'm sorry, Nana. I guess you really are lonely in here.'

After that, he came back to check on me another ten times. With Satoru popping in and out more often than the other owners, before long the dogs started teasing me about it. Every time Satoru left the room, there would be a noisy chorus of *Pampered! Pampered!*

Knock it off, you hounds! I growled, and was about to curl up again in the back of the cage when the chinchilla, directly below me, addressed the room.

Carrying on like a bunch of brats – you chaps are really starting to annoy me. Don't you understand? It's his *master* who's the lonely one?

For an expensive-looking long-haired breed, this cat had quite a mouth on him. The dogs all grumbled back, *Yeah, but . . . You see, Nana's master said Nana was lonely, didn't he?*

For dogs, you lot have a rubbish sense of smell. That master gives off a smell that says he's not going to be around for long. So he wants to spend as much time as possible with his darling cat.

In an instant, the dogs had piped down. *It's too bad. The poor guy,* they started to mumble in hushed voices. To tell you the truth, they weren't very subtle about it. But I forgave them. They were all young dogs, and none too bright.

Thank you for that.

I aimed this at the invisible cage below me, and the chinchilla shot back with a sullen *They were getting on my nerves, that's all.*

The next time Satoru appeared, the scolded hounds all wagged their tails enthusiastically at him. 'Wow,' Satoru said happily, 'you guys really are happy to see me, aren't you?' and he reached in through the bars of one or two of the cages to stroke the occupants. Not the sharpest pencils in the box, these dogs, but I'd have to say they were pretty docile and decent types.

After this, we cats occasionally joined in the dogs' idle chatter, and time passed by on our unremarkable sea voyage. Most of the time, though, we talked at cross purposes. We couldn't fathom, for instance, why the dogs were so into snacks like canine chewing gum and other stuff.

At midday the following day, the ferry arrived safely at its destination – the island of Hokkaido. Satoru came to fetch me first thing.

'I'm sorry, Nana. You must have been lonely.'

Not at all. I had a good chat with that barbed-tongued chinchilla. I was just thinking it would be great if I could say my goodbyes to him face to face, when Satoru turned my basket around so the open door was facing the room.

'Nana, say goodbye to everyone.'

See you all, I said, and the hounds' tails wagged in unison.

*Guddo rakku!*

This from the chinchilla, in some language I didn't understand.

Guddo . . . what?

It means 'good luck'. My master often says it.

Come to think of it, the chinchilla's master, a foreigner with a Japanese wife, had come to see him during the journey. The cat had learned human language mainly from Japanese people, but apparently understood a lot of what his master said, too.

Thanks. *Guddo rakku* to you, too.

We bid farewell to the pet room, made our way down to the car deck and climbed into our silver van.

When we emerged from the mouth of the ferry, we were greeted by wall-to-wall blue sky.

'Hokkaido, at last, Nana.'

The land was flat and sprawling. Outside the window was what looked like an ordinary city, but everything seemed much more spread out. The roads, for instance, were far wider than those around Tokyo.

We drove for a while before reaching the suburbs. There wasn't much traffic, and we enjoyed a leisurely drive, listening to upbeat music as we went.

The road was bordered with a lovely profusion of purple and yellow wildflowers.

You could just leave the roads in Hokkaido as they were and they'd look pretty gorgeous. Not at all like the roads in Tokyo, which are surrounded by endless concrete and asphalt. Even in the more built-up areas here, the hard shoulders are all dirt. Because of that, perhaps, it's easy for the soil to breathe and the flowers to thrive. The scenery was very soothing.

'The yellow ones are called goldenrods, but I don't know about the purple ones.'

The flowers had caught Satoru's eye, too. The jumble of colours was that striking. The purple wasn't one block of colour but various gradations from light to dark.

'What do you say we stop for a bit?'

Satoru pulled over in a layby. I got out, with Satoru carrying me. An occasional car passed by, so he held me safely in his arms and wouldn't let me down as he climbed up to the purple flowers.

'They might be wild chrysanthemums. I had imagined them to be a bit neater and tidier, though . . .'

The wildflowers pushing up vigorously from the soil had stems covered with blooms, like an upside-down broom. Not at all what you'd call graceful; more forceful and vigorous than that.

Oh!

As soon as I spotted it, I reached out my paw. A honey-bee was buzzing among the flowers.

'Careful, Nana. You might get stung.'

Hey, what are you going to do? It's instinct. I clawed at the bee and Satoru brought my paws together in his hand and held them there.

Damn it. It's exciting to play with the insects flying around. Let me go, I said, straightening my legs against his arms to get free, but Satoru held me tight and put me back in the van.

'If you just caught them, that would be fine, but I know you'll eat them, too. And we can't have you getting stung inside your mouth.'

Well, you catch something, you've got to take a bite out of it. Back in Tokyo, when I killed cockroaches I'd always take a bite. The hard wings were like cellophane so I didn't eat those, but the flesh was soft and savoury.

Every time Satoru found the remains of a cockroach I'd left, he'd scream. I don't understand why humans have such an aversion to them. Structurally, they're not so different from *kabutomushi* and drone beetles, the kind kids collect as pets. If it was one of those beetles, you can bet he wouldn't scream like that. But from a feline point of view, their speed makes them both challenging and fun to catch.

We continued our drive along a river, then down a hill, and emerged on a road that ran alongside the sea.

Waa—

'Wow.'

We both shouted out at almost the same instant.

'It looks just like the sea.'

He was talking about the pampas grass which spread out along both sides of the road. Its white ears covered the flat, sprawling fields from one end to the other, and swayed in the wind like white, cresting waves.

It hadn't been long since we last stopped, but Satoru pulled over again.

Even though there were so few cars on the road, Satoru came around to the passenger side and carried me out. He must have been afraid I might leap out. A little over-protective, I thought, but if that makes him feel better, I'm happy to let him take charge. Satoru had big hands and I felt secure and calm whenever he held me.

I wanted to see this scenery from a slightly higher vantage point, so I slipped from his hands on to his shoulder and stretched my neck. I was now just at Satoru's eye level.

The wind was rustling, the ears of the pampas grass swaying. The waves were rolling further than the eye could see.

It was just as Satoru had said. This was like a sea on land. Unlike the sea, though, there was no heavy booming sound. In this kind of sea, I might be able to swim.

From his shoulder, I leapt down to the ground and nosed my way into the pampas grass.

The path before me was blocked by the thick stems. I lifted my head and saw, far above me, the white ears waving against a clear blue sky.

'Nana?'

Satoru's worried voice reached my ears.

'Nana, where are you-uuu?'

There was the sound of dry grass being trampled so I knew that Satoru had entered the pampas grass sea, too. I'm here, just here, just near you.

But as he called me, Satoru's voice drifted further away. From where I was, I could see Satoru, but he couldn't see me, hidden as I was by the pampas.

I guess I have no choice, I thought, and followed quickly after Satoru so he wouldn't get lost.

'Nana?'

Right here! I answered him, but it seemed like my voice was being carried away by the wind and didn't reach him.

'Naaaaana!'

Satoru began to sound desperate.

'Nana! Nana, where are you-uuuuu?'

Satoru started to call out into the distance and, unable to bear it, I let out a loud shout, as big as I could make it.

I'm right heeeere!

And then there he was, framed against the sky, gazing down at me. The instant our eyes met, his stern look melted. His eyes softened and light caught the trails of water sliding down his cheeks.

Without a word, he knelt down on the earth, placed his big hands around my middle and hugged me. That hurts! My guts are going to squeeze out.

'You silly thing! If you wander off in here, I'll never be able to find you!'

Satoru's whole body shook with his sobs.

'For someone your size, this field is like a sea of trees!'

A 'sea of trees' is how Satoru had described it to me earlier. Inside a forest like that, internal compasses don't function and you totally lose your way.

*You're* the silly one. I'd never wander so far that I'd actually lose you.

'Don't leave me . . . Stay with me.'

Ah-hah! *Finally.*

Finally, he had said what he really meant.

I'd known for a long time how Satoru felt.

I knew he was searching hard for a new owner for me, but that as each attempt came to nothing, he felt hugely relieved to be taking me home again.

'It's such a shame I can't leave him here,' he'd tell each of his friends, but in the van on the way home he'd be all smiles. How could I ever leave him, having experienced that kind of love?

I will never, ever, leave him.

As Satoru wept silent tears, I licked his hand over and over, my rough tongue wandering over every knuckle and crevice.

It's okay, it's okay, it's okay. I realized how much Hachi would have regretted it – being separated from a child who loved him so much.

But Satoru was no longer a child. And I'm a former stray. So this time we should be able to make things work out.

Okay, let's get back on the road! This is our final journey.

On this last trip, let's see all sorts of wonderful things. Let's make a pledge to take in as many amazing sights as we can.

My seven-shaped crooked tail should be able to snag every single marvellous thing we pass.

Back in the van and driving off, the doves-about-to-appear CD came to an end. Then a woman's low, husky voice started to sing strangely and in a foreign-sounding language I couldn't understand.

The doves-about-to-appear song was one his mother liked, apparently, while his father preferred this one, with the husky-voiced woman singing.

The road was lined as far as the eye could see with those purple and yellow flowers.

We continued driving at a leisurely pace. Hmm . . . when was the last time we had to stop at a traffic light?

We were no longer by the seaside but heading inland, and sturdy-looking wilderness spread out on either side. Finally, we could see cultivated, rolling hills.

I was in awe of this land, so flat and magnificent. It was like nothing I'd ever seen.

Wooden fences lined the roads now, and in the plots behind them there were – well, I wasn't at all sure *what* they were. Large animals, noses to the ground, chomping away at the grass. What the hell *were* those things?

I put my paws up and pressed them against the passenger window, stretching up as far as I could. I often did that to check out the scenery outside, so Satoru had made a seat for me out of a large box with a cushion placed on top. Whenever I saw something that piqued my interest, I'd always lean forward like this.

'Ah, those are horses. This area is all pasture.'

Horses? *Those things?* I'd seen them on TV, but this was my first time seeing the real thing. On TV, they looked much bigger. The horses chewing grass along the road were certainly large, but they were also relatively slender.

I craned my neck around to take a last look back at the horses as we passed, and Satoru laughed.

'If you like them that much, let's park up for a closer look next time we see some.'

In the next pasture we came to, the horses were in an enclosure quite a long way from the road.

'It's a little far away,' Satoru said ruefully as he got out of the van, walked around to my side and picked me up.

When he slammed the van door shut, the horses, so distant they appeared smaller than Satoru's hands, stopped chewing grass and raised their long heads to look at us.

There was a tense moment. The horses' ears pricked up as they appraised us.

'Look, they're watching us, Nana.'

Not just watching, but carefully checking us out. They wanted to see if we were a danger to them. If we had been close enough for them to realize we were just a human and a cat, they would have been relieved.

Given their size, I didn't think they needed to worry. But animals have an instinct. Whatever their size, horses are grass eaters, and grass eaters have a long history of being hunted by meat eaters. This makes them timid and skittish.

On the other hand, we cats may be small, but we're hunters. And hunters are fighters. We're on our guard, too, with creatures we don't know, but when it comes to a fight we're more than willing to face up to animals much bigger than us.

That's why when dogs meddle with cats for fun, they end up whimpering, their tails between their legs. A dog ten times our size? Bring it on!

In my view, dogs have long since given up hunting. Even hunting dogs just chase their prey for the sake of their master these days, and they don't finish it off themselves. That's the crucial difference between them and us cats;

even if we're just hunting a bug, we're intent on making the kill ourselves.

This point about *killing* prey is a major divide between various animals. Horses are certainly dozens of times bigger than me, but they don't scare me.

A sense of pride suddenly swelled up in me. Pride in myself as a cat who still hadn't lost his identity as a hunter.

And for me, as a hunter, I can tell you that I'm not going to back away from what lies ahead for Satoru.

The horses stared at us for a while, then concluded perhaps that we weren't an immediate threat and returned to chomping on the grass.

'They're a bit far away, but I wonder if I could get a photo of them with my mobile phone.'

Satoru took his phone out of his pocket. Most of the photos he took with it, by the bye, were of me.

But I don't think you should take one of those horses, I thought.

When Satoru held the camera out towards them, the horses' heads popped up again. And their ears shot up, too.

They stood there, stock-still, gazing at us until Satoru had taken the photo.

'Yeah, they're definitely too far away.'

He gave up and put the phone away. The horses continued to stare silently.

They gazed at us right up to the moment we were back in the van and the doors were shut, before finally swinging lazily back to their meal. Apologies, my friends. Sorry to bother you, I called out.

I suppose there are animals who live like this, even though they could easily kick me, and Satoru, from here to the far end of Hokkaido.

If it is their instinct that makes them that way, then I'm glad I'm a cat and have the instinct to put up a fight. I'm happy to be a high-spirited, adventurous cat that will never be intimidated by other animals, even if they're bigger than me.

I've made my point, but just to reconfirm this: meeting those horses meant a lot to me.

On the drive, I saw even more lovely scenery for the first time.

White birches with pale trunks, mountain ash with red clusters of berries like bells.

Satoru told me what everything was called. And that the mountain-ash berries are bright red. I remember some expert on TV saying once, 'Cats have a hard time distinguishing the colour red.'

'Wow! Would you look at how red those berries are!' Satoru called out, and that's how I learned about the colour *red*. It no doubt appeared differently to Satoru, but I learned how what Satoru called red appeared to me.

'The ones over there aren't so red yet.'

Every time he saw trees through the window, Satoru would talk to me about them. So I became quite skilled at discriminating between different shades of red. I just learned to distinguish, in my own way of seeing things, the variations of red that Satoru pointed out, but also that they did all indeed share the same colour. For the rest of my life, I would remember all the shades of red Satoru mentioned that day.

We saw fields, too, of potatoes and pumpkins being harvested, and fields where the harvest was over.

The harvested potatoes were stuffed into bags so huge

they looked like they could hold several people, and the bags were then piled up in a corner of the field. Large pyramids of pumpkins were stacked up on top of the black, damp soil.

And here and there on the gentle hills were gigantic black or white plastic bundles. I was wondering why someone had left these toys behind, but they turned out to hold cut grass.

'They have a lot of snow in the winter here, so before it falls they have to harvest the grass so their cows and horses will have enough to eat.'

Snow – I've seen some of that white stuff falling in Tokyo. It melted pretty swiftly, though, so it was nothing to get worked up about. That's what I was thinking at the time. But once winter arrived, I began to realize, the snow here would be a whole other story. Whenever there was a snowstorm and you couldn't see anything in front of you, even I, strong as I am, would be tossed mercilessly into the air. But that's a tale for another time.

Countryside snow that piles up to the eaves, versus city snow that melts away in a few days. It made me wonder, honestly, how they could both go by the same name.

As we drove on, taking the occasional break at a small supermarket, the scenery became more mountainous. Finally, the sun began to set.

We crossed a mountain pass as it did so, and another town came into view. As the silver van drove on, the sky fell darker by the moment, as if playing tag with the night.

'It's too late today. And we can't buy any flowers,' murmured Satoru, sounding put out, though still he didn't head straight for our hotel but turned off the main road.

We continued down a minor road until we reached the end of the town, where we climbed a gentle hill. At the top was a wrought-iron gate. We drove straight through it.

The land here stretched out in all directions. It was neatly partitioned into squares, and in each square was a line of square stones. I knew what they were because I'd seen them on TV.

They were graves.

Apparently, humans like to have large stones put on top of them when they are dead. I remember thinking, as I watched a programme on TV about it, that it was a strange custom. The people on the programme were discussing how expensive graves were, and so on.

When an animal's life is over, it rests where it falls, and it often seems to me that humans are such worriers, to think of preparing a place for people to sleep when they are dead. If you have to consider what's going to happen after you die, life becomes doubly troublesome.

Satoru drove the van through this huge area as if he knew exactly where he was heading, and at last came to a halt somewhere in the centre of it all.

We got out, and Satoru walked slowly among the graves. After a while, he came to a halt in front of a grave with a whitish stone.

'This is my father and mother's grave.'

It was the final spot that Satoru had been so longing to visit.

I don't get why humans like to have a huge stone put on top of them when they kick the bucket. But I do understand why they might want to look after a splendid stone like this.

I got the sense that the long drive was becoming too

much for Satoru, but still, he had made it, in his silver van, with me by his side, his cat with the number-eight markings and the crooked tail like a seven.

Cats are not so heartless that they can't respect those sorts of emotions.

'I wanted to pay my respects with you here, Nana.'

I know, I said, rubbing my forehead vigorously along the edge of his parents' gravestone.

It's a great honour to meet you. Hachi was a wonderful cat, I'm sure, but don't you think I'm rather nice, too?

'I'm sorry. I was in a hurry, so I'll bring flowers tomorrow,' Satoru said, squatting down at the grave. There were some slightly wilted flowers in a vase.

'Ah, I see,' Satoru murmured. 'It was Higan recently, the time of year when people visit graves . . . My aunt must have come.'

Satoru tenderly stroked the wilting petals.

'I'm sorry I haven't been able to come here much. I should have visited you more often.'

I stepped away from the grave, to give Satoru some time alone. If I disappeared completely from sight, I knew he would become anxious, so I lingered where he could see me.

During the five years I'd lived with Satoru, he'd left home only a couple of times to visit this grave.

'Someday, I'll take you with me, Nana,' he had said. 'You look just like Hachi, and my father and mother will be so surprised.

'Someday,' he had promised me, 'we'll go on a long trip together.' And now it was happening.

'Nana, come here!' Satoru called me and put me on his lap. As he stroked me gently, running his wide hand across my whole body over and over, I wondered what he was talking about so silently with his parents.

This town was Satoru's mother's hometown, it seemed. His grandfather and grandmother, who were farmers, had passed away fairly young, and Satoru's mother and his aunt hadn't been able to keep up the farm, so they let it go. His mother had apparently regretted this for the rest of her life.

Especially after Satoru became part of their family.

A hometown where the only thing left is a grave has to be a bit sad for a child. But there were only a few relatives on Satoru's mother's side, and they had all moved away, so what could you do?

There are so many things in life that are beyond our control.

Satoru finally straightened his legs, enveloping me tightly in his arms.

'We'll be back tomorrow,' he said, then turned to the van. We drove in silence through the now completely dark town towards our lodgings for the night.

We were staying in a cosy hotel that had a few rooms reserved for humans who had pets with them. It was a very sensible little place, I must say.

Satoru must have been exhausted from all the driving, because he went out once to get something to eat but came back within the hour and fell heavily on to the bed and into a deep sleep.

The next morning, though, he got up early.

He swiftly packed his bags, and when we emerged from the hotel the sun was still just coming up.

'Darn, the florist's isn't open yet.'

Satoru made one circuit of the area in front of the station and seemed at a loss.

'Maybe somewhere will be open on the way to the cemetery...'

He'd sort of jumped the gun starting off so early, with the flower shop still closed. On the way, he pulled up at the side of the road.

'Guess we'll have to make do with these.'

And the flowers he started picking were the purple and yellow flowers that had decorated the road we had been driving on the previous day.

I liked them! They were much more beautiful than any you'd buy in a shop, and Satoru's father and mother would be thrilled to be given them.

I searched out some wild chrysanthemums with open blooms and showed him. 'So you're looking for flowers, too, eh?' He laughed and plucked the very ones I'd been rustling around in for him.

He gathered an armful and we continued on to the cemetery.

It had been dark yesterday, so I hadn't noticed, but from the top of the hill you could see the town in the distance. All the way to where the urban landscape became countryside.

The cemetery had a much more cheerful feeling in the early morning than it had the previous night, though, come to think of it, even when we'd visited in the dark yesterday, I hadn't felt at all frightened. One associates graves and temples with ghost stories, but this place had none of that gloominess, or any sense that a resentful spirit might appear at any moment.

You ask if we cats can see ghosts. Don't you know

that there are things in this world that are better left a mystery?

Satoru, with flowers and garden tools (he must have bought these last night) in his arms, got out of the van.

After cleaning the gravestone, he took the wilting flowers from the vase, changed the water and replaced them with the new ones he'd just picked, their colours bright and festive.

The vase was overflowing now, and half the flowers were left over. 'I'll use these later,' he said, and wrapped them in some damp newspaper and put them in the back of the van.

Satoru unwrapped the buns and cakes he'd bought and left these as offerings at the grave. Ants would no doubt soon swarm over them, and crows and weasels would come and whisk them away, but it was better than leaving them to rot.

Satoru then lit some incense at the grave. Apparently, in his family, it was the custom to light a whole bundle at once. I found it a bit too smoky, and slunk upwind to escape it.

Satoru sat down by the grave and gazed at it for a long time. Claws in and tucking my two front paws beneath my chest, I snuggled up on his knees, and he beamed at me and tickled under my chin with his fingertips.

'I'm glad I could bring you, Nana,' he whispered in a small voice that was barely audible.

He sounded really happy.

I stepped away from Satoru and took a stroll nearby, staying close so he could still see me. Below the low hedge that bordered the site, stringy butterburs grew. And below those a cricket or something was leaping around. I sniffed around in them until Satoru came over.

'What's up, Nana? You've burrowed pretty deeply into those butterburs.'

Well, the thing is, underneath here is . . .

'Something's in there?'

Yeah, something very nimble indeed. It was just a quick glimpse, but I saw it jump. And it left behind a strange smell.

I kept sniffing below the butterbur leaves, and Satoru laughed.

'It might be a Korobokkuru.'

Come again?

'Tiny people that live under the butterbur leaves.'

What? That's news to me. Are there really weird creatures like that in the world?

'They were in a picture book I loved as a child.'

Ah – it's just a story.

'My parents loved that story, too. As I recall, they were both really excited when I was able to read that book by myself.'

Satoru told me all kinds of things about those tiny people, but since it was all, from a feline point of view, less than enthralling, I yawned deeply, showing my pointed teeth, and Satoru smiled.

'I suppose you're not very interested.'

What can I tell you? Cats are realists.

'But if you do happen to see one, don't catch it, okay?'

Okay, okay. Message received. If they really are there, I'd be itching to grab them, but out of deference to you, Satoru, I'll hold back.

Satoru sat down in front of the grave one more time.

Then at last he stood up, and said, 'See you later.' He looked calm and refreshed, as if he had done what he had come to do.

We drove off again and before long Satoru was pulling up at another grave.

'My grandfather and grandmother.'

He placed all the leftover flowers at this grave and, as before, he unwrapped some buns and cakes and left them as offerings, then burned some incense.

'All right. Let's hit the road.'

The next destination was Sapporo, where his aunt lived.

The silver van was heading off on its final journey.

It happened as we were driving down a fairly nondescript stretch of road.

The road cut through a hill which sloped steeply on either side. Rows of white birches covered the embankments. From halfway down the trunks of the birches, the ground was covered with thick, striped bamboo.

In Hokkaido, this was entirely ordinary, nothing-special scenery.

We were driving along when suddenly Satoru gave a little yelp and braked to an abrupt stop. The sudden halt made me lurch forward and I pressed my claws into my cushion to steady myself.

Hey, what is going on?

'Nana, look over there!'

I turned to look out of the window in the direction of his pointing finger. And whoa, talk about surprising!

Two large deer, and a smaller one, with spots on their

backs. Probably parents and child. With the pattern on their backs, they blended in with the undergrowth. Pretty darn good camouflage.

'I didn't notice them at first, but then one of them moved.'

This particular deer had a puffy white heart-shaped bottom.

'Shall I roll down the window?'

Satoru leaned over to the passenger side, pushed the button and the window began to open with a mechanical whir. And with that, the deer family turned in unison in our direction.

There was tension in the air.

Ah – I get it. These animals are similar to those horses. If you were to divide animals into those two categories, they're the hunted.

'I must have put them on their guard.'

Satoru stopped the window and watched their reaction. All three deer were staring at us steadily, then the two parents began to lope away up the hill.

The young deer, left behind, held our gaze, its sense of wariness still not fully developed.

His parents, apparently exasperated, seemed to call down to him from the top of the embankment, and the young deer, flashing its white heart-shaped little rear end at us, bounded up the slope.

'Ah, it's gone . . .'

Satoru stared regretfully after it.

'But that was amazing. I've never seen deer like that beside the road.'

It's got to be thanks to my tail. Just you wait – my crooked, seven-shaped tail is bound to snag lots more wonderful things.

And the perfect example of this came not long after we had watched the deer disappear.

The scenery was, typically, nothing special for Hokkaido. Gentle hills with softly wooded areas running into one another.

Just as we were heading into a thin layer of grey cloud, it started to rain. The kind of rain you see on a sunny day, just a light scattering of drops.

'That's really something. That's the exact boundary where the rain begins.'

Satoru drove on, happy, but most cats find rain very depressing. I hoped it would stop soon, and, amazingly, it did start to let up and the sun fought its way through the clouds.

In the driver's seat, Satoru gave a massive gulp. I was napping and twitched my ears at the sound. He braked gradually before pulling over to the side of the road.

In the sky above a hill before us was a vivid rainbow.

One end of the rainbow was rooted in the hill. We followed that arc with our eyes and found the other end rooted in the opposite hill.

I'd never seen the end of a rainbow in my entire life. And Satoru hadn't either, I gathered, the way he was holding his breath.

We were both seeing something extraordinary together for the first time in our lives.

'Shall we get out?'

Gingerly, Satoru got out of the car, as though he was afraid any sudden move would disturb the rainbow.

With both hands, fingers widened, he lifted me up out of the passenger seat, and the two of us gazed upwards.

The rainbow's two ends were firmly anchored in the ground. The top was a little fainter, but the rainbow was entirely whole. It made a perfect arch.

I'd seen these colours somewhere before. I thought about it, and then it dawned on me.

The flowers at the graveyard that morning. The wild purple chrysanthemums, the colour of each slightly different, the bright-yellow goldenrod, and the cosmos.

Cover that bouquet of flowers with some light-coloured gauze and it would be just like a rainbow.

'We offered a rainbow, didn't we, at the grave?'

It made me happy when I heard Satoru say this. The two of us were on exactly the same wavelength.

Instead of getting all puffed up about it, I threw my head back and looked directly upwards, and saw one more extraordinary sight.

I gave a long meow, and Satoru looked up to see what had caught my attention.

Above the perfect arc of the rainbow was another – faint, but still continuous – rainbow.

Satoru gulped again. 'Isn't it amazing,' he said again, this time his voice a little husky.

To think that we'd see this kind of thing at the end of our journey.

Satoru and I would remember this rainbow for the rest of our lives.

We stood there for a long time, until the weather cleared and the rainbow evaporated into the sky.

This was our final journey.

*On our last journey, let's see all kinds of amazing things. Let's spend our time taking in as many wonderful sights as we can.* That's what I had pledged yesterday, when we set off. And what incredible sights we saw.

Shortly afterwards, we arrived in Sapporo, and our journey drew to an end.

# 4

# How Noriko Learned to Love

In her previous job, Noriko had often been posted to new places, so she was used to moving. She would take what she needed out of the cardboard boxes, steadily unpacking, always in the same order. When two or three boxes had been emptied, she would flatten them to give herself more space.

She had never liked to clutter her life with household objects, so she never had many boxes to unpack.

A wall clock emerged from a box she'd just opened. The hands showed it was midday. She hadn't yet unpacked a hook to hang it on, so she placed it on the sofa in the living room. Every time she unpacked after a move, she reminded herself to pack a hook with the clock next time, but every time she forgot.

Afraid she'd lose it somewhere, whenever she moved, she'd put her phone in her pocket, and now it was vibrating. An email.

It was from Satoru Miyawaki, her nephew. The child her older sister had left behind. Miyawaki had been her sister's husband's last name.

*I'm Sorry,* read the subject heading; it was ornamented with a cute little emoji.

*I'd hoped to arrive in the early afternoon, but it looks like it'll be later. Sorry to leave you to unpack everything yourself.*

He said he was going to pay a visit to his mother and

father's graves. He must have lost track of time there.

She typed in a subject for her reply: *Understood*. In the body of the message she wrote: *Everything's fine here. Drive carefully.*

After she sent it, she began to feel a little anxious. Had her reply been a bit curt? It wouldn't be good for Satoru to think she'd written a cold reply because she was angry with him for arriving late.

She opened the message she'd just sent and re-read it. They were both just short messages but, compared to the warmth in his, hers came across as rather blunt. Maybe she should add something?

She typed *PS* and was going to add a new message, but nothing light and chatty came to her. Still agonizing over it, she finally typed, *Don't rush, or you'll have an accident*, and sent it. But a moment later she regretted it, just like she had the last one.

Desperate to recover from this second mistake, she sent a third email. *PPS*, she typed. *I'm worried you'll be concerned about being late and drive too fast.* As soon as she sent it, she realized she'd got her priorities all wrong, since sending so many messages to him while he was driving might distract him from driving safely, the opposite of her intention.

Just then, another message came in. From Satoru. The title read *(Laughing)*. She breathed a sigh of relief.

*Thank you for being so concerned. I'll take you up on your offer and take my time.*

And another emoji at the end, a waving hand.

Worn out by her own indecisiveness, Noriko plonked herself down on the sofa. Her nephew was more than twenty-five years younger than she was, and how were they going to get on if she forced him to respond to each and every tiny little thing?

But it had always been this way between the two of them. Ever since her older sister and brother-in-law had died and she'd taken on the twelve-year-old boy they had left behind.

Her sister had always done her best for Noriko, and Noriko had tried to do the same for the son. But she could never shake off the feeling that all she'd ever done for him was to provide for him financially.

Her sister had been eight years older than her.

Noriko's mother had died when she was very young, so she could barely remember her, and her father had passed away when she was in her first year of high school. So, for Noriko, her sister had been her sole guardian.

When her father died, Noriko had said she wouldn't go on to college, but her sister had insisted that she did, arguing that it was a waste if she didn't, as she was so bright. After her older sister graduated from high school, she had worked at the local farmer's co-op, and it seemed she had given a lot of thought to the question of whether Noriko should go to college. Even if their father had still been alive, the family's financial situation would have made it difficult for both girls to go.

In the spring, when Noriko passed the exam to go and study law, the specialism she had chosen herself, straight after high school, her sister had been transferred from their hometown to Sapporo. Noriko's college was outside Hokkaido, so this meant that both of them were leaving their hometown. Her older sister had used this opportunity to sell off every piece of farmland and the woodlands her father had owned.

Selling it off piece by piece, her sister had explained, wouldn't bring in much money. Up until then, they'd been renting the land out to a neighbouring farmer, but the income was minimal. Selling it all as one lot would bring in a fair amount of money, enough to cover Noriko's tuition fees and living expenses.

At first, they had been reluctant to sell the house they'd grown up in, and had rented it out, but by the time Noriko graduated from college her older sister had let this go as well. Her sister had married and the sale would raise money for Noriko's remaining tuition fees. It wouldn't do for her sister's new family to have to continue supporting her.

Her sister always used to apologize for not having waited to get married until after Noriko had graduated. But Noriko knew how patiently her new brother-in-law had waited to marry her sister. He'd been transferred away from Hokkaido in his job and had proposed to her before he was due to leave.

That was the official reason, but there was another reason her sister couldn't reveal. The young man's family was opposed to him marrying this woman who not only had no parents but was supporting her younger sister. His family were well off, and knowing her older sister was struggling financially, they had decided she was after their money.

They'd set up any number of *omiai*, arranged meetings with other women, trying to get their son to leave her, and truth be told, it had been hard for both of them to resist the pressure.

Noriko was glad her brother-in-law was not the kind of man to buckle under pressure from his family and leave her sister. She was grateful to him for this, and it never crossed her mind to oppose her sister's marriage.

'But, sis,' she argued, 'can't we at least keep the old house?'

'No one wants to rent it any more. And it's getting really run-down. The person we're renting to now said if we sell it to him he'll renovate it, but otherwise they'll move out.'

'That's not a bad offer . . .'

'Both of us live outside Hokkaido and we can't afford the upkeep of an empty house. If we pay for the renovations, we might be able to find a new person to rent it, but financially it'll be tough. And an empty house wouldn't survive the winter snows.'

Her sister had never explained the situation to her before, and for the first time Noriko had understood that she had always done her best to provide her with everything she needed.

She had hoped one day to repay her sister for all she'd done for her. But well before she could, her sister and her brother-in-law were gone for ever.

At the very least, she wanted to do her best for the son they'd left behind, Satoru. That was what she had hoped, but, from the very start, she didn't feel she had managed to keep that particular ball in the air.

And it would all end with her never having done enough for Satoru either.

Sis, I am so very, very sorry.

I don't think I ever made Satoru happy.

All I do is make him worry over trivial things like this. The email with the title *(Laughing)*. He joked around, but you could sense the tender concern that was so typical of Satoru.

Ever since she had started looking after him, Satoru had been a reasonable, very perceptive, mature child. But was this really his true nature?

Her sister had always insisted he was a mischievous boy who gave her a lot of trouble, though she'd always smiled when she said this.

And it was true that, while his parents were still alive, Satoru had been pretty naughty. When Noriko went on the occasional visit, she had found him big-hearted and self-assured, as children who know how fiercely they are loved often are. 'Auntie, Auntie,' he'd say, clinging to her, and sometimes he'd throw a tantrum or sulk.

A typical child, in other words, yet when he came to live with her he never once acted selfishly. This seemed less because his parents' death had forced him to mature quickly than because Noriko had compelled him to be that way.

She had no idea how to overcome the distance she'd created between herself and the young Satoru, and she generally relied on him to paper over her sense of estrangement.

I hope he can at least spend these last days free of worry. She truly felt that way, and yet she couldn't even do a decent job of exchanging a few emails with her nephew.

At least, Noriko thought, as she got up from her short rest on the sofa, at least I can get everything in order here before Satoru arrives. She might be lousy at sorting out the subtleties of other people's feelings, but even an obstinate, unsociable person like her could buckle down and get the job done when she had to.

It was nearly three o'clock when Satoru finally drove up to the apartment.

'Sorry, Aunt Noriko, for being so late.'

'Don't worry. I get things done faster by myself.'

She'd meant to respond lightly to his apology, but Satoru looked a little embarrassed. Seeing his expression, she realized that, yet again, she'd said the wrong thing.

'I have no problem at all with us living together. I'm your legal guardian, after all.' She'd hurriedly added this, but again it was something that would have been better left unsaid. The more she tried to explain herself, the faster her speech became.

'The only things left unpacked are yours, Satoru. I put the boxes in your room. I've pretty much finished putting everything else away, so you don't need to help with that.'

When she saw Satoru's face, as he looked at her, blinking in surprise, she realized she'd been firing off one comment after another without giving him a chance to respond.

'I'm sorry. I'm afraid I'm the same as ever . . .'

Her shoulders slumped dejectedly, and Satoru suddenly let out a small laugh.

'I'm *glad* you haven't changed, Aunt Noriko. We haven't lived together for thirteen years and, to be honest, I've been feeling a bit nervous about it.'

Satoru then put the bag he had slung across his shoulder on the floor, and with both hands placed the basket carefully beside it.

'Nana, this is your new home.'

He opened the basket door and a cat leapt right out. The cat had markings shaped like the character for eight on his forehead, and a black hooked tail. Other than that, it was pure white. She had the feeling that the cat Satoru had had years ago, the one they'd had to give away when she took her nephew in, had looked similar.

The cat had its nose to the ground, sniffing tentatively.

'I'm sorry that taking me has meant taking in Nana as well.' Satoru frowned. 'I was hoping to find a place for him before we started living together, but I just couldn't find a decent new owner. Though a number of people did offer.'

'It's quite all right.'

'But it's meant you've had to move into a new apartment.'

He'd told her he would find someone to take Nana before he moved out of his place in Tokyo, but that hadn't worked out, so here he was, cat in tow. Noriko had moved out of the apartment she was in, which forbade pets, and had found a new place that allowed them.

This new apartment was also in a good location, convenient for Satoru's visits to the hospital.

'Ah, I see you found something nice, Nana.'

Satoru narrowed his eyes as he looked at the cat. Noriko looked over, too, and saw that the cat was sniffing around one of the cardboard boxes that had yet to be flattened.

'Why does he like that box, I wonder?' To Noriko, it was just a cardboard box.

'Cats like empty boxes and paper bags. And narrow spaces, too.'

Satoru squatted down next to the cat, and Noriko noticed how thin his neck was, like an old man's, far too small for the collar of his shirt.

And he's still so young.

Noriko felt a sharp pain deep in her nose and hurried off to the kitchen.

As she was more than twenty-five years older than Satoru, she felt it would have made more sense if she'd gone first.

\*

'I'm really sorry, Aunt Noriko.'

She recalled the day of that desperate phone call. A test had revealed a malignant tumour. He needed an operation immediately.

She'd travelled to Tokyo first thing. The doctor wasn't optimistic, and with each word he spoke, it felt as if all hope was fading.

Best to operate right away, she was told, and though they did, the operation turned out to be ineffective. Tumours had spread throughout his body and all they could do was close up the areas they'd cut open.

One year left to live.

After the surgery, Satoru had lain in the hospital ward, smiling with embarrassment.

'I'm sorry, Aunt Noriko.'

There he goes again.

She half told him off for apologizing. Satoru said he was sorry again, and was about to apologize for saying sorry, but swallowed back the words.

Satoru decided to leave his job, move from Tokyo and live with Noriko. When he finally had to be hospitalized, Noriko would go to the hospital to look after him.

Noriko worked as a judge in Sapporo but had stepped down from her job in order to be with Satoru. Judges are constantly being transferred and, if she hadn't stepped down, there was no guarantee that she wouldn't be transferred just as Satoru was breathing his last. Taking advantage of her connections, she found a job as a lawyer in a law firm in Sapporo.

Satoru worried about Noriko having to change jobs, but she had been thinking all along of working as a lawyer after the mandatory retirement age for a judge. This just speeded things up a bit.

In fact, she regretted not having thought about changing jobs long ago, when she had first started looking after Satoru.

If she was able to leave her position as a judge now, she could have done so back then. Back when Satoru was at an impressionable age, she'd forced him to transfer to a new school repeatedly, yanking him away from friends and places he'd grown comfortable in.

If he's going to leave this world at such a young age, she thought, the least I could have done was to give him a happier childhood.

Holding back the tears, she pretended to be straightening things up in the kitchen. Just then, Satoru called out to her from the other room.

'Aunt Noriko, is it okay if we leave one small cardboard box and don't flatten it? Nana really seems to like it.'

'When he gets tired of it, be sure to put it away.'

She said this intentionally loudly so he wouldn't notice the tears in her voice.

'Did you find the parking spot okay?' she went on.

She'd rented one space in the basement parking area for Satoru to park his van.

'I did. Number seven, on the corner. Did you pick number seven especially for me?'

Satoru seemed so pleased it was the same number as his cat's name.

'Not really. I thought the corner spot would be easy to find, that's all.'

Then she went ahead and asked a silly question.

'So Nana's name comes from *nana* – seven?'

'That's right. His tail is hooked like the number seven.'

Satoru went to pick Nana up and show him to his aunt, but the cat was nowhere to be seen. 'Nana?' he called, puzzled.

'EEEEEK!' This shriek emanated from Noriko. Something soft was rubbing against her calf.

She dropped the pan she was holding and it clattered loudly to the floor. She shrieked again as something small and furry scampered away.

Satoru scooped up the cat and burst out laughing. It seemed Noriko's shriek wasn't totally unexpected.

He spluttered painfully, he was laughing so much.

'You don't much like cats, but now you've got one in your own home.'

'It's not that I dislike them, I just don't know how to handle them,' she protested. Once, when she was little, she'd gone to stroke a stray cat and had been badly bitten. Her right hand – the one she had thoughtlessly touched the cat with – had swelled up to twice its usual size, and ever since then cats had been on her list of things she couldn't handle.

A sudden thought occurred to her. At what point had Satoru found out about her aversion to cats?

'But please understand that it wasn't because of my issues with cats that I didn't let you keep that cat all that time ago.'

'I know. I understand.'

When she'd taken Satoru in, they had to give up the cat because her job meant she was transferred so often. Most of the housing they lived in was provided by the government and didn't allow pets.

But if she had liked cats, would she have kept it? If she herself had been fond of animals – not just cats – would she have better understood the feelings of a child who had to be separated from his beloved pet?

When Satoru was on a junior-high-school trip to Fukuoka, he'd snuck out of the hotel one night. The teachers had caught him at the station, he was given a strict reprimand and his guardian was contacted, and when this happened Noriko had been shocked.

Had he been trying to visit the cat he'd had to give away? The distant relatives who had taken in the cat lived in Kokura, one stop away from Hakata on the Shinkansen train. Once Satoru had meekly mentioned wanting to see the cat, but she'd told him it was out of the question since she was too busy. As far as Noriko was concerned, the matter of the cat was settled. Now that they had someone they could trust to care for it, there was no need to travel so far just to see it.

Noriko felt a sudden rush of regret.

'I'm really sorry I didn't understand back then how much you loved that cat, Satoru. I should have taken the cat in like this for you when you were a child.'

'Hachi was well taken care of until the very end, and that's good enough. Because you found decent people to take care of him.'

Satoru stroked Nana, who was curled up on his lap, gently stroking each paw with the tips of his fingers and circling the central spot on his head.

'But Nana scuppered all the relationships at every home I was trying to make for him. You've really helped us by letting me bring him with me now.'

Satoru held Nana's head in two gentle hands and pointed his face towards Noriko.

'Nana, you get on nicely with Aunt Noriko now, okay?'

You can tell me to get on with her, but I'm still feeling a bit cross.

The reason is, Noriko is kind of rude. I'm going to live here with Satoru, and I just thought we should get on, so all I did was go ahead and say hello.

Rubbing yourself against someone's legs is the best a cat can do when it comes to a warm greeting, so what was with the big squeal, that 'EEEEEK!'? It gave me the fright of my life! Sounded like she'd run into a ghost on a dark night.

Well, she *is* taking in both Satoru and me, so I suppose I can overlook it.

Our first meeting was a disaster, but our new life with Noriko began nonetheless.

Noriko was the type of person who had no clue at all about cats, and it took us a while to find the appropriate distance to keep from each other.

'Good morning, Nana.'

In her own way, she tried to get used to me, and she started timidly reaching out a hand to me as she said hello. But what was she thinking, suddenly touching my tail like that? I mean, unless you're a special pal of mine, I'm not about to let anyone touch my tail. Normally, I'd give them a good whack – claws in, obviously – if they tried, but out of respect to the head of the household I confined myself to scowling and lowering my tail out of the way.

I hoped Noriko would get the message, but every time she reached out to touch me she inevitably zoomed in on my tail.

One particular morning, Satoru happened to see this and came to my rescue.

'You can't do that, Aunt Noriko, touching his tail all of a sudden like that. Nana hates it.'

'Then where should I touch him?'

'Start with his head, or behind his ears. When he gets used to you doing that, then you can do under his chin.'

A toothbrush in his other hand, Satoru demonstrated, stroking each area in turn around my head.

'The head, behind the ears, under the chin . . .'

You won't believe this, but as Noriko repeated these instructions, she took notes!

'Do you really need to take notes?' Satoru laughed.

Noriko was deadly serious. 'I don't want to forget,' she replied.

'Instead of notes, it would be better to practise by stroking him.'

'B-but it's near his mouth.'

So what if it's near my mouth?

'What if he bites me?'

The impertinence! You have the nerve to speak to me like that? A gentleman who, in spite of you suddenly touching his tail, refrained from swatting you? And you aimed for my tail more than just a couple of times!

What you said just now, now *that* deserves a bite.

'It's okay. Try it.'

At Satoru's urging, Noriko very timidly reached out a hand. If that didn't deserve a bite, I didn't know what did. However, I'm a grown-up cat and I restrained myself, so, everyone, feel free to shower me with praise.

Still, I now understood why she always went for my

tail. To Noriko's way of thinking, it was the furthest point from my mouth. Though, in actual fact, all animals will react more quickly if you touch their tails or back rather than hold your hand out right in front of them.

'He's so soft.'

I'd always prided myself on having fur as soft as velvet.

'See? He likes it.'

To be honest, Noriko's touch was awkward and not all that pleasant, but to help train her I was quite willing to pretend that it was. Plus, I certainly didn't want her targeting my tail each and every time.

'Eeek!'

Noriko screeched and pulled back her hand. I shrank back, too. What on earth?

'His throat! The bone in his throat is going up and down. Yuck!'

This is impertinence squared! The way you touch me doesn't even feel that good. I'm only purring to make you feel better about it!

'Not to worry,' Satoru explained. 'When he feels good, he purrs.'

As a rule, that is. This is an exception. I'm forcing myself here to give you a treat, so don't you forget it.

'But it's coming from all the way down his throat,' Noriko said.

Noriko rubbed my throat with the side of her finger.

'Where did you think it would come from, if not the throat?'

'I thought it came from the mouth,' she replied.

Purring from my *mouth*? What are you, an imbecile?!

Excuse me – the shock has made my language deteriorate. A thousand pardons.

Noriko stopped stroking me, so I stopped purring and popped into the cardboard box that had been placed specially for me in a corner of the living room.

This cardboard box that Satoru had left out for me fitted nice and tight and was really quite cosy.

'Satoru, how long do we have to keep that box there?'

'Nana likes it, so leave it there for a while.'

'But *I* don't like it; it feels like we're not totally unpacked. I mean, I bought him a nice cat bed and a scratching post.'

A box is totally different from a bed and a post, I'll have you know.

In this way, Noriko grew used to the presence of a cat in her house.

'How's this, then?'

Noriko said this the other day while bringing in what I took to be a replacement for the cardboard box, which by now was looking pretty shabby, what with me sharpening my claws on it.

She'd taken another cardboard box, opened it up and made it wider and shallower, then reinforced it with tape.

'This one is newer and wider,' she said. 'I've made it with two layers of cardboard so it'll last longer when he sharpens his claws on it. So what do you say to getting rid of that tattered old box? The corners are all bent out of shape where Nana's been sleeping.'

'Hmmm . . . I'm not sure.' Satoru shot me a glance. 'What do *you* think?'

I yawned back. Sorry. Zero interest. Noriko just doesn't

get it. A wide box spoils all the fun; it offers none of the charms of being inside a box.

Ignoring Noriko's creation, I slipped inside the old box, and Noriko looked deflated. Satoru laughed. 'Maybe it was better not to alter the box. Next time we get a cardboard box, how about just leaving it as it is?'

'But I did all that work on it.'

A waste of time. Cats the world over prefer to discover things they like on their own and rarely go for anything that's been provided for them.

For a while after this, Noriko's box sat there forlornly beside the old box, but before long it was put out with the recycling.

Satoru began to visit the hospital nearly every day. It was nearby, within walking distance, but he'd go there first thing in the morning and often not get back home until evening. Maybe there was lots of queuing, or the tests and treatment took a long time.

Satoru had lots of marks from all the injections on his right arm, bluish-black bruises that didn't fade, and soon his left arm was the same. I only get one vaccination shot a year, and I hate it, so I was amazed that Satoru could put up with getting a million of them.

And yet, no matter how often he went to the hospital, his smell didn't get any better. As several dogs and cats had told me earlier, that *doesn't smell like he's got much longer* scent was only getting stronger.

No creatures ever get better once they have that smell.

Sometimes, Noriko cried in secret, weeping gently beside the kitchen sink or in the bathroom. The only one who knew about it was me. She forced herself never to cry in front of Satoru, but she didn't think to include a cat in the equation.

When I rubbed against her legs after that, she didn't scream any more. And I was beginning to feel her appreciation when she fondled the back of my neck.

The town was completely white with snow, the mountain ashes that lined the streets even redder as they endured the freezing cold.

'Nana, let's go for a walk.'

Satoru's strength had faded, so much so that on the days when he went to the hospital he'd sleep for the rest of the day, but still he never missed out on our walks together.

It was freezing and slippery, but except for when he was at the hospital longer than usual or when there was a snowstorm, we went for a walk every day.

'You've never been through a winter in a place with so much snow, have you, Nana?'

The street was icy and the pads of my feet skidded on it. Icicles hung from the eaves of the buildings. The snow pushed up by the snowploughs looked like millefeuille pastry piled up along the streets.

Sparrows huddled in rows on the power lines. Dogs cheerfully ploughed their way through snow banks in the park. Cats in the town quietly slipped into the few spots that would keep them out of the cold: sheds, garages, warm kitchens.

There were still a lot of things the two of us had never seen before.

'My, what a cute cat. Out for a walk?'

It was a bright, clear day, and a charming old lady at the park had called out to us.

'What's his name?'

'He's called Nana. After the shape of his tail, like a seven.'

Satoru hadn't changed. He was still the same cat-loving guy, intent on explaining the origins of my name to every passer-by.

'He's very well behaved, isn't he, walking beside you like that?' said the old lady.

'He certainly is.'

After we'd said goodbye, Satoru picked me up, his fingers, no longer strong and broad but thinning and fragile, finding their way around my belly.

'You are very well behaved, so I know you'll be a good boy from now on.'

From now on? When *hadn't* I been a good boy? Kind of impolite to have to make sure of that now, don't you think?

The streets were filled with festive lights, and, as if that weren't enough, Christmas adverts spilled out of TVs everywhere. In the evening, Satoru and Noriko ate Christmas cake, and they gave me some tuna sashimi, to which I was more than a little partial. The next morning, all their energy turned to preparing for New Year.

On New Year's Day, they gave me some chicken breast, but after sniffing it a few times I kicked sand on top of it. There was no actual sand there, of course, so it was only air sand.

'What's wrong, Nana? Don't you like it?'

Satoru looked puzzled. I would have loved to have eaten it, but it smelled funny.

'Aunt Noriko, is this chicken the same kind you always give him?'

'Well, given the occasion, I splashed out. I steamed some special local free-range chicken.'

'Did you add something to it when you steamed it?'

'I poured in a bit of sake so it wouldn't smell so much.'

Humph. I rest my case, Noriko.

'Sorry, but it seems like Nana can't eat it because it smells like sake now.'

'Really? It was only a couple of drops.'

'Cats have an excellent sense of smell.'

'I thought that was dogs? Six thousand times more sensitive than humans, they say.'

Noriko's not a bad sort, but at times like this she tends to overthink things. It's true that dogs are known for their great sense of smell, but that doesn't mean cats don't have a good nose. I mean, no one needs a sense of smell six thousand times better than humans to discern that sake has been sprinkled on a chicken breast.

'Cats are way more sensitive to smell than humans as well.'

Satoru was in the kitchen, and he prepared my usual safe, high-quality chicken breast and brought it over to me on a clean plate, taking away the chicken that had had those unnecessary things done to it.

'That sake-steamed meat, I'll put it in my *ozoni*.'

Noriko let out a deep sigh.

'Until Nana came here, I never would have imagined that a person would eat a cat's leftovers.'

'It happens sometimes when you have a cat. And these aren't leftovers. He didn't touch it, so it's perfectly safe.'

Satoru put the meat in his bowl of *ozoni* soup as a topping.

'What will people think if they hear I gave you something to eat that even a cat wouldn't touch? Please don't mention it to anyone.'

'Anybody who has a cat will understand.'

Satoru and Noriko then said 'Happy New Year' to each other and started eating their *ozoni*.

'Nana's only been here three months, but in that time I've found that cats really are odd creatures.'

Ah, so *that's* how you think of me, and we're barely into the New Year? I'll have you know, that's the kind of rudeness I simply can't overlook.

'And that box . . .'

The cardboard box was still in the corner of the living room. Noriko had resentfully let it be known that she wanted to toss it out before the New Year.

'A new one would be so much better . . .'

Sorry to tell you this, but you're missing the point.

'And why does he go into a box that's clearly too small for him? It's obvious it's not big enough.'

Hit a sore spot, why don't you?

'The other day he thrust his front paw into a jewellery case.'

'Yep, that's the way cats are.' Satoru nodded happily.

'And once he tried putting his paw in a tiny box that had contained a watch.'

What can I say? It's instinct, pure and simple. Cats are always looking for a nice cosy space that will fit just right.

So when I spy a nice square box that's slightly open, instinct doesn't allow me to let it go. Because maybe – just maybe – if I stick my paw inside, some device in there might make it expand? 'Course, up till now, I haven't had any luck at all with that.

Though I do hear there's a cat in some cold foreign country who keeps on opening doors, thinking that, eventually, one of them will lead to summer.

'I'm sorry, but I can't eat any more.'

Satoru laid his chopsticks down. For a moment, I saw a sad look cross Noriko's face. She had only put one *omochi* in Satoru's bowl. And he had barely touched the lavish spread of New Year's delicacies she'd bought specially at a department store.

'It was delicious. My mum always used to include taro root, snow peas and carrots in her *ozoni*. And the way you season it is like the way Mum did it, too.'

'That's because, for me, my sister's cooking was the taste of home.'

'I remember when I first came to live with you, how relieved I was to find that the food tasted like Mum's cooking. I think that's why I got used to living with you so quickly.' Satoru smiled broadly. 'I'm glad you're the one who looked after me.'

Noriko gasped, as if surprised, and avoided his eyes. She looked down and murmured, 'I . . . I wasn't such a good guardian. If you had gone to live with someone else, maybe it would have been bet—'

'I'm *glad* you're the one who took me in,' said Satoru, ignoring her words.

Noriko gulped again, her throat pulsing like a frog's. Now who was it, when they first met me, who freaked out about *my* throat making a funny sound? *Hm?* That's a pretty funny sound you're making yourself, if you don't mind me saying.

'But that thing I said to you, when I first took you in.'

'I was going to find out some day. You didn't do anything wrong.'

'But . . .' Noriko sniffled as she continued to look down.

Still gulping over and over like a frog, and in between gulps murmuring, 'I'm sorry, I'm sorry,' over and over.

'I shouldn't have said that to you.'

Her voice had become husky.

∽

WHEN NORIKO HEARD THE NEWS of her sister and brother-in-law's deaths, she went to the funeral intent on taking Satoru in, even though she was single. Satoru was the one thing her sister would have been worried about and Noriko was determined to do whatever she could for him.

Relatives from her brother-in-law's side of the family made a token appearance at the funeral and left without touching on the issue of what was to be done with Satoru at all.

And on her side of the family there was no one else willing to take the decision to have him. When Noriko said she would, some of them were worried, saying a woman on her own might not be able to manage. Most of them suggested putting the boy in foster care.

Satoru was her sister's and brother-in-law's child. If he had no relatives, that would be one thing, but since there was a relative who had the financial resources to take him in, she would be shirking her duty if she put him into foster care, so she insisted, in spite of the resistance.

The funeral ended, the estate was settled and, soon afterwards, Noriko adopted Satoru. She told him:

'You're going to find out eventually, so I'm going to go ahead and tell you now. Satoru, you are not related by blood to your father or your mother.'

Reality is reality. That was her way of thinking, but when she saw the look on Satoru's face when she told him, she realized she'd made a big mistake.

Satoru grew pale, and his face contorted in shock.

It was the same blank look he had had after his parents' deaths. As he approached the two coffins set up in the local community centre, he'd looked as if he had lost everything he had in the world.

Even a tactless person like her knew instantly that in a matter of seconds, because of her, Satoru had lost everything all over again.

When his friends came for the wake, he cried for the first time. Afterwards, the expression on his face slowly returned to normal.

The realization that she had done something unspeakable upset her terribly.

'Then who are my real father and mother?' Satoru asked.

'Your real mother and father are indeed my sister and her husband. The others are just your birth parents.'

Obviously, Satoru had done nothing wrong, but still she spoke like this, as if scolding him. She was so confused, she couldn't control herself.

'Your real parents are my sister and her husband; your birth parents merely gave birth to you. They were utterly irresponsible and they were going to let you die when you were a baby.'

This had been Noriko's first big case as a judge. The couple had been quite young. It was more than a criminal case of child abandonment; it was so extreme that the birth parents had been charged with attempted murder. They'd stopped feeding the baby until he was no longer able even to cry, then had wrapped him in a black plastic bag and thrown him out on the day the rubbish was due to be collected. A neighbour had grown suspicious when he spotted the plastic bag moving and ripped it open. The couple had been walking away when the neighbour reported them.

The trial ended, and Satoru's birth parents were given the prison terms they deserved, but there was nowhere to place Satoru. The only option left was an orphanage.

The whole case had almost been too much for Noriko. Imposing a punishment that befitted the crime — that she could do, but it did nothing to secure a future for the innocent baby.

Her sister had been the one who helped her cope with this ordeal. It was a major case, and her sister had been following it since the start.

'People should really go through a vetting process in order to get married,' Noriko had grumbled at the time. 'If couples with kids were all like you and your husband, sis, then this type of crime would never happen.'

Just as she said this, she felt a cold trickle of sweat run down her back. After her sister had got married, she'd found out she wasn't able to have children. The criticism from her husband's family had been hurtful, and her husband had distanced himself from them, yet even so her sister remained anxious.

It was soon after this that Noriko's sister told her that she wanted to adopt Satoru. Just before he was due to be sent to an orphanage.

'It's because you told me we would be good parents,' she had said, smiling.

*

Satoru had been devastated by the news.

'Your birth parents just gave birth to you, that's all,' Noriko had reassured him. 'Your real parents were my sister and brother-in-law. So it was my duty to take you in.'

Noriko had said this to put Satoru's mind at ease, but she had instantly regretted using the word 'duty'. It sounded so stiff and formal.

'Satoru, you don't need to worry about a thing,' she had added, in an attempt to make up for it.

The criticism her male relatives had of Noriko — that she needed to be more careful about what she said — was spot on. From the very beginning, she'd got it all wrong with Satoru, telling him things she never should have.

'That's why she can't find a husband,' they had said. And, she thought now, they were probably quite right. At the time, she'd had a boyfriend, but soon after she adopted Satoru they split up. Her boyfriend seemed upset that she hadn't consulted him before making the decision.

'Why didn't you talk to me about this?' he had reproached her, and she had explained that, since Satoru was her nephew, she hadn't thought she needed to.

At that moment, the barriers had gone up, and she knew it. It seemed that, once again, she'd been incredibly insensitive.

Learning to have some insight into other people's sensitivities was, she concluded, more difficult than mastering the law.

The cat that Satoru had owned ended up being taken in by a distant relative.

This relative — such a distant relation that Noriko didn't

feel at all close to him – had tousled Satoru's hair and said, 'Don't worry. Everyone in our family loves cats, so we'll take good care of him.'

Satoru had given him a cheerful look and nodded. Not once since the day his parents died had Satoru looked at her in that way.

Occasionally, this relative would send them a photo of the cat. But before long, these letters became few and far between, though the annual New Year's card from them always had a photo of Hachi printed on it and a short message: *Hachi's doing well!*

The family were considerate enough to let them know when Hachi died, and when Satoru went to visit the grave they welcomed him warmly.

Maybe Satoru would have been happier if they had taken him in, too – even now, the thought occurred to her sometimes. When all the other relatives had hesitated to take in this child to whom they had no blood ties, this family had said, 'If only we had the means, we'd have liked to help out.' They had other children already, quite a lot in those days. 'It's a question of money, you know,' they'd said, smiling awkwardly.

But couldn't they have taken Satoru, if Noriko had helped them out financially? Was taking him in herself just egotistical, all about her not wanting to give up the one thing her sister had left behind?

She had thought about all these things for the longest time.

Noriko had started to weep.

'I think you would have been much happier if your relative in Kokura had adopted you.'

'Why?' Satoru blinked in surprise. 'He's a nice man and everything, but I'm glad *you* took me in, Aunt Noriko.'

Now it was her turn to ask why.

'Well, you're my mother's younger sister. You're the one who can tell me the most about my parents.'

'But right after they died, I went and told you that awful thing—'

Satoru cut her off. 'I *was* pretty shocked when I heard that, I grant you. But because you told me that, I was able to appreciate just how happy I'd been with them.'

Noriko looked dubious. Satoru laughed.

'I never, ever thought they weren't my real parents. That's how much they treated me like their own child. Though my birth parents didn't want me, another man and woman loved me that much – I mean, you don't find such incredible love very often.'

*That's why I'm so happy.* Satoru had said this to me, his face beaming, many times.

∽

I GET IT. HAVING HAD SATORU take me in as his cat, I think I felt as lucky as he did.

Strays, by definition, have been abandoned or left behind, but Satoru rescued me when I broke my leg.

He made me the happiest cat on earth.

I'll always remember those five years we had together. And I'll forever go by the name Nana, the name that – let's face it – is pretty unusual for a male cat.

The town where Satoru grew up, too, I would remember that.

And the green seedlings swaying in the fields.

The sea, with its frighteningly loud roar.
Mount Fuji, looming over us.
How cosy it felt on top of that boxy TV.
That wonderful lady cat, Momo.
That nervy but earnest hound, Toramaru.
That huge white ferry, which swallowed up cars into its stomach.
The dogs in the pet holding area, wagging their tails at Satoru.
That foul-mouthed chinchilla telling me *Guddo rakku!*
The land in Hokkaido stretching out for ever.
Those vibrant purple and yellow flowers by the side of the road.
The field of pampas grass like an ocean.
The horses chomping on grass.
The bright-red berries on the mountain-ash trees.
The shades of red on the mountain ash that Satoru taught me.
The stands of slender white birch.
The graveyard, with its wide-open vista.
The bouquet of flowers in rainbow colours.
The white heart-shaped bottom of the deer.
That huge, huge, huge double rainbow growing out of the ground.
I would remember these for the rest of my life.
And Kosuke, and Yoshimine, and Sugi and Chikako. And above all, the one who brought up Satoru and made it possible for us to meet – Noriko.
Could anyone be happier than this?

'It must have made you sad that we had to move all the time

because of my work. Every time you made friends, I had to tear you away.'

'But I made new friends wherever we went. I was sad to say goodbye to Kosuke, but in junior high I met Yoshimine, and in high school I met Sugi and Chikako. Our *omiai* meetings didn't go so well with any of them, but they all said they'd take Nana for me. I've been so lucky to have this many people willing to take care of my darling cat.'

Satoru reached out his thin hand and covered Noriko's fingers.

'None of the people who offered to take Nana were right for him, and in the end you took him in for me, Aunt Noriko.'

Noriko was still looking down at her lap when her shoulders began to shake.

'And even more than that, you found my parents for me, before adopting me yourself. So how could I *not* be happy?'

So – you shouldn't be crying there, Noriko.

Instead of sobbing like that, it would be better to keep a smile on your face till the end. And then I'm sure you'll be happier.

SATORU BEGAN TO STAY OVERNIGHT at the hospital more often.

'I'll be back in a few days.'

He'd say this, tickle me on the head, and leave the house, bag in hand. Gradually, the amount of time he stayed away grew longer. He'd say he'd be gone three or four days, but then would not come back for a week. Or he would say a week and return ten days later.

The clothes he had brought from Tokyo no longer fitted him. His trousers became so loose you could fit a couple of fists inside the waist.

He started wearing a wool cap at home. I don't know why, but his hair was getting thinner than ever, along with his body, and then one day he was completely bald. I thought maybe they'd shaved his hair off at the hospital, but he'd gone to the barber's himself and got them to do it.

One day, as Satoru was preparing for another stay in the hospital, he put a photograph into his suitcase. A photo of the two of us, taken on one of our trips, which he'd always kept beside his bed back in Tokyo.

And then it struck me.

I stood up on my hind legs and scratched at my basket in the corner of the living room and meowed. Come on, don't you need to bring this with you?

Satoru closed the clasp on his suitcase and smiled at me with a forlorn look.

'I guess you'd like to come with me, wouldn't you, Nana?'

Well, *of course*. Satoru opened the basket door, and I hurried inside. Then he turned the basket so the door was against the wall.

Just a second now! How am I supposed to get out? Enough with the silly jokes.

'You're very well behaved, so I know you'll be a good boy from now on.'

Hold on there! I clawed hard at the inside of the basket. What're you talking about, Satoru?

Satoru stood up with his suitcase. He opened the front door without taking my basket with him.

Wait, wait! I scratched even harder at the basket, my fur on end, and yowled.

'I know you'll be a good boy.'

Shut up – *a good boy*? What a load of hogwash! I'll never, ever let you leave me behind.

'You be a good boy now.'

What? Come back here! Come back right this minute! *Take me with you!*

'It's not like I want to leave you. I love you, you silly cat!'

I love you too, you dummy!

As if shaking off my yells, Satoru slowly left the room and closed the door firmly behind him.

Come back! Come back! *Come back!* COME BACK!

I'm your cat till the bitter end!

I screamed as loud as I could, but the door didn't open. I cried and cried and cried and cried, until my voice was completely hoarse.

After I'm not sure how long, when the room had turned dark, the door quietly clicked open.

It was Noriko. She moved my basket away from the wall and opened the door.

I stayed in the corner of the basket, sulking, and a small hand reached gingerly in.

With the tip of her finger she touched my head, scratched behind my ears, softly stroked my throat.

For someone who wasn't good with cats, she had come on quite well.

'Satoru said to take good care of you. Since you're his darling cat.'

I know. That I'm precious to him – that much I know.

'I put out some food for you. I crumbled some chicken breast on top, too. Satoru said to pamper you today.'

If he thinks that'll make up for leaving me behind, then he's got another thing coming.

'Satoru's room is kind of small, but it's a private room and very comfortable, not hospital-like at all. The nurses are all really kind, too. Satoru said he wants to spend his final days quietly.'

Noriko's voice was trembling as she stroked me.

'So Satoru said to tell Nana not to worry at all.'

Maybe I didn't need to worry, but without me there with him it must have been just awful.

'As soon as he got in the room he put up the photo of the two of you. Right next to his bed, just like at home. So he said everything's fine.'

Nonsense. Which is better – a photo of me, or the real flesh-and-blood cat? The answer's obvious.

Of course having the real me there – warm and velvety-soft me – is better.

I licked Noriko's hand. At first, she hadn't liked it when I licked her; she said my tongue was rough.

Since you're crying, I'll eat later, when I feel so inclined. I mean, you went to all the trouble of topping it with chicken breast and all.

Other than eating and using the litter tray, I pretty much stayed holed up in Satoru's room.

Whenever I was alone in the house and the door opened, I leapt out, hoping it was him, but it was always Noriko.

I would let my tail droop and head back to Satoru's room. I wasn't at all embarrassed about letting it droop when I couldn't see him. Because it was only natural to feel sad.

It seemed that Satoru had asked Noriko to take me for a walk every now and then, but if I couldn't go out with Satoru I didn't see the point of treading with the soft pads of my paws on streets covered with freezing white snow.

Satoru didn't seem to get it. How important he was to me.

Every day, I stared out of the window.

Hey, Satoru, how are things where you are?

There was an awful snowstorm today. A total whiteout outside the window. I couldn't even see the lights of the city. Was it the same where you are?

Now it's sunny. Not a cloud in the sky. But the clear, blue sky looks really cold.

Today, the puffed-up sparrows on the power lines set a new record for rotundity. There are some thin clouds and it isn't snowing, but I'll bet it's freezing outside.

I saw a bright-red car driving down the road. The colour of the berries on the mountain ash, the colour you taught me. But I get the feeling the mountain-ash berry is a deeper colour, the kind that takes your breath away. Humans are good at making colours, but they can't seem to reproduce the power of natural ones.

One day, Noriko walked into Satoru's room.

'Nana, let's go and visit Satoru.'

Come again?

'Satoru seems really lonely without you, so I went ahead and asked if I could bring you. The doctor said you can't come inside, but when Satoru is going for his walk in the garden we can see him.'

Bravo, Noriko!

Noriko held out the basket and I scurried inside. We drove there in the silver van. Noriko had been using it the whole time Satoru had been in hospital, apparently, and this was the first time I'd been in it since the last journey Satoru and I had taken together.

By car, it took all of twenty minutes.

Satoru was this close by.

If it were just me and Satoru in the van, I would have opened the basket instantly and slipped out, but since it was Noriko I stayed quietly inside. Unused to thinking about things from a cat's perspective, she put the basket on the floor in the back, so my only view was the van's dark interior.

'You stay here like a good boy, and I'll fetch Satoru.'

As instructed, I waited like a good boy.

Of *course* I did. I'm a wise cat. I know what to do in any and all situations.

Finally, Noriko returned and lifted the basket out of the van.

The hospital was a tranquil place in a quiet neighbourhood. Beyond the parking lot was a soft, snowy field. The trees and benches were decorated with a thick layer of snow. I imagined the grass and flowerbeds asleep underneath.

There were chairs and tables on a roofed-in terrace projecting out from the building, and this place seemed to be used as a rest area on days when the weather wasn't good. And then—

On the terrace, in a wheelchair, was Satoru.

I was impatient to leap out of the basket, but because Noriko was holding on to it, I refrained from unlocking the door myself.

'Nana!'

Satoru had a down jacket on and was all puffy, but he was even thinner and paler than the last time I'd seen him.

But then, a bit of colour came to those ghostly cheeks. I don't think I'm being conceited if I say that I was the one who brought that warm red glow to his face, but what do you all think?

'I'm so glad you came!'

Satoru half rose from his wheelchair. Like me, he couldn't stand the distance still separating us. I wanted to open up the basket and leap straight out. But Noriko still didn't know I could unlock it myself.

I sprang into Satoru's lap as soon as I could.

He pressed me close in his thin arms, unable to speak. I purred till my throat hurt, rubbing the top of my head over and over against his body.

The two of us were so very, very well matched, so don't you think it was strange we were kept apart from each other?

I wanted to lie in his arms for ever, but pretty soon the piercing cold became too much for Satoru, in his condition.

'Satoru,' Noriko said hesitantly. Satoru knew what she meant, but found it hard to let me go.

'I keep the photo of the two of us next to my bed.'

Um. Noriko told me.

'So I'm not lonely.'

That's not true. In fact, it's such an obvious lie that Enma, the Lord of Hell, who pulls out the tongues of liars, would be laughing too hard to do any tongue-pulling.

'You stay well, Nana.'

One more firm squeeze around my middle that nearly

brought the stuffing out of me, and Satoru finally let me go. At Noriko's urging, I stepped straight back into my basket, ever the good boy.

'Just a second. I'll put Nana in the car.'

Noriko left me on the back seat of the van before hurrying back to Satoru.

That was my moment. With my right paw, I flipped the basket door open. I sat down low in the driver's seat and waited for Noriko to return.

It was almost an hour later when she did. There was a light dusting of snow swirling in the air, and Noriko was hunching up her shoulders against the cold as she walked.

The door on the driver's side snapped open.

'Nana!?'

She chased after me, but when it comes to playing tag, humans are no match for four-legged animals. I avoided her easily and raced out into the parking lot.

'Come back here!'

Noriko's voice was nearly a scream. Sorry, but I'm not going to listen to you.

Because I'm a wise cat, who knows what to do in any and all situations.

When I had reached a safe distance, I stopped and turned to look, focusing my vision hard on her flailing, distant figure.

Then I put up my tail cheerily.

*See you! Bye!*

I scampered off into the snowy landscape and never looked back.

Now then. No matter how proud a stray cat I might be, winter in Hokkaido is pretty formidable.

The snow in Tokyo should never be called by the same name as the snow that falls here, so heavy sometimes you can't see your nose in front of your face.

Here's where all those walks I'd taken with Satoru came in useful.

The town cats I ran across were great at slipping into sheltered spaces to avoid the cold. And, of course, there were some heroic cats in the neighbourhood around the hospital as well.

That being the case, since I was always prepared to go back to being a stray, why wouldn't I survive?

Using the hospital as my base, I located several spots where I could keep out of the cold. As might be expected with large buildings, there were many cracks and gaps – in garage and warehouse walls, for instance – that a cat could slip through. The areas below the flooring in people's houses and underneath their boilers were both comfortable places. Sometimes, another cat had beaten me to it, but perhaps the severe winter cold helped foster a spirit of cooperation, and more often than not we would end up sharing the spot rather than disputing it.

I'd heard that the citizens of Hokkaido were particularly kind. Noriko had told Satoru that it was quite common for people to pick up drunks and travellers and let them stay in their home. Sure enough, I experienced how that principle operated in the cat world, too.

The local cats showed me where to scavenge for food, for example. Houses and shops where they'd give you tasty leftovers, and a park where a cat lover might feed you. There was a small supermarket near the hospital as well, and I often charmed my way into cadging treats there.

And, of course, there was always hunting. The cold made the puffed-up birds and mice move nice and slowly, so they were easy prey.

The cats around me thought I was a little odd for having intentionally given up the easy life for one as a stray. *Why do that?* they often asked. *It's such a waste.* They concluded I must be a little mad.

But, for me, there was something more important at stake.

The snow began to let up, and night was yet to fall. I crept around to the side of the warehouse from which the hospital was visible and – yes! Just as I thought.

Satoru, wheeling himself in his wheelchair, was coming out of the front door.

Tail straight up, I scampered over to him. His face broke into a tearful smile. Then he said, 'You need to go home now.'

You know what'll happen if you try to catch me, don't you? I'll scratch you – up and down and all over – until you look like they could play checkers on your face.

Satoru could see I was wary, and said, 'I give up.'

Turns out, when I escaped from Noriko, they had totally freaked out. Satoru was apparently so shocked when he heard I'd run away he broke out in a fever.

Noriko looked for me every day on the streets but, naturally, I was too stealthy for the likes of her to find me.

A few days passed, and when I turned up again in front of Satoru, despondently sitting on the terrace, boy was he surprised! His jaw dropped so far he looked like Donald Duck.

See? Didn't I tell you I'd stay with you to the end?

Satoru reached out from his wheelchair to grab me. I flailed around like a freshly caught salmon and slipped out of his grasp.

When I looked up at him from a safe spot on the floor a few yards away, Satoru's face looked like that of a child on the verge of tears.

'Nana, you're being foolish,' he said. 'You came to say hello, didn't you?'

I am Satoru's one and only cat. And Satoru is my one and only pal.

And a proud cat like me wasn't about to abandon his pal. If living as a stray was what it took to be Satoru's cat to the very end, then bring it on.

When Noriko heard the news from Satoru, she huffed and puffed and jumped in her car. I'm not sure where she found it, but she brought over a huge cage used to trap animals, left it in the garage and went back home. As if I would be stupid enough to get caught in a contraption like that!

For a while, I couldn't trust the hospital staff either. Apparently acting on instructions from Noriko and Satoru, they tried to coax me over, with the sole intention of capturing me.

They saw me appear whenever Satoru happened to be on the terrace, only to leave as soon as he went inside, so I think they finally understood.

After that, I became Satoru's commuting cat.

On days when it wasn't snowing, Satoru would come outside for a short while, and we'd spend some precious moments together. I chewed on the crunchies and chicken breast he brought me and curled up tightly in his lap.

Satoru would tickle me behind my ears and under my chin, and I'd purr for him.

Just like when we first met.

'Mr Miyawaki?'

The nurse was calling him back inside. She was about the same age as Noriko, but quite a bit rounder.

'Okay. I'll be in soon.'

Satoru held me tightly to his body. Whenever we parted, he would always give me a huge hug. I could tell from the way his thin arms clung around me that this might be the last time.

I licked Satoru's hands, each and every knuckle, and leapt down from his lap.

By the way, when I became a commuting cat, some of the other cats I got to know received extra perks as well.

The hospital staff and visitors started to leave little snacks around the yard for me. Each one thought they were the only one stealthily leaving me food, but actually there must have been a whole lot of them.

I couldn't eat it all myself, but took some to all the cats who'd been kind to me, to repay them.

It snowed for several days in a row.

When it finally let up, I sidled over to the side of the warehouse where I had a clear view of the hospital's front entrance.

It was the first sunny day in a while, yet Satoru didn't appear on the terrace.

When the sun began to set, Noriko pulled up in the silver van. Her face looked pale, her hair dishevelled.

I pattered up to her, but she said simply, 'Sorry, Nana. You'll have to wait,' and walked swiftly inside.

IN THE HOSPITAL ROOM, all Noriko could do was watch.

The waves on the ECG machine were getting steadily weaker.

She could just see the figure of Satoru lying on the bed, between the members of staff clustered around him.

As Noriko tried to slide between them, a nurse brushed against the bedside cabinet and two framed photos – a family photo with Noriko, and one of Nana – fell crashing to the floor. They were hurriedly retrieved and put back in place.

Just then, a cat's mewling from outside resounded around the ward. Mewling and mewling.

'Can I—'

Noriko spoke before thinking.

'Can I bring in the cat? Satoru's cat?'

She'd never made such an absurd request in her life.

'Please – let me bring in the cat.'

'Please don't ask!' the matron scolded. 'If you ask, then we'll have to say no!'

As if propelled by a cannon, Noriko raced out of the ward. Ignoring the No RUNNING IN THE CORRIDOR sign, she clattered down the stairs, two at a time.

Then she burst through the front entrance.

'Nana! *Naaana!*'

Nana leapt out of the darkness like a silver bullet. He jumped into Noriko's arms and snuggled into her body. Then Noriko raced back up to the ward.

'Satoru!'

The staff were reaching the final stages of the procedure. Noriko elbowed her way through them to Satoru's side.

'Satoru, it's Nana!'

Satoru's closed eyelids quivered. As if fighting against gravity, they slowly lifted.

Unable to move his head, his eyes searched from side to side.

Noriko clasped Satoru's hand and placed it gently on the top of Nana's small head.

Satoru's lips moved faintly. She thought she heard him say, 'Thank you.'

The ECG screen flat-lined.

Nana nuzzled the top of his head up and down against Satoru's lifeless hand.

'I'm afraid he's passed away,' the attending doctor said, and the matron added, 'We can't have you bringing a cat in here. You'll have to take him out now.'

Suddenly, the atmosphere seemed to lighten. Some of the nurses even gave a small smile.

And then, as though something loose had finally been wrenched open, the floodgates broke.

Not since she was a little girl had Noriko wept with such abandon.

The staff members finished unplugging the monitors and took them away.

'Make sure you take the cat outside immediately,' the matron reminded her, before swiftly leaving the room.

Noriko's throat throbbed, until she couldn't weep any more.

Suddenly, she felt a rough tongue licking the tops of her fingers. Gently, ever so gently.

'Let's take Satoru back, Nana.'

As if in response, Nana licked her hand again.

'Nana, is it okay for me to believe that Satoru was happy?'

Nana nuzzled his forehead against Noriko's palm, and then once more began to lick, ever so delicately.

# EPILOGUE

## Not the End of the Road

P̲URPLE AND YELLOW FLOWERS in bloom as far as the eye can see.

The earthy, warm colours of Hokkaido in autumn.

There I am, chasing a honeybee.

Stop it, Nana.

A voice sounding flustered. He grabs hold of me and carries me tightly in his two hands.

What if you get stung?

Satoru, smiling as he reprimands me.

Hey, it's been a while. You look good.

I rub my small cheeks against Satoru's arms.

All thanks to you. How about you, Nana?

I'm good – all thanks to you.

Ever since the day he departed on his journey, every time Satoru visits me it's always in this field. This open expanse, with its riot of flowers.

But I wonder how many more of these winters I can put up with.

You're getting on.

Don't say that. Just because you left this world when you were younger than me, don't get carried away.

A mellow sun shines but there is a dusting of snow fluttering in the air. Another winter is just around the corner.

And I'm finally coming to the end of my story.

Satoru left behind a list of people he was close to or who had helped him in one way or another, together with a note requesting that they all be contacted and thanked. Which Noriko duly did.

I was amazed by how many condolence letters and telegrams flooded in. Not just from friends, but from colleagues and former supervisors at work, and even from former school teachers of his. Even people Noriko didn't contact, but who had heard the news, got in touch.

Noriko was terribly busy dealing with them all. I think it was good for her to be busy so soon after Satoru passed away. I was worried she would become depressed after his death. 'She might age a whole decade,' Satoru told me when he was in hospital. 'So you've got to stay by her side, okay?'

In the end, Noriko aged maybe two or three years, max. I mean, she wasn't that young to begin with (about as old as Momo the cat, I imagine), so a couple of years wasn't going to make much difference. Oops. If Noriko or Momo heard that, I imagine they'd be pretty upset!

'Satoru knew so many kind and thoughtful people, Nana.'

As well as sending their condolences, people asked to come and light incense and pray in memory of him. They were all people I knew, and Satoru had left handwritten letters for all of them.

On Honshu, the main island, the cherry blossoms were blooming further and further northward. They wouldn't start blooming in Hokkaido for a while, though. On the streets of Sapporo, there was even some leftover snow in the shadier spots.

The weather was dodgy for a few days, but on the day

of the funeral the sun shone. It was as though Satoru was welcoming his guests. It was a quiet affair, with only Noriko and relatives on his mother's side attending. I waited at home while the funeral was taking place. I can't say I'm much interested in the ceremonies humans like to conduct.

I was in the hospital to see him off. But he's still here, in my heart, so I don't need a ceremony to remember him.

Later, several people I hadn't seen for a long time arrived at Noriko's and my apartment: Kosuke and Yoshimine, and Sugi and Chikako.

They all wore black and didn't say much, their lips drawn.

'Please – come on in. I ordered some sushi. It's fine to have some, now that the period of abstinence is over. And I'll make some soup to go with it, so please wait a moment.'

Noriko said this cheerfully, but the others were concerned they were causing too much trouble.

'I'm so sorry you have to do all this,' Kosuke said, and all the other guests murmured their agreement, bowing to her.

'Don't worry about it. I'm delighted to have Satoru's friends over.'

'Do you need some help?' Chikako said, standing up. But Noriko waved her offer away.

'Don't worry. I'm really not comfortable having people in my kitchen.'

As usual, Noriko didn't mean anything by this, but it made Chikako feel a little awkward. If Satoru had been there, he would have said, 'I'm sorry. Her heart's in the right place.' But Noriko kept her eyes fixed on the chopping board and didn't seem to notice.

If she had seen Chikako's reaction, she would no doubt have said something else and dug herself into an even deeper hole.

'Instead of helping, why don't you play with Nana?'

Oh – well played, Noriko, to get me in on the act. I went over to Chikako and rubbed the side of my body up against her leg.

'Hi, Nana. I wish we could have taken you in,' she said, reaching down to fondle my tummy.

'Hm?' Kosuke said. 'Did Satoru arrange a meeting with Nana for you, too?'

'He did,' said Chikako and Sugi together, both smiling wryly. 'Our dog and Nana didn't really get on, so it didn't work out.'

'For me, it was my kitten that was the problem.' This from Yoshimine.

This seemed to break the ice, and they all started telling each other their Nana stories. 'Nana is surprisingly fussy,' Kosuke said. An uncalled-for remark, if you ask me.

Oh, really? And who's the one who quarrels with his wife and gets all weepy about it, eh?

It seemed that Kosuke and his wife had adopted their own cat. Kosuke proudly showed a few photos on his phone of a pretty silver mackerel tabby. You and Satoru might have been childhood friends, but there's no need to show off your cat like that.

Then Yoshimine pulled out his mobile phone. 'Me too,' he said, passing it around.

*Et tu*, Yoshimine? That cat with the silly name, Chatran, had grown up to be a rugged young thing. He was an expert at catching mice now. Perhaps my efforts to train him had paid off.

'Satoru met him, so I thought I'd show him this photo.'

Yoshimine got up and went over to the altar in the corner of the room set up in memory of Satoru.

'If I'd known we were going to be bragging about our pets, I would have brought my photo album,' Chikako said, but she and Sugi weren't about to be left behind when it came to animal photos. Both of them pulled out their mobile phones to share photos of Momo and Toramaru.

'We run a bed and breakfast that welcomes pets, so please stop by sometime,' Sugi said, pulling out some business cards. They all exchanged addresses.

You know something, Satoru? After you passed away, the people who miss you all became connected.

'If you wouldn't mind taking one, too?' Sugi said to Noriko, handing her his business card as she brought in the sushi.

Yes, please, give her one, I thought. I'd like to lie down all snug on top of that boxy warm TV set again someday.

'Thanks. I haven't climbed Mount Fuji in ages, and that would be lovely.'

Go right ahead, Noriko. I'll hold the fort back at the Sugis', on top of that toasty TV.

They all sat around the table, eagerly sharing stories about Satoru.

'What? So Satoru didn't swim in junior high?' Kosuke blinked in surprise.

'That's right.' Yoshimine nodded. 'When he was with me, we were in the gardening club together. Was he that good at swimming?'

'He was in the swimming club all through elementary school. He won a lot of races in big galas, and people had high hopes for him . . . Did he swim in high school?'

Sugi and Chikako both shook their heads.

'He had a lot of friends, but he wasn't in any particular club.'

'Really? He was such a fast swimmer. I wonder why he gave it up.'

As she gave me some tuna sushi, minus the wasabi, Noriko casually murmured, 'Must have been because you were no longer with him, Kosuke.'

Oh, Noriko, what is *wrong* with you? You're usually so clumsy with words, but occasionally what you say is spot on and cuts right to the quick. Kosuke's face fell.

'As he was writing those letters, he told me a lot about all of you. About how he and you, Kosuke, ran away from home with the cat, and that he was a little bit worried about you since you and your wife had argued.'

Come on now – you didn't have to say that!

'We're fine now,' Kosuke hurriedly explained.

'He told me how much he enjoyed helping you, Yoshimine, and your grandmother in the fields, and how you always did things at your own pace and ran off in the middle of class to take care of the greenhouse, and how anxious that made him.'

Yoshimine looked out of the window, as if deep in thought.

'He also told me how Sugi and Chikako loved animals and were a great couple together, and how happy he was when he got to see you again in college.'

Kosuke's bottom lip began to tremble, and Chikako wiped away tears.

'But why . . .' Sugi muttered. 'Why didn't Satoru tell us he was sick?'

That's disappointing. Just like always, you stammer out things you shouldn't.

You really don't understand why?

'I kind of understand why,' Yoshimine said. 'He wanted to say farewell with everybody still smiling.'

Bingo!

Satoru loved all of you guys.

That's why he wanted to take your smiles with him.

Simple enough, I think.

'The letters . . .' Kosuke's voice was weepy, but he smiled all the same. 'In his letters, he wrote about all kinds of funny things. Silly jokes and gags, too. I laughed, thinking, This can't be his last letter, can it?'

They all chuckled.

When it was time for them to leave, Noriko drove them to the airport in the silver van. Satoru's silver van had become Noriko's silver van. Though no longer the magical vehicle that had shown Satoru and me so many amazing sights, it still did the job.

Okay, then. Before Noriko got back, I had something to do.

Noriko came home after dark, and as she wandered into the living room she let out a scream.

'EEEEK! Nana! You did it again!'

I'd removed every single tissue from the box and was sitting quietly in the corner contemplating the result of my actions.

'You don't use them, so why take them out?'

Good point. But as you focus on your anger and on tidying up the floor, don't all your sad feelings begin to lift a bit?

'What a waste! What a complete waste!' Noriko

muttered as she strutted around picking up the tissues, but then, as if letting out a soft puff of air, she laughed.

∽

SEVERAL YEARS HAVE PASSED.

Kosuke turned his shop into a studio specializing in pet photos. This was thanks to Satoru's advice, he told us, so I was welcome any time for a free photo session. But the New Year cards that arrive have begun to feature bizarre photos of his dressed-up mackerel tabby, who always looks so sullen. So I'll take a rain check.

Now and again, Yoshimine sends us vegetables he's grown. *I'm sure Hokkaido has great vegetables, too*, he writes in the short note he always includes in his vegetable box. It's more than Noriko could eat by herself, so she's kept busy running around, sharing them all out with her friends and acquaintances.

Noriko did take me once to stay at the Sugis' B&B. The purpose, though, was for her to climb Mount Fuji while the Sugis took care of me. While she was gone, I enjoyed the warmth of that boxy TV underneath my belly to my heart's content.

Momo had become a refined old lady cat, and nervy Toramaru had transformed into quite the sensible pooch. Sorry about back then, he apologized.

I almost forgot – the Sugis have a child now. A precocious little girl who greeted Noriko with a 'Welcome, Grandma,' which made her blush.

The berries on the mountain ash along the streets are bright red again this year. And pretty soon there'll be a constant layer of snow on the ground.

How many times, I wonder, have I seen this red that Satoru taught me?

One day, Noriko brought home a very unexpected guest.

'What should I do, Nana?'

A siren-like wail was coming from the cardboard box she was carrying. Inside was a calico kitten. Not an *almost*-calico, but a genuine one. And because it was a pure calico, it was, of course, a female.

'Someone abandoned it under the apartment building. I thought, since you're already here, Nana . . .'

I sniffed at the wailing siren and gently gave it a lick under its chin.

Welcome. You're the next cat, aren't you?

'We're just back from the vet. Nana, do you think you two will get on?'

Save that for later. Right now, you've got to get some milk into its tummy. The little gal seems hungry.

I got into the box and snuggled close to the little creature to warm it up, and she promptly tried to find some nipples on me. Sorry, sweetheart – no milk to be had here.

'Oh, she's hungry, isn't she? I've bought some milk for her. Let me warm it up.'

And so Noriko plunged into a life in which this demanding young kitten has her wrapped around her little finger every single day.

∽

PURPLE AND YELLOW LIKE A FLOOD.

The field I saw on our last journey, bursting all the way to the horizon with flowers.

When I dream about these colours, Satoru always appears.

Hey, Nana. How have you been? Aren't you a little worn out?

I suppose so. Momo at the Sugis' left us a few years ago. I might not last as long as she did. And we have a new cat that's arrived to take over.

Is Aunt Noriko doing okay?

Having that kitten seems to have put a spring in her step.

Noriko named the kitten Calico, after her looks. When it comes to giving the most obvious, second-rate names, you and Noriko are like two peas in a pod, I must say.

Really? It's hard to think that she'd take in a stray cat.

Satoru seems genuinely moved.

Surprisingly, she has the makings of a cat fanatic. Whenever she gets sushi, she always gives me the *toro*, the best part of the tuna.

Even I might have trouble handing over the *toro*, Satoru says, laughing.

This is the first cat of her own she's ever had.

That's right.

We live together, but I'm not Noriko's cat.

For ever and ever I am your cat, Satoru. That's why I can't become Noriko's.

So, about time, maybe, for you to come over here?

Yeah, but I have one more thing I need to do first.

Satoru looks puzzled. Ahem, I say, and twitch my whiskers.

I have to help little Calico get on her feet. Noriko isn't training her at all.

If she becomes too spoiled and ever tries to make it on

her own on the streets, she'll be toast. At the very least, I've got to hammer the basics of hunting into her.

To be fair, when you grab her by the scruff of the neck, her legs do immediately contract, so she clearly has potential. Much more than, say, Chatran at Yoshimine's.

Once Calico can make it on her own, I think I'll set off on my journey. To this place I see only in dreams.

Tell me, Satoru. What's out there beyond this field? A lot of wonderful things, I'm thinking. I wonder if I'll be able to go on a trip with you again.

Satoru grins, and picks me up, so I can see the far-off horizon from his eye level.

Ah – we saw so many things, didn't we?

My story will be over soon.

But it's not something to be sad about.

As we count up the memories from one journey, we head off on another.

Remembering those who went ahead. Remembering those who will follow after.

And someday, we will meet all those people again, out beyond the horizon.

If you're wondering why the cat on the front of this book does not resemble Nana, it's because we found this original Chinese brush painting while researching images online and fell in love with it.

Entitled 'Man and the World', it is painted by Shuai Liu, a Chinese painter with cerebral palsy whose work is supported by Chilture.com, a studio of disabled artists. If you'd like to know more about what they do and view other work by disabled artists from China, visit www.Chilture.com.

# The Goodbye Cat
## by HIRO ARIKAWA

**The uplifting new cat book from the bestselling author of**
*The Travelling Cat Chronicles*

**'Quirky and life-enhancing'**
*The Times* **Biggest Books of the Autumn**

---

*Against changing seasons in Japan, seven cats weave their way through their owners' lives.*

A needy kitten rescued from the recycling bin teaches a new father how to parent his own human baby.

An elderly cat hatches a plan to pass into the next world as a spirit so that he and his owner may be together for ever.

A colony of wild cats on a holiday island shows a young boy not to stand in nature's way.

A family is perplexed by their cat's devotion to their charismatic but uncaring father.

A woman curses how her cat constantly visits her at night.

**Bursting with empathy and love,** *The Goodbye Cat* **explores the unstoppable cycle of life as we see how the steadiness and devotion of a well-loved cat never let us down.**

www.penguin.co.uk

**HIRO ARIKAWA** is the million-copy-bestselling author of *The Travelling Cat Chronicles*. Her brand-new homage to cats, *The Goodbye Cat*, brings together seven cats as they weave their way through their owners' lives. Featuring all the irresistible wit, wisdom and warmth that thousands of readers across the world love so much in her storytelling, *The Goodbye Cat* is published into multiple languages. Arikawa's latest book, translated into English by Allison Markin Powell, is the bestselling, much-loved modern classic, *The Passengers on the Hankyu Line*. She lives in the city of Takarazuka, Japan.

**PHILIP GABRIEL** is a highly experienced translator from Japanese, and best known for his translation work with Haruki Murakami.

## Readers around the world love
# *The Goodbye Cat* by
## HIRO ARIKAWA

'Irresistible and warms your heart. Mitori is so cute,
so annoying, so sweet, that I am weeping'
★★★★★

'I'm grateful to have read this wonderful book'
★★★★★

'This is not human. It's full of cat flavour'
★★★★★

'An essential book for cat-owners'
★★★★★

'A wonderful and inspiring read for all cat-lovers'
★★★★★

'Seven stories: Ideal for when you want to read but
can't concentrate on a full novel'
★★★★★

'Thoroughly enjoyable. Difficult to put down'
★★★★★

'Got this as a remembrance of our little old puss who
passed away, beautiful book in looks and sentiment'
★★★★★

'Touched my heart and I'm not really a cat person'
★★★★★

'Interesting to get a glimpse into life in Japan.
Have bought two copies, one as a Christmas gift'
★★★★★

# The Goodbye Cat

## Seven Cat Stories

### HIRO ARIKAWA

Translated from the Japanese by Philip Gabriel

doubleday

# The
# Goodbye Cat

A SMALL DISH OF SOY sauce sat on the dining table. A couple of grains of rice floated in it, left over from breakfast, no doubt. The dining table was covered by a light-blue tablecloth printed with a random pattern of small flowers.

Kota Sakuraba placed a palm into the soy sauce, then pushed it firmly on to the tablecloth, being careful to avoid the flowers. He left his palm there for a bit, then lifted it to reveal a small, soy sauce-coloured plum blossom print.

*Not bad, not bad at all.*

Gazing at his work, Kota again dipped his palm in the soy sauce. Then again, and again. More and more soy sauce-coloured plum flowers bloomed on the blue cloth.

*I'm in the zone today.*

He was about to make a fourth and a fifth print when—

'Hiromi! Stop that!' Mum scolded.

*Damn, I'm busted*, thought Kota, ears pinned back against his head.

And then—

'Did I do something?'

It was Hiromi, in the hallway, peeking uncertainly into the living room. He was the Sakuraba family's second son.

Kota was the Sakurabas' third-eldest son – scratch that, *cat* – but Kota considered himself the second eldest, with Hiromi as the third in line.

'Goodness,' Mum said, seeing Hiromi in the doorway.

· 3 ·

She burst out laughing. 'Sorry! I'm wrong. It's Kota. He's being an artist again.'

That's what the Sakuraba family called it, when Kota made his little paw prints: he was *being an artist*.

Kota found this hard to fathom, since it wasn't like he was painting a picture.

'You're at it again, eh?' Hiromi said, coming over and giving Kota a gentle flick of the finger on his forehead.

'*Please don't do that*, Kota,' Mum said. 'Our tablecloths have your paw prints all over them.' She grabbed Kota under his belly and wiped his soy-soaked paw vigorously with a damp dish cloth. Kota didn't like feeling wet, and so quickly withdrew his paw and began to lick it.

'Hey, Mum, I wanted to say the same thing to you: *please don't do that*. I don't like these false accusations.'

'Ah, sorry. It just came out. I never make that mistake with Masahiro.'

The mistake Mum always made was to mix up Hiromi and Kota's names. She never called Masahiro, who was Hiromi's elder brother, *Kota* by mistake. All three shared the same Chinese character in their written names, though in Kota's case, it was pronounced differently.

'Well, it seems like it's the youngest child's fate to be confused with the family cat.'

'Really?' asked Mum.

'I looked into it,' said Hiromi. 'My friends and I talked about it at school. The ones that get called the wrong name are all the youngest in the family.'

'Well, what do you know,' Mum said, as she attempted to scrub away Kota's paw prints from the tablecloth. 'Masahiro's left home, hasn't he? So if I'm going to mistake anyone's name, Hiromi, you're the only one still around.'

· 4 ·

'What do you mean?' Hiromi shot back with a smile. 'You've been doing it since I was a kid. Mistaking me and Kota.'

Mum just laughed it off. 'I'm going to have to wash this,' she said, folding her arms and looking disapprovingly at the tablecloth. 'How did Kota learn to do that naughty trick, anyway?' she wondered aloud.

Mum's familiar response, to which Kota wrinkled his nose.

*That is no naughty trick. It's a dry run.*

Kota was honing his skills at making paw prints, readying himself for when the time came.

HIS EARLIEST MEMORY WAS OF being terribly cold.

During the rainy season twenty years ago, for whatever reason his mother had left him behind.

His eyes still hadn't fully opened. Crawling out of the space behind a wall where they'd been sleeping, he searched everywhere for the mother cat's warmth. Instead, he was hit by drops of cold, drizzly rain.

In the normal course of things he would have passed away soon after that, if he had not been rescued by the father of the Sakuraba family.

The Sakurabas already had a cat: a Persian with an abnormality in its iris that meant the pet shop was about to get rid of it. Mr Sakuraba rescued this cat, too. He was the kind of person who, if he crossed paths with a cat in trouble, could not simply walk on by.

*So you are one lucky cat*, the Persian, named Diana, said, as she let the motherless kitten suck at her teats. Mr Sakuraba, rather clumsily, often fed him milk, but the need

· 5 ·

to suck at a warm body with arms and legs like his mother's could not be met by a plastic bottle.

'I want to give him milk too!' their son, Masahiro, whined.

Diana told the kitten that a human sibling was on its way, and that Masahiro would become an older brother. The pregnant human was in the hospital, she added.

'No. It's too tricky for you to feed him, Masahiro – I'll do it.'

This was true, because once when Masahiro tried to feed him a bottle of milk, he stuck the teat so far down the kitten's throat, he coughed for hours afterwards.

Apparently while the father was out during the day, he'd asked Mrs Sakuraba's friends, women from the neighbourhood, to look after him.

He'd been drinking milk every three hours, which became every five hours and then three times a day, by which time the kitten's eyes had fully opened.

It was the day that Mrs Sakuraba and her new baby, their second son, came home from the hospital.

'Whoa, he looks like a monkey! What a weird face!' Masahiro yelled when he came back from kindergarten, earning a slap from his mother. Diana, though, was inclined to agree with him.

*You looked just like a monkey yourself,* she thought.

Mrs Sakuraba had really been looking forward to seeing the kitten her husband had rescued while she was at the hospital. After getting the new baby to sleep, she came over to take a proper look.

'My, what a beautiful silver tabby!'

This was the moment the kitten first learned what his fur colour was called.

'Have you decided on a name yet?'

· 6 ·

'Not yet,' Mr Sakuraba said a bit evasively.

'But hasn't it been two weeks since you found him?'

'I wasn't sure we were going to keep him, and if we give him a name, then we'll get attached.'

Mr Sakuraba had planned to wait until his wife was back before making a decision about keeping him. But she had no qualms at all.

'Let's adopt him,' she said. 'The kitten seems to get on well with Diana, too,' she added. 'You're such a sweet cat now, aren't you, Diana?'

The Persian cat puffed up with pride.

'So, what shall we call him?'

'We need to name the baby first.'

The family had to register a new baby's name with the city hall within two weeks, and so Mr and Mrs Sakuraba had been discussing the matter of the baby's name for quite a while. As the older boy's name was Masahiro, the one thing they'd agreed on was that the new baby's name should contain the same character, *hiro*.

Mr Sakuraba decided on the name Hiromi, while his wife, after much deliberation, wanted Kota – the *ko* being another reading of the character *hiro*. Neither would back down, and so finally they did paper-scissors-rock to reach a decision. Mr Sakuraba won.

Mrs Sakuraba seemed quite disappointed.

'Hiromi . . . isn't a bad choice, but won't people mistake it for a girl's name? I still think Kota might be better.'

'No complaints, please. I won the game, fair and square. If you like the name Kota so much, why don't we call the kitten that?'

And that's how he came to be named Kota.

\*

By the time little Kota was scampering around the house, baby Hiromi still had not learned to roll over. All he could do was shuffle his arms and legs around while swaddled in a blanket.

*Do you think he's okay?* Kota asked worriedly, but Diana reassured him. *Don't worry, he'll be fine.*

Masahiro had been exactly the same, according to her. Humans took longer to grow up than cats.

Even so it seemed to be taking a very long time. Kota often went to check on little Hiromi as he lay squirming around like a caterpillar.

*Wonder if today's the day he'll stand up*, thought Kota, fixing him with a good long stare. *Nope, he's still a caterpillar.*

*Hurry up and learn to stand. If your mother abandons you, then what?* Kota suddenly remembered that his mother had left him behind because he had been such a weak kitten with extremely wobbly hind legs.

One day as he was nervously scanning Hiromi's sleeping face, the baby's eyes popped wide open.

No one had been able to tell if the baby could actually see anything much, but now those unseeing dark eyes seemed to be focusing at last.

And then he gave a little laugh.

Mrs Sakuraba came scurrying over.

'I hope you're not trying to bite him,' she said.

*That's pretty rude*, Kota thought and was about to stalk off, when Hiromi suddenly burst into a loud wailing.

'Hmm . . . Do you want Kota to stay?'

Mrs Sakuraba patted Kota on the head, and put her hands together in apology. 'I'm sorry. And here you were getting along so nicely.'

*Ah well, she's the mum, so best to cut her some slack.*

· 8 ·

Kota nestled down beside the baby's pillow and Hiromi was now all smiles and contented gurgling.

'Isn't that nice, that Kota wants to have a cuddle with you?'

With a heart-melting smile, Mrs Sakuraba stroked Hiromi's cheeks, and then gave Kota's throat a fond scratch.

*Ah, I get it. From the way Mum is smiling, it doesn't look like she's going to get rid of this caterpillar any time soon. All's well that ends well*, Kota thought, giving Hiromi's milky-scented forehead a good lick, thus provoking another happy gurgle of laughter.

Kota began to curl up beside Hiromi every day, until Hiromi learned to roll over and around, then to crawl, then to stand on his own two feet, and finally to walk. Before you knew it, he was racing around the house like a member of some infant biker gang.

He fell down a lot though, and bumped into things, his motor skills still only half developed. Meanwhile, Kota was fast growing into a fully fledged adult cat.

*Humans really do grow up so slowly*, he lamented.

*You're right*, agreed Diana. *By the time the baby reaches Masahiro's age, you could have become an adult five times over.*

When Kota was still a kitten, Masahiro had looked huge to him, but now he seemed just like some young kid.

The *fusuma* sliding doors were by this time completely in shreds. They could repaper them all they wanted, but they still ended up in tatters. Mrs Sakuraba decided to let them stay ripped.

'We have two gangsters in our house,' she complained. This was about the time Hiromi was starting kindergarten and Masahiro had gone up to elementary school.

· 9 ·

Masahiro was more often now referred to as the *onee-san* – the older brother. Most of the time it was when he was being scolded: 'You're the *onee*-san, so you should behave yourself.' Masahiro would come back with a sullen, 'I hate being the *onee*-san.

'You never tell Hiromi to behave. It's not fair!' he'd protest.

His parents had to admit he had a point.

'Okay, so let's make Hiromi an *onee*-san, too,' Mrs Sakuraba proposed.

'But Hiromi doesn't have a younger brother.' Masahiro was pouting again.

'No, but he does have Kota,' Mrs Sakuraba said with a smile.

*What? Just a second!* Now it was Kota who was getting flustered. *I'm the older brother, actually. I was born first, and besides, I'm already an adult.* But Kota could protest all day – humans couldn't understand cat talk.

'Hiromi, you can be Kota's big brother, can't you?'

'You bet!'

*You bet wrong there, little man.*

But this cat protest, too, was completely ignored.

*You'd best give it up. Humans only understand their own language*, Diana said.

'So you'd better set a good example as an older brother for Kota,' said Mr Sakuraba.

Kota dropped his eyes and lay belly down on the floor.

*When it comes to walking, running, jumping, even grooming, a kid like Hiromi has absolutely nothing to teach me.*

'Before we have dinner, I'd like the two of you to clean up the room, okay? You're both older brothers now, after all.'

'*Okaay*,' the two boys answered, a more docile response than usual, and began to gather up the toys and picture books that lay scattered across the floor.

This is how Kota became the third son – *cat* – in the family hierarchy, even though by any measure nothing could have been further from the truth.

BUT NOW, YEARS LATER, HIROMI had grown properly big, Kota thought as he gazed up from where he sat at his feet. Hiromi had got up late this morning, but still did not seem to be in a hurry.

Hiromi had grown taller than Mr Sakuraba, even taller than Masahiro.

'Morning!' Hiromi greeted his mum, who immediately shot back with, 'Took your time getting up, that's for sure.' Hiromi shrugged. Being a college student seemed a pretty leisurely occupation.

Hiromi gave Kota's head a good pat as he passed by on his way to the fridge. He took out a carton of milk and started to glug it down.

'Don't drink straight from the carton!'

'But I'm going to finish it.'

Hiromi drained the milk, rinsed out the carton in the sink and dropped it in the recycling bin.

*Ah hah!*

As Hiromi was crouched down arranging items in the recycling bin, Kota, who had been sprawling on the sofa, suddenly saw his chance. He shot over to him and scrambled up Hiromi's back.

· 11 ·

'*OUCH!!*'

By the time Hiromi had let out this overblown yell, Kota was already at his shoulders.

'You scratched my back with your claws, Kota!'

*But I have to bare them – how else can I get a grip?*

Kota now had a good purchase on Hiromi's shoulders and was gazing down, his face inscrutable. Mrs Sakuraba, who had been rifling through the morning mail at the dining table, looked over and giggled. 'He's never satisfied until he's climbed on top of your shoulders at least once a day.'

'Kota has been doing that since he was little. Though it used to be Dad he preferred to climb.'

*No, you've got that all wrong.*

Kota stuck out a paw on the back of Hiromi's neck.

*Since he was little.* Kota had not been little at all. Only Hiromi and Masahiro had been little at the time. When he'd started to climb up Dad's back, he was already an adult.

'I wonder what it was that made him start that habit.'

'Diana never did anything like that, so he's not imitating her.'

He did it on purpose, so calling it a habit was a bit annoying. What made him do it? It was Hiromi himself (and Masahiro).

But Hiromi seemed to have forgotten all about it. *He might be big now, but he's still an unreliable little kid, as far as I'm concerned.*

At the time, the Sakuraba boys were crazy about riding on their dad's shoulders, and whenever their father had a day off, they pestered him.

And as Kota observed the boys in action, he caught on

to the rules. The one who got on top of Dad's shoulders was the winner. And it wasn't because he was lifted there.

So a few days later, Kota sat back, quivered his behind as he focused on his target, then took a leap and clambered up Mr Sakuraba's back. Ignoring Mr Sakuraba's shouts, Kota kept climbing, grabbing tightly with his claws on to the back of his neck, thus winning the cooing admiration of the boys.

Later, as Masahiro grew big enough to overtake Mr Sakuraba, so it was Masahiro he began to climb.

*I'm the tallest of all, guys. Cool, right? Who's lowest on the ladder now, eh?*

A few years later Hiromi outstripped Masahiro in height, so Kota switched again. Perceiving how Kota always chose the tallest person to climb, Masahiro wasn't best pleased that the cat was now perching on Hiromi.

'You'd better get down. You're getting heavy.'

As Hiromi tried to pull him off, Kota beat him to the punch and took a deep jump down to the floor, landing in a single beat.

*You wish!* He had judged the landing perfectly.

'Amazing, amazing,' said Mrs Sakuraba, clapping her hands.

'He's so agile it's hard to believe he'll be twenty this year. And his fur still looks brand new.'

'True. When I took him for shots at the vet's the other day, the people in the waiting room couldn't believe it. A cat with such fluffy fur and he's twenty?'

*You're spot on,* Kota thought proudly. *No signs of ageing here, thanks very much.*

*Pretty soon my tail will show signs of dividing in two.*

· 13 ·

'WHAT ABOUT LUNCH? WILL YOU eat at college?' Mrs Sakuraba asked her son as he gathered up his books.

'I'll eat before I go.'

'Would udon be okay?'

'Sure, anything's fine.' Hiromi sat down, and began to leaf through the newspaper.

*Oh!* Kota leaped on to the dining table. Silently stepping across the cloth, he plunked his behind on to the page that Hiromi was reading.

*Hey, how about looking at me instead of that paper? Better on the eyes to gaze at a beautiful grey tabby cat than at all that minuscule writing. And allow yourself to glide your hand down my glossy, fluffy fur.*

'Why are you squatting right where I'm reading?'

'Diana used to do the same thing.' Mrs Sakuraba smiled nostalgically as she chopped rhythmically with her kitchen knife. From the faint but sharp smell, she was clearly about to top the udon with thinly sliced spring onions. Not exactly the kind of thing to tempt a cat.

Diana had taught him that if cats ate spring onions, they'd get sick.

The irresistible smell of dashi stock wafted their way, as Mrs Sakuraba brought in two bowls heaped with udon, a bowl for her and one for Hiromi.

'Here you go.'

Kota sauntered off the newspaper and stepped down on to Hiromi's lap. Once Kota had settled down comfortably, Hiromi, as a matter of course, placed his left hand on the cat's spine to hold him.

'That's another strange habit that he's got back into,' Mrs Sakuraba said.

*What are you talking about?* Kota wasn't sitting on

· 14 ·

Hiromi's lap because he wanted to. *It was you, Mum, who first told me to sit with Hiromi while he ate.*

This was back when Hiromi was finally old enough to chew his food. He sat in a high chair and often grew bored of sitting and tried to escape, and so Mrs Sakuraba used to carry Kota over to accompany him at his meal.

'See? Kota's beside you. So be a good boy and eat your food.'

She picked the right person – scratch that, *cat* – for the job. Since he was a kitten, Kota had slept beside Hiromi every night, and the boy had grown attached to him.

When he got tired of sitting still, Mrs Sakuraba would pause in feeding him, and let him stroke Kota, and eventually Hiromi no longer tried to wriggle out of the seat.

*He can't even eat by himself,* Kota thought, a bit stunned, *but if he's this fond of me, I guess I have to pitch in, as part of the family.*

And ever since then, he always sat with Hiromi while he ate.

Around the time Hiromi stopped eating from a tray and began eating at the table, this whole ritual started to fade away, until, in recent years, Kota had felt inclined to revive this duty.

'Doesn't he make it awkward to eat?'

'Not really. Kota's getting old and maybe he's feeling a bit lonely, too.'

*Okay – go ahead and admit it. It's your habit, not mine – not being able to eat unless I'm with you.*

'But eating with one hand doesn't seem polite. You have to figure out another way.'

Mrs Sakuraba said this each time, but had yet to come up with any practical solution. Today, too, Hiromi ate with

his right hand, and when he had finished, he tickled Kota's throat.

*That's it, just there. A little more to the right.*

'Well, I guess I'd better be going.' Hiromi stood up and lowered Kota to the floor.

'Just a second – these are yours,' Mum said, handing him the letters she'd been sorting through earlier. 'You're getting a lot these days.'

'It's because I've been applying for seminars and things about job hunting.' Hiromi turned over a postcard and frowned. 'This one I don't need. An offer from some kind of beauty salon.'

'Ah, another person who thinks Hiromi is a girl.'

As Mrs Sakuraba had predicted, people often mistook Hiromi's name for a girl's.

'Around the time of the Adults' Day celebration, you got mail shots for women's kimonos, too.'

Hiromi handed the postcard back to his mother. 'You can chuck out this one.'

'Oh, there's a discount card attached. Can I use it?' she asked.

'Be my guest. Go get all your wrinkles and stuff smoothed out.'

'I wonder if it really does help with wrinkles,' his mother mused, a serious look on her face as she tugged at her cheeks.

'Hiromi's a nice name and all,' Hiromi said, 'but I guess there's nothing we can do about other people's mistakes.'

His mother stopped tugging at her skin and smiled. 'You think it's a nice name?'

'It's okay.'

'Tell your dad that next time.'

*Yeah*, Kota agreed. *It would be good to tell him.*

Hiromi gave an awkward smile. 'I'll get around to it,' he said and gave a little wave as he went out of the door.

'I HATE THE NAME HIROMI!'

Hiromi had begun to whine about his name around the time he started elementary school.

The first time their teacher took the register, he mistook Hiromi for a girl's name.

'Hiromi Sakuraba-chan,' he called, adding the *-chan* suffix used for girls. But the way he tried to correct his mistake made it even worse.

'Oh, I'm sorry. You're so cute with those long lashes, I mistook you for a girl.'

After that everyone in class would tease him with 'Hiromi-*chan!*' His self-respect took a dive.

But the person who was even more upset about it was his dad.

'I just hate the name Hiromi!'

Every time Hiromi threw a tantrum and yelled about his name, Mr Sakuraba looked about ready to cry as the choice of name had been his.

'Don't say that,' he said. 'It's a nice name. One of the characters in Mum's name is in it, too.'

Mrs Sakuraba's name was Akemi, sharing the same character, *mi*, as in Hiromi. For Masahiro they'd taken the *masa* part from Mr Sakuraba's name, Kazumasa, and he'd decided that for their second son they'd use the same character for *hiro*, and combine it with the *mi* in his wife's name. Mr Sakuraba had been quite pleased with the choice of

· 17 ·

name, even before they knew the sex of the baby. 'Hiromi will work whether it's a boy or a girl,' he said. 'We're good either way.'

'Maybe Akihiro or Hiroaki would have been good, too.' *Aki* being the same character as the *ake* in Akemi. Mrs Sakuraba chuckled as her husband's face crinkled up tearfully even more.

'At least we should have reversed the characters and named him Yoshihiro,' she said. *Yoshi* being another reading for the character *mi*.

'No way.'

She patted her disheartened husband on the head.

'For each of the boys we took one character from your name, and one from mine, and both brothers share the character *hiro* in their name, one in the end, one at the beginning. It's clear how we choose names in our family and I think it's a good name.'

'NO, IT IS NOT!' Hiromi yelled. 'Kota would have been a better name! Let's switch our names!'

Put on the spot, Kota was a bit confused. *Hey, don't involve me in your squabbles, okay?*

'Kota's a boy's name. And Mum wanted to name me Kota when I was born.'

His father was so dejected about the whole matter, he finally left the room.

'Oh – *poor Dad*,' Masahiro said, exaggeratedly, so they'd take notice. Hiromi felt a little put out, but the next thing his brother said was going too far.

'You're being a bad boy, Hiromi.'

'Am not! Let me switch names with Kota!'

'Absolutely not.' His mum wouldn't even consider it. 'He's been known as Kota for six years, so imagine how

· 18 ·

much confusion that would cause him to suddenly change names.'

'No, it won't. Kota's a cat.'

'I don't like it when you say such things – you think because Kota's a cat, you can do whatever you like to him.'

His mother's strict tone got to him, and Hiromi fell silent. When Kota gazed up at them from underneath the chair, Hiromi looked away, teary-eyed.

Thinking maybe she'd gone too far, Mrs Sakuraba gathered Hiromi up and gave him a cuddle.

'Kota's been called that for six years and taking away a name that has so much love wrapped up in it would be hard for him.'

Hiromi still looked unconvinced.

'Your name, too, Hiromi, is filled with six years' worth of love from your family. Do you want to throw away your mother's love for you?'

With her crocodile tears Mum was putting on quite a performance, and Hiromi became suddenly panicked. 'No!' he yelled.

Hiromi was yet to be persuaded, but the last thing he wanted was to make his mother cry, so he had to agree.

*Humans. I tell you – all this ruckus over a name.* Underneath the chair, Kota shrugged. Diana twitched her tail knowingly.

Names, she explained, were very important to humans. Back in the day when they named her, there was quite a commotion between the mother and father.

She herself, she explained, had become the Sakurabas' cat well before Masahiro arrived. His parents had made their decision to name her by paper-scissors-rock back then, too.

· 19 ·

Diana was the name of a character in the book *Anne of Green Gables* that Mrs Sakuraba liked. But Mr Sakuraba had suggested something else.

'*Furama?* That's a weird name,' was Mrs Sakuraba's response to her husband's suggestion.

Apparently, it was the name of the hotel they'd stayed at on their honeymoon abroad.

Mr Sakuraba had rescued Diana just after they'd come home. He wanted their new cat's name to remind them of their honeymoon, but what his wife most remembered about their hotel was forgetting her key and locking herself out for hours. Not a pleasant memory, so she had come up with Diana.

Mr Sakuraba had always been a bit of a romantic.

Just as they had used a character from his name for their eldest son, so he had wanted to include one of the characters from his wife's name for their second – a very sweet and charming gesture.

The evening after Hiromi's crying fit, Mr Sakuraba went to his son's room, looking as if he'd come to a painful decision. 'Here's the thing, Hiromi,' he began. 'We can't change your name right away, but after you grow up, if you still dislike it you can apply to the court and if they give you permission, you can change it. So even if you can't do it now, you can consider it when you're older.'

Lying curled at the foot of the bed, Kota poked his nose against the soles of Hiromi's feet.

*Hey, you're awake, aren't you? Tell him you don't need to change your name. You know it's no big deal – just some friends teasing you.*

Hiromi gently pushed Kota's head away with his feet,

all the while pretending to be asleep so he wouldn't have to answer his father.

All this commotion over names came to an abrupt halt thanks to their cousin Satsuki-chan, who came to visit during the summer.

Satsuki-chan, who was in the first year of junior high, was a gentle, good-natured girl, and the Sakuraba boys adored her.

Masahiro and Hiromi were continually scrambling around and competing for her attention. As they both vied to show her their good side, they sometimes ended up quarrelling.

For whatever reason, Masahiro had criticized Hiromi for whining about his name.

'*You're* the one who got upset just because the teacher called you Hiromi-*chan*.'

Hiromi went bright red and started pummelling Masahiro, and soon the boys were rolling around on the floor in a scuffle.

Satsuki-chan intervened and listened to each boy's side of the story in turn. Puzzled, she turned to Hiromi: 'Why do you hate your name, Hiromi-kun?'

'Everyone laughs at me because it's a girl's name.'

'But I think the name Hiromi is really nice,' Satsuki-chan said, smiling. 'When I was in kindergarten, the first boy I liked was called Hiromi. Written with different characters, though.'

These words hit Hiromi like a bottom-of-the-ninth, come-from-behind grand-slam home run. Even more so when she told him what a wonderful, handsome boy this first love of hers, Hiromi, had been.

'It's just a coincidence you two have the same first name. Don't think that means she actually likes you, Hiromi!'

Masahiro did his best to dampen Hiromi's good mood, but to no avail.

'Ahh, thank you so much,' Mrs Sakuraba said to her later. 'He seemed to really hate it when his friends teased him, and it's still bothering him. And it's made Mr Sakuraba doubtful as well.'

'Well, then, you'd better apologize to your dad,' Satsuki said, trying to persuade him.

'Maybe later,' Hiromi answered, awkwardly.

All this did put an end to Hiromi's crankiness about his name. And to his idea of switching names with Kota.

When the new school term began, his friends seemed to have stopped teasing him. They'd done it because it was fun to get a rise out of him, and now that it didn't seem to bother him any more, the teasing came to an end.

So Satsuki had helped Hiromi by teaching him how wonderful his name was. And his dad, too, after all his brooding over the issue.

It was in the summer of the following year that Satsuki-chan became a helpful influence on the family once again – this time for Kota.

The summer holidays the following year began on a depressing note.

The school's pet rabbit had died just before the summer break. And it had happened just when Hiromi's class had been looking after it.

Part of their duties involved bringing in vegetables to feed the rabbit, which was one of Hiromi's favourite tasks. The children also vied with each other over who would get

to clean out the rabbit hutch. Then, one morning, they discovered their beloved rabbit had given up the ghost, and was now lying stone cold in a corner of the hutch. The entire school was saddened, but Hiromi's class was especially hard hit.

'Mum, what does *lifespan* mean?' Hiromi asked, when he came back from school that day.

The children were considering holding a class meeting, convinced they'd done something wrong in their rabbit-care duties, but their teacher had told them that the cause of death was related to *lifespan*.

'It's no one's fault at all,' he'd explained. 'The rabbit was old and had reached the end of its lifespan.'

Rather than feeling relieved to hear it wasn't their fault, Hiromi grew concerned about this idea of lifespan and death.

His mother wracked her brains to explain, but Masahiro, entering the rebellious stage, butted in with a mean remark.

'Lifespan is lifespan. When you've reached the end of your lifespan, you die. Didn't you even know that?'

It hadn't been so long ago that Masahiro himself had lost sleep worrying over the same thing.

'Mum, are you and Dad really going to die someday?' he'd asked in the middle of the night, clinging to his mother and crying his eyes out. And now he wanted to act all high and mighty because of all the suffering he'd been through.

'It's not just the rabbit. Kota and Diana, too, will die sooner or later. And also—'

'Masahiro!' his mother said angrily and shooed him away. She wanted to get him out of the room before he finished what he was intending to say: *And also Mum and Dad*.

· 23 ·

But for Hiromi, the mere thought that Kota and Diana would die like the rabbit was a terrible shock.

'*No way!*' He burst into tears, for all the world like he did when he was a baby bawling his eyes out.

'NO! Kota can't die! Or Diana!'

He yelled Kota's name first, not because he wasn't fond of Diana, but because he and Kota had a special bond. Sure, they were cat and human, but really they were more like brothers. What child, suddenly confronted with the notion that his brother is going to die, wouldn't burst into tears?

*Say what you like*, Kota thought, *but Masahiro's carried his meanness too far this time*, and he whipped his tail around grumpily and furrowed his brows.

'Don't worry. Kota and Diana are super healthy. They won't die any time soon.'

Mrs Sakuraba did her best to soothe Hiromi, and after a while he became worn out from crying and stopped.

But that didn't change the fact that one day Kota and Diana would die. Hiromi was utterly dejected and that was his emotional state as the summer holidays came around.

There were times when the tears would roll down his cheeks as he slept. And at those times Kota, on his nightly patrols, would press his paws on the boy's cheeks and lick away the tears from either side of his nose.

His heart squeezed, Kota went to Diana. *Tell me*, he asked her as they were sitting under a chair in the living room in the middle of the night. *Is it possible for us to live longer than Hiromi?*

Surely, they just needed to live a single day longer than Hiromi to put an end to his terrible distress.

*Unfortunately, I think that may be tricky*, said Diana. *If*

· 24 ·

*they have a long life, humans can live to nearly a hundred years old. But I've never heard of a cat living that long.*

*Can't we do something? I can't stand to see Hiromi feeling so low. It's making me sad.*

As the two cats brooded over this, the summer holidays were about to begin and Satsuki-chan would be coming to visit again.

Hiromi liked Satsuki-chan so much, and having her around did cheer him up, yet still there were times when his face clouded over and he'd heave a deep sigh.

One day Satsuki-chan was checking the boys' holiday homework when Hiromi let out a particularly heartfelt sigh. He didn't seem to be focusing on his work.

'What's wrong?' That's all Satsuki-chan said, but it was enough for Hiromi's eyes to fill with tears. They trickled along those long eyelashes before rolling down his cheeks.

Hiromi explained how the school rabbit had died just before the summer break. He remembered how Masahiro had said some mean things at the time, but Hiromi was restrained and didn't say a word about this to Satsuki.

'And Kota and Diana will die someday too, won't they?' he asked.

'I suppose so . . .'

Satsuki-chan tilted her head, baffled how best to respond. You couldn't very well expect a second-year junior high student to give advice on a subject like this.

'But because Kota and Diana are cats . . .'

*So what if we're cats?* Unconsciously Kota leaned forward at her words. Diana was doing the same.

'When cats have lived for ten years, they transform completely. Or is it after twenty years?' Satsuki-chan pondered

· 25 ·

this question for a time but gave up. 'Anyway, they say that if they're brought up with humans for a long time, they turn into something else.'

'*I* know,' Masahiro jumped in, having kept quiet all this time. 'They change into *nekomata*, like *yokai*, supernatural spirits. And their tails split into two.'

'Right, right,' Satsuki-chan said, nodding. He'd hit the nail on the head.

Not convinced, Hiromi asked, 'So after they become *nekomata*, they can't die?'

'I don't imagine so. Because they're supernatural spirits. I've never heard of spirits dying.'

Hiromi's expression brightened, as if discovering light in the midst of unending darkness.

'Diana's already fourteen, isn't she? She's lived a long life, so it might be possible.'

'Right?' Satsuki-chan said, seeking Masahiro's agreement. Masahiro, concentrating on his homework, didn't reply.

But at least he didn't deny that spirits actually existed.

'Yay!' Hiromi sprang up, the first genuine smile breaking out on his face in weeks.

Now if Kota and Diana could become *nekomata*, then that would solve everything.

But how did you go about becoming a *nekomata*? Did it mean you just had to live a long life and you could turn into one?

There had to be some procedure, was Diana's opinion. Whenever there was a change in a human's life, they had to go through procedures at the city hall, she said. Like when someone was born, or they died, or got married. When Masahiro and Hiromi were born, the parents registered their names at

· 26 ·

the city hall. *You were just a kitten, then, Kota, so you might not remember.*

*Now that you mention it*, Kota said. He was thinking back to when Hiromi was whining about wanting to change his name. His father had told him that to change his name he'd have to apply to the court.

*I'm sure that's it*, said Diana. When a cat became a *nekomata*, it also had to apply to the city hall or court.

*But what are they, exactly – these procedures?* asked Kota.

There had to be *documents*, Diana said, suddenly brimming with confidence and twitching her ears excitedly. When Masahiro and Hiromi's names were given to the city hall, their parents had filled in these documents. Then they had stamped them with their *hanko* seals.

*What should we do? We can't write*, said Kota.

*But even cats can stamp a seal, can't they?* Diana replied.

*Okay, but where do cats get seals?*

This question stumped them for the longest time.

They didn't find a seal in time for Diana.

'I'M BACK!'

Hiromi had come home from college.

His mother called out from the kitchen, 'Good timing. Would you go shopping for me?'

Hiromi put his bag down on the sofa, unable to hide his irritation.

'You should have called or texted me before I got in.'

'But I only just remembered I'd forgotten to buy something.'

'Okay, okay. So what do you need?'

· 27 ·

He might grumble about it, but Hiromi always went along with his mother's requests.

'*Kanikama* – crab sticks.'

'Ah – right,' Hiromi said, getting it immediately.

'Today's the anniversary of her death.'

'So we need to offer some at our altar.'

Diana had died one winter a decade earlier when Hiromi was in elementary school and *kanikama* had been one of her favourite foods. The day she died, it had been a warm respite from the bitingly cold weather.

'Hard to believe it's been ten years since she passed.'

'She lived a long life – sixteen years.'

'She could almost have become a *nekomata*.'

Hiromi and his mother looked at each other and giggled.

*What's this?* Kota thought as he sat watching from under the dining table. It had been a long time since they'd mentioned *nekomata*.

*Hey guys, I'm still here, you know.*

With that, Kota decided to clamber up Hiromi's back, making him screech in pain and duck his head as Kota dug his front claws into his scalp.

'Not now, Kota. I have to go shopping.'

Hiromi lifted his arms to grab him, but Kota slipped from his grasp and lightly, deftly, landed on the floor. He rubbed the top of his head up against Hiromi's knees and Hiromi, with a resigned smile, scratched him under his chin.

'So you're already twenty-one, aren't you. About time you transformed, I'd say.'

*Leave it to me. So Diana didn't make it in time, but I've found a* hanko *seal.*

· 28 ·

Wallet in hand, Hiromi was about to walk out of the living room when he heard his mother's voice. 'Oh, one more thing.' She had a lot of *one more things* when someone was about to leave. 'Pick up your suit from the cleaner's. It's ready.'

'Oh, you got it cleaned for me? Thanks!'

Hiromi was knee deep in job applications now and often he'd go out dressed in a suit like his father.

'Hurry now. We'll have dinner as soon as your father gets back.'

'Boy, it's one request after another in this place.'

Laughing, he headed towards the front door, while Kota trotted at his heels, to see him off.

'Don't buy the wrong kind of *kanikama* now. Diana always liked the low-sodium kind,' called his Mum.

'Would you like something, too, Kota?' Hiromi patted Kota's head as he headed out, only to return with some of Kota's favourite cod-with-cheese.

DIANA'S CONGENITAL EYE PROBLEM HAD been getting worse. One eye had become so cloudy she could no longer see out of it. The good eye, too, had got steadily worse, and perhaps afraid of roaming around too much when her vision was so bad, Diana limited her movements to going to the litter tray or to her food bowl.

That made her lose her appetite, and her normally lustrous fur grew matted – she became the very picture of a decrepit cat.

The vet had apparently told them she was reaching the end of her lifespan.

· 29 ·

*It's a pity, but it looks like I won't become a* nekomata *after all,* Diana murmured as she hobbled around the house. She still hadn't figured out where to get a cat seal. Kota didn't offer any unnecessary words of consolation. Diana's lifetime was coming to an end.

Diana could never become a *nekomata*. That was all.

No cat could defy its fate.

*Will Hiromi cry his eyes out?*

*Of course he will. But it's okay – I'll be with him.*

*I'm counting on you.* Diana's voice was low.

The winter was harsh that year. The moment came when the biting cold was beginning to let up and the sun had begun to shine brightly.

Surrounded by them all as they said their final goodbyes, Diana quietly breathed her last.

*I hope you can become a* nekomata, *Kota.*

Moments before she died, she uttered these words.

Hiromi cried his eyes out, and did not eat the whole day, but then the next day, as if making up for it, he stuffed himself.

Kota reassured him. *If you eat a lot and sleep well, you'll be fine.*

As he ate a lot and slept well, little by little Hiromi grew bigger, stronger, able to handle more sadness. He no longer teared up at thoughts of missing Diana. Even with her gone, he was able to smile again.

Still, there were nights when he would cry in his sleep.

And Kota would secretly lean his paws on either side of his nose, and lick away those salty tears.

*It's okay. I'm here with you. I'll become a* nekomata *and watch over you, Hiromi.*

· 30 ·

This was what Diana had wanted.

A *hanko* seal, a seal, a cat seal. So where did you get hold of this cat seal, the kind you needed to carry out the procedure of becoming a *nekomata*?

All of a sudden, he found it.


'If you could stamp your seal here, please.'

It's what the package delivery boys always said.

Mrs Sakuraba kept the seal for deliveries near the front door, stamping it on to a receipt before taking in the package.

On that particular day, the seal was missing and she couldn't find it anywhere.

'Can I just do a fingerprint?' Mrs Sakuraba asked the delivery boy.

'Sure.'

She touched her index finger to the red ink pad and pressed it against the receipt.

From below, Kota watched the whole process with great interest.

How to put it? He'd found the bluebird of happiness, right here, in his own house.

A cat's seal was right here, in the paw he'd been born with.

Now that he knew, all that remained was to practise. Sometimes he saw Mrs Sakuraba mess up stamping a seal and being forced to redo it.

To avoid this, he'd have to master the art of stamping his print. And so Kota diligently went about practising paw prints.

Whenever Mrs Sakuraba left the red ink pad out, Kota jumped at it, and whenever Mr Sakuraba was stamping a template greeting on to his New Year cards, Kota stretched

· 31 ·

out his paw into the red ink and stamped his print on to the pristine white cards.

'KOTA!' Mr Sakuraba roared.

'It's okay,' his wife said. 'You can pretend they're plum blossoms.' She took out a calligraphy pen and added some branches.

Kota found lots of things worked for practising paw prints: the paints Hiromi used for art, spilled ketchup, and yes, soy sauce, even though it wasn't red.

The only thing he needed now was the document.

One day soon, while sorting through the mail, Mrs Sakuraba would surely say, 'Kota, this one's yours,' and pass him a document.

AFTER A LONG SEARCH, HIROMI finally decided to take a job at a travel agency. Whenever he helped organize trips for his club at college, he found he enjoyed it more than he'd expected.

On the day he received the still unofficial job offer, the family celebrated, and even though it wasn't exactly the anniversary of Diana's passing, they placed some of her favourite *kanikama* in front of her photo. Kota got some delicious chicken jerky to eat.

Masahiro wasn't there that day, but when he and his wife next came to visit, he brought a necktie as a present for his brother, to celebrate his new job.

His parents, naturally, also gave Hiromi a present. Mr Sakuraba gave him a wristwatch, while Mrs Sakuraba gave him a baby-carrier sling.

· 32 ·

Hiromi eyed it dubiously.

'What's this?'

'A sling. You use it like this.' She draped it diagonally across her body and placed Kota inside it. 'It's really to carry a baby with, but a cat fits too. Use this and you'll have both hands free, especially at mealtimes.'

'Makes sense. It's useful for sure. But is this really a present for me? Not for Kota?'

'I've been thinking about a solution for ages. And I happened to find this.'

'Well, I guess it's okay.'

During meals, Hiromi now placed Kota in the sling, keeping him close to his chest and freeing up his hands.

'But what a strange cat he is,' his dad said. 'A climbing cat, who also paints, and now that he's old, a cat you carry around.'

'He might soon start walking around on two legs,' added his mum.

'And finally turn into one of those magical cats.'

Hiromi smiled and patted Kota's forehead, which was poking out of the sling.

'Do your best to be a *nekomata*.'

Satsuki-chan, who'd first told him about *nekomata*, still phoned regularly. She'd taken a job at a company in her hometown and was even training the new employees.

Winter arrived, and so too the anniversary of Diana's passing, and then spring.

Hiromi began commuting to work wearing a suit.

'See you later!' he called, but his mum stopped him.

'You missed a bit shaving,' she said, tapping her own

chin. Hiromi ran back to the bathroom and picked up his electric shaver.

*Oh, his back is wide open!*

Kota quivered his tail in preparation to climb, but Hiromi, noticing him at the last minute, dodged aside. The jump failed to launch.

'Don't do that. I'm wearing a suit. It'd be awful if you ripped it.'

This newly ordered suit wasn't like the shirts and sweat-shirts he was used to wearing.

*Okay, I'll let it slide this time. But two times out of three, I'll look for my chance.*

Hiromi began to get used to Kota climbing up him even when he had a suit on and had started to shave with Kota squatting on his shoulder.

'Mum – could you make *tonkatsu* for dinner tonight?' Hiromi asked one day as he was coming in from work. This was in the autumn, and he'd been at the travel agency for six months.

'How come? Do you have a test coming up?'

Hiromi had never been picky about his food, so he didn't usually make requests like this – the only time being when he had an important exam, and then he'd ask for *tonkatsu,* or deep-fried breaded pork cutlets, considered lucky since the word *katsu* was a homonym for 'win'.

But he'd already graduated from college.

Looking up from below, Kota tilted his head, puzzled, until Hiromi revealed what was up.

'Yeah, I have an exam at work.'

Come to think of it, he had been staying up late these days, studying, thought Kota.

· 34 ·

His mother did her very best to make a nice meal of *tonkatsu*. When Kota was about to use the leftover sauce in a dish for his seal-stamping practice, Mrs Sakuraba screeched, '*Stop that!*' and Hiromi and his dad managed to block him.

The next morning, Hiromi set off for his exam in high spirits.

About a month later, Mrs Sakuraba was sorting through the mail. 'Oh!' she called out. 'Is this the exam results?'

She waited nervously until Hiromi got home, then did her best to hand him the notification calmly.

Looking tense, Hiromi opened the envelope.

Either because of his mother's *tonkatsu*, or perhaps because of Hiromi's own efforts, he'd passed with flying colours.

Kota looked askance as the parents whooped it up in celebration and instead placed his nose on the document to give it a sniff. *Don't you stamp a seal on this document?*

'What's the matter, Kota? You going to read it?'

*No, I was just wondering why it's taking so long for my document to come.*

Thinking, mistakenly, that Kota was interested in his notification, Hiromi explained its contents to him.

'This means I'm qualified to escort tours abroad.'

'When will your first trip be?' his mother asked, to which Hiromi shook his head.

'Who knows,' he said. 'The soonest people can escort a tour seems to be after a year with the company.'

He seemed excited, wondering when the first assignment would come, and what country it would take him to.

Winter arrived, and so too the anniversary of Diana's passing, and spring was now on its way.

· 35 ·

The following took place on one of those days before spring.

Hiromi was at the sink, shaving.

*His back is wide open!*

Kota jumped, trying to scramble up, but then—

*Oh gosh, what's wrong?*

He suddenly found himself falling off. Hiromi turned around, gazing down at him in shock.

*Couldn't do it – must be an off day for me.* Feeling awkward, Kota scuttled away.

From that day on, Kota could no longer climb up Hiromi's back. He tried over and over, but could never manage it again. Not only that, but he could no longer leap up on to the dining table. He had to jump on to a chair first.

The condition of old age that had caught up with Diana seemed to be grabbing hold of Kota as well.

*I guess I was a bit too complacent, since Satsuki-chan had said that if I ever reached twenty, I'd become transformed.*

And here was Kota, aged twenty-three. The next rainy season, he'd turn twenty-four.

He'd been so positive that once he'd got to this age, he'd become a *nekomata*.

But Kota's document never arrived.

*After all that practice stamping my print.*

Spring was around the corner. The cold snaps and warmer breezes contended with each other, the temperature fluctuating from day to day. There would be three cold days, followed by four warm ones, and in the midst of this, Kota carelessly caught a cold. His eyes became coated with an unusual film and Mrs Sakuraba took him hurriedly to the vet's.

· 36 ·

The vet put eyedrops in, but the cold lingered and Kota's strength began to fade.

*I get it. I don't have long to go.*

Just then, Hiromi's first foreign tour came through.

'Where is it?'

'France. A tour around Mont Saint-Michel.'

'That's wonderful! You wanted to go there, didn't you,' his mum said, but it was clear she was forcing herself to sound cheerful.

'Yes, I really did. But why *now*?'

'It can't be helped. If you tell them you can't go because you're worried about your cat, they'll fire you.'

Mrs Sakuraba used a dropper in the corner of his mouth to feed Kota his medicine. At first he struggled mightily, but then he gave in and let her have her way.

*If I waste time struggling, the little time I have left will slip away.*

'It'll be okay. It's only for one week, isn't it? I'm sure he'll wait for you.'

His mum might have said this, but her heart told her otherwise.

*No one believes it, but I believe in myself. I can hold out until Hiromi comes home.*

'So go and enjoy your trip. How can a cat who's lived twenty-three years not hold out one more week?'

Hiromi caressed Kota's fluffy fur, as if this was their final farewell, then he set out on his tour.

He called home every day. Morning and evening.

Sometimes the phone would ring just before dawn, and his mother would answer, never sounding annoyed.

'Don't worry. He's taking his medicine the way he should.'

Masahiro, who lived far away, came one time to see how Kota was doing.

'I think this is the end,' he said, before getting back in his car regretfully and driving home in the middle of the night.

*One night. Two nights. How many days has it been?*

Waves of gentle drowsiness kept washing over him, over and over.

*If I were engulfed by these waves, I would probably never wake up again.*

*But I'm not afraid. Because it's the place where Diana went.*

*Everyone goes there eventually. Father will, and Mother, and Masahiro . . . and Hiromi, too.*

*It's a shame I can't be here to see Hiromi on his way. After how Satsuki-chan told me about becoming a* nekomata *and all.*

*And here I am, so expert at making a paw-print seal.*

*I only wish I could have outlived Hiromi – even by a single day.*

*But Hiromi's all grown up now. Big and strong, the tallest one in the family. So tall, I can't climb up him any more.*

*So he'll be fine.*

*With that healthy body, he can surely handle any amount of sorrow.*

Another wave of drowsiness swept over him.

Suddenly a large hand stroked his head. Fingers tickled at his throat and slipped behind his ears to scratch.

A purr came out on its own.

*Stop it, I'll feel so good it'll make me sleep. And I won't be able to wake up.*

*Kota.*

· 38 ·

He felt like Hiromi was calling him.

*Hiromi.*

*Hiromi, Hiromi. Hi-ro-mi.*

*It's a nice name. So what if your friends teased you. No big deal.*

*The* masa *in Masahiro comes from your father's name, the* mi *in Hiromi from your mother's. And you and Masahiro both share the* hiro *part. It's like that game where you make a new word from the last syllable of the previous one.*

*And my name, too, has the same character for* hiro *in it. We're a matching set.*

*There is no other name that could connect you so completely to your family.*

*So, come on, go and tell your dad what a great name it is.*

HIS FATHER WENT TO THE airport to fetch him.

They took the highway and were home within the hour.

'Go now,' his father said, and Hiromi opened the door and rushed to the house while his father parked the car in the garage.

The front door was unlocked; he kicked off his shoes and ran in.

They'd made Kota's bed in the living room, in the warmest spot.

Mrs Sakuraba was tending him, her eyes swollen from crying.

'Is he still . . .?'

She nodded. Still alive.

Hiromi came closer. Trembling, he knelt down and,

· 39 ·

with the tips of his four fingers, started to stroke the little silver tabby head.

He tickled his throat and scratched behind his ear.

And Kota purred.

'Kota.'

The voice croaked. Kota, too, gave a feeble, hoarse meow.

The family had all taken turns stroking him, over and over, coaxing an occasional brief purr.

Near dawn the purrs suddenly stopped.

'Oh. I thought he was asleep—'

But he'd passed, and never purred again.

Hiromi was not sure why, but he didn't feel sad.

Just grateful.

'He waited for you, Hiromi.'

His mother's voice was gentle.

'So your first big job wouldn't be a sad memory.'

His father laughed.

'A climbing cat, a drawing cat, a carried cat and, to the very end, a considerate cat. A cat of many talents, for sure.'

'*Dad.*'

He didn't know why it happened then, at that moment. But the words spilled out, as if he had to get them out.

'My name is really nice.'

'What's this all about?'

'I really do think it's nice.'

He gently stroked Kota's still-warm body.

'Even if I were reborn, I'd want to be your child. And be named Hiromi and bring Kota up all over again.'

'You're leaving out Masahiro,' his mum teased.

· 40 ·

'If he asks me, I'll let him be my older brother.'

And if Hiromi asked his older brother, he would surely let him be his younger brother.

'So name him Masahiro again, and name me Hiromi.'

'Sure. That sounds good, I guess . . .'

# Bringing Up Baby

WHEN KAORI TSUKUDA CAME home from her parents' house, where she'd gone to stay when she was about to give birth, she found something major had happened in her absence.

Her husband Keisuke had stayed behind to take care of their home while she was gone. Keisuke, under the name *Keisuke Tsukuda*, written in katakana, was a mid-level manga artist who contributed to a boys' monthly magazine. A few years before, he'd had a hit series, but ever since then he had been confined to one-shot manga or short-term series, toiling away as the epitome of a reliable cartoonist.

He was, from the outset, the type of person who put his heart and soul into manga. The manga world was a harsh one, though, and you could give it everything you had and still never have any success. Kaori had laid down the law before she went to her parents' place: use this opportunity to sharpen up your domestic skills, she told her husband, though she didn't really expect the house to be shipshape when she got back.

Keisuke was supposed to collect her today at the Ueno station, but just before she got off the Bullet train, he had called, apologizing profusely for not being able to make it. He didn't have any looming deadlines, as far as she recalled, but with someone so completely dedicated to manga this was nothing new. With his wife away for a month, it was probably beyond him to straighten out the now messy, cluttered house

in a single day. This was a man who kept putting off his manga assignments, so expecting him to handle the housework on his own was a total pipe dream.

With the baby to carry and still not feeling a hundred per cent, she decided to grab a taxi from the station.

Before she left home, she'd ordered all the baby-related items she'd need. The only thing Keisuke had to do was assemble the crib before they returned, and she made it emphatically clear that if he didn't, he was a dead man. As long as he took care of this single task, she figured his life would be mercifully spared.

They lived in an odd house that they'd managed to acquire when Keisuke had his hit series. They knew they couldn't let the chance slip by and scraped together as big a deposit as they could.

When Kaori got home and rang the front doorbell, her husband wasn't in. Maybe he'd stepped out to the local convenience store? She opened the door with her own key.

She steeled herself for an appalling sight, but when she actually stepped inside, the house was a bit dusty, for sure, and there were opened cardboard boxes randomly piled up in the hallway, but overall the place was in decent order.

The cardboard boxes were mainly baby goods Kaori had ordered. Formula, diapers, baby wipes, a litter tray for a cat . . .

*Wait, what?*

She did a double-take but nothing had changed. A cardboard box that had held a cat-litter tray was right there, as clear as day.

Just then, the front door clicked open behind her.

'Oh . . .'

She turned, and when their eyes met, her husband let out a guilty little yelp.

· 46 ·

In one hand, he held a bag. No, not a bag, exactly, but a carrier for an animal. Out of which issued a siren-like wail.

'What on earth is – *that*!?' Kaori squealed, and the baby in her arms joined in the wailing.

THEIR BABY'S NAME WAS SHIORI.

Keisuke had named her.

They'd agreed from the beginning that Keisuke would choose the baby's name. Otherwise, Kaori felt he'd remain for ever an unreliable cartoonist focused solely on his work. When she first told him she was pregnant, he just looked vacant, and it was impossible for her to tell if he was happy or not.

On top of that he'd asked, 'Is it mine?' and war broke out between them. She'd fired off an instant 'I want a divorce!' machine-gun burst; Keisuke had yelled out, 'Mayday! Mayday!' and that was the extent of their hostilities.

'No – *no*, that's not what I meant,' Keisuke kept on saying, repeating himself like a broken record.

Kaori, exhausted by her anger, asked, 'If that's not it, then *what*?'

To which he snapped, 'I just can't believe it.'

'Okay, then we'll get divorced,' she replied, and laughed almost sneeringly at him.

He waved his hand. 'No, you don't understand.'

'Don't understand *what*?'

Keisuke said something along the lines of not being able to believe that he was going to be a parent. Or at least she thought so. She'd been so upset that now she couldn't really recall his exact words.

'I couldn't believe someone as hopeless as me was going to be a parent,' he explained over and over through his tears. A complaint you might very well expect from Keisuke, whose whole life was manga and who tended to be a bull in a china shop in any social situation.

'ALL I DO IS DRAW manga but I'm involved in tax evasion? Me?'

When his big hit series came out and his income sky-rocketed, Keisuke was so pressed by work that he forgot to submit his latest income tax return. But the fact remained that he'd let it slip and had therefore defaulted on paying a hefty amount of tax.

At the time, Kaori, who worked as an editor at the same publishing company, had been selected as the personal assistant to Keisuke, in charge of managing his affairs, and her very first task was to find an accountant to resolve this non-payment problem.

'Paying taxes is the duty of every citizen. *Comprenez-vous?*' said Kaori.

Having the writer of their signature series involved in tax evasion was a blow to the publishing company's reputation. They could replace his series with another, but there was no stand-in for a scandal. *Whatever you do, get him to pay his back taxes* was the eyes-only order that came down from the company president.

After that, she didn't receive a single manga manuscript from him. Kaori's job now as his personal assistant meant dealing with the accountant, her tasks entailing such things as unearthing utility bills and receipts for work expenses from his studio and getting them in some kind of

order, as well as the extra task of keeping a record of his expenses.

Around this time the accountant urged them to file an income tax return, and when she reported this to Keisuke, he said, 'For goodness' sake,' and left it all up to her. Kaori had to devise a company name for him and register his business officially. Around the time the manga series was reaching its grand finale, Kaori was transferred to a different section within the publishing company. The accounting department. Considering what she'd achieved as personal assistant to *Keisuke Tsukuda*, it made sense.

When he heard she was going to continue to be in charge of his accounts, Keisuke grew pale and apologized to her in tears. Turning on the tears was standard operating procedure for him, in all kinds of situations.

'I don't get why you're making me the head of a company all of a sudden,' he said.

'How dare you say that! You're the one who created this mess, and I was the one who had to clean it all up.'

She didn't owe him anything, she thought, so she could have just slugged him one and left. But just as these feelings welled up, Keisuke told her, *I don't know what I'd do without you*. And this led to a proposal to *Marry me*, which only reinforced what an idiot he was when it came to social interactions.

Even so, for her there was none of that starry-eyed *I love you more than ever* type of development.

Except—

Kaori had really liked the *Keisuke Tsukuda* manga and had read them even before his big hit series.

Throughout the years she'd been working as his personal assistant, she'd seen how socially inept he was, and

was sure that if she stepped aside, the time would come when he would be ruined financially. For one reason or another – non-payment of taxes or tax evasion, or perhaps because a friend or some woman had tricked him out of his savings. Whatever the reason, it was inevitable.

If that happened, she wouldn't be able to read his manga any more, she thought, which would be a great shame.

And that thought made her blurt out, to his sudden marriage proposal, 'Sure, if you like me . . .' And the deed was done.

'Someone like me can be a dad?' he'd asked.

Keisuke's tears continued to flow. *It isn't a question of* can you, *pal*, she thought. *You're* going *to be one and that's that.*

In the end, her response boiled down to just two words: *Be one.*

Keisuke may have noticed how worked up she was – that she would only accept *Yes!* as an answer – and so he nodded his assent.

But her pregnancy went by with no visible change in him, Keisuke still his usual undependable self. His seed had been sown and taken root, but that wasn't enough for him, she concluded.

When their daughter was born and she was in the maternity hospital, Keisuke seemed less moved by the experience than a little afraid. Out of a sense of awe for a new life? Maybe that would explain his reaction to becoming a father.

At least he could be given the task of naming the baby, she decided. The way he'd incorporated the character *ri* from her name, Kaori, into the baby's, Shiori, was something a father might come up with, and she was impressed. Kaori's parents, and Keisuke's too, praised him to the moon

· 50 ·

for coming up with it. The unspoken understanding being that praising him might finally help him grow up.

Please be patient with him, her parents-in-law had said, asking her to take good care of him. And she planned to – but still she thought, *Shiori, your papa is a harder nut to crack than I reckoned.*

'WHAT'S GOING ON HERE?'

Kaori had given milk to the crying Shiori and laid her to sleep in the bouncer in the living room, and now was the time to face each other.

'Right . . . so, can I let it out?'

The kitten inside the carrier, is what he meant. It was an orange tabby cat. Its nose was pink, so the pads of its feet were probably pink too. Kaori was familiar enough with cats to deduce this much from a quick glance. They'd always had cats when she was growing up and even now her parents had one.

'Keep it shut.'

Now that they were in the same room, she knew she'd lose her resolve if the cat started wandering around.

'Until when?'

*When, where, who, what, why, how?* At this point the only answers were to *who* and *what*. *When, where, why* and *how* had Keisuke picked up a stray cat?

'Well . . . it was about three weeks ago, maybe?'

*Hey – you've been keeping it that long!* she was about to yell, but stopped at *Hey*, seeing how it made Keisuke flinch and, her common sense working, realizing she might wake Shiori.

· 51 ·

'Where?'

'The rubbish collection point.'

The local neighbourhood bins were diagonally opposite their house. What trap lay in wait in the space of just a few dozen metres?

'Because you told me never to let the kitchen waste pile up.'

Three weeks ago, Keisuke had, at Kaori's insistence that the rubbish not pile up, picked up a cat.

*Wait a second – that doesn't make sense.*

'I went to dispose of the rubbish and I spotted a cat that'd been thrown away.'

'You don't have to use that *Don't let the kitchen waste pile up* line any more. It has nothing to do with it.'

'It was in a Mikkabi brand tangerine box.'

*An amazing memory for detail.*

'I was the very first one to take out the rubbish.'

Keisuke tended to be a night owl, so it was easiest for him to take the rubbish out early in the morning after he'd stayed up all night. That way he wouldn't forget.

'As I was the first to arrive, the Mikkabi tangerine label kind of leaped out at me. I thought, *Hey, today's not the day for recyclable waste.* I wondered if it was okay to leave it out like that.'

Amazing that he'd remembered the waste collection schedule, and she couldn't help a few tears welling up at how he was awakening – at long last – to what society expected of him.

'I thought, *Hmm, maybe I should flatten the box.*'

The kind of consideration an adult would show, but hard to say if that was good or bad. It wouldn't do to have others think he'd been the one to violate the rules about

what kind of rubbish on which day, but adult wisdom dictated that he should just tut, make a face and let it pass. How things worked normally in their neighbourhood was that, in a case like this, if someone else showed up, you should say something like, 'Isn't it non-recyclable waste today?' and just ignore the tangerine box so that when the rubbish truck arrived and slapped a *Cannot Be Collected* label on the box, leaving it behind, the person who'd put it there would realize his mistake and take it back.

In any event, Keisuke, wanting to display a civic-responsibility spirit, was about to crush the tangerine box.

'I thought, *Hey, there's still a couple of tangerines inside*, but when I looked, it turned out that one was a marmalade kitten, and the other was a tiny black one that looked a bit like a mouldy tangerine . . .'

'They call that a tortoiseshell.'

'The kittens' eyes weren't open yet, and the tortoiseshell one was already cold. It was probably too small to survive. So I brought the other one back home for the time being and thought I'd take it to a vet.'

The vet disposed of the dead kitten. He instructed Keisuke on how to feed the other one with milk and how to deal with its waste. Its fur was clean, with no fleas or ticks, so it seemed like it'd been a house pet and then discarded. Maybe the kittens had been too much for the mother cat to cope with.

'The vet said that if it were a stray, it'd be full of fleas and ticks by now, since its sibling had died before it.'

When a host dies, fleas and ticks immediately move to another host. And here the destination might have been the warm little orange tabby in the same box.

'The vet said that, when it's weaned, to bring it in for a blood and stool test.'

*Weaned? What are you talking about?*

'When your own daughter is still an infant?' Kaori asked incredulously.

Back at her parents' home, they'd waited on her hand and foot, but now it was all up to her and she wasn't sure what to do. Add to that managing their home every day, a husband with few social skills – and now an unweaned kitten? It was all too much.

Inside the carrier, the kitten meowed and started to scrape at the lid. *Let me out, let me out.*

*For goodness' sake, I can't think straight.*

'Two unweaned infants – it's like some impossible game . . .'

'It's not two. Spin's already eating solid food . . .'

'What the – you've already *named* it? Give it a name and you'll grow attached to it. That's a problem. Why do you think I put you in charge of naming Shiori? Anyway, we need to find someone to take it.'

Taking the kitten to her parents' was a last resort. They used to have two cats, and now only had one, so there was an opening. It'd be a problem if the cats didn't get along, but they could always keep them in separate rooms if they had to.

Mention of someone else taking Spin had Keisuke protectively shifting the carrier behind him. The hands can be as eloquent as the mouth.

'I . . . I thought if I abandoned it, I wouldn't be qualified any more.'

'What do you mean, *qualified*?'

'I mean, Shiori's been born and all . . .' He looked at her pleadingly. 'I thought, *Shiori's been born now, but if I abandon this little kitten I couldn't be a parent.*'

*You didn't have to take it in – it wasn't necessarily going*

· 54 ·

*to die.* But that was too much sophistry and she couldn't voice it. The sibling kitten in the Mikkabi tangerine box, the tortoiseshell one, had indeed died.

If he'd abandoned this orange tabby, it would have died and he'd be the one who'd left it to its fate. Having the mindset to come up with such a compelling story with such speed was what made Keisuke Tsukuda *Keisuke Tsukuda*. The kind of story where you relied on others – where someone else was sure to rescue the kitten if you didn't – that would never make a convincing manga. It was the mindset of a person who'd take the initiative and crush the box. A person who wasn't a hero would have nothing to do with the tangerine box and would therefore not discover the kittens inside.

'It's a Schrödinger's Kitten, isn't it,' said Keisuke.

Until the kittens were actually observed, it was unclear whether they were dead or alive. If Kaori had been the one taking out the rubbish that day, she would have followed the waste collection rules and never noticed them, and the cat would never have existed as part of the Tsukuda household's universe.

*Keisuke Tsukuda,* though, did observe the kitten and even gave it a name, so the kitten in the Mikkabi tangerine box became a fixed part of the Tsukuda family.

*Show the same mindset when it comes to Shiori, okay? Otherwise you're dead.*

'Why weren't you here when we arrived?'

'I had to pick it up at the vet's . . . they called me.'

It goes without saying that Keisuke at this point was blubbering. His emotions fluctuated so wildly that what he said had to be true.

'Yesterday morning, Spin started vomiting.'

· 55 ·

Cats were creatures that did a lot of vomiting – vomiting after eating, after drinking, vomiting up hairballs – but when a little kitten vomited it was scary.

'I checked and it had chewed an eraser, and there was part of an eraser mixed in with the vomit.'

That required going to the vet's.

'They did an X-ray and an ultrasound but didn't find any foreign object inside. I checked the piece of eraser the cat had vomited against the original eraser and I think it had vomited up everything. The vet told me that if there's any left, it'll come out in the cat's stool, but advised me to let them keep it there overnight for observation. And I just got the call a while ago saying that it was fine and to come pick it up.'

Keisuke's shoulders shook with a sob.

'I . . . if it had died, I don't know what I'd . . .'

He broke down, crying, and didn't finish the thought.

Piecing together his broken words between the sobs, Kaori realized he was saying that it had been his fault for leaving the eraser out.

It was true that he'd never taken care of a pet before. If the kitten happened to die on him, it would be like a giant axe had split apart his hero's sensibility.

The orange tabby kitten was scratching at the gaps in the carrier.

*Good thing you're a strong cat, you.*

'I'm sorry I couldn't pick you guys up at the station.'

'Well . . . I guess it couldn't be helped. Its name is *Spi—*?'

'*Spin.*'

'Spin? Like turning, rotating?' She rotated a finger, asking him how he'd come up with the name. Was it connected to the way a cat would spin round and round chasing a toy?

'Exactly.'

Keisuke pointed at a book on the low table. One of Kaori's books.

*I remember – I was reading it just before I left the house,* she thought. It'd been lying there a whole month and he hadn't put it away?

'When the kitten first opened its eyes, the first thing it played with was the ribbon *shiori* – the bookmark – in that book.'

There was a blue ribbon bookmark poking an inch or two out of the bottom of the book.

'It kept on batting at it. It was so cute.'

'Then let that cute thing out.'

As Keisuke opened the carrier, the orange tabby batted at Keisuke's hand. Keisuke seemed used to this.

As Kaori picked up the kitten, she realized it had been decades since she'd felt this kind of soft, downy fur. Below the forlorn little butt hole, which looked like a small line made in clay with a tiny spatula, there were no fluffy little cat balls.

'So it's . . . female?'

'Good catch.'

'But doesn't Spin sound more like a boy's name?'

'But she's Shiori's little sister.' She was playing with the *shiori* bookmark.

So when he'd named the cat, thoughts of Shiori had indeed crossed his mind. For Keisuke this was quite an achievement.

'Shiori, look. It's your little sister!'

He held up the kitten and swung her towards Shiori's pillow. Spin gave the baby's head a gentle sniff. Spin had soft downy hair, and so did Shiori.

· 57 ·

Perhaps because Shiori had a milky odour, Spin began to purr and groom Shiori's soft hair.

Shiori woke up, her eyes swivelling towards the kitten. She shouldn't be able to see properly yet, but she did seem to be staring at Spin. She shouldn't be able to smile yet either, but she seemed somehow to be smiling.

The two of them seemed to hit it off.

One reason the house had been cleaned up more efficiently than Kaori had anticipated was so that Spin wouldn't mistakenly swallow something she shouldn't. The vet had drilled into Keisuke's head how dangerous it was for cats to eat something they shouldn't, and Keisuke told her how while Spin was at the vet's he'd stayed up all night tidying the house to avoid history repeating itself.

'When I was cleaning up, I came across all kinds of things on the floor that Spin might accidentally swallow. If she swallowed, say, a piece of string, the vet told me they'd have to operate and cut open her stomach.'

Kaori suddenly noticed that the Lego and plastic models that had been piled up on the sideboard in the living room were now stored away in a clear plastic case. Many was the time she'd cut her foot when she stepped on a fallen piece, and she'd told him either to put them away or get rid of them, and had bought him the plastic case. But for years the case had just sat there, gathering dust.

One little cat could convince him when a million rants from his wife could not. *Well*, she thought, *I can live with that*. Was there a woman, or a man, in this world who could beat a cat?

'And the things that Spin might swallow Shiori might

as well. So I thought I'd better straighten out the house before Spin and Shiori came home.'

Goodness. What had happened to the Keisuke she knew? When it came to the cat, he'd got the master–servant relationship back to front but he had worked out, nonetheless, that what was dangerous for Spin would be equally dangerous for Shiori.

'All that's left is to vacuum,' Keisuke said, getting to his feet. He was even taking the initiative when it came to housework.

'The mop should be enough. You'll wake Shiori.'

After Spin had raked her claws softly a few times through Shiori's downy hair, the baby had fallen asleep again in the baby bouncer.

'Good point. Spin would be frightened too.'

Kaori suddenly thought of something.

'Now, did *I* buy that bouncer?'

She recalled that when she'd been checking out all the baby-related goods she'd need, she'd put it lower down on the list since it might not be used all that long.

'Oh, I bought that. I figured if Spin's running around, she might step on Shiori.' After her eyes had opened, she'd become more active and mischievous, Keisuke explained. 'It came a couple of days ago and I assembled it. I'm glad it arrived in time.'

'Now you're acting like a proper human being!' The words just slipped out.

Keisuke smiled in embarrassment.

Should he feel embarrassment at this moment, Kaori wondered. Wouldn't most people feel offended?

'I don't want Spin or Shiori dying or getting injured.'

· 59 ·

Again the master–servant relationship had the cat on top. But that was okay. Nothing to worry about. What keeps the cat safe keeps the baby safe. And what keeps the baby safe keeps the cat safe. Two sides of the same coin. Yin and yang. A safe, happy family.

As Keisuke started to wipe the floor, Spin began to meow. *Right* – this *cry I recognize*, Kaori thought, wondering if the kitten had been fed.

'What about Spin's food?' she asked.

'It's in a drawer underneath the oven. It's in pouches, and I take out half a pouch and warm it up a bit. You're smart to know she's hungry!' Keisuke added, eyes wide.

'She sounds just like Shiori when she's hungry. The same sort of crying.'

Maybe because they couldn't speak, the urgent need in their tone struck you all the more.

Kaori went out to the kitchen and Spin skipped through after her. She didn't seem in the least bit shy. Maybe because she knew she was a member of the family? Animals and babies are said to pick up on the relationship with new people from the vibe they get from other family members.

Spin's matching food and water bowls and her litter tray were lined up neatly along the floor in the kitchen, proof of how determined Keisuke had been to keep the kitten.

Spin's little tail described a figure of eight as it brushed against Kaori's feet, then stuck straight up, the tip quivering. A happy tail. There were all kinds of tails on cats – long ones, short ones, hooked ones. All good, but longer tails were more expressive.

When Spin smelled the warmed-up food in her bowl,

her purring moved up a gear and she was all over it. Maybe she'd been too tense at the vet's to eat anything.

Seen from above, the head and body were like two downy balls, with two triangles for the ears attached to the smaller ball. Any way you looked at it, this was a miraculous creature – a winner of a Good Design award. She wouldn't be a kitten much longer; crouching over the little cat, Kaori found she could study her for ever.

'This won't do – I'm wasting time.'

She shook off the spell and stood up.

'I'm going to go crush those cardboard boxes in the entrance,' she announced and was heading in that direction when Keisuke stopped her.

'No, I'll do it,' he said. 'The Bullet train must have been tiring. You go and lie down, and I'll let you know if Shiori starts crying.'

He really had become more human, she mused, even shivering a little at the thought.

Taking him at his word, she headed to the bedroom. The set-up there had changed in her absence. Immediately inside, along the wall, was the crib, and in order to accommodate it their own two beds had been shifted to face in a different direction from before. An adjustment of the layout done with the logistics of babycare in mind.

*Assemble the baby's crib. Otherwise, you're a dead man!* He'd not only passed the test, but had done so in medal-worthy fashion.

The bedclothes seemed untouched since Kaori had left, the pillowcase retaining her scent, but that was trivial. She'd got the bed because taking out futons and then storing them away every day was a pain, and she wasn't proud of how seldom even she changed the sheets. Once while chatting with

· 61 ·

people at work, the topic of how often they changed the futon covers had come up, and she was in the corner that hemmed and hawed about it, before beating a hasty retreat.

Not long after she had got into bed, she heard the soft padding of approaching feet. She'd been wondering when the kitten would come. Sensing a presence near her bed, she lifted her head before the feet pattered away again.

The feeling of having a tiny living creature moving about the house as it pleased filled her with a surprising warmth. Perhaps because it had been so many years since she'd had a cat in her life.

And, she thought, being brought up with that warm little creature maybe wouldn't be such a bad thing for a baby.

She trimmed Shiori's fingernails every day. A baby's nails were like razor blades, and if you let them grow out even a little, they'd tear to pieces the skin of whoever was taking care of them. A mother's chest would be covered in cuts. But what was scariest of all was how the baby, in moving her hands and feet, could cut her own skin. Shiori wasn't moving them that much, but she could still reach her face.

It was a frightening business trimming those nails, like tiny grains of Swarovski crystal, or even tinier than that. She was using special nail scissors for babies, but the force you had to apply to these was in inverse proportion to their size.

'Oh, this is scary,' Kaori groaned, which made Keisuke glance up from the notebook where he was writing something in pencil. He used little notebooks to jot down reminders and sketches he came up with. He carried them about with him everywhere, and there were always a few dotted around the living room. Even little sketches and

· 62 ·

scribbles could become ideas for manga, so these were part of his bread and butter.

'Shall I trim them?'

*Seriously? Three years of marriage and finally showing some initiative?*

'Just do it as much as you can.'

He did it bit by bit, and managed to do several fingers, making an excellent job of it at that. From that moment, he did a nail check every day.

Keisuke would take Shiori in his arms and settle down on the floor, legs crossed and nail scissors in hand.

'Don't cut her fingers, and don't trim them down too far.'

'I'll be okay, I think.'

The *I think* was a little scary, but he was quite proficient by this time. When her little balled fists opened, he'd quickly grab a hand and trim one or two fingers. When he was able to, he'd do three or four fingers at a time.

'Wow, you're really good.'

'Like back when I used to paste tone film.'

Manga artists had switched to digital now, but back in the analogue age *Keisuke Tsukuda* was known for his beautiful tone work, in which thin pieces of film would be pasted on to a scene in a manga.

'Goodness, you're much better at it than me.'

'At this kind of thing, yeah— And it's easier than with Spin.'

Spin was on the sofa, flashing her furry belly.

'Kitten's claws are proper weapons, aren't they,' Keisuke went on.

If a baby's nails were razors, then a kitten's were hooks. And they were thin, so they could really pierce. When a young cat's tendons had grown enough to allow it to extend

and retract its claws, the muscle strength in its paws also developed and it could mercilessly stick them into anything, like hooks sinking in.

'I looked into it after Spin arrived. Cats' claws are curved, so if they leave them extended they could dig into their own pads, right?'

'Yeah, if they keep them extended. Cats brought up indoors don't walk around enough for their nails to be naturally whittled down, and so some of them have terrible talons,' said Kaori.

'It makes you cry just thinking about a cat's claws cutting into those cute, squishy little pink paws . . .'

'Would you focus now on those cute, squishy little pink *fingers* for me?'

'And with cats' claws if you cut them too much, they'll bleed, won't they?' Keisuke mused. 'They hate getting them cut, and struggle so much I'd be scared of hurting them.'

'If Shiori gets hurt, I'm going to kill you.'

'Compared to Spin, Shiori minds her manners. It's easy.'

*The cat first, eh? The cat's the boss after all.*

Meanwhile, all the fingers and toes had been done, and Kaori declared Keisuke to be their official nail trimmer.

As she discovered, raising a cat helped them in many ways.

During the day, babies needed to be nursed every two or three hours, a relentless schedule that never let up. And the same held true in the middle of the night. Kaori would be in bed, having just fallen asleep, when that distinctive siren wail blasted out.

Her breast milk had dried up while she was still at her parents' house and so she'd crawl out of bed to get *Milk! Milk!*

Kaori was just getting out of bed, when—

'I'll make it, you go back to sleep,' murmured Keisuke.

She would have loved to, but the blaring milk siren was too insistent to ignore, so she lifted Shiori out of the crib and stroked her forehead. She could hear a faint clatter from the kitchen downstairs as Keisuke bustled about.

*Husbands never get up at night*, a mother at her workplace at the publishing company had warned her. In other words, don't count on them to join the battle in the middle of the night. But until now, Keisuke had never once failed to attend to the baby siren.

'Because, you know – Spin,' he said.

*Again with the cat.*

Spin, who'd been abandoned before she was weaned, had, in the space of two weeks, adjusted to drinking milk, he told her. Spin was on a two-hour timer, too, he added.

A kitten's siren was piercing, like a warning alarm on a machine, and it was impossible to sleep through it. Shiori's was much easier on the ears.

'If I don't take care of Spin, she'll die.'

Kaori was amazed at how meticulously he carried out the operation of feeding Spin. He'd heat up milk, ensuring it was the right temperature, and before giving it to her, he'd wet her tiny bottom with a tissue dipped in warm water to stimulate her to poop. She could choke if he fed her when she was lying on her back, so he got her to crouch like a miniature Sphinx and fed her that way, not forgetting to sterilize the bottle afterwards. Kaori was astonished at how perfectly he had mastered it.

Even at Kaori's parental home, where they'd never lived without a cat, she'd not seen such sensitive caring for a kitten. And she had never done it herself; she'd always let her mother handle it.

There was no excuse for cutting corners. And this clearly helpless little ball of fur had changed Keisuke so much.

'You really did a good job, for *you*,' Kaori commented.

Her comment implied a lot more, and Keisuke gave an embarrassed smile.

'These days, we've got Dr Google and Master Yahoo to help us,' he said.

Intrigued by his comment, Kaori opened the website history on the tablet they shared and marvelled at how active Keisuke's private Yahoo account had been.

QUESTION: *I found an abandoned kitten. The vet said to use damp cotton wool to get her to pee, but I don't have any in the house. What should I do?*

ANSWER: *Tissues work just as well.*

ANSWER: *If there are any women in the house, wouldn't you have some make-up wipes? They sell them at convenience stores, you know.*

ANSWER: *Make sure you use warm water to wet the cotton wool or tissues! Cold water won't work and the kitten will catch a cold.*

QUESTION: *Sorry to bother you again. The kitten-pee guy here. The kitten won't drink milk from the bottle. It will put the teat in its mouth but then turn away. What should I do?*

ANSWER: *Is the milk at the right temperature? It should be slightly warmer than a person's body temperature (38–40°C). Check the temperature on your wrist.*

· 66 ·

ANSWER: *Is it too warm? Mix it with cooled-down hot water, shake the bottle and let it cool.*

QUESTION: *Hot water that's been cooled down? What's that?*
ANSWER: *Google it, stupid!*
ANSWER: *It means water that's been boiled and left to cool. You boil it at about 70°C. Pour it into a baby-feeding bottle and cool it under cold running water.*

QUESTION: *If the temperature for drinking is 40°C, can't you just heat it up in a microwave?*
ANSWER: *You boil it to get rid of the chlorine and chalk in the water, so do that and then cool it down.*
ANSWER: *Are you trying to kill the cat?*
ANSWER: *You could just set your electric hot-water dispenser to keep the water at 70°C. After it boils, it will keep it at that temperature.*

QUESTION: *So it has that kind of convenient setting? I'll check it out!*
ANSWER: *Are you saying you've never used your hot-water dispenser?*

QUESTION: *My wife's always taken care of things around the house . . . Right now she's back at her parents' place to have our baby. So until she gets back, I have to take care of the kitten by myself.*
ANSWER: *Whoa, that's some terrible wife, I'd say.*
ANSWER: *She wants you to do everything. Grounds for divorce.*

QUESTION: *Really, grounds for divorce?*
ANSWER: *I'll see you in family court! From your wife.*
ANSWER: *I predict that you'll let the cat die before your wife gets home.*

QUESTION: *I don't want it to die. So, which is better – to cool down the milk, or heat it up?*

ANSWER: *You have to decide, kitten-pee guy! How are we supposed to know what temperature your milk is?*

ANSWER: *Is this guy phishing?*

ANSWER: *Faster to just make up a new bottle. Stop posting – go and do it right now.*

ANSWER: *He's phishing. This cat does not exist.*

ANSWER: *If he's not phishing, this little cat is gonna die. That's why I'm responding – for the baby cat that* might *exist.*

This led to a minor flurry of comments on the blog, an uproar about this may-or-may-not-actually-exist cat, with a few *screw you*-type responses mixed in. In the end, the class assembly decided he had to confess all this to his wife. 'My apologies, everyone, for being a hopeless husband.'

QUESTION: *Sorry to keep bothering you. Cat Pee here . . .*

Cat Pee finally became his online pseudonym.

*. . . Thank you so much for the advice about milk the other day. By the way, though she pees fine every day, I haven't seen anything that looks like poop. I wonder if she's sick?*

ANSWER: *Is she drinking all the milk? If she is, then I wouldn't worry about it. Kittens' poop is so thin, you're just not noticing it.*

ANSWER: *Golden Milk for little cats is nearly 100 per cent absorbed by them, so while they're still on milk they sometimes don't poop.*

ANSWER: *When you wiped her butt to get her to poop, was there ever a thin yellow line? That's poop. But tell me, have you confessed to your wife?*

· 68 ·

QUESTION: *A thin yellow line! So that's poop! I haven't been able to say anything to my wife yet . . .*
ANSWER: *Hurry up and tell her. What'll you do if your wife gets angry and orders you to get rid of the cat?*

QUESTION: *My wife isn't that kind of person. At least she wouldn't make a kitten suffer, I know that.*
ANSWER: *Then why not tell her?*

QUESTION: *I'm sure she'll blow her top . . .*
ANSWER: *They say people bring it on themselves.*
ANSWER: *Well, she might say to put the kitten in a foster home.*

QUESTION: *That would be hard . . . I can't imagine giving her up after all this . . . She's coming back next week with our child, and I think I'd prefer to let her know first . . .*
ANSWER: *You're a kind of procrastinator, aren't you, when things are tough.*

They had no way of knowing how he'd once put things off so much, he'd nearly been charged with tax evasion.

ANSWER: *I reckon he'll never ever tell her. I'm willing to bet a million Zimbabwean dollars on it!*

In the end everything had worked out, even if they'd bet yen on it. After the million Zimbabwean dollars remark, there were occasional responses on the thread, such as 'How's the cat's pee now?' and 'Wonder if he's in the family court?'

Kaori heard footsteps hurrying up the stairs.
'Oh, that must be Spin, on her way!'
They put Spin in a cage in the living room at night, but Keisuke seemed to have let her out. Maybe he was planning

· 69 ·

to stay up and work. His deadline wasn't for a while, but he did have a one-shot manga assignment he had to complete.

Spin placed her front paws on Kaori's shin and dropped her head to sniff, seemingly concerned about what was taking place above her. She seemed to be worried about Shiori crying. During the day, too, if Shiori was nearby, Spin often padded inquisitively over. Shiori didn't show signs of reacting badly to the cat, so they were more often taking her out of the bouncer and letting her lie down on a baby futon on the floor, and when she was, Spin could be found snuggling up next to her, grooming her own furry undercarriage, the picture of a harmonious twosome.

*Because of all of you, we're getting along well*, Kaori thought, silently thanking all those online respondents.

'Sorry to keep you waiting,' Keisuke said, finally making an appearance, milk bottle in hand. The milk was at just the right temperature for the baby.

Kaori gave Shiori the teat and the siren came to an abrupt halt. She gurgled and cooed as she sucked down the milk.

'You see that, Spin? How Shiori's drinking her milk? What a good girl—'

His hands wrapped around her belly, Keisuke lifted Spin up and she must have smelled the milk since she extended her paws and scratched at the bottle.

'You've graduated from milk, right?'

Her teeth had grown in, strong enough to bite off a teat on a bottle. A cat's teeth came through much faster than a human's did.

'Are you going to do some work?'

'I'm wide awake now, so I reckoned why not.'

Keisuke was basically a night owl to begin with. During

Kaori's maternity leave this was helpful, as they could divide up the daytime and night-time duties.

'I want to tweak the plot of my new work a bit. But it's kind of hard.'

This was a touchy subject. Ever since his one big hit a few years ago, he'd had no long-running series. His other series were seen as okay pieces of work, but never went beyond more than a few volumes when they were published as separate books. The editorial department was hoping he'd come up with a new series that was even better, but the word online was that he'd never write anything to top that earlier hit, and Keisuke didn't have a strong enough will to avoid egosurfing the net – and telling a creative not to ego-surf was ignoring human nature, plain and simple.

Creators were human beings, and human beings instinct-ively cared how others reacted to what they created. How many people in the world, when ordered to put a lid on that instinct, could actually comply?

The attitude of the editorial staff had changed substan-tially. In the past, they'd tell their authors not to worry about what was being said online, because if the authors did get to know, they'd either be inflated by praise or worn down by criticism. This was especially true of newcomers. Older hands weren't yet as affected. It was a different era now from the days when editors could conceal critical feedback from their authors.

Kaori's record in accounting surpassed what she'd done as an editor, but still she had once harboured ambitions as an editor.

'I love *Keisuke Tsukuda*'s manga,' she'd said.

Even though it wasn't what had pushed her into marry-ing him, it's true she had said, 'When *Keisuke Tsukuda*'s

work comes out, I'll buy *Keisuke Tsukuda*'s work, no matter what the genre.'

His earlier hit had been an action manga featuring characters with special powers. She had wanted to read whatever he wrote, be it a rom-com manga or one set in the workplace.

'Nor does it have to be science fiction, necessarily.'

Kaori had also liked a serialization he'd done earlier, a teen rom-com story. He seemed to be able to pull off every-day, realistic manga as well.

'If you aim for a long-term serialization, it'll be obvious how you think you should stick to the genre you're especially good at . . . So it's best not to plan things out too much.'

That wasn't what he was cut out for. He was the type who, left to dig where he wanted, would eventually hit the motherlode.

As Shiori drained her bottle, the online chat room still lingered in her mind.

'Good girl – now give me a burp, a little burp.'

Kaori jiggled her a bit and patted her back, and Keisuke picked up the bottle she'd put aside and got up to take it to the kitchen. The guy was well trained, she thought.

'I'm going to my study to work. Go back to sleep if you can.'

As he toddled out of the room, another set of feet followed him. The drill instructor. The three weeks they'd spent together had been extremely bonding, and Spin gravitated much more towards Keisuke than to Kaori.

Kaori's drill instructor had been the midwife. For her mother this was her first grandchild and it had been years since she'd had anything to do with babies, so she was

relegated to assistant drill instructor. The head instructor, the midwife, had been the one who drummed the basic principles into Kaori's head.

One thing she'd told her was: whether it's using the toilet, eating or making sure you're presentable, don't cut these activities short even if the baby is crying.

It was human nature for young mothers to want to rush to their baby's side as soon as it started crying, but as long as it's crying it's alive, the midwife had taught her, so prioritize your own needs, including going to the toilet, making sure to eat, and keeping yourself clean and presentable.

When a baby was really in trouble it wouldn't cry, but fall silently into a life-threatening state.

*Talk about frightening!*

Even with crying, there were very different types.

There was your ordinary, business-as-usual crying and the declaring-a-state-of-emergency crying, and a mother needed to be able to distinguish between the two. No one else takes care of a mother's need to use the bathroom or eat or look after herself. You have to listen attentively to your baby's crying while you're using the toilet, eating, applying a little lipstick.

*Seriously?*

Making yourself presentable couldn't be so important, could it, was Kaori's thought, but a mother's emotional health was vital.

And more than that—

If you were just wearing any old thing and suddenly had a visitor and couldn't greet him or her, that would be a problem. In other words, she should make sure she looked neat enough to at least go to the door if there was a mail delivery.

*

Even with her husband with his lack of social skills added to the mix, by the time she left her parents' home, Kaori had accrued enough experience to prevent her baby being in danger, and things were less stressful than she'd thought.

And much of the credit for this had to go to their wonderful drill instructor, Spin.

Spin, who'd grown up at a rate that far outstripped that of her little human companion, had reached the point where she was coordinated enough to climb to the top of their net curtains. A skill they had hoped she wouldn't acquire. Going up was one thing but she couldn't climb down and would hang there, upside down at the top, meowing. Not a *Help!* sort of meow but more of a desperate plea to *Get me down!*

'What's going to happen when she gets heavier?' Keisuke asked. 'If her claws get caught they'll be torn out . . .'

'You really want to know?' Kaori laughed with a snort. 'What'll happen is the curtain will tear.'

At her parents' home, every time they got a new kitten the curtains would soon be in tatters. Even the *fusuma* sliding doors got ripped.

'I wonder if we should put in blinds instead.'

'They'll just snap off.'

Interior furnishings were definitely not designed with cats in mind.

'Should I make some lunch?' Keisuke suggested. Kaori had been cradling the baby for nearly an hour.

'No, it's about time to put her down.'

She was happy Keisuke was concerned about her, but he hadn't progressed beyond the kind of cuisine that required just pouring in hot water and waiting three minutes. Kaori herself wasn't exactly a great cook, but she always kept some

· 74 ·

udon noodles in the freezer. She figured she'd zap them in the microwave, and make *kamatama* udon with a raw egg and soy sauce and, to really liven it up, add some chopped spring onions.

When it was ready, she'd add some crushed nori or ground sesame seeds, or even a little grated cheese to give a richer, Western taste. Wait – if she wanted richer, she could put in *tenkasu*, the crunchy bits of dough from tempura, she thought.

Searching for the point of overlap between what was quick and what she wanted to eat, she steeled herself and lowered Shiori on to the bed. The moment the baby's back had actually touched the futon, her eyes popped wide open and she showed an *Et tu, Brute?* look she'd been saving up and let out a lusty war cry.

'If she's crying, that means she's alive.'

'If she's crying, that means she's not dead.'

They voiced these watchwords to buck each other up.

And just then Spin padded over. They expected she might try to groom Shiori's hair, but instead she pressed her cheek into Shiori's side. Shiori let out a little cooing sound they hadn't heard before.

Spin began gently kneading Shiori's tummy with her paws making the adults call out, '*Whoa! Wow!*'

They pulled out their mobile phones and began snapping rapid-fire shots. After several dozen clicks, they realized something: 'No – we should *video* this!' and switched over.

They suddenly noticed Shiori's war cries had ceased. Her eyelids were drooping and finally they closed.

*Seriously?* they murmured simultaneously.

Spin's little pats finally slowed down and she herself went to sleep.

Fully savouring the afterglow, Kaori quietly got to her feet and made her way stealthily to the kitchen.

She zapped the noodles in the microwave, added a raw egg, soy sauce, chopped up some spring onions and shook in a good amount of grated cheese, with a final flourish of freshly ground pepper. She mixed these late-afternoon udon carbonara-style noodles with her chopsticks and she and Keisuke began slurping them up.

It would never make it on to a café menu but was excellent for a busy couple juggling two small creatures.

After that they often observed Spin's little baby-soothing pats. When Spin kneaded lightly on Shiori's side, it never failed to put her straight to sleep. Figuring that lightly patting their baby's side was the trick to get her to sleep, the adults began to imitate Spin with their fingertips, but only Spin could make it work. Perhaps because they couldn't reproduce the advanced pitter-patter movements that Spin had down to a tee, or maybe it was because they were too caught up in a desire to rush their baby and make her *go to sleep*!

While Shiori was sleeping, it was the ideal time for cleaning the house. As Kaori pushed the mop around on the first floor, she heard footsteps tramping up the stairs.

*Don't wake Shiori!* she thought, and a head-on collision of scolding was just about to happen when Keisuke called out, 'Kaori, what should I do?!'

'About *what*?'

'This!'

He held out the tablet. The screen displayed the 'Yahoo! Japan' app.

What really startled her was how many sketches he'd

· 76 ·

posted, all executed in a style she knew so well, of a sleeping baby and a kitten.

'What have you done?' she wanted to yell, but with no time for fury, she scrolled down the thread.

QUESTION: *Thank you so much, everyone, for your help the other day. Thanks to you all, the kitten has become a real member of our family. And she gets along with our baby so well, too. As a thank-you, I've uploaded a few sketches.*
ANSWER: *Wow, they're great!*
ANSWER: *I'm glad everything worked out. The drawings are amazing!*
ANSWER: *I'm guessing these aren't the work of an amateur . . .*
ANSWER: *Are you a pro? An illustrator? A manga artist?*
ANSWER: *Thanking us with sketches – now that takes some confidence. It's possible he is a pro.*
ANSWER: *Already married, with a new baby, a man . . . so not someone doing shojo manga . . .*

The thread bounced around speculating about his identity.

*Oh no! No, no, no!*

A quick scan showed nobody had brought up the name *Keisuke Tsukuda*. They were quick, rough sketches, so it was hard to pinpoint the artist. Thankfully, too, there were no social-networking sites under the name *Keisuke Tsukuda*. If he had been regularly posting drawings online, then that might have given away his identity.

'A few sketches to thank you? Are you kidding me?'

Kaori almost whacked him on the head.

'I just wanted to thank them, that's all . . .'

'You've got to understand you're much, much better than just anyone. At least at drawing!'

· 77 ·

'What should I do? Delete them? My name hasn't come up yet.'

To delete or not to delete. This was the crucial question when it came to keeping it from blowing up. *They're by someone else, make it someone else. Decide calmly, like you're an uninvolved third party.*

'I think it's best not to delete.'

Suppressing the fear that seemed to be welling up, that he'd be recognized, he managed to wring out this decision. Delete them and it was very possible this would prod people to correctly identify him. But even if the name *Keisuke Tsukuda* did come up, it would just be mentioned in passing as one of many possible candidates.

'Don't ever enter this thread again. From now on, official *Keisuke Tsukuda* SNS sites are strictly off limits.'

'Okay, I won't touch them. Too scary.'

With his lack of social skills and general pessimism, what he feared more than anything was a back and forth online with other manga artists. In some areas, he was very conscious that his inability to read the room might lead to a sticky situation. His own SNS accounts were all under his personalized name K@rom and locked, and besides he hadn't posted on them at all.

When Kaori had finished cleaning, she came downstairs and found Keisuke fast asleep, curled up like a bug next to Shiori on her futon, probably worn out by the fear that he would be outed.

The source of all this must be the notebook in the living room, she thought, and went to fetch it. The pictures in question must be towards the back of the notebook.

*Goodness, he's become a real parent now, hasn't he.*

· 78 ·

Kaori's eyes started to get itchy. No, it was more a feeling in her chest.

It was Shiori and Spin all over the place. Drawings of them covered the pages of the notebook, which was about to run out of space.

Out of the corner of her eye she spied an orange furball coming towards her. Spin then curved her back upwards in an elegant stretch. Every time she needed a stretch, she would come over where they could see her.

Kaori clicked her fingers to beckon her over and Spin responded, skipping towards her, happy tail trembling.

'It's all thanks to you,' Kaori said.

Because it was Keisuke who'd gone to take out the rubbish that day, this tiny Schrödinger's kitten made itself observed. What a happy Uncertainty Principle it had turned out to be.

Kaori took a felt-tip pen from the stand on the table. She wrote 'Excellent!' under the final sketch in the notebook. And added: 'What's not to love!'

A sudden thought came to her – it was in ink so it was there to stay. *Don't get me wrong*, she thought – *I'm evaluating the drawing, not you.*

She closed the notebook and left it where she'd found it. When she opened it again a few days later, it was full of new sketches. Fearing she might see something scary, she turned back to the spot where she'd written her comments. There Keisuke had shyly added a self-portrait and the words *Me too*. Wait a second – this had been her comment on the drawing, not on him.

Kaori would occasionally jot down some notes when she saw Shiori and Spin together. Kind of like an exchange of diaries. A few days would pass, and she'd see how Keisuke

had taken an idea from her note, one easy to draw, and made a one-panel comic out of it.

'How does her tail stick up exactly?'

Sometimes she'd check the details.

*So cute, so very, very cute. Adorable. Cute and adorable, adorable, adorable.*

A lovefest filling page after page. A new notebook began, and from the first page it was a flood of love.

Shiori's weight had doubled now. She'd graduated from infant diapers to size S. She could support her head by herself. And she could laugh. When her poop leaked out from the diaper, it was like the end of the world and she'd wail. *She could see well now, right? The way her eyes followed Spin. Today she'd looked Kaori in the eye and could see her!*

As predicted, the net curtain got ripped. Torn from top to bottom, three claws' worth. Spin started eating crunchy cat food. When her poop stuck to her backside, she'd race about in a panic, meowing her head off. She slept with Shiori's crotch as a pillow. *The diaper was a cushion? Didn't it smell?*

Not every day was a good day. There were times when Keisuke felt down in the dumps or under pressure. He and Kaori quarrelled occasionally over what was best for their baby, and for their cat. But he only put things in the notebook they could laugh over someday.

They filled the notebook only with items that, if Shiori were to see them later, would show their love for her.

Keisuke had a break from the short-term serialized manga he'd been working on. He was now planning a new work. Kaori was busy gathering information on childcare, kindergarten hunting.

When she was less than a year old, Spin was spayed. When she came home after the operation, her expression

· 80 ·

was one of betrayal. *You humans. I'm never going to trust you ever again.* About an hour later, she was rolling and rubbing herself against them like always. 'Who could have done such a horrible thing to our little Spin,' Kaori cooed over and over, doing her best to offer comfort.

Shiori started to crawl and had to be watched even more closely. The words of an experienced mother friend hit home: 'Wait until they start to move around. That's when the "fun" really begins.' Every five minutes brought a new way of dying by suicide. Even a plastic spoon could be lethal for a small human with a death wish.

In the midst of all this, Keisuke came to her one day, a serious look on his face. 'I have something I need to ask you,' he said. 'My editor asked me if I'd write something for *Healthy Child*.'

This was a high-profile magazine for bringing up babies published by Kaori's company.

When he'd gone to the editorial offices to talk about a new manga series and was asked what theme he was interested in these days, Keisuke had said, 'Well, if it's about kids and cats, I've got a ton of material.' He'd said it as a joke, but his editor took him at his word, the upshot being a commission for *Healthy Child*.

Comic articles about a husband who enjoys spending time with his own child? He and Kaori laughed uproariously at the idea.

'Hmm,' said Keisuke. 'I guess that wouldn't work, would it?'

'Well – it might.'

She found it funny to think of Keisuke as one of those gung-ho fathers, a man who fully engaged with the real world.

'Why not give it a try? The material you have in your notebooks is great.'

· 81 ·

At some point, he'd moved from just sketches to framing the drawings like manga, and she was thinking it was a waste not to share these with the world.

'I think a kind of full-blown comic article could be really popular.'

They settled on *The Schrödinger Daddy* as the series title.

*Hello. My name's Keisuke Tsukuda. I usually write sci-fi action manga . . .* went the intro for the opening piece.

SCHRÖDINGER'S LAW STATED THAT UNTIL you observed the cat inside the box, you couldn't know whether it was alive or dead, in the same way that Kaori wouldn't know if her husband would pass, or fail, as a new father, until she tried opening the box. His wife, before she observed anything, was sure he'd fail.

He wrote about it all: how when she found out she was pregnant, they squabbled to the point where divorce seemed imminent, how he worried that even when he saw his baby's face, he still wouldn't have any fatherly feeling, the first episode ending as he rescued a still unweaned kitten. And readers lapped it up, a survey later ranking this first episode the most popular story in the magazine.

*Everyone, I really want to thank you for helping me,* he wrote – and the 'Yahoo! Japan' thread buzzed to life again with posts such as *I never imagined it was Keisuke Tsukuda!*

Concerned that he wasn't so well known to readers of a magazine aimed at parents of young children, he opened each episode with the same *I usually write sci-fi action manga* introduction until finally Editorial updated the by-line to *An article by a manga artist who also writes sci-fi action manga.*

· 82 ·

He was the type of manga artist who beavered away at whatever he fancied until he happened to strike a rich vein of ore, and though this time the vein he'd unearthed wasn't a major hit, it did look like it might have a long shelf life. He'd always had an eye for the magic of the everyday.

Its popularity led to cat-related manga drawings, and unusually he and Spin were featured in a TV report about the relationship between a manga artist and his cat. The production team were eager to include his baby daughter and wife, but Keisuke turned them down with a firm *No.*

Instead, the reporter concentrated on his other work, and so his earlier books began to shift more copies.

'Spin-chan, you've been our *lucky-cat charm,* haven't you now, you liddle cutey . . .' Keisuke said, in an embarrassing baby voice, giving firm strokes along her back, until he ended up with a claws-in cat-punch to the side of his head.

'Daddy's such a liddle dummy now, isn't he . . .' Kaori said to Shiori.

Kaori herself had become completely inured to this kind of baby talk. Baby Shiori, though, shot her a look of disgust.

'Tha's how babies talk, Mummy,' she said.


Sometimes Kaori wondered what would have happened if Keisuke hadn't rescued Spin that day.

The inside of the Mikkabi tangerine box. What was observed was a live cat whose sibling had just passed away. Perhaps also notable was what would happen to the very observer whose life was touched by that very cat.

# Good Father – Bad Father

D AD WAS NEVER THAT fond of cats to begin with.
Even when pressure came from the kids to get a cat, and they found one advertised in the *Free Giveaways* newspaper under the 'Kittens Available' section, still Dad didn't show much interest.

The pale-brown kitten that arrived was a male, advertised as just two months old, but must have been three times that age.

The man who dropped off the kitten by car said his hobby was fishing, and just as he was leaving, bent over the kitten and said, 'Next time I'll bring over a fish I caught for you,' though he never showed up again. As an aside, the man spoke the local dialect, which tacked on a *nyaa* or a *chuu* to the end of each word, and was mocked for sounding like 'a cat and a mouse having a conversation'.

According to the man, the kitten had been living with another family for a while, but they gave him back, which might explain the kitten's slightly sulky vibe. After the man left, the kitten lay down on the floor beside the sliding glass doors in the living room, a nice sunny spot, with a *Well, I'm only here temporarily* look.

He didn't try to scratch you or anything, but he certainly didn't seem to go out of his way to ingratiate himself with his new family, and the kids, who'd been looking forward to getting a cute kitten, were frankly disappointed. Mum, who had dealt with the kitten's owner when he first

came by, was, she admitted, hesitant about taking him initially.

'I thought he seemed pretty damn big for two months,' she said.

Mum was a timid person and perhaps couldn't bring herself to say to the kitten's owner, 'Thanks for bringing him over, but he's too big and we don't need him.'

'It's a little unfair on your father,' she said.

No one in the family found this past-his-prime kitten very appealing. Dad, though, was the most outspoken of all.

He had given the kitten a long stare, listened as Mum explained the background, before coming out with:

'The first family must have sent him back because of his looks.'

Everyone was thinking the same but didn't dare say so. At the time there was a popular male singer with a smooth voice who appeared on TV a lot, and when Dad saw him he'd said, *This guy certainly isn't getting by on his looks, that's for sure.* In typical Dad fashion, he was trying to say that the guy was a very good singer.

'I bet the guy who dropped off the kitten thought, *Good riddance.*' He seemed to find it amusing, perhaps picturing to himself the old guy sighing in relief as he walked out of the door. 'If we give back this kitten, I doubt he'll be able to find anyone else to take him.'

In his roundabout way, Dad was telling them to keep him. So the pale-brown cat became a member of the family and with his tiger stripes they named him, simply, Tora – *Tiger.*

Mum and the kids had been thinking that if they were getting a kitten, they should have at least got a cuter, more lovable one, but Dad was totally unconcerned. This was a man who, after all, didn't care much about animals. A guy

who, when asked what was his favourite animal, replied, *A hyena*. Not exactly what most people would say. Ask him what he liked about hyenas and he'd answer, *They keep low to the ground*.

'We could learn a lot from them. Hyenas don't stay low like that because it's in their nature, but because of their skeletal structure. I like the spotted hyenas better than the striped ones. Because they're more seedy-looking and melancholy,' he added.

Most people would lump striped and spotted hyenas together. But not Dad, who often went to a zoo in the next prefecture, where they had both. This was, typically, just a passing fad on his part, and didn't mean he was becoming soft on animals. He was the type who, when he found something interesting, would obsess about it for a while, but the obsession never lasted. He was good at discovering little hobbies for himself like that.

The construction company where he worked was involved in the massive Seto Bridge project, building a link between Okayama and the island of Shikoku, and just before the bridge was completed, he became totally obsessive about it, collecting posters and picture postcards of it, and without first obtaining permission signed up his whole family for a special day-long bus tour that would allow them to walk across the bridge before it opened for business. They hadn't heard a thing about it until one morning when he woke them all up at the crack of dawn to board the bus. Since it was a tour, they couldn't very well give up and go home halfway through, so they had to march like troopers along the dark and shining asphalt of the bridge.

When they asked which part of the bridge Dad's company had been involved in building, it turned out to be the

stretch that connected the bridge to the road. His company had somehow wormed its way into building a small part of this massive public-works project in another prefecture. Come to think of it, his company must have been a pretty ambitious firm to land that kind of contract, however small.

Besides Dad, there were plenty of other parents rash enough – since final checks were still to be made – to bring their families along on the tour, and so there were a lot of visitors walking about on the bridge, literally as far as the eye could see. On the way back, almost everyone fell asleep, but one girl was woken up by the swaying of the bus and saw that, for some reason, the TV was showing *The Story of Hachi-ko*, a film about the famous dog also commemorated in the form of a bronze statue in Tokyo. She had no idea about what happened to the dog or its master, because she dropped off again shortly afterwards and by the time she woke up, the credits were rolling.

But this story is about a cat, not a dog.

Most people at the time kept their dogs outside and let their cats roam wherever they wanted and so, in line with tradition, Tora had a pretty random upbringing. When he reached puberty and was neutered, there was no cat carrier in the house, so he was placed in a cardboard box, which was then wedged into the pannier on Mum's little motor scooter and off they went to the vet's. Naturally any cat suddenly finding itself shut up in a box would panic and Tora struggled so mightily it made it hard for Mum to steer. Finally, Tora managed to thrust a paw between the cardboard flaps at the top of the box, and with the vet's only one traffic light away, it looked as if he was about to escape. They'd underestimated their cat's athletic ability.

Dad had said: 'A box is perfectly good for a cat. Plus the

vet's not so far away, so it's a waste of money to buy a carrier.'
But Mum had had enough, so by the time Tora was dis-
charged from the vet's, she'd already ordered a carrier from
the nearest DIY store.

'Hard to believe you made it all the way here,' the vet
had told her, a bit stunned at the sight of the box, and his
comment had obviously got to her.

'Dad was so stingy, it made me so embarrassed,' she said
when she got back home, clearly upset. 'And if Tora-chan
had ripped open the box and escaped, he might very well
have been hit by a car and badly hurt.'

'Okay, okay, but he came out of it all right, didn't he? So
all's well that ends well.'

If all this had happened now, Dad would have been
roundly abused by one of those animal-rights groups. And it
wasn't as if he didn't like Tora or anything.

'He had those cute little plump balls before,' Dad said,
poking and prodding at Tora's deflated little scrotum. He
moved Tora's thick, crooked tail around like a gear lever:
'Look, he's changing gears.' Tora gave him a look but just let
him carry on. The cat wasn't exactly very friendly, but you
had to admit he was pretty tolerant.

Once, Tora had been put inside a carrier bag hanging
from a hook on the back of a door. It wasn't the kids who
had put him there, but Dad.

'He'd stuck his face inside the bag, and seemed to be
sniffing around, and when I gave him a little push so that he
ended up inside the bag, he seemed surprisingly okay about
it, so I hung the bag from the hook.'

Until the moment Mum found him and let him out, he
hadn't made a peep, and had curled up inside the bag. Hard

to tell if he was just being stoical, or whether he actually liked it in there. When she put him down, he unhurriedly sauntered off, his tail quivering as he went.

This unfriendly, long-suffering cat lived with them for eighteen years. The children had all grown up and flown the nest by then, and though Tora had always niftily made himself at home wherever he pleased, now he had all of a sudden become quite weak.

He had always been an inactive cat and his back legs, even from the outset, were never that sturdy. But they now became seriously unsteady, his knees so feeble he'd have to rest after each step on his way upstairs.

He got to the point where he couldn't even step over the side of the litter tray, and often soiled the floor. They got rid of the litter tray and spread plastic sheets on the floor, but he seemed at a loss as to what to do and tended to find somewhere else to relieve himself. Usually on the carpet or the futon cushions. Cleaning up after him became too laborious, so they made diapers for him. In those days, pet diapers didn't exist, so Mum cut a hole for his tail in a baby's diaper and put it on him.

When it looked like he was not long for this world, the children were contacted by phone. The eldest daughter lived far way and only came over when she had time off, so it was the cool, detached daughter number two who stopped by their house regularly.

When Dad came home in the evenings, he'd look at Tora and say, 'You still alive and kicking?' Mum scolded him for his lack of delicacy, but that's the way he was.

The eldest daughter was at college in the Kansai region when the huge earthquake hit the area in 1995. She'd taken refuge in a park, and when the shaking finally ceased and

she had got back home, the first thing she did was to phone Mum and Dad. Never having experienced such violent tremors before, she was convinced all of Japan was about to get swallowed up.

It was just a little past 6 a.m. Still half asleep, Mum answered the phone and, clearly a touch irritated, asked what was wrong. The daughter wanted to know if they'd got through the earthquake unscathed, but Mum hadn't realized anything was wrong. Finally convinced Japan hadn't been engulfed yet, the daughter hung up.

Immediately after their phone call, the phone lines to Kansai went down.

'She's pretty smart,' Dad said, praising his eldest daughter for calling so quickly. Terrible scenes of the aftermath began to appear on TV, and when they tried to call their daughter back, they couldn't get through.

*She's pretty smart – what kind of remark is that?* their daughter had thought at the time. She knew that even when it came to well-meaning praise, Dad always approached things in a left-field way. Normal parents would probably have said something like, *Our daughter always has her act together.*

After the earthquake, when the phone lines were restored, Dad said to her, 'Sure, you went through a lot, but you got through it, and now you have quite a story to tell.' She'd thought that herself, though she didn't say it, nor did she think it was the kind of thing any dad would say to his daughter when she was stuck in lodgings without a proper flushing toilet, where fear of aftershocks meant she went to bed with her shoes on. The younger daughter summed it up neatly: 'The man's got no heart.'

Tora, in a diaper, spent the night in Mum's arms, and just before dawn, he passed away, peaceful to the end.

When he heard that Tora was gone, the dad with no heart simply nodded and said, 'Oh, really?' It was as if he meant to say, *Well, he lived a good life.* Or maybe not.

This was a dad who liked hyenas. And so Tora's death did not affect him, not one bit.

Mum was the one who suffered what people now call *pet bereavement.* The kids had pestered her for a cat, and she had been the one to look after him.

So while the loss of Tora had no effect on Dad, he did notice, in his own way, that Mum was seriously upset. He happened to have reached mandatory retirement age and had begun to work at a part-time job that let him come and go as he pleased, and so he often took Mum on a drive for a change of scenery. He had always loved car trips and would spend time looking for places to take her.

On this particular day, they were on their way to scoop up jellyfish from the ocean. A while back, the local post office and other shops that retailed local products had been selling special packs that enabled you to raise and observe jellyfish in your own home. Order one and you'd get a plastic fish tank with an actual live jellyfish inside it. According to their advertising, if you refilled it with fresh seawater, the jellyfish would live for a while, and when it began to weaken, you could return it to the sea. The pack came with a container of seawater to freshen the tank. It was a pretty shoddy product, if you think about it.

When jellyfish grow weak, and can no longer swim, they turn a bluish black. Manufacturers of the packs expected that at this point you'd return the jellyfish to the sea, but Dad preferred to see it through to the bitter end.

'Why don't you take it back to the sea?' Mum urged him,

· 94 ·

but he ignored her. So the jellyfish met its end, floating life-lessly in the corner of the fish tank. Such a cruel way to go.

Even after this short-lived craze for keeping jellyfish blew over, Dad didn't give up on his hobby.

'You don't need to buy anything,' he insisted. 'There are tons of jellyfish we can scoop up inside the breakwater.'

And so off he'd go with a net to drag the sea for glossy little jellyfish.

He soon realized it wouldn't do to catch anything that was too big. The fish tank being small and the oxygen insufficient, a large jellyfish would soon keel over.

'They've come up with a really nasty product,' Mum sighed. 'It was the same with the silkworms.' This was when the kids were still in elementary school, where they were raising silkworms to try to get them to spin a silk fan.

The school had purchased a silkworm pack that came with mulberry leaves for the caterpillars. When they reached the terminal larval stage, the caterpillars could be placed on the ribs of a fan where they were supposed to excrete enough silk thread to create a fan. Whoever had come up with this system was clearly not firing on all cylinders.

Placed on top of the spokes, the silkworms were driven to produce cocoons, but because the ribs of the fan were flat, there was no way the caterpillars could manage it, and so they'd try all sorts of methods of excreting their thread, until they ended up crucified on top of the spokes.

'This is pretty awful,' Dad had muttered, but without offering any help, so that Mum was left to cut the threads and rescue the worms. Later, she prepared a small cocooning frame in a box so they could spin their cocoons there.

Hard to tell what the difference was for him – why he'd expressed compassion for the silkworms but none for the

jellyfish. This being the case, Mum had decided it was best to go along with him on his trips to scoop up jellyfish.

On one particular day, they were on a road that cut right across some fields when the line of cars in front started to slow down. They seemed to be making a detour around something.

'What's going on?' Dad said, peering ahead uncertainly, but it was Mum who spotted it first.

'Honey, it's a cat!'

Barely the size of a fist, a tiny kitten had crawled out from the grove beside the road and the cars ahead had been swerving widely to avoid it.

Mum figured Dad was about to swerve too, but instead he pulled over on to the verge, just inches away from where the little cat sat mewling and waving its tail.

He put the handbrake on and got out.

*Pyaoww! Pyaoww!* went the cat, like a wailing siren. It was a light tortoiseshell mixed with patches of cream.

Mum, wanting to help it back into the bushes for its own safety, pushed it gently towards the grove, but the kitten could not be persuaded and crawled straight back on to the road, and even after several pushes, it re-emerged every time.

'Maybe we should take it home with us.'

*What?*

Mum couldn't believe her ears. Here they were, on the way to massacre some jellyfish. And now?

After watching Tora pass away, Mum had decided she didn't want another cat. She just didn't have the strength to say goodbye in that way ever again.

But once the decision had been made to take the kitten home, the tiny creature clung to Mum's hand with all its might.

· 96 ·

'We still have Tora's litter tray, too,' said Dad.

Getting rid of all their cat-related paraphernalia would have meant erasing all traces of Tora, which they couldn't bring themselves to do.

So that day they put a hold on the jellyfish massacres, and the kitten came home with them.

The kitten was a veritable paradise for fleas – you could spot them scampering around in its whisker pads – so the vet prescribed a strong anti-flea treatment. The kitten turned out to be female, and her eyes were only just opening. Nevertheless, during her examination by the vet, she protested loudly, her claws out.

The second daughter, who lived nearby, came over straight away, her toddler in tow.

'You have to give her a name. What about *Ten* – Sky, or Heaven? Wouldn't that be cute?'

It had very nearly been her daughter's name, though they hadn't ended up choosing it. It didn't sound good alongside her married surname.

With no suggestions from anyone else, *Ten* became the cat's name.

Ten ate voraciously and soon had chewed off the teat of the baby's bottle. Later, she started to chow down proper canned cat food. *Now you're talking! Why'd you all wait so long to give me this?* she seemed to be saying.

Their eldest daughter left her husband at home by himself just to come over to cuddle the kitten.

'And you hardly ever come to visit,' her father told her.

'Well, kittens are only a limited-time offer, so you've got to catch them while you can.'

For all that, the main topic of conversation in their

house was Dad. They each wondered what had got into him. They all had their own theories about what had made him take home a stray.

'Maybe he really did love Tora after all.'

'Mmm. Don't think so. The day he died, all Dad said was, *Oh, really?*'

'And with all his killing of jellyfish, ceaselessly and ruthlessly.'

Mum's wish had been simply that he'd stop with the jellyfish slaughter, and a cat, of all things, had turned out to be the answer to her prayers.

When his jellyfish obsession had finally subsided, they'd left the empty fish tank in a corner of the living room and Ten would climb inside, in raptures, purring and mewling. For a cat, the dry, empty fish tank was simply a transparent box.

'Dad seems to like Ten a lot.'

Whenever Ten clambered into the fish tank, Dad never said a thing. It seemed he'd given up enslaving jellyfish and no longer had any use for it.

Ten eventually grew tired of the fish tank and it was disposed of. Dad didn't complain then either.

It was their son who came up with an answer of sorts to solve the puzzle about Dad's unpredictable behaviour.

'Mum's been looking pretty down – maybe a new cat will perk her up?'

Apparently, Dad had muttered this to his son a while back, but with no intention of actually getting a cat, so when a kitten crawled in front of the car, it had been a genuine godsend.

For some strange reason, the kitten, at the height of her cute period, was very attached to Dad, and would rub up against his legs whenever he got up. Dad never did anything

· 98 ·

to look after the cat. He found all that touchy-feely business annoying and would lightly kick her aside, so the cat's devotion to him was hard to fathom.

All that kittenish attention did actually move this man with no heart, this lover of hyenas (especially the spotted variety). He even started to buy toys for it.

Ten was still at the stage where she loved to play with toys, so every time Dad went out, he'd come home with something new. There were a couple Ten showed no interest in, and Dad seemed to enjoy trying to figure out why certain toys weren't in favour. He got heavily into rifling through the hundred-yen shops to find something that would capture the kitten's fickle attention. He'd often come home with carrier bags bursting with absurd little items, and Mum found the whole thing quite a pain.

DAD HAD ALWAYS LOVED GOING out on car trips, but he finally reached the age where he had to give up driving and so, against his will, he got rid of the car.

'I must be getting old. I'll be driving along and suddenly find there's too much space between me and the car in front.'

He'd come out with this statement a few years earlier, when grazing the side of the car was becoming an everyday occurrence, as was shaving off parts of other people's walls.

'If you ever hit somebody, you won't recover from it,' the son told him, almost forcibly taking the car from him and selling it.

Now without a car, he aged overnight. His wasn't the type of sunny personality who would make do with the bus

· 99 ·

or train, and since he didn't go out any more, he started to lounge around the house in his pyjamas, his legs getting visibly wobbly and his back weaker. The only old people who were as bent over and stooped as he was were the old grandpas from old-time fairytale manga.

The second daughter, who had a tendency to be snide, said he reminded her of a *hairpin*, which had Mum in stitches. That was a bit over the top, but he was so bent over, it made you wonder if he wasn't turning into a hunchback.

Nor was Dad the type to listen to any advice about getting some exercise. The son, who'd quarrelled quite a bit with him after he'd taken away the car, commented, 'As long as he doesn't kill anyone, we should let him do what he wants.'

Since Dad had enjoyed jellyfish so much, Mum kept suggesting that they take him to the jellyfish aquarium in Yamagata before he became completely immobile, and so the eldest daughter and her husband took on the task of arranging the outing.

As there was no direct flight to Yamagata from their area, they stayed at their daughter's place in Kansai, from which they would set off on their trip the following day.

When their daughter came to greet them at the arrivals gate, she had to wait what felt like hours for them to appear. The rest of the passengers had long since deplaned, but there was still no sign of Mum and Dad.

When finally they hobbled into view, she almost didn't recognize them.

'I thought it was an invalid and his carer.'

Dad's burning interest in jellyfish seemed to have faded long ago, and so he wasn't all that keen to visit the aquarium.

In fact, the trip was a total failure, Dad being his usual wilful self.

Meanwhile, Ten was growing up. The wildcat side she'd first displayed on her visit to the vet's only strengthened, and soon it was impossible to get her into the pet carrier as she was too big.

'If Ten gets sick,' Mum said, 'I'll do my best for her at home, but that's really all I can do.'

The last time she'd taken Ten to the vet's had been a few years earlier, and according to her, the vet was clearly none too happy to see the cat. The vet and her staff never got through a visit from Ten without a bit of bloodshed.

Looking back on it, Tora now seemed an accomplished, gentle cat, and their nostalgia for him only increased.

Ten had grown up among butterflies and flowers, so how did she end up such a ferocious character? When their eldest daughter came home on a rare visit, she'd flash her claws at her as she passed. She'd leap on her, too, when the daughter was napping on the sofa, aiming for her windpipe, clearly out for the kill.

Mum could not just stand by and watch, so she gave her daughter a can of luxury cat food.

'She cannot resist it, so give it a go,' she said. But Ten wouldn't come near, watching from a safe distance with her eyes half closed. *No way am I going to touch anything* you *give me*, she seemed to be saying to the daughter.

'Animals are a good judge of people,' was Dad's smug remark, as Ten continued, as always, to be his fan alone.

When it got to the point where going upstairs was too much for him, they moved Dad's bed down to the Buddhist

altar room just off the living room, and this space became his lair. And except for coming to the dining table or going to the toilet, he was like a bagworm, ensconced in his cocoon. As soon as Dad woke up, Ten would leap out from wherever she had chosen to rest, and coil around his legs as he tottered about. Dad went on lightly kicking her aside, but Ten's devotion showed no signs of abating.

'This cat is no judge of people,' their daughter said angrily – clearly a case of sour grapes. 'The only good thing about her is her face.'

And it was true, she was a beautiful-looking cat. Irresistibly cute from the time she was a kitten.

'Maybe she remembers it was Dad who brought her back home. She *is* pretty intelligent,' she said.

Being wary, too, was a sign of intelligence, according to her.

The eldest daughter, never having conquered her discomfort around Ten, finally got a cat of her own. A different breed, with a different face from Ten's, but hers, too, was quite the looker.

'My cat's cute, too, Dad,' she said, opening the photos on her smartphone to show him, but he only snorted.

'Every cat in the world is cute,' he shot back.

*What did you say?* The whole family was stunned. 'Where's our dad, and what have you done with him?' Even in a worst-case scenario, Dad wasn't the type to say something so indulgent about cats. Despite what he said, when Ten got in his way he'd still give her a little kick.

Him tottering along, her rubbing up against him. Totter, totter, rub, rub. As if this scenario of old man and devoted cat would go on for a hundred years or more.

\*

· 102 ·

Dad's upbringing had led him to be a drinker, and he'd been a heavy smoker, too. He'd been told either cirrhosis of the liver or lung cancer would get him. In the end, it was both.

At one point, he seemed to cut back on his drinking, and though he always coughed when he inhaled on a cigarette, he didn't appear unwell. He was kind of holding his own against the passage of time, and his family took this as part of the ageing process.

What was a far bigger problem for them was how his legs were giving way. Until one day he took to his bed, refused to get up and was hospitalized.

Humoured by a lovely nurse, he did his rehabilitation and managed slowly to get back on his feet and to totter around again. At the rehab centre, they called it a miraculous resurrection.

The lovely nurse urged Dad to have a check-up and that's when they discovered the diseases. Both were terminal, and both inoperable. The doctors seemed amazed he was still alive.

Since there was nothing to be done, it seemed cruel to put Dad in a hospital again. Without giving him the details of his condition, they decided to take care of him at home in his final days.

He'd spent his life drinking incessantly, and smoking like a chimney, so it felt like it was all inevitable.

Mum took care of various end-of-life things for him. Just as she'd watched over their cat as it passed, she was full of generosity and kindness. And so he didn't seem to suffer much. Their son, a confirmed bachelor, came home to help.

Dad slept, and got up. Then he slept, slept, slept some more, then he got up. Spending his days in this routine, he began to grow a bit senile. 'When's dinner?' he'd ask. 'You

already had it, Dad,' came the answer. This kind of back and forth became a daily occurrence. The sensation of having eaten had perhaps deteriorated, because he often complained of being hungry.

Mum would hear sounds from the kitchen and, going to investigate, would find him rummaging through the cupboards. He'd happily haul any sweets he'd discovered back to his bed, but the problem was that in among them were some of Ten's treats.

'Honey, those are Ten's snacks,' Mum would say as she removed them. Often she'd make tea and they'd have a little night-time drink while she bent over to give Ten the snacks Dad had accidentally pilfered.

Right up until the day he lost consciousness, Mum supported him when he went to the bathroom. Ten would wind herself around his unsteady legs as he walked, and Dad would, as usual, kick her away.

They thought he'd totter around for ever, hanging in there, but once the pain took hold, it was the end of the road. He was the type who couldn't stand any pain or suffering, and had always avoided the dentist, even to the point where, by the time he turned sixty, he didn't have a tooth left in his head.

At some point during the marathon consumption of painkillers, he finally passed away. His eldest daughter and her husband hurried over, but arrived too late.

'He never did have any patience,' she said.

They kept his body at home for two days, waiting for an opening at the crematorium, and he looked as though he was just sleeping. The room was maintained at a very low temperature with an air conditioner and dry ice, but everything else remained the same.

Dad had always hated formality, so they had a small private funeral. He was taken out of the altar room that had been his lair, and he came back to it again, this time as ashes.

While they were at the crematorium, the rental people came and took away the hospital bed. In its place, they set up a simple altar where Mum placed his funerary tablet and an urn for his ashes.

Ten, who'd stayed at home all the while, joined them, unnoticed.

It was hard to tell if she understood what had happened, but she sat in the doorway staring for a time at the altar. Then she disappeared.

A year went by.

Their son, the confirmed bachelor, said he'd leave home after Dad died, but he ended up staying, and the three of them embarked on a new life together – Mum, son and cat.

Probably because her son was around, Mum didn't lose heart and stayed healthy.

Their son was always a quiet soul, so it was to her two daughters that she spoke the most. In a good mood, Mum said that when the weather improved, she wanted to see the Pallas's cat at Kobe Zoo. She'd heard about it some years before in a television documentary and was completely taken with it, being extremely curious about it before interest in the cat became a thing.

She'd clipped out newspaper articles about the cat and kept them under a table mat. If it hadn't been for Dad, she would have gone much earlier to see it. She stayed with their eldest daughter instead of at a hotel.

'That reminds me, how's Scary Cat doing?'

That was the daughter's name for Ten, who'd attacked her throat that time.

'She really does have a cute side to her, you know.'

Mum always defended Ten, bragging about little things she did that, frankly, any cat would do.

'Now that you mention her . . .' Mum said. That day she had a new titbit to share. Since it was winter, they kept the sliding glass doors between the altar room and the living room closed to keep the warm air from escaping. When Dad was alive, they'd left the doors open so it was essentially one big room.

'If we close the doors, Ten-chan starts to scratch, asking us to open them.'

When they opened the sliding doors, Ten would pace around where Dad's bed had been and sit under the altar for a while, her tail wrapped around her body, her ears turned forwards as if sensing something.

Even when left behind by him, the cat's devotion to the old man refused to fade.

'She was really close to Dad. Maybe Ten's the one who misses him the most?'

Dad's human family had accepted his passing, had cried soft tears at his funeral, yet they had made a quick recovery, knowing his time had come.

'But this cat really isn't a good judge of people. I mean, Dad never fed her, not even once.'

'He didn't do a single thing to look after her. But Ten-chan really adored him.'

Dad, who always did what he liked, whose words and manner were always so left-field, whose actions were often so preposterous, that even other families noticed.

Whenever their daughters talked about Dad, their friends would unfailingly chime in with: *If other people's dads do something, it seems funny, but if your own dad does the same, you don't like it.*

But there was a cat who loved Dad unconditionally, so if you were to have the good-father/bad-father debate, this would be enough to push him over to the good-father side.

It wasn't as if he even liked cats that much – he didn't – but in his later years, he had taken his family completely aback with his surprise comment *Every cat in the world is cute.*

Merciless to jellyfish, merciful to cats. They could cancel each other out.

He was, when all was said and done, a good father. Troubled, troublesome, yet utterly adored by a lone cat who could love no one else.

No more to be said.

# Cat Island

'RYO, WHY DON'T WE go to Cat Island?'
   We were eating dinner when my father, a freelance photographer, suddenly came out with this.

It was not long after my father had remarried following the death of my mother and we'd moved from Hokkaido to Okinawa.

Haruko, his new wife, was a lovely woman whose smile, like the sun, could light up a room. But I couldn't forget my real mother and couldn't bring myself to call Haruko *Mum*.

Looking back on it, it's hard for me to believe there ever was a time when I felt uncomfortable around her.

At the time, my father wanted me to get closer to Haruko, and at every opportunity would push us to *go out as a family*, which frankly got a little tiresome.

I was at a sensitive age then for a boy. The more he pushed me, the more I resisted the idea of calling Haruko *Mum*.

But the name *Cat Island* intrigued me. It sounded like the beginning of a fantasy adventure or something.

'What's Cat Island?' I asked Haruko, who was working as a tour guide. I was being considerate, drawing out her expertise, as a child will, at the dinner table.

'Its real name is Taketomijima,' my father jumped in. 'There are hundreds of cats there and there's been a bit of a buzz about it among cat lovers recently.'

I had been trying to include Haruko, but my father,

· 111 ·

butting in with his usual adult thoughtlessness, torpedoed my efforts. My eyes met Haruko's, and we couldn't help but share a smile.

*What a pain he can be, right?*

*I know.*

'How do you get there?'

It was Haruko who responded to my question. Finally, my attempts to include her were paying off.

'You take a plane from Naha to Ishigakijima, then a high-speed boat that takes about ten minutes.'

There are so many little islands in Okinawa, with lots of small planes hopping between them. I was finally getting a sense of the geography of the place, and how people could travel in small planes that buzzed back and forth between the islands.

'Katsu-san, so you accepted the job? To photograph the cats?' Haruko asked my father, who was holding out his empty tea cup for a refill.

'Yeah. I couldn't say no,' he replied, pulling a long face.

'Is that right?' Haruko said, tilting her head as she poured more tea into his cup.

'I told them I don't specialize in animal photography, but they said it would be okay.'

Apparently an editor my father knew had asked him to take the assignment. Their magazine was doing a special feature on cats, with one section on cats and travel. Taketomijima was one of the possible sites, but the company didn't have the budget to send their own in-house photographer on the assignment. So they picked one they knew who'd moved to Okinawa.

Taketomijima later became better known as an island with a lot of cats, but back then it was not yet famous, and

· 112 ·

the editorial staff had done a good job in spotting its potential before anyone else.

'That sounds good, Katsu-san. You like animals, don't you?'

Haruko still had a lot to learn about my father, I thought.

'I guess, but . . . if it's for work . . . Cats and I don't exactly hit it off . . .'

'Oh, so you don't like cats?'

My father seemed at a loss for a reply, so I piped up: 'Dad doesn't dislike cats, but they don't usually like *him*.'

'Shut up!' Dad growled as he wolfed down some of the Okinawan *chanpuru* stir-fry he'd piled on top of his rice.

His problem with cats was that he overdid it with the touching and playing. He'd rush over to them and they'd run away. Or else hiss in anger.

'Dogs I'm better with,' he added.

Still, even with dogs the ones that would respond well to him were the gentler types, or older. Dogs that were bashful around strangers felt scared by him, and hard-to-please dogs would bark.

In the past we'd visited Nara, famous for its deer, and when he rushed at one, crying out *It's Bambi!*, an angry parent deer had bulldozed him aside.

I was wondering whether to tell Haruko about this incident – but when I remembered that my late mother had been with us at the time, I decided not to.

'If they were salamanders, you might be able to photograph them well,' I teased.

But Dad took it seriously. 'Yeah, they don't seem to run away so fast.' As a photographer, maybe you shouldn't admit defeat like that.

'If all of us go, it should be at the weekend or during the

· 113 ·

holidays.' Haruko laid down her chopsticks and started leafing through her planner. During most school holidays, she had to work as a guide.

'The weekend after next I have free. That Monday is Founders' Day, so we could stay for two nights and three days. Does that sound good?'

She was referring to Founders' Day at my elementary school. It wasn't on the calendar so until Haruko mentioned it, I'd totally forgotten about it.

So Haruko had all my school activities written down in her planner, did she? The thought made me a bit uneasy. She had all these written down because she'd become my *mother*. She cooked for me every day, washed my clothes. And whenever there was a school event, there she was. If it was up to Dad, he'd get all the notifications and info messed up, that was obvious, so it was the correct division of labour.

Every day, Haruko was being my *mother*.

So how long would I keep calling her *Haruko-san*?

I still felt confused about calling her *Mum*. It was only two years since my mother had passed away.

Haruko didn't say anything, and always smiled cheerfully, and I let her spoil me, and got away with not calling her *Mum*.

'Okay, then, the week after next,' Dad said, excited at the prospect. Our trip to Cat Island was set.

***

IT WAS SUNNY, FORTUNATELY, ON the day we departed.

We took the first flight of the morning from Naha to Ishigakijima, then a thirty-minute bus ride from Ishigakijima

airport to where we would catch the ferry. Haruko had arranged for all the transfers to be smooth, so barely three hours after we'd left home, we were on the high-speed boat to Cat Island.

As ever, the colour of the sea around Okinawa shimmered turquoise. The thing that surprised me most after we started to move wasn't all the incredible tropical flowers, or the blazing light, but the harbours.

Even the sea filling each little harbour was a bright blue, as if paint had been dissolved into it. This blue, like coloured water a child would make for fun, spread all the way from the wharf to the far-off shore.

The high-speed boat seemed to fly over this unbelievable turquoise sea like a stone skipping across the water. It took about ten minutes to reach the island.

Thinking he needed to be taking photos of the scenery, Dad had been snapping away since before we got on the ferry.

The boat arrived at the pier at Taketomijima and we and our fellow passengers all crowded off. Here small shuttle buses were waiting to pick up guests already booked into the local inns. It was a tiny island, a mere 9.2 kilometres in circumference, and so there were no taxis.

While passengers were getting into their various rides, we waited for Dad to take his photos.

'Where are all the cats?' I asked Haruko as we waited in the shade for him to finish. I'd been picturing cats lined up at the harbour to greet us, and felt a bit disappointed.

'There are plenty of them in the villages and around the beach. People don't linger at the harbour, so that's why.'

Even if they decided to take up residence here, they wouldn't reap much from the tourists in the way of food.

· 115 ·

A van had just pulled up at the bus stop and Haruko waved at it.

'I asked them to come when you were about to finish taking pictures, Katsu-san,' she said.

She'd timed it perfectly. Before they got married, Haruko had been Dad's guide many times on photo trips to Okinawa.

The van trundled along slowly, but it was still only a matter of minutes before we arrived at the village in the centre of the island. We hadn't yet passed a single car.

The asphalt road began to peter out and now we were driving along a track of white sand that weaved its way past a terrace of houses with their low stone walls and the distinctive Okinawan red tiles, *shisa* guardian lion figures perching on the roofs.

The van pulled up in front of a house with particularly crazy-looking *shisa* on its roof.

'Oh, I'm so happy you chose this one,' my father said excitedly. 'The first time Haruko ever guided me on a photo trip, this was the place we stayed,' he added.

'It looks like an ordinary house . . . Is it like a guest house?' I asked. For a guest house it seemed quite cosy, as if one family would barely fit inside.

Haruko explained: 'People have family homes in Taketomijima that they rent out to tourists. Think of it as a kind of holiday cottage.'

Apparently an acquaintance of Haruko's managed it as a part-time business.

My father leaped out of the van in high spirits and started heaving our luggage out with the help of the driver. What with all the camera equipment we had more bags than your usual family on a three-day trip.

· 116 ·

Haruko strode across the lawn and thrust her hand into a gap in the stone wall. After a rummage, she brought out a wooden tag with a key attached. The whole set-up was so analogue, I exclaimed in surprise and Haruko smiled.

'When they're here they hand me the key, but when they're not, this is how we do it.'

'And that's okay? No one minds on the island?' I meant in terms of security.

'No one minds,' she confirmed.

'I guess it's unlikely there are any thieves who'd bother coming all this way.'

Once we had stepped into the house, you could take in the whole of the interior in a single glance. Three tatami rooms, a tiny kitchen, and beyond that what I imagined must be the bathroom. Just right for one family.

So they had stayed here together before, I mused. Dad had come on a photo trip to Okinawa for the first time about six months after Mum died.

Just as I was thinking this, Haruko smiled and whispered, 'I stayed at a different friend's house.'

'Oh!' I nodded and went to the front door to help Dad haul in the luggage. Our van had already left.

'Were you able to get some good cat shots the last time you were here?' I asked him.

'Cats weren't what I was after then.'

The assignment had apparently been to photograph typical island scenery to go in a guidebook, with cats just as an added extra.

They had laid out three sets of futon for us, which had been aired in a dryer and were nice and fluffy.

'Oh – this'll be the first time we'll all sleep lined up in one room together.'

It's when he says things like that that Dad makes me feel bad. I wasn't sure if, out of duty to my mum, I should have whinged a bit about the sleeping arrangements. He should have just let it pass without comment.

'This room faces east and the rising sun feels really good. We can look forward to getting up in the morning,' said Haruko. Now I no longer needed to make a fuss about the sleeping arrangements. I was looking forward to getting up in the morning, too.

'We have all the ingredients, so I'll throw together something for lunch.'

The fridge and kitchen shelves were packed. The system was that the owner stocked whatever food they thought appropriate, and we could help ourselves. All the necessities were provided, making you feel really at home, like staying at a relative's house where they had laid on everything.

'Well, I'm going to go rent us some bicycles,' Dad said.

Tourists on the island mainly got around either on foot or using rental bikes. You could call the bike shop and they'd bring them over, but since the shop was nearby, Dad said he'd go for a walk and drop in on the way.

'Why don't you leave the camera behind?' Haruko said. 'I'm making *somen chanpuru* and it will be ready soon.'

'Don't worry. I won't be long,' Dad said, and set off, a camera slung over his shoulder.

'I'd better reckon on about thirty minutes, I guess.'

Haruko's prediction was on the right track. If he came back in thirty minutes, that would be fast for him.

'Ryo-chan, you should go check out the area too,' she said to me.

'I might sleep for a while,' I replied.

· 118 ·

We'd got up so early, I was feeling a bit sleepy. And the lounger in the garden looked pretty inviting.

I went out and lay down, but then quickly got up again as the sun was shining right in my eyes. I tried moving the chair around and adjusting the angle of the back, searching for a comfortable position.

I'd finally found the best spot when I saw someone gazing at me from the gate. It was a bent-over old woman. She must live in the neighbourhood, I reckoned, but she was scrutinizing me so intently I began to feel uncomfortable.

'Excuse me, but may I help you?' I got up and walked over to the old woman. With a jolt, I saw that her right eye was all cloudy.

The old woman seemed to notice how I tried to hide my shock and brought up a hand to cover her right eye. 'I'm sorry if it makes you feel bad.'

'No, I'm okay.' I may have said this, but it's true I was taken aback.

'I was sick when I was a child,' she explained.

She apparently couldn't see at all out of her right eye, and I thought how hard it must have been for her to live with this all her life.

'Are the people you came with your parents?'

She seemed to be referring to Dad and Haruko. Did she know them, I wondered.

'I'm my father's child from a previous marriage.'

'Ah, I see. That explains it. Even if they had a child soon after they got married, you're a bit too big.'

So she *did* know them. 'Are you friendly with my dad and Haruko?' I asked.

'You might say that,' the old woman answered vaguely. 'Are you all happy?' she added.

This sudden question threw me completely, and I fumbled for an answer. Did she mean me? Or Dad? Or Haruko?

'Haruko is cooking right now. And Dad went out to hire bikes for us . . .'

My reply was as weird as if I'd said *Once upon a time there was a grandpa and grandma, and the grandpa went out gathering firewood in the hills while Granny stayed by the river washing clothes*, like some old folktale. I mentioned Haruko first since she was in the house. I thought maybe the woman wanted me to fetch her.

The old woman's face creased into a smile, buried so deep in all the wrinkles it took me a moment to realize.

'I'm glad you're all happy.' I hadn't said anything about us being happy. 'I was a bit concerned about them, you see.'

'If you want to have a chat with Haruko, she's here. Should I get her?'

'Nah, that's fine,' she said, brushing off the question, and abruptly walked away. I stood there, watching her shuffle off.

I made my way back to the lounger I'd spent so long getting in the right position and flopped down on it.

A few minutes later Dad came back.

'Hey, Ryo. You look very cosy.'

'Dad! If you'd got here a few moments ago, you'd have seen someone you know.'

'Oh really? Who?!'

'An old lady.'

I hesitated to mention her cloudy eye. 'Her sight wasn't so good,' is how I put it, but Dad didn't seem to have a clue.

'Someone Haruko knows, maybe.' He stepped into the house with a quizzical look on his face. I followed after him.

· 120 ·

'Ohh – good timing,' Haruko's voice greeted us from the kitchen. 'It's just about ready.'

The smell of *somen chanpuru* being sautéed in sesame oil wafted towards us.

'Someone you know stopped by apparently. An old lady.'

'I wonder who it was. Saying it's an old lady doesn't really tell me anything . . .'

'She had a bad eye,' I added, but that didn't seem to help narrow down the field.

'That's not uncommon.'

'Well, I guess she might come by again since she lives in the neighbourhood.'

'Yes, maybe,' Haruko said, carrying two plates of noodles. She placed them in front of us, and I fetched the third plate and set it down for Haruko.

'You have one hand free, so you could have brought the chopsticks.' Dad got up after me and came back in with three sets of disposable chopsticks.

'You have a hand free, so you could have brought the tea, too.' Haruko smiled and headed back to the kitchen. She came back balancing two cups neatly in one hand as I went to fetch the third cup from the kitchen.

'Don't they have a tray?' Dad asked. Maybe he was feeling a bit ashamed, having brought back only the chopsticks.

'No, there isn't one. Even though they've provided pretty much everything else. I'll let the owner know, since it'll be nice for others who stay here.'

Even though she had cooked it in someone else's kitchen, the *somen chanpuru*, made with canned tuna, onions and carrots, tasted just as if she had cooked it at home.

The food was delicious, but Dad still had to say, 'You

· 121 ·

know, when we make *chanpuru* I'd like to include some of those island spring onions too.'

Haruko had recently rustled up a special dish of sautéed spring onions and bacon mixed with noodles. Spring onions went well with any kind of noodle – *somen chanpuru*, spaghetti, yakisoba, whatever.

'If you go shopping over in Ishigakijima, buy some and I'll make it,' Haruko said, letting any perceived negative comment pass. There wasn't a supermarket on Taketomijima, and the islanders went over to Ishigakijima by boat to do their shopping.

'The tuna works well, too, so just be quiet and eat,' I said.

Dad and I often had this kind of role reversal, where I said what an adult would say as if he were the child. My late mother used to tell him, laughingly, 'Take a lesson from Ryo.'

Haruko and my mother shared this trait, being able to accept my often childlike father. In other words, the capacity for patience and generosity needed to be Dad's wife.

Haruko let it all go as a joke, but my mum, an elementary-school teacher, would smilingly tell him not to be so selfish. When I thought about this, I realized it was one of the reasons why I found it hard to call Haruko *Mum*.

Mum and Haruko were similar. They might express themselves differently, but what lay behind their words was very similar. A warmth, a gentleness, a generosity, a bigheartedness . . . that was the very least of it.

If they had had more contrasting personalities, aside from whether I could actually open up or not, I might have been able to come to a decision more quickly. But the uncanny resemblance between them made Haruko overlap

· 122 ·

with Mum in my mind. In a sense, Dad's taste in women remained constant, you could say.

And it was because Haruko and Mum were so similar that, every time I was on the verge of calling Haruko *Mum*, confusion and hesitation took hold of me.

While we were having our meal, a small truck pulled up outside with our rental bikes. Three red city bicycles, the kind with baskets on the front.

Haruko seemed to know the deliveryman and went out to sign the receipt.

Immediately after we'd finished eating, we set out in search of cats.

'Maybe we should bring some food for them?' I said as we stepped out of the house, the thought just occurring to me.

'Great idea!' Dad said. I don't think he was all that confident the cats would take to him.

Naturally there was no designated cat food in the house, so we rummaged around for something the cats would like.

We picked out some *chikuwa* fish cakes and processed cheese, which Haruko cut up into small pieces and placed in a plastic ziplock bag. We then set off on our rental bikes.

'The tyres can get stuck in the sand, so be careful not to fall off,' Dad instructed me, though with his camera bag slung over his shoulder and single-lens reflex camera hanging from his neck, *he* looked like the one who was about to topple over.

The sand along the alleyways lay quite thickly, and we couldn't glide down as on a paved road. On both sides, our tyres would sink into the sand, making ruts and

· 123 ·

slowing us down. We were heading to a particular beach that was said to have a lot of cats. It was about five minutes by bike from our house. Once we'd got out of the village, we emerged on to a paved road that encircled the island. Over time this road, too, had begun to crack and weeds were shooting up.

We carried on pedalling, over a stretch of compacted sand. Just beyond, we caught sight of the sparkling blue sea. We parked our bikes, close to the water's edge, near a mini arbour. As we walked closer, we saw them. Over twenty, at least. Kittens and grown-up cats. Everywhere. As many as thirty of them.

'I see them, I see them!'

Dad rushed towards the arbour. The cats, cooling off in the shade, began to creep stealthily backwards at the sight of this excited old guy intruding on their space.

'Damn, they don't like me.'

Haruko and I walked tentatively towards them; the cats didn't move a whisker.

A black-and-white tuxedo cat lay flat on a nearby bench, its paws folded under. Haruko stroked it lightly with her fingertips; the cat waved its tail once in response.

'Oh, that's what I would like to do. Just casually pet them,' Dad said.

'Then just go ahead,' Haruko said, laughing.

Dad reached out but the tuxedo cat furrowed its brows, turned its head away and leaped off the bench.

'See. I don't know why, but they always do that to me.' It was hardly surprising – he was too forceful about getting to pet them.

'Ah, but today I have a secret weapon.' Dad took out the plastic pouch filled with food from his camera bag.

· 124 ·

I was the one who'd suggested bringing food along, Haruko was the one who'd prepared the food, but Dad was the one who made use of it. He was quite shameless about taking a piece of the action. He wasn't even aware of it. I guess, that's what you had to expect from a child.

'Are you going to feed them now?' Haruko asked.

'When else am I supposed to?' Dad laughed. 'Hey, guys, here's some food for you. It's really tasty!'

Dad opened up the bag and the ears of the cats shot straight up and swivelled towards the source of the sound. From every direction all eyes were focused on him. The cats waiting at a distance began to pad forwards. Dad was swiftly and silently encircled.

Instinctively, I backed off a bit, moving over towards Haruko. These prowling cats weren't about to cutely coax any food from him. The scene reminded me of something. A TV documentary about wild animals that hunt in packs and behave just like this . . .

'Ha ha ha, they're just cats after all. Isn't it cute how they're going for the food!'

Innocent, triumphant, Dad pulled some titbits from the plastic bag. Just at that moment – the pack moved. Swarming around Dad from all directions. Not a single sweetly begging miaow, but the whole pack advancing with silent intent, an awful energy focused on Dad, demanding that he *hand it over*.

'What the—?'

Dad began to shake and dropped a piece of *chikuwa* fish cake. It rolled away on the ground. A number of cats made a dash for it and it quickly disappeared into one of their mouths.

The cats closed in further on Dad, moving to cut him

off. One bold cat reached up and batted at Dad's knuckles. Another made a leap for the plastic bag. All a bit demonic.

'Haruko-san! These guys are harassing me!'

'They're wild animals.'

'Get back!' Dad tossed some bits of food further away. The siege fell apart as a number of cats dashed towards the titbits rolling on the ground. Others were anticipating that Dad was still holding more food. They gathered in an even tighter circle around him. Exactly as if they were on the hunt.

'Whoa—!'

In a flash, a particularly brazen cat had yanked the plastic bag from Dad's hands. The food scattered and the cats ran amok. A massive brown tiger-striped cat, clearly the boss, growled at his companions as he gulped down the food.

'Hey, you! You've had plenty! Give some to the kittens!' Dad shouted, and when he tried to shoo the boss away, the cat flashed its front claws. It raked Dad's right hand and left other deep scratches.

In an instant, the cats had devoured the food, and their wild frenzy began to subside. They scattered to their preferred spots and collapsed.

'You damn cats!' Dad railed at them. They'd grabbed all his food for free and he hadn't managed to get a single photo.

'But I thought you said they were cute,' Haruko teased.

'Those are – wild animals.'

'It's not easy for them to survive, you know. The islanders feed them, but it's never enough, and the stronger ones get most of it.'

'So that boss cat's always eating. He should share some with the smaller cats.'

'That logic doesn't work in the wild.' I couldn't help a jab at Dad.

'I mean, you should have warned me that they were going to be so fierce.' Dad directed his petulance at Haruko.

'Well, I didn't think you were going to feed them right there and then,' Haruko said. 'I was sure you'd take the bag out to feed a smaller group or if you saw a kitten by itself.'

It's true Haruko had expressed her surprise that he was feeding them so quickly. She'd known there was going to be carnage.

'Enough of this.' Dad was beginning to sulk. 'I can take photos without the need to bribe them. I'm a professional. Plus I have a telephoto lens.'

As he was speaking, Dad started to change lenses. He did this not in the cats' headquarters, the arbour, but safely outside on a bench.

When he finally started on his photo shoot, both Dad and cats were professional about it. Dad nifty behind the camera, the cats natural at lounging and licking, staring into the distance and lazily twitching their tails.

When Dad suppressed his desire to touch the cats and just focused on photographing them, they went about their business, oblivious to him, grooming, napping and enjoying their space.

Nowadays with digital cameras you can take as many photos as you like and curate them later, but at the time film cameras were what most people used, and you wouldn't know how well the photos you had taken would turn out until they were developed. Each photo cost money, so it wasn't so easy to continuously click the shutter. Photographers showed their stuff when they captured the perfect moment.

Dozing, contented cats, the occasional click of the shutter when Dad, in his own way, thought the moment was right.

'I'd like to see a little more movement,' he muttered after a while. Left to their own devices, the cats sprawled listlessly, showing no intention of doing anything interesting for the camera.

With his telephoto lens he did follow a couple of kittens who were climbing on each other's backs as they headed playfully towards the beach, but back at the arbour things remained laid back.

'Ryo, could you engage with one of them for a bit? As if you're an island kid playing with a cat?'

'No way!' I replied in an instant. 'It'll be in a magazine, right?'

A more outgoing child would have leaped at the chance, but I wasn't one of them, and there was no way I wanted to be featured in a magazine. No thanks.

'The editor will make the final selection, so there's no guarantee.'

'But it might. So I don't want to. I mean, it would be fake, anyway? I'm not an islander or anything.'

'Then how about we list you as a child of one of the tourists?'

'*No. Way!*'

Dad and I kept sparring until we heard a loud flutter of flapping wings coming from the beach.

'*Noooo!*' It was Haruko screaming.

The kittens on the beach were now surrounded by crows. One kitten had failed to get away and they were pecking at it.

'Get away, you—!' Dad put his camera down and

scurried towards the beach. At times like this, he could really move. Haruko took off after him.

The two adults had vanished, leaving the expensive camera equipment behind them, so I ended up staying there to mind it. We couldn't just leave Dad's camera, no matter how laid back the island was.

'*Gya*—!' Dad yelled as the crows tried to attack him.

'Hang on, Katsu-san!' Haruko, arms windmilling, joined in as the crows continued their assault.

'They never change, those two.' I turned at the sound of the voice behind me and saw the old woman I'd met earlier. The brightness of the sea and sand made her cloudy, whitish eye stand out even more.

'Never change?'

'When they came here the last time, they did the same thing, getting all flustered trying to save something that didn't need to be saved.'

'That didn't need to be saved . . .'

Wasn't it just human nature to try to save a poor little cat being pecked at by crows?

'The weak get hunted down. That's the way it is.' The old woman's words were heartless but for some reason didn't feel harsh.

'If the weak don't die, things will come to a dead end.'

What would come to a dead end? I didn't dare ask. It felt like if I did, I'd get some terrible, bleak response.

'So have they tried to rescue a kitten before?'

'It was a fully grown cat. It had lived a long life, and it would have been okay if it had gone.'

'Dammit!' My dad's cries came from the beach. He was throwing sand at the crows.

'Ryo, get some stones!'

· 129 ·

'What?'

I looked around. The ground around the arbour was sandy; there were no stones big enough to use.

'I can see some over there.' The old woman pointed at a thicket with a line of low shrubs.

I hesitated. I wanted to hear more of what she had to say. What would this old woman, with her heartless vision, make of Dad and Haruko? I was especially curious about when Dad and Haruko first met. And about how they had rescued an adult cat that had lived long enough.

'Go on,' the old woman urged me. 'If you want to hear more, go out into the garden and look at the stars this evening. I take walks around there at night too.'

It turned out that while I was gathering stones for a counter-attack, our intervention had already made the crows give up on the kitten.

'Not a word of thanks from him, even though we saved his life,' muttered Dad.

As soon as the crows had flown off, the kitten made a desperate dash back towards the arbour.

'What do you expect? It's a cat living out in nature,' Haruko said, laughing, and without thinking I came back with, 'Since it's part of nature, isn't it better not to rescue it?'

The old woman's words had stayed with me.

*The weak get hunted down. That's the way it is . . . If the weak don't die, things will come to a dead end.*

'I suppose so,' Haruko said with a smile. 'But us being here is also a natural part of things.'

'You're right!' Dad said, interrupting. 'That kitten was lucky. If your luck's good, you get saved; if not, you die. That's fine. I mean, you would have a guilty conscience if you just stood by and watched crows peck a defenceless

· 130 ·

kitten to death, right? Especially during what's meant to be a relaxing family trip.'

'Isn't this trip a work-related photo shoot?' I said.

'It's a family trip which I'm paying for, so that's entirely within the scope of my discretion!'

The lucky little kitten had by now been absorbed by the group and we could no longer see which one it was. There might be days when the crows came out on top and the kitten didn't. Today, however, it was lucky – the logic was simple and I completely understood.

Dad and Haruko lived according to the same logic. That's the thought that occurred to me.

Dad lingered at the beach until evening.

A few tourists wandered by, some of whom fell prey to the cats just as Dad had, and occasionally mini-spats broke out among the cats.

Camera in hand, he caught it all.

'That's one clumsy cat.' Dad pointed to a beautiful brown tabby with well-defined markings around the eyes. He wasn't as tiny as a kitten, nor as large as the fully grown cats. Must be around six months old, was Haruko's guess.

Haruko and I noticed something about that brown tabby. Perhaps because his position in the group was tenuous, when tourists dropped by with food the other cats would growl at him and drive him away, even before they went for the food.

Whenever a titbit happened to land nearby, he'd hesitate and, in that instant, it would be snatched away.

'I wish we still had some food.'

Dad had spotted how some tourists offered food to the cats they liked most. They'd scatter titbits to distract the

· 131 ·

main group of cats, and approach the single cat they had picked out. Then they'd bring out food hidden in their hand, crouch down casually and drop it by its paws.

'Using that method you should be able to target that clumsy cat and get him some food,' he suggested.

The sun had turned a luminous orange. Dad changed the exposure setting on his camera and squinted, hoping to catch the cats and the setting sun together.

Right then I made a great discovery.

'Dad,' I called quietly, but he'd noticed too.

A cat had backed into the low line of shrubs. In its jaws was a plover, the bird's head hanging down limply.

The cat had withdrawn into the bushes so the others wouldn't attempt to grab the prey. And wonder of wonders, this cat was the clumsy brown tabby.

Dad continued snapping away.

The brown tabby had now safely brought its catch into the bushes. An unlucky plover. With the brown tabby it wasn't luck, but skill. It was the plover's bad luck to have caught the eye of a hunter.

'What do you expect? He's wild,' Dad murmured.

Being lucky. Being unlucky. Being skilled. Each of these combined to determine who survived in this tiny wild kingdom that coexisted beside the humans.

'Should we go back?' Dad put down his camera. He'd taken the best photo of the day.

On the way home, a few cats were padding around, but Dad left his camera in its case.

For dinner Haruko used whatever was in the fridge to rustle up tofu *chanpuru* and papaya *irichi*.

'Ryo-chan, do you want to have a bath first?' she asked as she tidied up after the meal.

'I'll have it later. Is it okay if I lie out in the garden?'

'It can get pretty chilly here at night.'

'I thought if I lie down on the beach chair, I'll get a good view of the stars.'

'That sounds good,' Haruko said, allowing me to enjoy the cool of the evening as long as I wrapped myself in a blanket.

'That looks nice. I might check the stars out myself,' my dad said, seeing me cosily ensconced in my chair.

There were two beach chairs lined up in the garden, but I said, 'You should have a bath first. If we both put it off, then Haruko won't be able to have one until much later.'

Haruko always had a bath last. She liked to drain the water when she was done and do a quick scrub of the tub.

'But if I have a bath first and then join you outside, I might catch a cold. I want to see the stars, too, you know.'

*What a child he is.*

'If you dry your hair well and wrap yourself in a towel, you should be okay.'

'I'll get another bottle of beer ready for you when you get out of the bath,' Haruko said, joining forces with me, and somehow we managed to hustle Dad back inside the house.

I had no idea when the old woman would pass by on her walk, but old people tend to go to bed pretty early, so I figured it wouldn't be that late. We'd finished dinner, and it was a little before 8 p.m. If the old woman did go for a walk, this would be about the right time. So if I didn't see her, it would mean I was just unlucky.

When I lay down on the beach chair, the stars looked surprisingly close, as if they would fall to the ground at any moment.

If I turned off the porch light, I could see them even better, I realized, so I went back inside for a second and hit the switch. And *wow!* – the stars now looked close enough to touch. I lay sprawled on the beach chair, for all the world like a king.

I began to recall snatches of the Tanabata song of the star festival when the celestial lovers would meet once a year. It described the stars as gold and silver powder sprinkled across the sky.

'Ah, so you're there, are you.' Over by the gate, the old woman peeked in.

'You said you take walks at night, and so I thought it'd be around now.'

'Good thinking,' she said.

'Here, you can sit down.' I motioned for her to come through the gate, which she did, and she sat down on the other beach chair.

'We were talking about those two, weren't we?'

And the old woman launched into the story of when Dad and Haruko first came to the island.

DAD HAD ARRIVED ON THE island looking totally dispirited, she said.

From the moment they met, Haruko had been worried about him. This was the first time he'd visited Okinawa, and it was, unfortunately, rainy from the start. Quite stormy, in fact. Haruko suggested that he take advantage of the weather

to photograph Okinawa in a storm, and took him to a spot well known for its large waves.

I'd heard all this before and figured it must have been a good trip.

But the old woman shook her head. 'Far from it,' she said. 'Your father looked in bad shape. As if his *mapui*, his soul, had fallen away.'

The idea that the soul could fall away was a concept unique to Okinawa, where they believed it could be triggered by a great shock or surprise. In that event, you had to pick up the fallen soul and return it to the body. If you didn't, you'd become depressed, your body would start to ache and, in the worst case, you could become seriously ill.

I knew the reason why Dad's soul had fallen away. Mum had died, and he was at a total loss. To escape from the reality of her death, he'd travelled all over Japan taking photographs, like a kind of pilgrimage.

When he first met Haruko, his soul had probably still not returned to his body.

'Your mum took such loving care of him, you know.'

I was still uncomfortable hearing Haruko referred to as my *mum*, but I didn't tell the old woman this. Legally, Haruko was already my mother, and a child complaining to a third party soon after his father remarried was itself pretty childish.

I wouldn't be able to laugh at Dad any more for being such a *child*.

The old woman went on. The storm began to clear, but soon enough, the seas around the island began to turn rough and choppy as a new storm approached. Dad gave up photographing the sea, which had begun to look murky, and spent his time taking pictures of the houses with their red roof tiles.

On that visit, Dad had stayed in this very same house.

· 135 ·

Haruko seemed to regret that she hadn't booked him into a regular inn that provided meals.

'I'll come back later so we can wander around the island at night, so have some dinner first. You can eat any of the food stocked in the house. If it's too much trouble to cook, there's always instant noodles.'

After several reminders, Haruko left, seemingly still a bit concerned.

'She asked me to keep an eye on him when she left,' the old woman said with a laugh. 'She must have been quite worried to ask the neighbours to look out for him.'

Haruko ended up coming back earlier than she'd planned. She'd packed a few dishes in Tupperware containers for him to eat.

The lights were still on.

'Mr Sakamoto,' she called at the front door, but Dad wasn't in. Pushing open the door and entering, she came across a note lying on the low table in the living room.

*I've gone to watch the ocean.*

A guidebook was left open on the table at the page that described the pier on the west side.

Haruko placed the Tupperware boxes in the fridge and sat down to wait, but there was no sign of his return. She decided to go to the western pier to find him.

'It turned out I went along with her,' the old woman said, somewhat cryptically.

The western pier lay in darkness. He said he was going to watch the ocean but that was impossible. The sea was completely black, and everything offshore was lost in darkness. Great waves broke against the pier, the spray glittering white in the moonlight.

Dad was seated at the base of the pier, looking vacant. Relieved, Haruko walked over to him.

'Mr Sakamoto,' she called, and he looked up. Haruko stopped walking. Dad's face was wet with tears.

'Uh, the thing is . . .' he said, hurriedly wiping his face. 'I happened to be remembering my late wife. Pretty unseemly, huh,' he added, sniffing. 'I know it's time to get over it, but still . . .'

All Haruko could do was stand silently beside him.

'My son's much stronger than I am. I'm just a no-good . . .'

'It must have been so hard for you,' Haruko murmured, the words just slipping out.

And then, shoulders heaving, Dad began to sob uncontrollably.

Haruko crouched down beside him, stroking his back. It was an entirely natural gesture, as if she were treating someone who had been wounded. If there's someone injured in front of you, it's human nature to go to them.

Dad continued to wail.

Haruko remained beside him until the tears finally began to slow.

'I'll head back to your lodgings,' she said. 'So please take your time,' and she left.

Dad gave himself up to the tears that overwhelmed him once again.

Time passed but still no sign of Dad.

Haruko waited almost an hour before going back out to the pier to get him. She was worried, the way he'd been sobbing so relentlessly.

· 137 ·

When she reached him, she found him standing, stock-still, on the beach.

She watched as he started to run towards the sea. Haruko tried to call out, but her voice cracked. She raced after him.

Dad pushed through the waves straight into the sea.

'Mr Sakamoto!'

Dad kept wading.

Splashing feverishly through the waves, Haruko finally made it to his side. The sea was still shallow at this point, the water up to her chest.

'Come back!' she cried, but the wind snatched her words away. The waves beating against her, she grabbed Dad by the collar.

'Think about your son, before you go after her!'

'Le– let go of me . . .'

'No!'

'The cat!' he yelled. 'It's going to die!'

She looked over to where he was pointing, where the waves were crashing against the pier, the spray surging upwards.

A cat was floundering in the waves.

Half wading, half swimming, Dad and Haruko together managed to scoop up the drowning cat. The waves tossed them about as they made their way back to shore.

'This doesn't look good,' Dad said. The drenched cat lay limp in his arms, its eyes closed.

'It must have swallowed a lot of water.'

'How do you do CPR on a cat?' Dad asked, and then dangled the cat by its rear legs, giving it a vigorous shake up and down.

'That's not the way to do it,' said Haruko. 'When kids

· 138 ·

choke on a sweet, this is what you do. You slap them firmly a few times between the shoulder blades. Do it right and they'll spit it out.'

Dad's emergency treatment actually worked and the cat began to vomit up water. Having got all the water out, it collapsed in exhaustion.

'We should take it back to my place.'

'Good idea. It's cold here.'

Dad and Haruko both looked like drowned rats themselves.

Back at the house, they showered the cat with warm water, and dried it off with towels and a hair dryer.

They made a bed for the cat in a cardboard box and put it down to sleep, then the two of them took turns having a shower. Dad rummaged around in the closet and came up with a pair of pyjamas, which Haruko put on.

Once they'd both changed, the cat, too, had settled – no longer a half-drowned wreck but simply an ordinary sleeping cat, sacked out for the night.

'Um . . .' Haruko began awkwardly later. 'I'm sorry. I totally misunderstood what was going on.'

'Don't worry at all, it's okay,' Dad said, himself apologetic. 'Of course you'd think that – with a grown-up man bawling his eyes out, and then walking out to sea.'

He peered into the cardboard box.

'This cat seems to have eye problems.'

'I think you're right. And it must live somewhere nearby.'

'It sort of hung around me for a while when I was down at the pier, and after I'd stopped crying, it started wandering around. Then it lost its footing and fell off the pier.'

· 139 ·

'It's because it followed me. I shouldn't have let it,' said Haruko.

'No, it's my fault. It really seemed to want to keep me company.'

'No, I'm to blame.'

'No – it's my fault.'

They argued for a while, then finally looked at each other and burst out laughing.

'What should we do about the night excursion we were planning around the island?' Haruko asked.

'Let's save that for next time,' Dad said. 'Please take me around then. I'll bring my son with me.'

'I'd love to. I look forward to it.'

'I put some food in the fridge for you,' Haruko added on her way out, still worried about his dinner.

'WHAT A DUMB, CLUMSY CAT. Imagine losing its footing and falling into the sea – its time was up, I'd say.' No words of sympathy for the cat from the old woman.

'It was lucky.' I went with Dad's and Haruko's logic. 'It was natural, too, that Dad and Haruko got together.'

A wild kingdom right next to where people lived. If humans dropped in every once in a while, well, that was okay.

'Luck . . . Right.'

'Well, I guess we'll just leave it at that.' The old woman chuckled. 'After all that commotion, it seems your father's *mapui* came back. That makes sense.

'Right,' she added. 'If you do something for other people, it'll be good for you too.'

· 140 ·

It wasn't *people*, though, in this case, but a cat.

With a grunt, the old woman got to her feet.

'Shall I go and fetch Dad and Haruko?' I asked.

'No, it's fine. I'd better get back or the people at home will start to worry.'

The old woman shuffled slowly over to the gate. After a moment, she turned round.

'Are you going to start calling her *Mum* soon?'

'What?'

'Someone's waiting for it.'

I knew, of course. That Dad was wanting me to call Haruko *Mum*.

'Very patient, they are, so I don't think they'll be pushing you into it.'

'What?' I blurted out again.

*Patient? Since when did that describe Dad?*

'By *they*, do you mean Haruko?'

There was no reply, for the old woman had tottered out through the gate.

I was standing there, stock-still, when Haruko came outside.

'Ryo-chan, time for your bath.'

'My turn, my turn,' Dad said as he came outside. His hair was dry, and he was holding a bottle of beer. 'Whoa, now this is a bed fit for a king,' he murmured as he sank into the beach chair, his reaction the same as mine.

The next day we made another trip around the island in search of cats.

There were cats living on a beach where you could scoop up star-shaped grains of sand; Dad photographed the cats from many different angles. We competed to see who

· 141 ·

could scoop up the most star-shaped sand, and predictably Dad was the one who took it far too seriously.

That evening we went on our final excursion to the arbour. The beach lay glowing white in the moonlight, while the cats lay stretched out at random.

'This is a scene you don't see every day,' Dad said, quickly setting up his tripod, and snapping the cats on a long exposure.

On a slower setting of twenty seconds, the lens took in that much more light, making the night look even more astonishing, with the available brightness coming only from the moon and stars.

Even after he had stowed away the camera, we sat motionless on the beach, gazing at the cats.

'Finally, we managed to get around the entire island at night,' Dad commented.

*We'll go around the island at night at the next opportunity. Someday, I'll bring my son.*

His previous trip to Cat Island had ended with this promise.

'Back then . . . you rescued a cat from a stormy sea, didn't you?' I started to speak but then swallowed my words.

The story about how Dad had cried his eyes out over my dead mother. Not the right story to bring up when we were on a family trip like this with Haruko.

'What?' Dad asked, urging me to go on, and I changed tack.

'So before, when you were here, you didn't walk around the whole island at night?'

This was all I could do to change tack and not make it sound weird. I mean, I was a kid, after all.

Dad and Haruko exchanged a look, and then the faintest of smiles.

'When I was here before . . . there was a big storm and the waves were huge,' said Dad.

Which was true, but not the whole story. Not by a long shot.

This is how adults smooth over certain topics, I realized. So even Dad had some adult qualities after all, I thought.

'I wanted you to be there the next time I visited, Ryo.'

*Yeah, I know*, I thought, but left the rest unsaid.

'I'm glad we could all be here together.'

Not the whole story. But it wasn't a lie.

Dad had taken enough photographs of cats, so the next day we decided to wander around Ishigakijima before heading home.

We left our lodgings in time to make the ferry arriving at the island just after 9 a.m.

Haruko left the key in the same spot as before and we were loading our luggage into the van that had come for us, when an elderly cat came tottering up the sandy path towards us.

It was a dark tabby, its paler patches of fur yellowed by the sun and the sea.

'Goodness!' Haruko shouted. 'Katsu-san, look!'

Dad took a good look at the cat. 'Well, what do you know,' he said. 'So how've you been?'

The old cat meekly let Dad pet it, super friendly as it rubbed its cheeks and the top of its head against his hand.

'When we were here last time, this cat was about to drown, and Katsu-san rescued it.'

· 143 ·

*Yeah, I know*, I thought, without saying so. 'I've seen it several times.'

The cat's right eye was whitish, and clouded over.

'So you're still living round here, eh?' said Dad.

'A little while after that, one of the neighbours took it in,' said Haruko.

'Really? Lucky you, eh? You'll spend your final days nice and snug.'

As if to say *thanks to you* the cat rubbed its head even more vigorously against Dad's hand. It began to push its flank against Haruko, too, and me as well.

'Thank you,' I murmured. 'Thank you for telling me so many stories.'

'I'll call her *Mum* soon,' I whispered as I ran my fingers along its side, and the cat rubbed its whole body against me, right side and left, backwards and forwards, as if it was praising me for my decision.

THE DAY AFTER WE GOT back home, Dad wasted no time in developing out the photographs and sending them to his magazine editor.

A month later, we received copies of the special cat issue.

As Dad flipped through its pages, he began to frown, then he looked up at the ceiling. 'Ah – damn it!'

Haruko and I both peered over at the magazine and knew in an instant what he meant. The single photo Dad was most proud of had been left out – the one of the hunter with the plover in its mouth.

The photos they had used were of the cats playing on

· 144 ·

the beach at night, and pictures of cute little kittens. He was paid the same no matter which photos they ended up using, but he did feel slightly down.

'Cheer up,' Haruko said. 'I like that photo best of all too. It's the one that really captures Okinawan cats.'

'Me too,' I chimed in. 'I definitely like that one the most.'

It would be a pain if Dad moped around, so the two of us teamed up, trying to lift his spirits.

The way we were so in sync, it was like we really had become a mother and son.

The day wasn't too far off, now, when I'd call her *Mum*.

*So, not to worry*, I said, silently sending out a message to that old cat with the cloudy right eye.

# The Night Visitor

*Date: –th of ——*

In the middle of the night, I heard this heavy sniffing sound. Then a brush of whiskers. When I opened my eyes, Tom was stretched on his side, gazing at me.

His black eyes were urging me to *Get up!* Leading the way, turning occasionally to make sure I was following, he led me to the living-room cupboard. *I'm hungry, so bring out some snacks!* he was saying. It was 3 a.m.

That damn Tom. Damn, cute Tom.

*Date: –th of ——*

Getting woken up at 3 a.m. made me sleep deprived and I decided tonight was the night I would ignore him. I feigned sleep while he sniffed but then he leaped on to my pillow and walked all over it. I tried not to notice, but that didn't work because then he pretended to accidentally tramp across my face with each fifth step. I gave in and got out of bed.

That damn Tom. Damn, cute Tom.

*Date: –th of ——*

Yesterday I decided I was definitely not going to get up. My mind made up, I went to bed. I ignored all the sniffing. And Tom retreated.

I was sure tonight I'd be able to get a peaceful night's

sleep, when out of nowhere there was this *Pyopyo! Pyopyo!*
screeching sound, an electronic bird noise. A toy that
screeched like a bird when it was shaken. He was using it as
an alarm. He was clearly some kind of genius.

That damn Tom. Damn, cute Tom.

*Date: –th of ——*

I will not give in. I ignored the sniffing. Ignored the
tramping. Ignored all the *pyopyo* racket. He made a temporary retreat.

He leaped on to my pillow once again. Tramping around
didn't work any more, so he straddled my face with all four
legs. His belly fur was at the height where it rustled just
above my nose, brushing it. Nothing to do but get up.

That damn Tom. Damn, cute Tom.

*Date: –th of ——*

I will not give in. The sniffing, the tramping, the *pyopyo*
noise – consider them ignored. The tummy-fuzz attack I
avoided by turning on my side. And Tom retreated. Then
from the living room came the crazed bird cry – *Pyopyo!
Pyopyo!* – ad infinitum. Enraged, he was intentionally making it squawk again and again so I would hear. That insistent
angry beat made it impossible to sleep.

That damn Tom. Damn, cute Tom.

*Date: –th of ——*

I ignored the sniffing, ignored the tramping, and when
it came to the *pyopyo* noise I simply grabbed the toy and hid
it under the futon covers. I turned away from the tummy
fur. Tom stepped over to the opposite side of the pillow,
pushed his forehead against mine and twisted it vigorously

around. I never imagined he'd try such an outrageously coquettish move. If I ignored it, maybe he wouldn't try it again, I figured. I had to weigh up the pros and cons.

That damn Tom. Damn, cute Tom.

*Date: –th of ――*

Lack of sleep led to daytime naps. Tom was reclining out in the sun beside the screen door.

Everything seemed so calm, when all of a sudden his fur was standing on end and he was making a huge ruckus. I looked through the window and saw we had a cute little visitor.

'My, what a cute thing you are,' I said to the newcomer, and Tom glared up at me with this scary expression on his face. The eyes speak more than the mouth, and his were saying, *What are you talking about, eh?*

That damn Tom. Damn, cute Tom.

After our cute little visitor left, cherry blossom petals began to flutter down against the screen door.

The cherry tree that graced the centre of our garden was dropping petals for the first time this spring.

Tom is a cat.

In 2020 the world was besieged by something terrible – not exactly a nuclear firestorm but awful all the same.

For all that, the winter daphne still bloomed, as did the magnolias and the cherry tree.

And next spring they'll bloom again.

And next year, too, Tom and I will continue our night-time battles.

A YEAR HAS PASSED NOW.

The plum trees have blossomed, but the cherry blossom has yet to appear.

And predictably Tom and I still do battle each and every night.

From behind comes a mysterious, low-frequency humming sound looping over and over.

I look behind me and see that Tom is kneading the boa cushion on the couch, purring all the while, and staring directly at me, his pupils reduced to tiny slits in the sunlight.

What is it? I ask, as I come over and bring my face close to his. As he goes on kneading the cushion, he rubs my forehead with his own.

That damn Tom. Damn, cute Tom.

This is all just one big brag, so I don't mind if you forget everything I've said.

# Finding Hachi

W HEN HE WOKE UP, he was inside a cardboard box.
He looked around and spotted another kitten, a
brother born at the same time. White downy fur with a black
tail, just like him. There should have been several other siblings alongside him but it was just him and the one other
kitten.

The top of the box had not been closed properly, and
light was filtering in through the cracks.

If he meowed, his mother should appear. He mewled a
bit, his brother joining in.

Finally, the top of the box opened. It wasn't his mother
who was peering in, though, but a child, a boy he'd never
seen before. Behind the boy's head was a boundless blue
sky. He was gazing silently into the box with a surprised look
on his face.

Just then—

'Whoa – cats!' a voice called out. Another boy was now
peering inside.

'I wonder why they're here.'

'Somebody must have left them.'

'Wow – they're so cute!'

The boy who'd just arrived reached out a hand and
stroked the downy fur of both kittens with the tips of his
fingers. The first boy followed suit.

'Do you want to pick one up?'

This from the second boy. He scooped up the first

· 155 ·

kitten in his cupped hands, while the other boy scooped up his brother.

'Do you think somebody wanted to get rid of them?' the second boy asked.

'Probably.'

'That's terrible.'

'We'd better get going. We'll be late for swimming.'

'Yeah, you're right.'

But they stayed, crouched over the kittens.

The one who lingered the longest was the boy who'd arrived last.

'Come on, Satoru,' the first boy said, prodding his friend, and the boy named Satoru reluctantly let his kitten go.

The boys trotted off, the sound of their footsteps fading in the distance.

After a while a shadow loomed over the box. A couple of little girls in yellow hats peered in.

'They're sooo sweet!' a voice said from above. A hand abruptly reached inside and lifted the first kitten up. His brother was lifted up, too.

'I wonder if they've been thrown away. The poor things.'

'I might take one home.'

'Will they let you have a cat in your house?'

'I don't know. But they're so lovely. When Mum sees the kitten, I bet she'll let me keep it.'

'If you do, let me play with it, okay?'

'Sure! But which one should I take? Which one's cuter?'

The two girls began to compare the kittens. They picked them up, one at a time, and turned them over.

'I think I'll take this one.'

'Really? That one? But its tail is bent. It looks weird.'

'You think so? Then I'll take this one.'

· 156 ·

The girl placed the first kitten back in the box and picked up his brother. Unlike his own sharply angled tail, his brother's was perfectly straight.

His brother never came back.

All by himself now, he began to feel lonely and started mewling. Until now if he mewled, the mother cat would make her way quickly over to him, but now she didn't come, no matter how much he called.

The kitten began to grow tired, his mewls weakening. He curled up and started to nod off. He wasn't sure when, but at some point he fell asleep.

He was woken up by two voices shushing each other. He raised his head to see the two boys from before.

'What do you think happened to the other one?'

They seemed to be talking about his brother cat.

'Could we keep this one? How great would that be!'

The boys whispered together, watching him steadily. Finally, the one named Satoru said, as if making a decision, 'I'm going to ask my mum.'

'Hey, that's not fair!' the other boy exclaimed, and when Satoru flinched at his outburst, he added, 'I mean, I'm the one who saw them first.'

Satoru apologized. 'You're right, you saw them first, Ko-chan, so he's your cat.'

Ko-chan picked him up, box and all, and made his way home.

But later—

'A cat? Absolutely not. No. Way!' The man that Ko-chan called Dad wouldn't let the kitten into the house.

After persisting for some time, Ko-chan gave up. Tears sliding down his cheeks, he carried away the box with the

· 157 ·

kitten. It looked as if it was going to be left outside again, but Ko-chan was heading for Satoru's house.

'What's wrong, Ko-chan?'

'Dad said I can't keep the cat,' Ko-chan sobbed.

'I get it,' Satoru said to his friend. 'Leave it to me. I have a great idea!'

As Satoru dragged Ko-chan from the house, a voice called out, asking where he was going.

'Ko-chan and I are going to run away from home for a bit!' he called back.

'I have a plan,' Satoru explained to his friend. 'I read it in a book at school. A boy found a stray dog, but his father refused to keep it and told him to take it back where he had found it. But the boy didn't want to, so he ran away. His father came looking for him, searching late into the night before he found him. He finally allowed the boy to keep the dog. *But you've got to make sure you take care of him yourself!* his dad told him.'

In other words, Ko-chan should do likewise: take the kitten and run away from home. Ko-chan had his doubts, but Satoru was so insistent he finally gave in.

In a nearby park, the two boys sat down for a snack and opened a can of cat food they'd bought at a small supermarket along the way. The kitten was starving and gulped down the tasty, nutritious paste. In his frenzy, he stuck his nose into the paste and gave a sudden sneeze, making Satoru and Ko-chan burst out laughing.

Satoru's plan, though, didn't work out quite as expected.

'Hey!' came the angry voice of Ko-chan's father. 'How much longer are you going to sulk, eh? It's about time you called it quits and came home.'

· 158 ·

'It's the enemy! Run!' Satoru commanded.

The box bumped around as the two of them raced off with it. Inside, the cat was rolling about, no longer able to tell which way was up and which down. After some time, the shaking finally stopped, and the top of the box opened. The two boys peered in, frowning.

'Is he okay? We shook him up a lot, climbing those stairs.'

The kitten couldn't take any more. *Piao!* he howled in protest.

'I heard a cat!' came a voice from below, where a crowd was starting to gather.

'It's coming from the roof of the school!' came another voice. It was Ko-chan's father, growing angry again. 'Kosuke, enough!'

Ko-chan began to cry again.

'This isn't working out at all, Satoru. You lied!'

'No, it's too soon to say! We can still pull this off!'

'No, we can't!'

As they started to argue, the people below were discussing how to get hold of the boys.

'I'm going up the fire escape over there.'

Ko-chan's father, fuelled by anger, started to climb the stairs.

'We're done for!' exclaimed Ko-chan, while Satoru rushed over to the railing on the edge of the roof.

What was *done for* wasn't clear, but as long as they didn't shake him around any more, the kitten didn't care.

Satoru's voice rang out suddenly.

'Don't come any closer! If you do, he'll jump!'

A commotion arose among the crowd below.

'. . . is what Ko-chan said!'

'What the—?'

· 159 ·

Satoru's announcement wasn't at all what Ko-chan had in mind. 'What are you talking about?' he shouted at Satoru and the two began arguing again.

'Do you really mean to keep this up, Satoru?!'

'I do, I do. *Hey, he just took off his shoes!*'

A gasp arose again from the people huddled below.

'Stop right now!' It was Ko-chan's father. 'Enough of the tantrums. I'm coming up there and dragging you down if I have to.'

'Don't do it!' Satoru countered. 'Ko-chan's going to jump! Come any further and he's ready to commit double suicide with the cat!'

The kitten didn't know what *double suicide* meant, but it looked like he was going to be a part of it. And whatever it was, it didn't sound good. *Run for it!* instinct whispered, but the walls of the box were too high for him to scramble over.

As for the two boys, they were bickering again.

'How about not gambling away my life, eh?'

'Look, Ko-chan, you want to keep the cat, don't you?'

'Sure I do, but still. I mean – shouldn't you first ask your parents to let you keep him at your house?'

'What?' Satoru gulped. 'You mean it'll be okay if I keep the cat?'

'Wouldn't most people think of that before coming up with the idea of making their friend kill himself?'

'You should have said so!'

The upshot was that the kitten became Satoru's family cat.

When he got home, Satoru's parents gave him a piece of their mind.

Satoru listened as he wolfed down a plateful of food.

The kitten had his own food, too, which they'd placed in

· 160 ·

a bowl for him. As he was chewing, the paste-like cat food got steadily pushed into a corner of the bowl and he couldn't quite reach the last few bites. Satoru's mother gathered the pieces with her fingers and held them to his mouth.

The kitten finished his meal and was tidying up around his mouth with his tongue and front paw. Satoru seemed to have finished his meal, too.

'He looks like maybe he's two months old?' Satoru's mother said as she scratched delicately behind the kitten's ears. It felt just like a mother cat licking him, and he couldn't help purring.

'Whoa – he's purring.' Satoru, eyes wide, gazed at him.

'They purr when they feel good.'

'Really?'

'Here, too,' his mother said, stroking under the kitten's chin with her fingertips. Satoru tried it, but his touch was awkward and not as deft.

'He has a hooked tail, doesn't he.'

'A hooked tail?'

'The tip is bent like a hook, right?'

Satoru's mother traced the bent end of his tail with her finger. This tail, which bent sharply halfway down, was the reason those girls hadn't chosen him earlier in the day. But here, no one seemed to mind.

'We have to give him a name,' the father said, and Satoru's hand shot up.

'I've got it, I've got it!' he shouted. 'Lamborghini! Lamborghini!'

'It's too long and hard to say.'

'McLaren! McLaren!'

'Something other than car names!'

'But they're cool!'

· 161 ·

As Satoru and his mother argued over it, his father interjected.

'I prefer a Japanese name instead of a Western one. He's sort of got spots on his face, so how about Buchi – Spot?'

'Nah, that sounds cheesy.'

The mother's quick comeback left the father deflated.

Satoru gazed hard at the kitten's face – and then said: 'How about Hachi?'

His parents blinked in surprise.

'Look, there's a marking on his forehead like the character *hachi* – eight 八.'

'You guys are as bad as each other when it comes to cheesy names,' the mother said. 'I guess boys take after their fathers.' She looked pointedly at Satoru's father and he flinched.

'They may be cheesy names, but Satoru's suggestion has an extra twist to it, since the character *hachi* is a lucky number, the way it spreads out as if gathering in good fortune.'

And so it was decided. Holding the kitten with his hands under the front legs, Satoru lifted him up to his face and pressed his nose against his.

'Hachi! Your name is now Hachi! Speak to me, Hachi!'

When the kitten gave a little *meow!* Satoru's face lit up, his cheeks shining.

'He answered! He understands!'

Satoru pressed his cheeks against Hachi's whiskers.

And that's how he became the family's Hachi.

HACHI FAINTLY REMEMBERED THE HOME in which the mother cat and his siblings had once lived, but after three days at Satoru's he'd forgotten them completely.

· 162 ·

Ko-chan came over almost every day to play. One time he brought a cat teaser toy as a little present.

'My mum bought it for me at the supermarket. It's made with rabbit fur.'

Ko-chan waved the toy in front of Hachi, the grey furry part waving wildly from side to side. A hectic back and forth for sure, but the movement was too monotonous to be enticing.

'It won't work that way.'

Satoru took the cat teaser from Ko-chan and placed the grey furry part under the zabuton cushion, with just the tip of it peeking out. He brought it out for a moment, then hid it, then poked it out again.

Hachi instinctively raised his hips. His bent tail waved and he went into a crouch, his haunches quivering. Then he pounced and held down the toy with his front paws. Just when he thought he had it, the cat teaser slipped from his paws and wiggled away.

He pounced again, but the toy had slipped under the cushion and vanished. But then it peeped out at the other end of the cushion and Hachi, enthralled, dodged and pounced again. He'd almost grabbed it, but it eluded his grasp, and he couldn't quite get hold of it.

Ko-chan sighed in admiration.

'Boy, you're good, Satoru.'

'He he!' Satoru laughed.

He was proud of his skill with the cat teaser, though it was his mother who'd shown him how. She was even better at it. She'd had cats, she said, when she was a child.

'I get how to do it. Let me try,' said Ko-chan.

He copied Satoru, moving the toy around, but he moved it too quickly. Hachi's eyes swivelled around, watching the toy, but he couldn't time his leaps to grab it.

· 163 ·

'Move it more slowly.'

'Is Hachi maybe a bit slow?'

'No way. Hachi's just laid back.'

*Laid back* was the way Satoru's parents had put it. It meant something like *slow* but was a kinder way of saying it.

Ko-chan made the tip of the cat teaser pop out from under the sofa, then disappear. This was easier for Hachi to catch.


'Snack time, boys—'

Satoru's mother brought in warm steamed buns. Momentarily distracted, Ko-chan slowed down the game, and spotting his chance, Hachi made a lunge, snagging the fur toy in his paws. He began to chew on it, carefully working from the base upwards.

'Did you put raisins in the buns?'

'Not this time. I don't always.'

'Oh,' Satoru wailed, pouting, and his mother flicked a finger against his forehead. 'No complaints,' she said.

'I like the chocolate-flavoured ones.'

This from Ko-chan.

'We've run out of cocoa powder, I'm afraid. Just eat what's put in front of you—'

Ko-chan got his own forehead flick. He seemed happy to receive it, though.

Concentrating on their snacks, the boys ignored the cat toy, so Hachi took a flying leap at Satoru's fingertips and started chewing on them instead.

'Ouch! Stop it!'

But Hachi was determined to catch the moving fingertips. 'Okay, okay, I get it,' Satoru said. He rummaged around in the cloth box containing Hachi's toys and took out a mouse with white fur and a skinny leather tail.

· 164 ·

'You like this, don't you?' Satoru held the mouse by the leather tail and swung it around. 'Go get it!' he yelled and tossed it down the hall. Hachi scrambled after it, skidding on his way. Once the mouse was trapped, he pushed it down the polished hallway.

'Hachi really likes that mouse.'

'It will keep him busy for a while.'

'Do you think he could catch a real mouse?'

'I wonder.'

A couple of months later, Ko-chan's question was answered.

'*Eeeek – a mouse!*' Satoru's mother screamed as she was tidying up inside a cupboard. She'd just opened the storage space above it when a mouse dashed out.

It sped across the room and ran straight at Hachi.

'Go on. Grab it, Hachi!'

All well and good, but this mouse was three times the size of his white toy mouse. And it was a dirty grey. Above all, though, it ran around on its own without being pushed or slapped.

Unsure what to do, he instinctively edged away.

The mouse hurtled right between Hachi's legs towards the front door. Shocked by the sensation of the mouse racing under him, Hachi plunked his belly down on the floor.

'Let's chase him outside!' Satoru's father yelled, striding to the front door with a rolled-up newspaper clutched in his hand.

'Satoru, close the door!' his mother called. Satoru pulled the door from the living room to the hallway shut, and crouched down in front of Hachi.

'You're a cat, but you lost out to a mouse. That's pathetic.'

· 165 ·

For Hachi this was withering criticism. But this wasn't the kind of mouse that Hachi was familiar with.

'I suppose it was the first ever mouse you've seen, Hachi. You've led a pretty sheltered life, haven't you?'

*I'm telling you, that was no mouse,* Hachi meowed in protest, but neither Satoru nor his mother paid any attention.

'Hey, I chased it out of the house, guys,' Satoru's father said. 'That mouse tunnelled right under you, didn't he, Hachi?' He stroked the cat's head consolingly.

*But that was no mouse!* Hachi wanted to say, but who would listen?

'Even when mice appear in our house, our cat's no help at all.'

*Just ignore them,* Hachi said to himself as he curled up at one end of the sofa. *They don't get it, so take no notice.*

'It's okay. We don't have a cat, we have Hachi.'

'Are you upset, Hachi?'

Satoru came over and tickled his belly. A little late in the day, it seemed to Hachi.

'It's okay that you can't catch mice, Hachi. Because you're our family's darling cat.'

Hachi had planned to sulk for a while, but with all the scratching behind his ears and stroking under his chin by Satoru, he was overcome and before long started purring.

WHEN HACHI WAS FIRST BROUGHT home, Satoru had been a big boy, but before he knew it, Satoru had become more of a child than him.

Cat time and human time seemed to move at a different pace. Around the moment he realized that cat time

· 166 ·

moved more quickly, Hachi had passed Satoru and was already a fully grown adult.

The cat teaser and toy mouse didn't excite him as much as they had when he was a kitten. Whenever Satoru tried to get him to play, he couldn't always be bothered.

'And he was so, so tiny when we first got him.'

Back then, he'd fit snugly into Ko-chan's cupped hands; he'd been no bigger than the size of a fist, Satoru commented.

He must have been a bit bigger than that, but Satoru seemed to like to emphasize how small Hachi had been. Memories of when he was a kitten must have been deeply etched into his mind. From Hachi's perspective, when he was a kitten Satoru had loomed over him like a mountain.

Compared with Hachi, Satoru and Ko-chan were growing up quite slowly. In the space of a year, a young cat would grow many times larger than its kitten size, but for the boys, after a year, they had still only put on an inch or two.

*How many years are they planning to take before they are grown up?* Hachi wondered, finding it all extremely puzzling.

Spring arrived, the second since the boys had found him.

The school backpacks the boys carried were starting to look tight on them. Hachi hadn't noticed it on a daily basis, but suddenly he realized how their arms and legs had sprouted.

Spring passed and early summer arrived, and Satoru came home with a golden trophy. He'd brought home a few over the last few years, but never one this big.

Dinner that night consisted of all Satoru's favourite food. *Kara-age* chicken nuggets and potato salad, plus takeaway

assorted sushi, minus the wasabi, and nigiri sushi topped with omelette strips.

Hachi too was given a feast – a large bowl of steamed chicken breast.

As the family sat down to their meal, they made a toast, Satoru with orange juice, his father and mother with beer.

'Congratulations, Satoru, on winning!'

He'd apparently taken part in a big competition at the swimming club he and Ko-chan attended. It was the biggest swimming competition he'd ever taken part in, and Satoru had come first.

'You're amazing, Satoru,' his father said. 'When I was at elementary school, the furthest I could swim was twenty-five metres.'

'It makes sense,' his mother said, 'given that we grew up in Hokkaido.'

From what Satoru's mother said, the ocean and rivers in Hokkaido were so cold that there were few opportunities to swim, even in the summer, and not many people from Hokkaido were therefore able to do so.

'The swimming coach said he hopes you carry on when you go to junior high. Will you, do you think?'

Happily chewing on his mother's *kara-age*, Satoru looked a little dazed. He'd had three large nuggets already, with some nigiri sushi in between.

'Mmm . . . if Ko-chan does, too,' he answered absently, biting down on his fourth chicken nugget. For his part, Ko-chan didn't seem to be that keen on swimming. He was among the cheerleaders at today's competition.

'There's a swimming team in junior high, isn't there?' Satoru's father said, trying to arouse his son's interest, but

· 168 ·

again Satoru just said, 'If Ko-chan does,' before digging into the nigiri sushi.

'Did Ko-chan say he would?'

'He's not sure yet.'

For Satoru the appeal of swimming seemed to boil down to the question of whether he could be together with Ko-chan.

His father seemed disappointed that Satoru wasn't more enthusiastic.

'Well, Satoru should carry on if he wants to,' he said, before pestering his wife to bring him another bottle of beer. 'Keeper of the Purse Strings, if you would be so kind!' he pleaded, and his wife smiled and went through to the kitchen.

Having had his fill of nigiri sushi, Satoru helped himself to a tuna roll. Hachi scratched at his sleeve and Satoru peeled off a slice of tuna and handed it to him, leaving just the sushi rice for himself.

It wasn't clear if Satoru and Ko-chan would carry on swimming in junior high, but Hachi knew one thing for sure: he would keep watch over these two boys as they continued to grow.

He and his brother had been abandoned, and he'd ended up in this home, over all others. This had to be so he could watch over Satoru and Ko-chan as they edged towards adulthood.

'Hachi—'

Tired after his big meal, perhaps, Satoru rested his fingers on Hachi's tail. Satoru liked the cat's hooked tail and enjoyed playing with it.

The little girl who'd picked his brother to take home

· 169 ·

had left Hachi behind because of this bent tail. But it was this crooked tail that turned out to be Hachi's saving grace.

THE SAUNA-LIKE HEAT OF SUMMER had passed, and the wind was finally growing cooler.

On a cloudless autumn day, the sky looked so high.

'Mum? What about my bag? You said you'd buy it for me today!'

Satoru was back from school, and pestering his mother.

'All right, all right . . .'

Laughing, his mother fetched the travel bag she'd bought earlier in the day. A big blue bag made of a crinkly fabric.

'Can I start packing?'

'But your school trip isn't for another week.'

'But if I get ready early, I won't have to rush later on!'

The upcoming school trip to Kyoto was a major event for Satoru.

'I need three days' worth of clothes, so how many pairs of underpants should I take?'

'Two, I would think.'

'Not three?'

'The first day's pair you'll be wearing when you leave, won't you?'

'But will that be enough?'

'Then why not take three pairs? If you wet your bed, you'll be in trouble.'

His mother said this teasingly, and Satoru went red. 'I don't do that any more!' he insisted, slapping her arm in protest. 'I haven't done that for years!'

· 170 ·

Satoru was right. Hachi had still been a kitten when Satoru had drawn a world map on his bedding. Back then Hachi, too, had had some toilet mishaps of his own. Ancient memories that were fading away now.

But now Hachi had no more toilet accidents, and neither did Satoru.

'I'm not going to wet the bed, but it feels like two's not enough.'

'Then why don't you ask Ko-chan?'

When Ko-chan came over, Satoru asked him how many pairs of underpants he planned to take for the three days. He drew pictures of underpants in a sketchbook as they discussed the matter.

'The first day we'll take a bath so that's the first pair. After the second day's bath, that's two. And the third day . . .'

'The third day we'll be coming home, so we won't need another pair.'

Ko-chan was in the two-pair camp, to which Satoru countered, 'But we're going for three days,' though he didn't sound so confident any more. In fine lines, he drew several pairs of underpants in a corner of the sketchbook.

'Here's why—' his mother cut in as she passed by. She took the pencil from Satoru and drew a figure with underpants on and wearing a baseball cap. 'You'll have one pair to start off with, the underpants you'll be wearing when you leave here. Then the pair you'll change into after your bath on the first day, and the pair you'll change into after the bath on the second day. See? That makes three pairs altogether.'

His mother pointed at each pair in the sketchbook, counting them, and the two boys finally seemed convinced.

'So we'll only need to take two pairs!'

'That's right,' his mother replied, beaming, but when

she got to the kitchen, she paused. 'Wait a second!' She was reading the handout for the trip that was taped to the fridge. 'I'm sorry, boys! The guidelines for the trip say to take an extra pair! So it's three pairs, after all!'

'What?!'

The boys were none too happy to find the decision overturned.

'Okay – so three days' worth of underpants comes to how many pairs?' said Satoru.

'Basically two pairs. *Basically.*'

His mother came over, took the pencil and next to the second day's pair of underpants drew, in parentheses, another pair.

'You're taking one more pair, just in case.'

'Just in case?'

'Like I said, if you wet the bed, for instance . . .'

'*I don't wet the bed!!*'

After all the fuss, they finally settled on three pairs.

'What about socks? Three pairs too?' Satoru asked, and his mother went to the fridge again to check the guidelines.

'It doesn't say anything about extra socks. Two should be enough, I would think.'

'But what if it rains hard and they get wet?'

'If you're so worried, take three pairs.'

Satoru and Ko-chan launched into another discussion.

Cats get by just the way they are, but humans can have it tough. With one ear twitching at the boys, Hachi stepped inside the wide-open travel bag and curled up.

The day of the school trip loomed.

'So next is . . . a toothbrush!'

'Check!'

· 172 ·

Satoru and Ko-chan brought out their toothbrush sets from their bags and held them up like *inro*, the small cases that hang from the *obi* or belt of a kimono. Ko-chan had lugged his travel bag all the way over to Satoru's so they could go through the checklist together the day before the trip.

Ko-chan read it aloud, and they extracted each item from their bags in turn, showing each other.

'You sure you want to take everything out like that?' Satoru's mother called as she took in the laundry.

'We're good to go,' the boys called back, not really listening.

'Underpants?'

'Three pairs!'

'Socks?'

'Two pairs!'

They'd apparently settled on two pairs.

Satisfied, they zipped up their bags. Behind Ko-chan lay his toothbrush set, left out in all the excitement.

*Look what happened.* Hachi rolled his body over the toothbrush set a bit.

'Hey! Ko-chan – you forgot your toothbrush!' Satoru called out.

'Oh, my gosh!' Ko-chan said and grabbed the tooth-brush from Hachi. 'You shouldn't play with that, Hachi. It's not a toy.'

*I showed you it's missing and that's how you react? That's not nice.* Hachi narrowed his eyes.

'Let's play with something else,' suggested Satoru quickly and brought over the cat teaser toy.

Hachi was still a little put out but decided that, with the boys away for three days, if they thought he was upset when they left him, they'd worry about him on their trip, so

· 173 ·

he should cut them some slack. When all was said and done, Satoru and Ko-chan were still children, and you couldn't expect them to be totally considerate.

Not to mention how enticing the cat teaser toy was when Satoru wielded it, the way his mother had shown him.

Hachi bounded boisterously after the toy as it sped away, then he came to an abrupt stop, keeping a close eye on it as it leaped around. Ko-chan took over a few times, but his handling of the cat teaser was, as always, not as deft as Satoru's. He never let Hachi catch it, for one thing, which made it boring.

'It's almost time for dinner,' Satoru's mother called from the kitchen. 'You should go home soon, Ko-chan,' she added, 'since the trip is tomorrow. You're all meeting up pretty early in the morning.'

'Do I have to? But Hachi's in such a good mood.'

*Ahh – no need to worry. I'm good*, Hachi thought. He let go of the cat teaser and Satoru's mother added, 'You can play with Hachi any time.'

'Okaay—'

'See you,' Ko-chan said to Hachi, stroking the top of his head, and left, lugging his travel bag with him. Once Satoru had waved Ko-chan through the front door, he sorted out his own bag. Neither one of the boys had noticed Hachi stepping over their things and sniffing around to ensure they still hadn't left anything behind. They were, after all, still children.

That evening while they were having dinner, Satoru was feeling excited.

'So, Dad, what souvenir would you like me to bring back for you?'

'I'll be happy with anything as long as you choose it.'

His father was trying to please him, but Satoru shot back, *'Boooring!'* and his father looked dejected.

· 174 ·

'What about you, Mum?'

'I'd like some Yojiya facial blotting paper.'

'Facial blotting paper?'

His mother stood up and fetched her shopping tote bag. She opened up a little pouch where she kept her powder compact and lipstick and took out a small folder full of translucent sheets of paper.

'Here, this is what I mean. The Yojiya brand has a drawing of a woman's face on the outside.'

'What does it look like?'

'Well . . .'

On a memo pad, his mother drew him a face like that of a crude but charming *kokeshi* doll. Satoru studied the drawing.

'If there's a different, cuter brand, is it okay if I buy that?'

'No, it has to be the Yojiya brand,' his mother insisted.

'I guess I have no choice, then,' Satoru said, nodding seriously.

That night Satoru was so worked up he couldn't sleep. He kept turning over and every time he did, Hachi had to find a new spot on the bed.

'What should I do? I have to get up so early tomorrow . . .'

Satoru picked up his bedside clock to see the time and seemed about to burst into tears. Finally he threw back the covers and got up. Worriedly, Hachi padded silently behind as Satoru left his bedroom and headed for the living room. The light was still on, his mother still up.

'Mum . . .'

'Okay, I get it.' His mother smiled and stood up. She'd been writing something at the table but now went into the

kitchen. Satoru heard her moving about and the *ding* of the microwave, out of which emerged a steaming mug, the scent of hot milk wafting from it.

This was the *special sleep medicine* his mother made for him the night before a school outing or family trip.

'Today's drink is special, with two teaspoons of honey. That should do the trick.'

Satoru nodded and sat down on the sofa, blowing on the hot milk to cool it down.

'Mum, have you ever been to Kyoto?'

'Many times.'

'Did you go to Kiyomizu Temple?'

'I did, yes. The boiled tofu there was delicious. If you have time on the trip, you should try some.'

'Tofu? Boring!'

Satoru sipped at his milk as they chatted, and finally his eyelids started to droop.

'Night, Mum,' he said, and headed back to his room. He rolled over a few times before finally falling fast asleep. Hachi waited before moving towards his feet, and curling up.

The next morning, Ko-chan came to fetch Satoru and he got up on time and set off happily with his friend.

Two days later, he would be back home with all his souvenirs.

At least that was the plan.

THE DAY AFTER SATORU LEFT, it didn't stop raining.

And naturally Hachi felt his eyelids grow heavy, for rain always made cats sleepy.

· 176 ·

Hachi had just eaten his breakfast and had curled up on the sofa when Satoru's father came over and looked out of the window as he fastened his necktie.

'Wow, it's really coming down. Do you think Satoru will be okay?'

'The weather report says it'll be clear in western Japan,' his wife replied.

'I hope so. If it's raining like this over there, it will spoil their trip. I'm going to get soaked just walking to the station.'

'Don't worry, I'll drive you.'

After he'd eaten, Satoru's father put on his suit jacket while his mother took the plates to the kitchen and left them to soak.

And then the two of them hurried out. 'See you later!' Satoru's father called to Hachi. His wife didn't say anything. She planned to come right back.

The disheartening sound of falling rain didn't seem to let up. Cats spent rainy days like this fast asleep. Pouring rain, *zaa zaa*. Dozing cat, *zzz zzz*. Pouring rain, dozing cat, *zaa zaa*, *zzz zzz*.

At some point, amid the unceasing rain, Hachi's ears twitched, as he thought he heard a muted siren far off, though he could have been imagining it.

Finally he'd had enough of sleeping. He gave a wide yawn and dropped his back in a downward cat stretch, then leaped down from the sofa and padded gracefully towards the kitchen. His stomach was telling him it must be lunchtime.

In his little food bowl, in its usual spot next to the sink, there were a few crunchy leftovers from breakfast. Not enough to fill him up, but he went ahead and ate them. Satoru's mother would soon notice and refill the bowl.

But even after he had licked the bowl clean, she didn't

· 177 ·

appear in the kitchen. The room was filled with the sound of rainfall, but no sign of Satoru's mother moving around elsewhere in the house.

Hachi wondered what was going on but, unable to fight the heaviness in his eyes that crept up on him, he curled up and went to sleep.

*Zaaa zaaa, zzz zzz, zaa zaa, zzz zzz, zzz zzz, zzz zzz.*

Before he realized it, the sound of the rain had begun to slacken off. His ears twitched at the clatter of the key in the front door.

*You're so late – do you have any idea how hungry I am?* But when Hachi strolled over to the front door, it wasn't Satoru's mother. The face of the woman slightly resembled her but looked a lot younger.

This was Satoru's aunt, his mother's younger sister. She was always visiting.

The aunt gave a small flinch when she spotted Hachi. He was aware from past experience that she seemed uneasy around cats, so he didn't venture any closer.

'Satoru.'

Urged on by his aunt, Satoru appeared in the entrance lugging his travel bag.

Hachi was about to welcome him back by brushing against his knees, but instead he froze just inside the door—

Was this really Satoru?

The boy's face was pale, expressionless.

His face usually flitted rapidly from one expression to another, but now it had set into just one, his eyes wide open and mouth tight shut.

'Change into these clothes,' the aunt instructed, handing him a paper bag. Satoru awkwardly reached out and

· 178 ·

took it. Like some unoiled machine, you could almost hear his joints squeaking as he moved.

Hachi waited a moment, then followed him as he headed to his room. This didn't seem like Satoru at all and his fur began to prick up in mild fright, yet he wasn't about to leave him on his own when he was looking like that.

Inside the paper bag his aunt had given him was a suit like the one his father was always wearing. Except for the shirt, all the clothes were black – the jacket, the trousers and the tie. Even the socks were black.

Satoru tugged off his colourful sweatshirt and put on the close-fitting white shirt. He pulled on the trousers and jacket and snapped on the clip-on tie.

Finally, he exchanged his red-striped socks for the black ones. He threw the red-striped socks on top of his sweatshirt. Then, all of a sudden, he began to hurl himself around the room. He kicked at the sweatshirt and sent it flying. The red socks on top took off in another direction.

Hachi scampered under the bed, belly low. Usually Satoru would quickly apologize if he startled the cat. But not this time. He completely ignored him.

Face blank, Satoru stamped on the sweatshirt over and over again. Soundlessly, but no less violently, he continued to abuse the sweatshirt. As if it were to blame for everything.

Someone knocked at the door.

'Satoru, are you ready?'

At the sound of his aunt Noriko's voice, Satoru suddenly stopped stamping on the sweatshirt and left the room calmly as if nothing had happened.

His aunt was dressed from head to foot in black.

· 179 ·

'Let's go to where your father and mother are.'

Satoru nodded and started walking behind her. Hachi paused, before setting off after them.

Satoru was slipping on his shoes when he ran back inside as if he'd forgotten something. He was heading for the kitchen. He poured a mountain of crunchy cat food into Hachi's bowl and changed his water.

Then he made his way to the bathroom where he cleaned up Hachi's litter tray and poured in a bit more sand.

Even though his face was expressionless, and even though he'd silently tortured his sweatshirt, Satoru was still Satoru. Hachi rubbed the top of his head against Satoru's knees. Satoru didn't say anything, his face remained blank, but he did scratch Hachi's ears a little.

Hachi saw Satoru and his aunt off. As the front door shut behind them, he heard the sound of their footsteps receding. He had no idea where they had gone, but he did know it was somewhere sad.

Satoru had forgotten to turn on the lights, and the house eventually grew pitch black. Hachi ate his cat food in the dark, lapped a little water and spent the rest of the time napping or looking out of the window.

It was late at night when Satoru returned with his aunt.

When Hachi padded to the front door, Satoru seemed to shudder at how dark it was inside. His aunt went in first, switching on the lights, and finally Satoru took off his shoes and walked in.

The aunt went around turning on the lights in the hallway, the living room and the kitchen. Satoru followed as the lights came on. In the kitchen he saw that half of the cat food was left.

Satoru and his aunt took turns taking a shower and went to bed without eating. Satoru slept in his own room, while his aunt spread out a futon in the living room.

Hachi slid into Satoru's room, where the crumpled, mistreated sweatshirt still lay.

Satoru had gone to bed but when Hachi landed beside him by his pillow, he found him wide awake, staring, his eyes like vacant dark holes, at the glow from the small light bulb.

Satoru moved his pillow aside to make room for Hachi, but Hachi heard no gentle snoring coming from him as he usually did. Hachi fell asleep first, so he had no idea when those vacant eyes of Satoru's finally did close.

The next morning was bright, brilliant sunlight streaming in through the gaps in the curtains.

Satoru and his aunt again changed into their black clothes and left, but not before Satoru had filled Hachi's food bowl to overflowing and left the light on in the living room.

Hachi thought they'd come back late that day, as before, but it was different this time.

As the sun was setting, from outside the house came a loud voice, like a howling animal. And gradually, inescapably, the voice grew more shrill, echoing louder and louder against the walls.

Hachi sat in the entrance, ready to greet it.

It was Ko-chan who opened the door. As he walked in, he was propping up the wailing Satoru.

He stumbled slowly towards the living room. An animal howl rang from him. He sat down, shoulders heaving.

Ko-chan might have helped him home, but he had no idea what to do now. He stood wavering beside Satoru.

In a single leap, Hachi was on Satoru's lap. Satoru

· 181 ·

rested his palm on Hachi's cheek, and Hachi licked his hand carefully, very carefully.

*It's okay. It's okay.*

*I'm here. I'm here.*

He carried on licking his hand, and finally, as if worn out, Satoru's howls began to subside.

FATHER AND MOTHER CAME BACK home in two identical white urns.

Satoru was taken in by his aunt and was moving house.

'But you'll take Hachi with you, won't you?' Ko-chan sounded like he was praying this would be the case. 'If Hachi's with you . . . Even in your new home you won't be alone, Satoru. You won't be as lonely.'

'I can't take Hachi with me. 'Cause my aunt is transferred around a lot with her work.'

Satoru seemed to have resigned himself to it long ago. But it was painful for him to have to say so to Ko-chan.

'Then what about Hachi?'

'Some other relatives of mine said they'd take him.'

'Do you know these relatives well, Satoru?'

Satoru shook his head. Ko-chan bit his lip.

'I – I'm going to go see if we can keep Hachi at our house!' Ko-chan called as he left, but after dark he was back, clearly having cried his eyes out.

'Dad said no way.'

From his thick, swollen eyelids it was obvious how bravely Ko-chan must have battled to convince him.

'It's okay,' Satoru said, his tearful face smiling. 'I'm happy that you tried.'

· 182 ·

The two of them wept silently as they stroked Hachi, and Hachi let them stroke him as much as they wanted.

He'd been so sure he'd stay in this house and watch over the two boys as they grew up. But for both children and cats, life never seemed to turn out the way you wanted.

Later, an older man, an uncle of Satoru's, came to collect Hachi. He was tall, with a deeply lined face, and when he smiled his eyes disappeared into the wrinkles around them.

Satoru was in the living room, his arms tight around Hachi's belly. The man tousled Satoru's hair.

'Don't worry about a thing. Everyone in our family loves cats. We'll take good care of him, don't you worry.'

Satoru's face lit up. It was the first time since his parents had disappeared into those two white urns that he'd looked like that.

'Be sure to make Hachi happy.'

'Leave it to me,' the man said.

Even so, when it came time to say goodbye, Satoru wept as if his tear ducts were broken.

'I wonder if there's really no way Noriko-chan can take him.'

The man said this out of pity for Satoru, but his aunt's current place didn't allow pets, apparently.

'Look, let the last thing Hachi sees from you be a smile, or he'll worry about you,' the man said, and Satoru tried to smile through his tears. He forced the corners of his lips up into a grin, even if it was a bit lopsided and weird-looking.

'Hachi, take care!' Satoru called out, giving a big wave.

That was the last Hachi ever saw of him.

· 183 ·

FOR ABOUT THREE HOURS, HACHI swayed back and forth in
his carrier before they finally arrived at the uncle's house,
where there were four children.

The eldest boy was even taller than his father. Next was
a girl, then a boy, and another boy, each progressively
smaller, the youngest about the same age as Satoru.

Which is perhaps why the first name Hachi remembered belonged to this youngest boy. He was named
Tsutomu. Like Satoru, his expression changed by the minute. He didn't go swimming but was into baseball.

And he fought with his older brothers and sister every
day. Being the smallest, he always came off worst, whether
it be wrestling with them, or arguing. Hachi's daily routine
included sidling up to him as he cried, and licking his hands
and knees. Tsutomu lost every day, so blubbering was an
everyday occurrence.

'Usually cats get most attached to the person who feeds
them.' Both Tsutomu's parents found it odd that Hachi
would favour Tsutomu over anybody else.

'Hachi is sorry for Tsutomu since he's such a wimp,' his
sister said with a burst of laughter. When they argued, she
was the one who most often made her little brother cry.

'Shut up!' Tsutomu yelled and gave her a swift kick
from behind.

'Now you're for it!' she shouted and chased after him.

He'd end up crying no matter what, so why the boy
would get involved with her was a complete mystery to Hachi.

'Hachi doesn't seem to like going out much.' The
mother seemed to find this odd. 'When I clean the flat and
open the window, he'll go out into the garden but that's
about it. With our apartment being on the ground floor, he
should go out for a little stroll at least.'

· 184 ·

'Maybe he was an indoor cat at his previous place?' the father said.

'The poor thing,' the mother replied, frowning slightly.

'I wouldn't say that,' their eldest son chimed in. 'People are afraid of accidents and things, so there are more and more households that keep their cats indoors all the time.'

'Well, our little Milk was in an accident, too, wasn't he,' the boy next in age piped up.

Milk was the name of the very first cat this family had. The sister had named the cat, though the boys found the name too cutesy and hadn't been very fond of him as a result.

'Hachi's a bit slow. Maybe it's good he doesn't want to go outside.'

His sister gently poked Hachi's cheek with her forefinger.

'Stop it!' It was Tsutomu who broke in. 'He's not slow. He's just laid back!'

Hearing Tsutomu speak, Hachi recalled another boy the same age.

*No, what Hachi is is laid back.*

It was Satoru who had rephrased *slow* as *laid back*.

Hachi looked up to see a child smiling down at him, using the same words as Satoru as he scratched him behind his ear.

*Ah – I get it,* Hachi thought.

*My job now is to watch over Tsutomu in this place as he grows.*

*Satoru and Tsutomu are the same age. They use the same gentle words. As Tsutomu gets bigger, so will Satoru.*

Tsutomu replaced Satoru in his mind, naturally, and that was that.

It did bother him that he had left Satoru, but he was finally able to feel at home here.

Tsutomu tickled his throat with his fingers and for the first time since he'd arrived in this new family, Hachi purred to his heart's content.

SPRING FOLLOWED WINTER AND THE cherry blossom was out. Tsutomu now wore a school jacket with a stand-up collar and had started going to junior high.

As before, he continued playing baseball. When had he stopped swimming, Hachi wondered. Doing both was hard, so it couldn't be helped. Seemed he'd put away that golden trophy somewhere.

He played sports every day and ate loads. He shot up in height too. It was hard to believe there used to be a time when he had grown so slowly each year, since the following year, he shot up four whole inches.

Their baseball practice always seemed to be outside, and his skin became so dark it looked like it was boiled in soy sauce. 'When the light is behind him,' his mother said, 'his face is so dark I can't tell where his eyes and nose are!'

'He's even darker than me. Imagine that!' his father added with a laugh.

As always, though, Tsutomu's expression changed by the minute. And the fights with his older brothers and sister never let up. But the quarrels with his sister were more verbal now than physical. His sister's sharp tongue had become even sharper, incorrigible. Tsutomu no longer burst into tears when they fought, though on occasion a few did well up in his eyes.

Hachi loved Tsutomu, beaten to the punch by his

sister, and teary-eyed. He loved all of them – the father, the mother, the eldest brother, the second-eldest brother and the sister – but he loved Tsutomu most of all.

When Hachi ran, his hind legs got all tangled up, but Tsutomu and that other boy were nice enough to call him *laid back*. When Hachi came across a mouse for the first time in his life and stood there, frozen, wasn't that boy the one who said, 'Maybe he can't catch mice, but Hachi's our darling cat.'

He told anyone who wiggled the cat teaser toy too fast, to *Move it more slowly*. Now, what was that boy's name again? Who was he? Tsutomu's friend. He'd come over to play every day, a long, long time ago, when Hachi was still just a kitten. When had he stopped coming?

Cat time passed fast. The time when he was a kitten was so long ago it was like back before he was born.

He couldn't remember the other boy's name. Even so, he must be okay somewhere. *I mean, look at how much Tsutomu has shot up.*

*Please, let them all be well, and happy.*

Spring came around once more, and the eldest brother left home. He had passed his entrance exam to college and would be living in the city.

The apartment grew a bit quieter. The absence of the eldest brother was one reason, but the other children's quarrels had grown slightly less boisterous. Tsutomu and the second-oldest brother would occasionally tussle, but that was about it.

Tsutomu's arms and legs grew even longer because he got a daily workout at baseball practice and packed away so much food every day.

· 187 ·

In the summer baseball tournament, his team got as far as the semi-finals. Tsutomu came home crying tears of regret.

'Isn't making the semi-finals good enough?' his mother said, and his sister chimed in with, 'That's right. You can try again when you're in high school.'

'Shut up!' Tsutomu yelled, losing his temper. 'This is the only time I'll play with these teammates!'

'Hey, I'm only trying to make you feel better,' his sister shot back and threw a cushion at him.

*I don't think you should have reacted that way, Tsutomu,* Hachi thought, rubbing his side up against the boy's knees. As Tsutomu gave the cat a soft stroke, he gradually calmed down. Later, he apologized to his sister.

'But making it to the semi-finals is still quite an achievement,' his mother said, and ordered takeaway sushi for dinner. To which she added her own chicken nuggets and potato salad – his favourite meal since he was little.

The exact same menu as they'd eaten when he first won the swimming competition, Hachi seemed to recall.

But now he didn't seem to like nigiri sushi that much. Tsutomu ate only the tuna. When Hachi tugged at his sleeve, he carefully scraped off the wasabi from a piece of tuna sushi, gave it to Hachi, and swallowed down the sushi rice in a single gulp.

'Are you going to keep playing baseball in high school?' his father asked, to which Tsutomu grunted a yes.

'Didn't you say you didn't want to unless you could play with the friends you're with now?' His sister still seemed to be holding a grudge against him for snapping at her when she'd only been trying to cheer him up.

'I'm not that childish. And a few of them will be going to the same high school as me.'

'*Stop it*, all of you!' their mother shouted, and they reluctantly simmered down.

*My goodness – they've all grown so big, but at heart they're still just kids*, Hachi thought. *How big do humans have to get, anyway, before they're grown up?*

As for Hachi, he had only faint memories of the days when he was a kitten.

*We'll call you Hachi!* Was that Tsutomu who'd said that, pressing his cheek against his? And had he scooped him out of his box? No – that's not how it was. The other boy's uncle had brought him to this apartment in a pet carrier. Okay, then, what about that memory of being in a cardboard box? Of being in the box for a long time, and being shaken around and feeling queasy?

Why had he been shaken around so much? They wouldn't let him keep Hachi, so the boy pretended to run away from home, but it didn't work out and they had started arguing—

*This isn't working out at all. You lied!*

*Look, you want to keep the cat, don't you?!*

*I mean – shouldn't you first ask your parents to let you keep him at your house?*

So who was it that was being criticized when things didn't work out?

Tsutomu? Tsutomu played baseball. When did he quit swimming? *If ——-chan does it with me. But if ——-chan doesn't . . .*

'Hachi, how about some tuna?'

The sister waved a piece of tuna held between chopsticks. *Well, if she's going to the trouble, how can I refuse?* Hachi thought. She was holding the tuna up pretty high, so Hachi stood on his hind legs and gave it a good sniff. But his

· 189 ·

mouth wouldn't quite reach, and he lost his balance and ended up falling back on to his bottom.

'Ha ha! You're so slow.'

'He's *laid back*, not slow. Don't tease him like that.'

Tsutomu grabbed the slice of tuna from his sister's chopsticks. Bending down, using his palm as a plate, he held out the tuna for Hachi.

'But the way he's so slow is cute.'

'What an awful girl she is, right, Hachi?'

As before, Tsutomu had gently rephrased the word *slow* as *laid back*. Being called *laid back* was something Hachi had grown used to from a long time ago.

'Does it taste good?'

Hachi tipped his head sideways and licked the tuna in Tsutomu's hand.

The way time moved was certainly different for cats and humans. It was much faster for cats. When had he first realized this?

Tsutomu had grown much bigger, but was apparently still not an adult. Before he became one, he had to get through a test called a high-school entrance exam, so in the autumn and winter all he did was study, study, study.

At New Year, a man came to visit; he had a beard like a bear's fur.

'How've you been, Hachi?' he asked, but when he bent down to pick him up, Hachi flinched.

'What the—? Have you forgotten me? Even though you saw me during the summer break, too?'

'You were only back for a week, and a cat's little brain forgets. Plus you've now grown that beard.'

· 190 ·

Hearing the mother and the man talking, Hachi finally realized this was the eldest son.

*I'm sorry, I should have recognized you sooner*, Hachi thought. To apologize, he rubbed himself up against the eldest brother's knees and the brother, having regained his good humour, pulled Hachi on to his chest. When he rubbed his cheek against Hachi's whiskers, the beard scratched and Hachi thrust his legs into the brother's chest and scampered off.

Tsutomu spent New Year with his nose in his books and passed his exam. When the single cherry tree in the garden began to blossom, he swapped his jacket with the stand-up collar for a blazer and started his new school.

He immediately joined the baseball team and came back every day covered in mud. His new school apparently had a strong baseball team, and the practice schedule was intense.

The cherry blossoms scattered, and all that was left on the tree were the leaves. Caterpillars were plopping down from the branches. Every year at this time, the mother and sister insisted that they cut the tree down – that's how much they hated caterpillars.

'What are you talking about? It's a symbol, this tree.' This was the father's line every year as he soothed the female contingent.

On one occasion, Tsutomu came into the apartment with a caterpillar perched on his shoulder and the mother and sister screamed until the doors shook.

Another day, a caterpillar had somehow crawled into the hallway. When the mother and sister spotted it, they went berserk. Thinking he'd get rid of it for them, Hachi gave it a couple of good whacks with one of his front paws.

A burning pain shot through his paw pads. When he screeched, it was Tsutomu who raced to his side.

'Hachi, what's wrong?'

Tsutomu figured out at a glance what had happened.

'Did the caterpillar sting you?'

'No way! You mean the caterpillars from the cherry tree? They sting?' His sister raised a ruckus, and the second-eldest brother answered her.

'Most of them don't sting, but some of them do.'

'Eugh! Get rid of it! *Get rid of it!*'

While the second-eldest brother removed the caterpillar, Tsutomu knelt down to apply disinfectant to Hachi's paw.

'Maybe I should put on some cream for insect bites, too?' he asked his mother.

'It would be better not to,' she declaimed, like an oracle. 'Because he might lick it. If it swells up, I'll take him to the vet's tomorrow.'

The second-eldest brother came back in, having disposed of the caterpillar, and gave Hachi's head a gentle stroke.

'You silly cat, you shouldn't touch one of those guys if they can sting you.'

'He thought it would be even slower than he is,' the sister said. 'He thought he could beat it and got carried away.'

Hachi's head drooped at these unkind words, and Tsutomu grimaced.

'Don't say that! He tried to kill it because he knows you all hate caterpillars. I'm sure of it.'

'Sorry,' the sister said, chastened. Later, she gave Hachi a snack.

The pads on his paw continued to sting, but not so badly that he had to be taken to the vet's.

· 192 ·

Caterpillar season was drawing to a close when the phone rang one evening.

The father answered. He'd just finished taking a bath.

'Hey, it's been so long! How have you been? I see. And Noriko-chan's well, too?'

The father happily chatted on, decked out in just his underpants and oblivious to the horrified look his wife shot him.

'Oh, that sounds fine. Please, come over. Hachi would love to see you.'

The father hung up, and the mother asked, 'Who was that?'

'It was Satoru-kun. You remember – he sends us a New Year's card every year.'

Hachi's ears pricked up. That name shot through him like an electric current.

*Satoru.*

'Oh, the boy who lives with Noriko-chan . . .'

'Right, right. That's the one.'

'He's the boy who first had Hachi,' Tsutomu said. 'He's the same age as me, I think?'

'Really? He said he's going to work part time in the summer and come to see Hachi.'

'Where does he live now? His aunt was always being transferred for work, wasn't she?'

'He said they're in Yamanashi now.'

'Wow, so he's working to earn money just to come to see Hachi! The guy must really love cats.'

*Satoru. Satoru. Satoru.*

'In his New Year's card every year he always asks us to say hello to Hachi. He must have really loved him.'

· 193 ·

'If that's the case, he should have had his aunt bring him here sooner.'

'Noriko-chan's so busy, though. And since she took him in and all, I don't think he felt he could ask her to.'

*Hachi, take care!*

He'd smiled through his tears, waving and waving.

'When Satoru comes over, you be nice to him, Tsutomu.'

'Well, I'll treat him like anyone else. But – he loved Hachi so much, so I guess he must be a pretty good guy.'

The first person to call him *laid back* wasn't Tsutomu.

Hachi's memory rewound clearly to the moment when Tsutomu and Satoru had overlapped.

Satoru must surely have grown like Tsutomu, healthy and tall.

So Satoru was coming to visit this summer.

When would the summer holidays begin? The days were growing steadily longer, the shadows steadily deeper.

This was the season when Tsutomu's face became the darkest.

Every day was so hot now, the holidays should begin soon, right?

*I hope he comes soon*, Hachi thought. *When Satoru and Tsutomu meet, I'm sure they'll get along.*

Hachi had waited so long, he couldn't wait any longer.

*Maybe he got lost on his way over*, Hachi thought, deciding to take a little look around the neighbourhood. It

was evening, when the heat of the sun was finally letting up.

He'd never been outside in the garden and decided not to overdo it. He'd start with one circuit around the building, and then gradually go a little further each time.

'Hachi seems to be going for walks these days,' reported the mother at dinner.

Tsutomu frowned.

'I just hope he doesn't get lost.'

*Not to worry*, Hachi thought, proudly. *I'm pushing the boundaries of my walks, one step at a time.*

'Just in case, let's put a collar on him, an ID tag,' proposed the sister, buying one the very next day.

'He might hate it.'

Hesitantly, the sister attached the collar around Hachi's neck. He knew in an instant he could wriggle out of it if he made the effort, but he figured it would be too much trouble and so left it on.

'Well, he's always been the type of cat who goes with the flow,' the second-eldest brother said, laughing.

Hachi had now got used to strolling around outside, and thinking that Satoru might still have trouble finding them, decided to expand the scope of his walks even further.

There was a big road he had never crossed. So many people seemed to cross over that road in his direction. When Satoru arrived, he would surely use this road too.

Observing for a while how things were done, Hachi understood that if humans timed it right, they could cross safely on the striped part of the road without being in danger from any cars.

He tried it himself a few times and crossed safely over.

\*

One day he was waiting for someone to walk over with when a young man suddenly sprinted across the striped section. Thinking he could make it too, Hachi darted after him. Just then, a car blared its horn.

The young man had made a dash, but Hachi froze on the spot.

With a huge *bang*, Hachi was sent flying. As he realized what had happened, he began to spit up blood. The pain in his chest was so intense, he couldn't cope.

'My God, it's a cat!' screamed a woman.

'Hachi!'

In a flash, someone ran over and scooped him up.

Was he not able to see the dark face because his eyes were blurry, or was it because it was backlit by the setting sun? *Gosh*, he thought, *I can't tell if this is Satoru, or Tsutomu.*

*But either one is okay*, he decided.

SATORU FIGURED HE COULD FIND their place by just asking for directions as he went, but his relatives had said they'd come to meet him at the station, at the exit for the Bullet train. Satoru went to where they were supposed to meet and a tanned-looking boy – or would you say young man? he was at a kind of in-between age – called out to him.

'Hey, are you Satoru Miyawaki?'

'Yes, I am.'

'Nice to meet you. I'm Tsutomu.'

Tsutomu turned out to be the same age as Satoru, which made Satoru realize – a little late, perhaps – that he, too, was at the same indeterminate age.

· 196 ·

'I'm so sorry you came all this way and – this happened.'

'It's okay. None of you are to blame.'

They had already told him that the very day before Satoru was due to arrive, Hachi had died after being hit by a car.

Tsutomu led Satoru home, where the uncle and aunt gave him a warm-hearted welcome. 'We're happy to see you,' they said. 'But we're so sorry this happened.'

The same words that Tsutomu had used, and this made Satoru smile.

'And after I'd promised to make sure Hachi was happy,' the uncle said.

'I'm sure he was happy, being raised with your family,' Satoru replied.

In the living room, they had displayed a photo of Hachi, along with some offerings at the family's little Buddhist altar, just as you would for a deceased relative. Dotted around were photos of previous cats.

Living with this family, Hachi must have been happy and contented until the very end of his life.

'And his grave is where?'

'We couldn't afford anything fancy like a plot at a pet cemetery. Instead, we buried him in the mountains,' the uncle replied. 'Tsutomu said he'd take you there tomorrow.'

Tsutomu nodded. 'It's a half hour by train.'

'Thank you.'

That night the sister and eldest brother came home, and plates of delicious food were served for dinner, in a sort of celebratory feast.

They all shared stories about Hachi.

'He was kind of slow, which I thought was cute,' the sister said.

· 197 ·

'Don't ever say he was slow,' Tsutomu snapped at her. 'Hachi was a laid-back, gentle cat.'

Satoru couldn't help but laugh.

'Exactly that. He was a laid-back, gentle cat.'

The next morning, after breakfast, Satoru and Tsutomu set off for the grave.

They were bounced around in the train along an old branch line, and after half an hour they were out in the countryside, among hills and valleys. The station where they got off was surrounded by fields.

For a while, they hiked along a farm track, Tsutomu leading the way towards the hills.

'It'd be a lot easier if we had come by car, but Dad has to work today,' he explained.

As they climbed up the slope of a woodland path, they naturally fell into talking about Hachi. They'd already discussed their schools and the clubs they were in, and Hachi was the only shared topic left.

'Once when a mouse appeared all of a sudden, Hachi was so shocked he fell backwards on his behind,' Satoru said.

'Really? Yeah, I can imagine that.'

'Because he was so laid back. Being hit by a car is also something I could see happening to him. He must have been so shocked when he saw it coming.'

'No, that's not how it was.' Tsutomu's face was screwed up in regret. 'I got there right after he was hit. I was just passing by after baseball practice on my way home. A woman who saw it all told me. Hachi was following a man who had crossed against the traffic signal. Hachi was smart and cautious and I'm sure he thought that, if he crossed with a human, he'd be safe.'

· 198 ·

Tsutomu was staring straight ahead, trying his best to hold back the tears.

'If that idiot hadn't done that, I'm sure Hachi wouldn't have tried to cross. If I find that guy, I'm going to beat him to a pulp.'

'If you find him, let me know, too.'

Tsutomu shot him a look of surprise. 'You don't look like you'd be tough in a fight.'

'You're right. So I'll wait until you've beaten him up, Tsutomu-kun, and then I'll give him a final punch.'

'You're nuts.' Tsutomu burst out laughing. He turned away quickly, and wiped his eyes with his arm, pretending it was sweat.

At the top of the hill was a sunny, open field. Tsutomu led Satoru over to the furthest corner.

Dotted around were small granite blocks, one of which was brand new.

'Dad got an end piece from a friend of his who's a stone mason. We couldn't afford to buy a plot in a real pet cemetery.'

'This is perfect. It's so pleasant and sunny.'

They scattered crunchy cat food in front of Hachi's grave and opened packets of cooked chicken breast and cheese, which they placed carefully around. They'd brought along extra cat food and offered it at the graves of their other cats, all of whom were buried there.

'My parents died in a car accident too.'

'Yeah,' Tsutomu murmured. He seemed to know already.

'When I got back from a school trip, they were gone.'

'Yeah,' Tsutomu said, nodding again.

'The souvenir I'd bought for my dad was a good-luck amulet to prevent car accidents.'

· 199 ·

Tsutomu could no longer simply nod, and hung his head in silence.

'This one.'

Satoru pulled an amulet out of his bag. It was a keyring with a good-luck *maneki-neko* figure attached, the kind with one paw raised, beckoning you.

'Have you kept it all this time?'

'The one I brought back originally is in his coffin, which got burned when he was cremated. Before I got here, I stopped off in Kyoto where we'd been for our school trip and looked for another one. I don't know if it's exactly the same, but it looks like it.'

The keyring was the kind you could find anywhere. A childish-looking thing, the type kids would choose. These trinkets never changed, even over time.

'That *maneki-neko* looks like Hachi,' Tsutomu murmured as he rolled the amulet in his fingers. Satoru knew he would notice the resemblance right away. Because Tsutomu also called Hachi a laid-back, gentle cat.

'That's why I bought it. Though it wasn't in time to give to Dad.'

At the time, so many thoughts had raced through his mind.

He'd been angry at himself for buying an amulet that didn't get there in time. *What an idiot I was.*

Another thought: maybe it was because he'd bought this cheap little amulet that his mum and dad had been in that accident.

'But when I heard about Hachi's accident . . .' He firmly pushed down the lump rising in his throat. 'I thought maybe I should have given the amulet to Hachi.'

Too late now. He was fully aware of it.

· 200 ·

But he had intended to give the amulet to Hachi. He knew Tsutomu would understand why. Hachi was a laid-back, gentle cat, after all.

'Would you keep it, Tsutomu-kun?'

Tsutomu blinked in surprise.

'I'm sure Hachi will be happy if you take it.'

He hadn't arrived in time for his father. Or for Hachi.

If Tsutomu would take it, though, it would be in time, finally.

'All right.'

Tsutomu slipped the amulet into his back pocket.

'We should be heading back. If we miss the return train, we'll have to wait a long time.'

Satoru put his hands together in front of Hachi's grave.

'I'm counting on you, Hachi.'

As they made their way back across the field, he thought he heard a cat meowing. He looked over at Tsutomu.

'Might be Hachi,' Tsutomu murmured.

'Might be,' Satoru replied.

They sauntered back down the mountain path, and their laughter continued to ring out as they went.

# Life Is Not Always Kind

ALLOW ME TO INTRODUCE myself. I am a cat. The name is Nana.

That's me trying to imitate the greatest-ever cat in Japan, the one in Natsume Soseki's famous book *I Am a Cat*. But introducing myself like this is a bit lame, because that cat didn't have a name, whereas I do. And it would have to be a fairly elderly cat to say something like *Allow me to introduce myself*. I'm still a young cat, after all, so let me put a lid on any nostalgia right here and right now.

I am, by the way, an upstanding male cat, but with the girlish name of Nana, if you can believe it. I had nothing to do with it.

Satoru, my owner, gave me the name without asking me. He's a good guy, though sometimes a bit oblivious. The name came from my cute, hooked tail. The reason he gave me this name is a bit absurd – my hooked tail from above looks like the number seven, *nana* in Japanese.

Satoru might lack good sense when it comes to names, but as a human he's the perfect roommate. And I'm the perfect cat for a human's roommate.

We've been sharing a pleasant life together for five years now, but something came up recently that cast a shadow across it.

Unavoidable circumstances meant Satoru would no longer be able to look after me. Once he found out this was the case, he wasted no time in sorting it out. He used all his

contacts to find someone new to take care of me. As soon as anyone showed willing, he took me round to see them, as if he was matchmaking, setting up a *miai* or formal marriage interview.

Honestly, he didn't need to go to the trouble. Satoru adopted me when I was already a grown-up cat. In other words, until that moment, I had been living the life of a fully fledged alley cat. Even though I settled down quickly as a house cat, I still had a touch of the feral in me.

If I couldn't live with Satoru any more, then all I had to do was go back to my previous life. But Satoru had already shrugged off his own worries to focus on finding me a new home, though in doing so, he had totally underestimated me, in all honesty.

So Satoru began taking me around to see all these people he seemed to know. Naturally, I had no intention of letting any of these *miai* succeed. So far we've had three such meetings, and I made sure every single one of them was a failure.

In our travels, we've always taken the silver van. When it's a long trip, we bring along a cat-litter tray, and all the facilities are top-notch as far as a cat is concerned.

I was hoping he'd give up on all these meetings, but driving around in the silver van wasn't so bad, so I went along without complaint.

The upshot is I've glimpsed way more of the world than your average cat. I've seen two towns where Satoru grew up when he was a child, one farming village, some rice fields, the ocean and Mount Fuji. I grew up in the city, so ordinarily I should go my whole life without seeing anything beyond my day-to-day surroundings.

· 206 ·

But I've now seen more of the world than any other cat in Japan. And for the rest of my life I'll never forget the experiences Satoru and I have shared.

And now we were off on our fourth journey together.

The silver van was heading west. We drove out of Tokyo in the late afternoon, chasing after the evening sun as it was setting. Behind the wheel, Satoru's face glowed orange in the light. Even with the visor lowered, it was too bright for him, and he blinked over and over.

He glanced over at me, curled up in the passenger seat, and laughed.

'Your pupils are like the thinnest of threads, Nana.'

Cats' eyes have amazing pupils. They can adjust the amount of light that gets in. In bright light our pupils become really narrow, and then grow big and round when it's dark.

My pupils right now would be vertical slits, as thin as they could be.

'There's a saying that a man's eyes should be narrow and straight, while a woman's should be round as a ball, but your eyes are pretty adaptable, Nana, since your pupils can go thin like that if need be.'

*I suppose you're right*, I thought, twitching my whiskers. Satoru's eyes weren't adaptable at all, since even when it was bright his pupils didn't grow thin like mine. At times like this, I wished I could trade eyeballs with him. Because all I have to do when it's too bright is curl up in the passenger seat and sleep.

'Oh, we're almost in Kyoto,' murmured Satoru as he glanced up, apparently reading the road signs as they flashed by. 'If we took the Bullet train, it'd only take about thirty minutes to get all the way to Kobe.'

· 207 ·

Satoru was looking a bit tired, what with heading into the sunset for so long.

'Why don't we take a break in Otsu?'

*Fine by me. I could do with a snack.*

First, though, I thought I'd take a toilet break, and was about to slip through on to the back seat where the cat-litter tray was.

In the glow of the setting sun, a huge body of water suddenly appeared up ahead.

*What the—?* With my paws on the dashboard and my hind legs on the seat, I craned my neck forward.

'Caught your attention, did it?' Satoru laughed. 'Isn't it amazing? It's the biggest lake in all Japan.'

*Isn't this the ocean? You're saying this huge body of water isn't the ocean?*

'Let's stop and check it out.'

*No, thanks, I'm good.* The ocean from afar looked pretty, and there were all those fish swimming around – yum – and it was all very romantic, but when we got closer there was the frightening roar of those giant waves. Like in a horror film or something.

'Actually, if we stop here, we'll be late getting to the other side.'

*Yes, indeed, best not to overdo things.*

So Satoru stopped at a rest area for a break until the setting sun wasn't so bright any more. He gave the lake a miss, and we continued on our way.

Dinner for me that evening had been a simple healthy cat tuna blend, but Satoru sprinkled some *katsuobushi* flakes on top and I ended up eating way too much and feeling stuffed.

It's a physical fact that animals become sleepy when they've eaten a lot.

I curled up on the passenger seat, and after that I don't remember a thing. Only that at some point Satoru was stroking my back like he was at a loose end, and I thought drowsily that he must have hit a traffic jam.

I woke to the sound of the engine groaning to a halt and when I lifted up my head, I saw Satoru unbuckling his seat belt. Had we arrived at our hotel?

'Are you awake? I took a little detour before we get to the hotel.'

Satoru reached out his arms and, after I'd arched my back to get the kinks out, he scooped me up. As I got out of the car, the cool night air tickled my nose and I let out a sneeze.

The sun was long gone, the mountain ridges etched in deep shadows that seemed to suck up the darkness.

'See?'

Resting in his arms, I turned around in the direction he indicated. *Whoa!*

At the foot of the hills below us was a sea of sparkling lights. As if it was still daytime in that single spot.

Amazing. Humans could make night into day.

'They call this a million-dollar view.'

So they used a currency to express this, something that was tuned to a human value system alone. And a foreigner's currency, to boot. I let out a big yawn.

'Okay, so a million dollars at today's exchange rate would be what? About 800 million yen?'

Satoru went through some mental arithmetic until he figured it out.

'That would come to about 4.8 million cans of soft, savoury chicken cat food.'

Now *that* was something. I studied his face again. I could eat, what? – a can a day – and still not finish the pile before I died.

Hmm – a night view worth 4.8 million cans of tasty chicken breast meat. I looked down again on the sea of lights with fresh eyes.

Still – given a choice between the view and 4.8 million cans of tasty meat?

I'd take the cans, any day.

'What? You're tired of it already?'

Well, lights were just . . . lights, I thought, and once again let out a huge yawn.

Our hotel advertised itself as the only place in the area that was pet friendly, allowing animals to stay in the same room. Sure enough, when we checked in I caught a whiff of all the dogs and cats that had passed through.

We'd both eaten dinner at the rest area earlier, so all that was needed was to get ready for bed and go to sleep.

The room was on the smallish side but clean, and comfortable enough, though I deducted points for the fact that the TV wasn't one of those boxy-shaped ones I preferred.

The B&B we had stayed at before, run by Satoru's friends, was, by those standards, much better. You could look all over Japan, but hotels and suchlike offering boxy TVs for cats to sleep on were few and far between. We weren't allowed to walk down the corridor here, but the fact that it allowed people to stay with their cats made this one of the better hotels, in my book.

As I was slinking around the room, inspecting it, Satoru took a bath. From behind the closed door, I could hear him humming 20 per cent louder than usual, so I

· 210 ·

knew he'd filled up the tub and was having a nice leisurely soak.

He finally emerged from the bathroom, and I slid by him to have a look for myself. After running a bath, there had to be some water still left in the tap.

I'm not sure why, but for some reason the water left inside a turned-off tap always tastes better than the water in my bowl. After Satoru finishes his bath, I always drink the water from the tap.

So at that point I simply followed my usual habit. I had no idea what a terrible miscalculation this would turn out to be.

'Nana! You can't drink that water!' screamed Satoru.

It's a universal given that a cat can drink whatever water he likes, in whatever way he prefers, so I ignored Satoru as he tried to stop me, and took a flying jump up on to the bath. I had figured the tub had a cover over it to keep the water hot, the way it usually does.

Not this one.

I had a split second to let out a screech before I took an unexpected dive into the hot bubbly water. It had been draining out and the bath was only half full, but that was enough for me to get completely soaked.

'Hotel baths don't have covers like at home!'

*You should have told me that!*

I tried to scramble up on to the edge of the tub, but was so drenched I couldn't keep my footing. The bath was too slippery for my claws to get a foothold, and boosting myself up solely on leg power was, naturally, beyond me.

As I splashed about in the hot water, Satoru ran in and scooped me up.

He put me down on the floor and I gave myself a big shake, trying to get as much of the water off my wet, matted

fur as I could. I dashed out of the bathroom and was about to settle down to groom myself when Satoru strode quickly over again.

'Don't do that, Nana! The water's still soapy!'

He picked me up and took me back to the bathroom.

*Don't do that? Okay, but what about my soaked torso?*

Holding me tightly below my belly, Satoru closed the bathroom door behind him with his foot.

'This is a good chance to give you a shampoo – I'll just use a little soap.'

*Help!!!!!!!!!!!*

I scrambled free of him, but the door to the bathroom was closed, like a wall before me. I scratched and scratched, but it did not budge open even a crack.

'There's no running away!'

Satoru lathered up the soap and pinned me down firmly with his big hands. Then he lifted me back into the now-drained bath tub and began to scrub me.

*Aaaaargh!*

Satoru ended up having to get fresh pyjamas and towels from the hotel. Water had been splashed all over the tiny bathroom.

I was resting on a towel, doing my best to groom myself, when Satoru brought over a hair dryer. I furrowed my brows in a fierce glare and wrinkled my nose.

*If you aim that rackety thing at me, there will be a rift in our relationship that won't be restored by tomorrow. Are you willing to risk that?*

'You'll catch a cold,' Satoru tried to explain weakly, but he seemed to pick up on my vibes and meekly put the dryer away.

Satoru's mobile phone started to play a light-hearted melody. The kind of tune where you expect a dove to fly out.

· 212 ·

'Hello . . . Yes, we just got here a little while ago! Thank you so much for checking.'

I gathered this was the person we'd be meeting tomorrow. Satoru's professor from when he was in college, who was now working in a nearby part of Japan.

'All right, then we'll see you after one o'clock tomorrow!'

After hanging up, Satoru turned to me.

'If things work out, then tomorrow I guess we'll be saying goodbye . . . I shouldn't have made you so mad.'

Not to worry. I'd make sure the meeting tomorrow was a disaster.

I'd pretty much dried myself off and my tongue was getting tired, so I took possession of the armchair and curled up.

I woke up in the middle of the night feeling chilly, since my fur was still a little damp.

Nothing I could do about it, I thought, figuring all I could do was sulk until the next morning.

I stepped off the armchair and headed to Satoru's bed. Leaping up to his pillow, I sniffed around the edge of the futon cover. Satoru lifted the cover up to make space for me to crawl under. I'd trained him well.

I snuggled through towards his feet, turned around and shuffled back up to his pillow and lay down. Satoru, still prone, scratched the top of my head.

He was mumbling something and when I looked over, I realized it was my name. And in the darkness I could see his eyes were gleaming with tears.

Good grief. If he was going to cry about it, then why let me go? Humans were always so chock-full of contradictions.

How nice it would be if humans, like us animals, were multilingual. Then I could explain why he didn't have to go

· 213 ·

to the trouble of finding a new owner for me. I'd tell him that, as an unabashed former alley cat, I would simply go back to being a proud stray.

I stretched my neck forwards and licked around Satoru's eyes. My tongue tasted a slight saltiness.

'Nana, that hurts,' Satoru said, pressing his fingers on my whiskers to push me away.

Now what kind of response was that?

SATORU MIYAWAKI WAS IN A bit of a bind and had to give his cat away so was urgently looking for someone to adopt him. This news had reached a couple of friends who had attended the same seminar on regional industrial development with Satoru at a Tokyo university ten years earlier.

The couple – students at the seminar who had later got married but who now ran a B&B in Kofu – had made an attempt to adopt Satoru's cat, but their own dog had not approved and they couldn't cope with both.

The couple had since been in touch with Hisashi Kubota, an assistant professor in the economics department at the time of the seminar. The wife had remembered that the professor was fond of animals.

Satoru Miyawaki still hadn't found anyone to take the cat from him, they explained to Kubota, so if he felt able to, would he consider doing so himself?

The professor was living in a condo with his dog Lily, who had been brought up alongside an elderly cat and had grown fond of it. Whenever he spotted a cat on one of their walks, he'd wander over, only to be harshly rebuffed, leaving him discouraged.

· 214 ·

After the old cat passed away and there was no longer another around at home, Kubota thought that if he could find another to replace it, Lily might stop chasing cats outside and getting his nose scratched.

Would Satoru Miyawaki be willing to entrust his beloved cat to him? Concerned that he might not, Kubota didn't contact him directly but replied to the couple who'd first been in touch.

'Please tell Miyawaki that if he'll allow me to adopt his cat, then I'm ready,' he told them.

A reply came back not from the couple but from Satoru himself, and by phone.

'Professor, it's been ages!'

From the sound of his cheerful, friendly voice, he hadn't changed at all, even though Kubota felt sure they hadn't parted on very good terms all those years ago, that there had been some ill-feeling about something. Had he sent him off with a smile on graduation day? Kubota thought that he must not have done.

'Since we'd parted on such awkward terms,' Satoru said, 'I definitely wanted to see you again.'

Ahhh. So there really had been some ill-feeling, Kubota realized, as he was immediately yanked back to reality.

'I'm thrilled, of course, that you'd consider taking in Nana for me,' Satoru said, 'but I'm happier still about having this opportunity to see you again.'

He did seem genuinely happy. That made Kubota happy, but a bit ashamed, too. This guy was more than twenty years younger than him, he thought, and yet so much more generous and mature.

'Right. Well, when I hear that one of my former

students needs help, I can't very well ignore him, now can I? I love animals, and my dog loves cats, too.'

Kubota tried to sound as kindly as he could.

They checked their calendars to arrange a date, but Kubota's weekends were full, and since Satoru said a weekday was fine, Kubota looked at his teaching schedule and found an opening in the middle of the week.

'How will you get here? If you're taking the Bullet train, shall I pick you up at the station?'

But Satoru said he'd be driving.

'You wouldn't expect it of a cat, but Nana loves to go for drives,' he said. 'If you do take him in, Professor, please take him out for a drive every once in a while.'

'I often go to the dog park, so I could take Nana along,' Kubota suggested.

After their casual chat, they hung up, and now the day had arrived when Satoru would actually be coming to his apartment.

The previous evening after getting home from his teaching, Kubota had done some cleaning, hauling out the vacuum cleaner sooner in the week than he normally would. After vacuuming, he noticed the dust on the furniture and brought out the feather duster. For the first time in a long while, he remembered how his wife would scold him: *Use the duster* before *you vacuum!*

*Cut me some slack here*, he thought. Wanting to dust in the first place proved how motivated he was to clean, didn't it?

He planned to have tea and cakes waiting, but wondered if Satoru would have eaten lunch already. One o'clock was an awkward time. Maybe he should have invited him for lunch? He'd ask him when he got there, and if he hadn't eaten, then maybe he could have some sushi delivered?

· 216 ·

Which meant he'd have to restrict himself to a small lunch to leave room for the sushi.

After his morning classes had finished, Kubota stopped by the student cafeteria and, after much deliberation, decided to go with the tempura udon. But this didn't seem enough, so he added a three-pack of Inarizushi to his order. Maybe I shouldn't have added the rice balls, he thought, gazing at his protruding stomach, but if Satoru had already eaten lunch and they didn't get to have the sushi, this would turn out to be light fare.

Thinking it would be best for Lily and Nana to meet after Nana had had a moment to get used to his new surroundings, he put Lily in his cage in a back room.

The front doorbell chimed. He answered the intercom and the same voice he'd heard on the phone announced: 'Hello, it's me, Satoru Miyawaki.'

He opened the door and there was Satoru standing on the mat, cat carrier in hand. His lanky build hadn't changed since his student days. And neither had his winning smile.

'Welcome. Come on in.'

Kubota was thinking his voice sounded a bit shrill. Satoru looked at him, eyes widening. 'My goodness, Professor. You've grown so plump!'

Caught off guard, Kubota burst out laughing. That's right – that's the kind of student he was. Friendly, but with a mouth on him, too. This had often had the other seminar students in stitches.

'Somehow I've managed to put on twenty kilos in the last ten years.'

'That's not good at all. You'd better go on a diet.'

'It's too much trouble to cook for myself, so I end up

· 217 ·

eating out all the time,' Kubota said as he showed Satoru into the living room.

'Wow, your place is neat as a pin! Hard to believe you live all by yourself here.'

'Well, so far so good. I've been a widower for so long.' He didn't breathe a word about all the cleaning he'd done the day before.

'And your children?'

'Both went to college in Tokyo.'

'So they're that grown up now. How old are they?'

'My son just graduated from university, and my daughter has just started.'

As he placed Nana's carrier on the floor, Satoru sighed. 'I used to think there was such a big age gap between a college student and an elementary-school pupil, but now that I'm out and working, the gap doesn't seem that great any more.'

The year Satoru had graduated, Kubota's son would have been in his last year of elementary school.

'It wouldn't be so strange if he and I ended up working together. My company hired new college graduates this year.'

The thought occurred to Kubota that it wouldn't be odd either if he had a son Satoru's age. If he'd got married earlier, that was.

And this made him realize what a childish attack he'd made on Satoru back when he was the same age his son was now.

Satoru opened the carrier and peered inside. But Nana showed no sign of emerging.

'Sorry, but he never wants to come out right away,' Satoru apologized. 'Hey, Nana,' he said.

'That's okay. Let him be as cautious as he wants. It's a

· 218 ·

sign of intelligence,' Kubota said, touching his arm to stop him pulling Nana out.

Satoru smiled, seemingly happy to hear his cat being praised.

'Have you had lunch?' Kubota asked.

'I did. I figured you would grab a bite at college.'

'Come to think of it, are there any restaurants that allow you to bring a cat in?'

'I left Nana back at the hotel, and went out by myself before driving over here.'

He explained that he'd parked in the spot suggested by Kubota.

'Sorry we don't have a spot for guests in front of our building.'

Whenever anyone parked in front of the condo, the driver would get a ticket.

'Well, why don't you sit down. I'll make some tea. I'm sure Nana will choose to emerge at some stage.'

As a teatime snack Kubota had bought some *imagawayaki* sweets on the way back from campus. As soon as Satoru saw them, he broke into a smile. 'So they still have these!' he exclaimed. 'I haven't had them in such a long time. I don't know why, but having *imagawayaki* or those fish-shaped *taiyaki* cakes as a snack really makes me happy.'

'In this part of Japan they call them *kaitenyaki*,' Kubota said, displaying some trivia he'd picked up after moving there.

Satoru looked genuinely surprised. 'Is that right?' he said.

Kubota smiled at his interest. As a student, he'd always struck him as someone who listened carefully. He had also been a bit of a disrupter who clowned around and made

· 219 ·

people laugh, but he always took his studies seriously. Which is why Kubota had given him special attention. He'd liked him so much that, at times, he worried that he was favouring him over the other students.

So why hadn't he realized it at the time? That when such a sensitive student as Satoru was refusing to back down, there must have been a very good reason for it.

If he could rewind time . . . he wished even now he had bitten his tongue and not said anything.

THE FIRST TIME KUBOTA WAS aware of this student named Satoru Miyawaki was at a series of introductory lectures he was giving on the local economy.

In one of his classes, he happened to mention a book about a village that had once been successful in raising the profile of local industry, a book that was particularly relevant to the subject they were discussing.

Some time later, a student had come up to him.

'I really enjoyed the book that you mentioned in your class the other day,' he said.

He hadn't brought it up as assigned reading or anything, and frankly Kubota himself had forgotten he'd even mentioned it.

'So you went to the trouble of reading it, did you?'

'Yes, they had a copy in the university library.'

Kubota's first thoughts were sceptical, that this was someone who had possibly missed a lot of classes and was trying to earn extra points, but the student had then launched into a lengthy monologue about the book, which he had clearly enjoyed reading.

· 220 ·

'It seemed less like a straight factual account than a kind of adventure story. Like turning adversity into a positive way forward, and it reminded me a bit of an RPG.'

'RPG? Meaning?'

'Ah – that's right. People your age don't play video games much, do they. I'm talking about role-playing games – *Dragon Quest*, *Final Fantasy*, things like that.'

*Ah*, Kubota thought, *I get it now.*

'The ones my kids are always pestering me to buy for them.'

'Right, right – that's what I mean.'

The way he described his response to the book was so typical of young people, and Kubota found it refreshing.

'You finish one mission and then another begins. And you build up experience points every time. I haven't read much non-fiction, but I was amazed how dramatic the book was.'

'Truth can be stranger than fiction, like they say. Documentaries about successful projects are especially compelling. They can make you feel hopeful. When ambitious people get together, the future can seem full of opportunity.'

The bell rang, signalling the end of break.

'I'm sorry, I've taken up all your time.'

The student was walking away when Kubota stopped him.

'What is your name and what are you studying?' he asked.

'My name's Satoru Miyawaki. I'm a second-year student in economics.'

If Kubota hadn't asked him, Satoru might well have walked away without ever introducing himself. He'd just wanted to share his thoughts on a book with someone else who'd enjoyed it, it seemed.

· 221 ·

From then on, Kubota would occasionally lend Satoru books from his own personal library.

'There are lots of great books in the seminar room as well, so feel free to borrow those, too.'

Another professor was nominally in charge of the seminar, but he was such a well-known economist, busy with external TV appearances and speaking engagements, that he was rarely on campus. So Kubota was, in reality, leading the seminar, and had taken over most of the bookshelves in the room.

It would be great if this student were in his seminar, Kubota thought, and the following year his wish came true.

Satoru applied for Kubota's seminar with two friends, a boy and girl, to whom Satoru had recommended it. The young woman's family ran a fruit orchard in Yamanashi, as Satoru happily explained to Kubota: 'When I suggested that she apply, I told her the seminar would be helpful in running their family business.' The other friend, the young man, seemed to be a tag-along, going wherever the girl went. That happened all the time with young people.

Kubota's seminar focused on fieldwork, and very soon it was Satoru who proposed a theme for their summer training camp.

'Miss Sakita said her family's happy for us to use their place as a practice location,' he announced. Sakita was the girl whose family ran the fruit farm.

She and Satoru, and their fellow student, Sugi, turned out to be friends from high school.

The fieldwork that Satoru proposed was to divide the seminar students into two teams who would compete with each other to see who could sell the most fruit from a roadside stand. In exchange for helping with farm work in the

orchard, Sakita's family had said they'd be willing to finance the project by providing the produce. This way, they also got free labour during their busy season.

The orchard had already set up roadside stands at several locations, and on the days of the students' competition they let them take over the stands.

It was unclear how they should divide up the students to form the two teams.

Seniors versus juniors was one idea, but then the juniors, with the orchard owner's daughter plus the two boys who'd already worked there, would have an advantage, wouldn't they? But that said, the seniors had a year's more fieldwork experience, right? Okay, but what about grades? If one team didn't sell as much, would that affect their grades?

Kubota told them clearly that their grades would be based solely on the reports they turned in. Finally the details of the proposed competition were settled.

'Sir, even if our grades are based on our written work, if you give the winning team some sort of prize, that'd be a great motivator.' This from one of the bratty seniors.

'Okay, what do you suggest? We don't want it all to get too serious.'

'We're not kids. If we lose, we'll simply accept it.'

'In that case—' It was Satoru who raised his hand. 'How about giving the winning team premium Pilsner beer when we make the toast?'

The Pilsner brand was not in the all-you-can-drink promotion at the local *izakaya* and was an aspirational beer well out of reach of the students. But it wouldn't be too expensive for their supervisor to treat them to it. Satoru had been very tactful when it came to coming up with a compromise.

'Yeah, that'd be great,' the students agreed.

'It's agreed, then – the winning team will have premium Pilsner.' Kubota accepted the idea straight away, since it would not be a strain on his pocket, and inwardly he was grateful to Satoru.

During the students' summer training camp, the farm supplied peaches from its orchard and grapes from its vineyard.

The senior and junior teams each came up with their own strategy.

The seniors would provide free samples to potential customers, while the juniors went with selling sub-standard produce which they'd offer at a discount. Each team would put up one sign only for attracting customers.

The junior team, however, wasn't allowed to put 'Bargain Prices' on their sign, which they'd been planning on. And everything else they came up with to lure their customers with low prices was similarly vetoed. The juniors were none too happy with this decision, but there was too much of an advantage in advertising sale items compared to regular products.

In the end, the senior team chose 'Try Your Samples Here' for their sign, while the juniors wrote 'B Grade Fruit' on theirs.

From morning until evening, they worked at their roadside stands, and in the end the junior team won the day. This wasn't due to the price difference, it turned out, but to the position of the stands and the visibility of the signs. Their target customers were drivers on the highway, and the phrase 'Try Your Samples Here' was a little too long for people to take in as they drove past.

'B Grade Fruit', written in three simple characters in

Japanese, was pithier. The phrase also raised customers' expectations since it gave them the idea of getting a bargain.

If these had been stands aimed at pedestrian traffic, it was decided, the results may very well have been different. For browsers on foot the idea of free samples had a lot more appeal.

At any rate, the students gathered a wealth of material from the fieldwork to put in their reports.

That was the final day of their summer training camp, and the farm staff prepared a delicious dinner for them.

'Sir, thank you for all the help you've given my daughter,' the orchard owner said, pouring some locally made wine into Kubota's glass. Kubota had forgotten to tell him that he wasn't much of a drinker. 'A friend of mine who runs a winery gave it to me, especially for this evening.'

This made it even harder for Kubota to turn it down. Besides, the wine was quite tasty, and before he knew it he had become somewhat tipsy.

When he was just about to topple over, Satoru was there to lead him away from the party.

'Sir, we've laid out a futon for you.'

Their lodgings were in an annexe near the orchard. Just as they got in, Kubota's legs gave way and he collapsed on to the futon.

'Thank you,' he said. 'I was about to make a fool of myself.'

'People who can drink a lot have trouble imagining that others can't hold their alcohol. I'm not much of a drinker either, so I kept my eye on you, Sir. What I tend to do to avoid being given too much to drink is to help out as a server, but you didn't have that option.'

Kubota had noticed that Satoru had indeed been

cheerfully scurrying around like a busy mouse. But he hadn't realized why.

'I don't need to drink to have a good time, and I just wish they'd let me be.'

Satoru seemed the type for whom the party atmosphere was enough.

'Is Miss Sakita's father a heavy drinker?' asked Kubota.

'He certainly is. Back in high school, his son and I often got smashed together.'

'Wait just a second. You were still minors, right?'

'Let's not go there. Sakita's father's the one who urged us on, so best take that up with him, not me.' Satoru looked a bit ruffled, as if trying to avoid a subject he'd rather not discuss. 'The person who really ended up being a drinker because of Sakita's father was Sakita herself,' he went on after a pause, and laughed. 'That's why she was complaining throughout this whole fieldwork project. She complained to me that since we're staying at hers, she's been made to help out so much she hasn't been able to relax and have a drink.'

'I see. Maybe I pushed her too hard,' Kubota said. 'But it did turn out to be a very meaningful experience. Thanks to you, for proposing it.' He paused. 'I'm so happy you ended up joining our seminar,' he added suddenly, the alcohol doing the talking.

'Well, I had been thinking of attending a different seminar.' Satoru was such an affable student that other professors had had their eye on him as well. 'But I decided pretty early on to join yours.'

'How come?' Kubota asked.

'I enjoyed discussing books with you, and when I first visited the seminar room, I got a good feeling about it.'

· 226 ·

Kubota mulled this over. What could have made him think that way, he wondered.

'The thing is, Sir, you have photos of your family on your desk, don't you? Photos of you with your cat and dog, too, which really struck me.'

'So you're a cat lover?'

Satoru blinked in surprise, the remark seemingly spot on.

'Because you mentioned cats first.'

Satoru nodded. 'I like both, but if I could have a pet it would be a cat. I had one when I was a child.'

'What was it like?' Kubota asked, and Satoru was only too happy to answer.

'His name was Hachi. A sensible cat, very gentle. There was a mark on his forehead shaped like the character for eight – 八 – while his body was white and his tail was black and hooked.'

'A hooked tail, eh? Cats like that bring good luck.'

'Is that right?'

Satoru seemed unaware of the concept of lucky cats. Kubota couldn't recall where he'd heard about it.

'The idea is that the hooked tail snags good fortune and brings it to you.'

'Is that so,' Satoru murmured, as if heaving a sigh. His eyes seemed to melt into a smile.

'So cats with hooked tails should definitely be content, right? With good fortune hanging down from their tails.'

'Well, logically, I suppose so.'

'Mmm,' Satoru said, nodding, and his eyes looked shiny.

'When I saw your photos, Sir, it made me wish I had had my cat for longer.'

· 227 ·

Circumstances had forced him to give up his cat, he said, and ask some relatives to adopt him.

'In any case, he had a hooked tail, so I'm sure he was happy.'

'I'm glad!'

They passed the time contentedly talking about cats. That night Kubota had a dream about cats. The cat Satoru had talked about made an appearance.

The next morning when he told Satoru about it, his eyes lit up. 'Really?' he asked. 'Did he seem happy?'

'Hmm. I only saw him from afar. He was lying in the sun so I can't really say.'

'If he was lying in the sun, he was definitely happy.'

But Satoru still looked a bit put out.

'Hachi's a little cruel, though, to appear in *your* dreams, Sir, and not in *mine*.'

Satoru seemed seriously put out by this, which Kubota found amusing.

'WELL, HE DID, DIDN'T HE? He appeared in your dreams, Professor, but not in mine.'

'I remember thinking it was funny how much that upset you.'

As I listened to their conversation, I found it all pretty funny. *Yep, Satoru's the type who does get miffed at things like that, Professor.* But I don't think that's what Hachi intended. He wouldn't have liked it at all that Satoru didn't dream about him.

From where he was sitting on the sofa, with his legs crossed, the professor turned to look at me. His voice was a

· 228 ·

little muffled so I couldn't catch everything, and so while they were deep in conversation, I decided to step out of the carrier.

'He really does look exactly like Hachi. When I first saw him, I was so surprised. His tail hooks in the opposite direction, though. But if you look at it from above, it's shaped like the number seven.'

*A lucky-seven hooked tail, Professor. I pride myself that it snags more luck for me than Hachi's did.*

'I see. So you were fated to meet Nana.'

*Good point, Professor. Keep up the preaching. Satoru, how can you even consider getting rid of me when fate, in the guise of a lucky-seven hooked tail, brought us together?*

'Oh, yeah – I bought some cake, too. Would you like some?'

The professor stood up, but Satoru stopped him. 'No, really, I'm fine.'

'You don't eat enough. Young people need to fill up more.'

*No, exactly! It's true, Satoru's appetite has got smaller these days, but the amount of sweet things you've brought out is nuts.*

Satoru was at a loss from the start, just with the *imagawayaki*.

'Are you sure? Word among the students at college is that the cakes from that store are really tasty . . .'

The professor looked so deflated that Satoru gave in. 'Oh, okay, just one small piece, then.'

When the professor left the room, I strolled towards Satoru and leaped up on to his lap.

'Ah, so you're out now, Nana. Does that mean you might like it here?'

· 229 ·

*Not at all – I just couldn't properly hear what you were saying. The professor has a dog somewhere, I gather, and if I pick a fight with him, that'll be more than a good enough reason for this plan to fall apart.*

Watching the professor stroll back in after clattering around the kitchen, Satoru murmured, 'Whatever happened between us when I was a student still seems to be bothering him.'

I also thought he was acting a bit oddly.

He kept whipping out one sweet after another as if he wasn't sure what to do with himself. Any break in the conversation and the professor escaped to the kitchen. The outcome being this massive snack attack.

You didn't have to be a cat to understand what was going on. The man must have had some lingering sense of guilt towards Satoru.

'Here you go. Take as much as you like.'

The professor had brought over a box with six slices of cake. Way too many for just the two of them.

Satoru seemed to shudder, but exclaimed softly when he spied a thin slice of tangerine jelly. He seemed relieved to find something he might be able to stuff down.

'I'll have this one, thank you.'

'That's one of their specials, available only this month.'

The professor placed a large piece of rich Mont Blanc cake on to his own plate. He'd been gobbling one sweet after another and didn't seem to show any signs of stopping.

It was so funny to watch Satoru taking tiny bites of the jelly, by contrast, so he wouldn't finish it too quickly.

· 230 ·

SATORU AND THE KUBOTAS HAD always got along well, but things unfolded in Kubota's family that had soured their relationship.

His wife was found to have a malignant tumour. Satoru had just entered his senior year when the doctor told Kubota's wife she had only a year left to live.

At first Kubota didn't tell anyone, but when his wife was admitted to hospital at the beginning of the autumn of that year, he could no longer keep it a secret. Kubota found himself running the house while looking after his two children and the pets, and wasn't able to hide from his students the fact that he was paying frequent visits to the hospital as well. Even if all this hadn't been going on in the background, his seminar involved a lot of fieldwork, with a lot of close interaction with the students.

When he revealed what had been going on, the students took the initiative and rearranged the way the seminar was run to lighten the burden for the professor.

Satoru was the student who helped out most. He also took over a variety of domestic chores, food shopping and suchlike. And when Kubota couldn't arrange for a babysitter, Satoru would stay with the children at their home.

Satoru had a knack with children, and the kids grew fond of him. Until his wife went into hospital, Kubota had asked his parents to look after their pets, but once Satoru had started coming over to the house every week, the kids announced they could manage the animals themselves.

'Uncle Satoru', as they called him, seemed to enjoy looking after the pets so much that the kids wanted to copy him. Soon, the older boy was walking the dog. He'd go out with him after school, while it was still light outside.

· 231 ·

'I'm sorry you have to go to all this trouble,' Kubota said, gratefully.

'Not a problem,' Satoru said with a smile. 'I look forward to seeing Mi-chan and John, too, and this year I only have one seminar left.'

Impressively, he'd completed all his courses the previous year, and already had a post-graduate job lined up.

Satoru made it easy for people to lean on him, and that's exactly what Kubota did, updating him on his wife's condition, and generally using him as a sounding board for his worries.

Like a low-flying paper aeroplane stalling in mid-flight, there was a lull in the severity of her condition, but then in the New Year she went downhill quickly.

'I doubt she'll live to see the cherry blossom,' the doctor declared.

In the middle of it all, Satoru, who'd long since handed in his final thesis, came over to the seminar room unexpectedly. He was looking serious.

'What in the world is wrong?' Kubota asked. It would soon be visiting time at the hospital.

As if he'd made an important decision, Satoru said, 'Sir, will you please tell your children about your wife.'

'What on earth are you talking about?'

Kubota had never told his children his wife had a terminal illness. His son was still only in sixth grade, his daughter was four years younger. He couldn't bring himself to confront them with the fact that their mother was dying.

Kubota was determined, till the very end, to take on the burden himself to keep the children from experiencing anything so bitter. The kids could find out when she was about to die, he had decided. He didn't want them to visit her, and to feel tormented by the inevitability of her death. He had

· 232 ·

always insisted that, until that unavoidable final moment, the children's contact with their mother would be a happy time for them.

'Stop meddling!' Kubota burst out.

'But, Sir!'

The very thought of Satoru of all people intruding like this, and so late in the day! Kubota's anger surged all the more. He'd always thought Satoru had understood him best.

'Mind your own business!' he shouted.

But Satoru wasn't about to give up so easily.

'Sir, the kids already know!'

Kubota's blood began to boil.

'You haven't told them already, have you?'

'I haven't. But the kids sense it, that she doesn't have much time left.'

If he'd listened to Satoru, he knew he would have understood his point. But by this stage he was jumping at anything.

*He says he hasn't told them, but is that actually true? Even if he hasn't yet, there will come a time when he can't stay silent about it,* thought Kubota.

'Just as your wife is important to you, that's how important their mother is to the kids! If their mother's going to die, the kids will want to say a proper goodbye! Please – let your children say goodbye to their mother!'

Satoru was making it sound as if Kubota didn't understand his kids' feelings, and that made him even more angry.

Satoru didn't even have children, so what was he talking about? It was as if he was saying he was the one who was closer to the kids.

· 233 ·

'A parent should do what they need to do so their kids don't have any regrets!'

'You have no idea how a parent feels, so shut up!'

If only Kubota could rewind time and take back those words. How many times he had regretted them.

But Satoru continued to pick at his wound – he didn't back down a single step.

'I don't know how parents feel, but I know how *kids* feel! Because I am closer in age to your children, I understand how they feel more than you do!'

What feelings had wrung these words out of that young man that day?

'If they can make it in time, then kids, too, want to say goodbye! They'll want to tell her, *I love you* and *Thank you!*'

Satoru's wailing voice rushed through his ears. He slammed down the shutter on the matter.

'Don't ever show your face here again! Don't you dare come near my children! And there's no need for you to come back to the seminar either!'

Despair was written all over Satoru's face.

*This isn't any of his business, yet he looks so devastated.*

Facing him, with this end-of-the-world expression, was frightening, and Kubota fairly ran out of the seminar room.

Until now, that was the last time they had seen each other.

It was true that Satoru didn't need to attend the seminar, because as previously stated, he'd already submitted his graduation thesis.

And it was an outstanding thesis.

Satoru went along with Kubota's demand and never

· 234 ·

came back. At first the other students wondered why he'd stopped coming, but Satoru glossed over his absence, telling them he had training to do for the job he had lined up.

Satoru's almost threatening insistence that he tell the children had stirred something up in Kubota, however. He mentioned it to Satoru's best friend, Sugi.

'He's so very worried about my children. Is there a particular reason why?'

Sugi seemed to understand. Maybe he'd heard something about it from Satoru.

'His parents died in a car accident when Satoru was a child. I heard it was when he was the same age as your son, Sir. Maybe his feelings about it were so strong he couldn't help interfering . . .'

*Please try to understand him.* Sugi sounded as if he wanted to add this, if he could have done.

'I understand. Thank you,' Kubota said, feeling utterly defeated.

The last time he'd been so stricken by someone's words was when he'd heard his wife's days were numbered.

The words he'd hurled at Satoru came back to haunt him.

*You have no idea how a parent feels.*

How did Satoru, who had lost both his parents when he was a child, feel when he heard this?

*Because I am closer in age to your children, I understand how they feel more than you do.*

Satoru understood all too well how children felt when they were suddenly told one day that their parents were dead.

He wavered. Should he tell the kids, or not?

Then, when her final days were approaching, he told his son the truth.

'Mum doesn't have much longer to live.'

· 235 ·

His son began to weep, but he wasn't that shaken by the news. Maybe, as Satoru had said, he had a premonition of this already.

When they went to visit his wife in the hospital, most of the time she wasn't aware of her surroundings.

During the few moments when she was alert, his son repeated, over and over, *Thank you, Mum, I love you, Mum.* Then he more or less ordered his younger sister to do the same.

Kubota's wife could hardly speak, but the small nod she gave showed that she had heard.

If you can make it in time, you want to say *goodbye.* Want to say *thank you,* and *I love you.* The children had chosen the exact same words Satoru had used, so Kubota thought that maybe he *had* told them about his wife's condition after all, but when he heard his son repeat these for all he was worth, he felt it was okay even if Satoru had told them after all.

His wife died at the end of February, on a bitterly cold day.

After the funeral his son said, 'Dad, thank you for telling me.'

Kubota began to weep uncontrollably.

It was a burden lifted to know that he'd done the right thing. His daughter was still too young to understand what was going on, but he was relieved that his son hadn't had his chance to say a final goodbye snatched away from him.

About a month later, Satoru graduated.

Because he was still officially in mourning, Kubota wasn't at the thank-you party held for the teachers, but he did attend the graduation.

After the ceremony his seminar students came over to say hello. Unsure what to say to him since he was still in mourning, they kept it short.

Satoru was with them, but Kubota didn't speak to him. The situation made it fine not to do so.

Kubota had hurt Satoru, terribly, and he feared talking to him about it.

On his way out, Satoru bowed wordlessly to him.

Kubota acknowledged him with a nod.

'ACTUALLY, I ENDED UP TELLING my son that his mother didn't have long to live.'

'Is that right?' Satoru responded to this confession with a small smile.

'If you hadn't told me to, I never would have let the children and their mother say a proper goodbye. But nevertheless . . .'

Kubota suddenly bowed his head.

'I am so, so sorry!'

'Please don't be, Sir!'

In that moment, forgetting I was on his lap, Satoru rose to his feet. I mean, if it were any other cat, it would have tumbled to the floor, but I clung on.

The professor raised his head, and Satoru looked relieved. He sat back down on the sofa.

'I'm to blame too. I just vented because of what I went through myself as a child . . . But – you listened, and I'm thankful for that.' Satoru bobbed his head. 'I'm so sorry.'

Kubota looked blank as he took in the unexpected apology.

'Recently I've been feeling like I finally understand how you and your wife must have felt. If, for instance, I were the one who had to say goodbye, I don't think I'd want my final

· 237 ·

hours to be sad. I would want to see my loved ones' smiles to the very end.'

As a cat, I've noticed that people, young or old, always put themselves first: *This is the end, so I want to say goodbye, but until the very end I don't want to say a sad farewell.*

The boundary between adults and children is kind of vague. It's kids who believe in that boundary who announce that this is how adults should behave. Okay, so when do those kids become such mature adults?

'Still, it was as if I was preventing any other choice for you and your wife.'

I'd say it's at the point where human beings let feelings and not instinct dictate how they should behave that they lose sight of the boundaries between adults and children that we animals have.

The only choice for humans is to flounder around, searching for a vague boundary, certain that they are right, and creatures like these only think they know what it means to be an adult.

At the time when Satoru thought he knew what a parent should do for his children, and by expressing these thoughts placed the professor in an awkward bind, he was behaving like a child. But another thing about humans is that it's when they are children they can shake things up. With animals it's always the older ones who are the wisest.

'That's why I came here today. Not just to ask you to take care of Nana. I'm happy to be able to talk to you again, Sir, and to be able to apologize.'

Looking down, the professor shook his head. He was sniffling and seemed to be crying. He'd stopped rolling out the sweets in an attempt to cover up any silence.

· 238 ·

He sat back and, looking Satoru in the eyes, began to reminisce. Then he began to laugh.

'There is no end to regrets, but it's time now. Time to bring my dog out to meet Nana.' The professor stood up.

'What was his name again?'

'It's Lily. He loves cats, so not to worry.'

The professor walked out of the living room, then came back, bringing the dog with him on a lead. In an instant, the dog had shaken off the professor and rushed into the room.

*A CAT! It's a cat, a cat, a cat – let's play!*

The creature that leaped at us, excitement ramped to the max, was a huge Great Dane.

Say what you will, but this guy was *way* too big.

So much so that Satoru stood up, ready to leave, and at the speed of light I clambered on top of his head. My back arched, my fur bristling, I did my best to threaten this Great Dane jumping for joy in front of us.

*I mean, consider the size difference here. You think I can play with you when you're knocking us over?*

With the Great Dane's front paws pushing at his waist, Satoru collapsed back on the sofa.

*It's a cat!*

Driven into a corner, I was in total crisis mode. Even if he didn't mean any harm, there was no way I could play with him when he was this worked up, and I got out of control too, hissing and brandishing my claws at him.

*Kyan!* the dog screamed.

*Don't get any closer! Back OFF!*

The Great Dane finally took a step back, but was still looking for his chance to play. *That hurt just now, you know! But anyway, when will you be in a better mood? When you're*

· 239 ·

*in a good mood, will you play with me?* Obviously itching for action, his tail spoke a million words.

How was I supposed to be in a better mood in a situation like this, eh?

'Umm. Maybe Nana isn't so good with dogs?'

*That's not the issue here, people!*

'No, I don't think that's the problem . . .'

*Thanks for interpreting for me!*

Because I was forced into threatening the monstrously huge Lily, it seemed I wouldn't end up staying with the professor.

'Umm. It's too bad, but I don't think this is going to work for Nana,' said Satoru.

'You think?'

The professor finally forced Lily into a back room in the apartment, getting pulled down himself in the process as Lily struggled to go back into the living room. But I digress.

'It's too bad about Nana's *miai*, but I'm so happy we could meet again.'

'Me too.'

No ill-feeling left at all, teacher and pupil shook hands.

'Can I ask one question?' the professor said, hesitantly, as they said goodbye.

'Of course, what is it?'

'Just before my wife died, my son said *thank you* and *I love you* over and over. The same words you said you would have spoken, if only you could have got there in time. Did you, perhaps, tell the children about my wife?'

'No, I did not,' Satoru said, and smiled. 'It's only natural he used the same words. Those are the only last words a child wants to say to a parent, if they are loved – *thank you* and *I love you*. Don't you think so?'

· 240 ·

'I see,' the professor said, understanding at last.

'You're the only one, Professor, who had the right to tell your children about their mother. That's why I quarrelled with you so much.'

'I see,' the professor nodded several times, and smiled. 'Thank you, for quarrelling with me.'

*No, thank you, Professor, for saying these words to Satoru.*

Satoru seemed choked up, so to say *thank you* on his behalf, I purred vigorously from inside my carrier.

After we left the professor's apartment, Satoru took a walk down the flagstone streets of the nearby town with its foreign look. We were sort of off the main road, so there weren't many cars about.

I was thinking of getting out of the carrier and stretching my legs a bit myself. Lily had got his slobber all over me, and if I didn't do something about it, my carrier would stink of dog.

With my paws, I fiddled with the lock on the carrier and, seeing what I was up to, Satoru said, 'Oh, Nana, do you want to come out?' and he unlatched it.

The white flagstones felt different on my pads from the asphalt streets I usually walked on. The stones were cool and pressing my paws against them felt good. Just walking on them made me feel healthier.

I heard the click of a camera and turned around to find Satoru training his mobile phone on me.

'It's like a painting, Nana.' Satoru seemed to be checking his photo.

'Why don't we take the long way home,' he added.

As we walked, he took a few more photos of me. And I posed cutely to help him out.

By the time we had arrived back at the parking lot and

· 241 ·

climbed into the silver van, the dog smell had been blown away by the wind.

Trying to push back on that vigorous, calf-sized dog had worn me out, and as soon as Satoru had driven off, I slipped into a deep sleep.

'We're going to take a break, Nana.'

Satoru's voice woke me gently and I yawned and shook out my ears. Where were we? I stretched up to look out of the window and saw a huge body of water right next to us.

'It's Lake Biwa. Remember I talked about stopping here on our way?'

*But I told you we don't need to!*

'Come on, let's get out.'

Even if it wasn't like the horror movie of the sea, I still wasn't prepared to buy into it. But Satoru picked me up from my seat.

I braced myself for the heavy, gut-pounding crash of waves. But what I got was kind of anticlimactic.

On the lake there were just quiet little waves lapping at the shore, and no terrifying roar. The horizon looked the same, but the sea and a lake were totally different. You know, taking a walk here wouldn't be so bad, I thought, and wriggled out of Satoru's arms for a stroll along the shore.

There were other people strolling about too, sightseeing at the lake like us.

An older man with a camera was wandering around. He looked over at Satoru and when their eyes met, his expression brightened.

'Excuse me, but would you mind taking our picture?'

He seemed to want a photo of himself and his wife as a memento.

· 242 ·

Satoru was often asked for a favour like this by passers-by. Maybe because he seemed approachable.

'No trouble at all.'

Satoru took the camera from the man, and as he looked through the view finder, he called out to the couple, 'Move just a smidgen to your right, if you would. There you go. Perfect.'

He snapped a photo of the elderly couple, smiling for all they were worth. 'One more, just in case,' Satoru said and clicked another photo.

'Thank you very much.'

Thinking they were done, I sidled over to Satoru, and the old lady said, 'Goodness. What have we here? Is this your cat?'

'He is. His name is Nana. Because his tail is hooked like the number seven.'

The thought occurred to me each and every time: *Does he really have to explain my name to everyone he meets? Well – I suppose it makes him happy when people show an interest in me.*

'Is he travelling with you?'

'That's right.'

The old lady clapped her hands, as if she had suddenly had some great idea.

'If you like, we can take a photo of the two of you together. We'll send it to you later.'

'Oh, that's a great idea.' The old man was into it, too.

'You don't mind?' Satoru clearly liked the idea as well.

He swooped down to pick me up and positioned himself where the lake could be seen in the background.

The old man took several photos and had Satoru check them.

'Are these okay?'

· 243 ·

'Wow. Isn't this great, Nana? You look so cute in the photos.'

Could he have made it any more obvious he was cat crazy? TMI, if you ask me.

Satoru gave the old couple his address, thanked them, and we left.

Not long after we got back to Tokyo, we received the photos.

To me the address written on the envelope looked like wriggling worms, but according to Satoru the handwriting was *superb*.

Included was a short note: 'Thank you for the other day. I hope you're keeping well,' it said, according to Satoru.

He scrutinized the three photos inside.

'These are the first-ever photos of us together, aren't they, Nana?'

Satoru lived alone, so we'd never had someone to take any.

'I'm so happy,' he said, and straight away put them in a frame and displayed it in our flat.

We moved out of the apartment not long afterwards, but in his next home, Satoru continued to display the photos. When the day came for Satoru to move into the hospital ward, which I wasn't allowed to enter, he took them with him there too.

And when Satoru no longer needed the photos any more, they found their way back to me.

I lived a happy life, looking at those photographs.

But that's another story.